MIDNIGHT BITES

MIDNIGHT BITES

Midnight Whispers
Series Book 3

L.K. LATHAM

L.K. Latham

Contents

For my readers: Thank you.

I

Maria ran until her lungs burned and legs trembled. Fatigue slapped her in the face. She wobbled, slipping until her hands grabbed the coarse wood of a lamp pole hiding in the dark. Wrapping herself in the shadows, she filled her lungs with deep, quick breaths. Fear trickled down her back with each drop of sweat. The monster had killed her brother.

She leaned her forehead into the pole as burning embers flowed down her cheeks from her eyes. "Oh, Louis. What did we do?"

A motorcycle puttered past her on the street. Curls like flames tossed in the wind from beneath a helmet. The woman driving the motorcycle didn't see her, but the huge, white dog sitting in the sidecar did. Pink eyes glowed beneath goggles as it passed Maria. The dog barked once.

Maria jumped, afraid of what the dog saw. She ran across the street onto a residential road. Large houses with dark windows watched her run. The top of her foot hit the curb as she jogged between two parked cars to avoid a car driving down the street. She tripped, landing on her hands and knees.

She crawled into the bushes and sat beneath a closed gate. If she pulled her knees to her chin, she could just squeeze into a hole beneath the bushes. Blood oozed from both knees and hands, but top of her foot and ankle throbbed as hundreds of tiny spikes pushed on her muscles. She rubbed her foot with her sore hands.

Footsteps soft and hurried patted in her direction. From beneath the bushes, a young woman, not a girl, close to her own age, jogged along the sidewalk. The girl stopped in front of the gate. The light of her watch lit the girl's face, but Maria couldn't see her face, only the blue light.

"Best time yet," the girl said with pride. "Now, to bed."

The girl walked through the gate. A light from above the front door flashed on. The girl froze, breathing, "Argh! Security light. Who turned that on? Up the tree in back." The girl stepped off the path to the dark side of the house.

Maria twisted her head to look over the bushes. The girl disappeared behind the side of the house.

Maria felt the chill of fear wash over her. "He's near," she whispered.

Maria pushed herself out from under the bushes. She stood ready to run, but her foot would not allow any weight on it. The chill in her heart grew.

She pushed forward, forcing her foot to walk or limp forward. She had to get away. As she hobbled away from the house, she saw the girl climbing into a window on the second floor.

Maria opened her mouth to call for help, but only shook her head. The demon was too close.

Another block, and the streetlights went out. Maria stopped moving, letting the darkness swallow her. Her sore foot surrendered to the pain, and Maria fell to the ground. Tears blocked her vision. A footfall and then another and then the sound of something, close.

Maria pushed herself up with her right arm. *Just move.* She pushed herself forward.

But it was too late. A hand - a claw, cold, hard, grabbed her shoulder, lifting her off the grown. Blackness filled her senses. Putrid, wet breath filled her face. "Where's the others?" the voice, coarse and cruel asked. These were the last words Maria heard before she died.

Another story begins,
The seasons change,
Dreams tease.
As the nights grow long, and winds whisper songs of dances long and old.

Look to depths where the city waits between night and dawn,
Where the moon hides a face eyes refuse to see.
On this night, three women pass, unseeing but aware.
Tonight their lives mingle as Death takes her due.
The battle for the night, for peace rests with the victor,
A victor will fail alone.
But who will wear the victor's crown?
You're listening to Mary Midnight online and in your mind.
Walk the streets with care, my children.
Join the righteous unseen and unbidden,
Or wallow in the hidden agony of a Victor's dirge.

Luna leaned over the pastry counter, bathed in the light of her cell phone as her wrath abated. Her fingers banged out a message to Lisa, her cousin. *OMG! Hate work!*

She jumped and stood straight as Marcus walked out of the kitchen carrying a tray of clean cups and saucers. The dull light from the kitchen flowed into the darkness of the cafe, stabbing her eyes.

Her phone vibrated in her hand. Lisa replied, *What did Marcus do?*

Luna sighed. *I petted a cat.*

Marcus set the tray on the counter next to her with a bang and whispered. "Luna! Customer. And you still have cat hair on your apron."

Luna lifted her gaze, following Marcus' gaze to the far corner near the crumbling stage hidden by large green hostas and palms. The plants were her idea, *to breathe some life in this place.* It didn't help, but they gave her something to do in the afternoons while she was stuck working. They even thrived in the bright sunshine that streamed from the large front windows in the afternoons. She liked to see them, but just like Marcus had said they would, they hid the farthest corner of the cafe.

And then she saw the long, thin legs stretched out from under a table reflecting the dull, yellow light from above. The man leaned forward and waved.

"Him, again?" she sighed.

"Put the phone away and do your job." Marcus put clean cups and plates into the side cupboard with the spare dishes.

She typed: *Gotta work. Marcus = ass,* and didn't care if she had cat hair on her apron. Mr. Thin Man, as she had named him after his third visit to the coffee shop, sat at his usual table in the darkest corner in the café, reading his ebook. He was far too skinny to be attractive, and his pasty white complexion, especially with the blue light from his book, freaked her out. He looked ill, but then he'd say something with that deep, melodious voice and peculiar accent. His voice stirred something deep inside her, unfamiliar but not unwelcome.

It was as though she stepped into a different world when he spoke, transfixing her far away from the cafe. She had yet to decide where he was from, so sometimes she referred to him as Mr. Mystery Man. But when he looked at her as she took his order, large, beautiful, clear eyes glared into her. Sometimes she felt he was looking at something going on behind her. Sometimes she felt he was looking at her soul. The feelings both unnerved and fascinated her.

"Good evening, Luna," said Mr. Thin Man.

"I guess you really like this place or something." Luna didn't bother to smile. After serving him a different coffee and pastry every night for almost a week, he saw through the false, cheery façade she wore for her mother's sake.

"Or something, I would say."

Mr. Thin Man's being Mr. Mystery Man tonight. Luna raised an eyebrow. "There's hardly any cash here, so you can't be here scoping out the place to rob. You eyeing me? Or maybe you're eyeing my brother? Either will get you kicked out of here faster than you can spit."

Mr. Thin Man laughed. She hadn't heard him laugh before. The richness reverberated through the air, tickling the hairs on her neck.

"I would do nothing nefarious where your family is concerned, Luna. What will I have tonight?"

And so their game began. The first time she waited on him, he'd asked her what she would have. Since she didn't like coffee and she wouldn't do carbs, she had no suggestions, so he ordered a coffee and a donut. The next night, he told her to bring her something he hadn't had before.

"You've had each of the coffee drinks. Want to start on teas?"

"Excellent suggestion."

"And let's see." Luna put her finger to her lips and twisted to examine at the pastry counter. "You've had all the chocolate and plain croissants, eclairs, biscuits, donuts. Oh, Aunt Jasmine brought in some lemon scones yesterday. She says they're good."

"I'll take your suggestion." Mr. Thin Man returned his gaze to the screen in his hands. The game was over.

She went back to the counter to fix his tea. Marcus watched her approach as he wiped down the counters. "What's your Mr. Thin Man want tonight?"

"Tea and lemon scone. And he's not *my* Mr. Thin Man."

"You always wait on him." Marcus's eyes narrowed as he watched the man leaning back in his chair, watching them. "He's not messing with you, is he?"

Luna rolled her eyes, opening a tea bag and placing it in a cup of hot water. "I always wait on him because you always make me wait on tables. You going to stand there or hand me one of those lemon scones?"

Marcus took a clean cloth from under the cabinet and used it to pick up a plate, still warm from cleaning. He used the same clean cloth to pick up the tongs and place the pastry on the plate.

Luna put her hands on her hips. "And what are you so bent out of shape about? He's a paying customer. Probably works somewhere around here and is taking a break. About time we had someone come in here more than once."

"We're just getting started." Marcus slammed the door to the warming oven. "Once fall term starts, we'll have plenty of customers."

Luna placed the steaming teacup on a tray. "Right. Just like last fall," she said, not looking at her brother. She took her phone out of her back pocket and tapped, *Get me out of here.*

Marcus grabbed her phone from her hands. "Will you stop! This is serious. You know we've got to make this place work. Professionals don't text when they're supposed to be serving."

The warming oven dinged. Luna gritted her teeth, pulled the cleaning towel off the cabinet, and reached for the oven.

"Not with that towel!" Marcus pushed her aside. "I'm cleaning with that one. Think!" He grabbed a new towel to wrap around the tongs and pulled the heated scone out of the oven.

Luna's teeth remained locked together. "I am not a professional server. I'm only doing this 'til classes start. Then you and Mama can hire a real server."

"We do not have the money to..."

"I don't care!" Luna grabbed the plated pastry and banged it on the tray. "Mama promised. I'm doing my part, Marcus."

Luna carried the tray to Mr. Thin Man. She tried to smile and serve the way Mama taught her, but her hands shook.

"Let me," Mr. Thin Man said, taking the cup and plate from the tray. He smiled, and once again, his clear eyes reflected not only the room with its dim lights but her face. She saw her own angry eyes looking back at her and took in a deep breath. Her anger, entirely justified, would not get the better of her.

"Thank you," he said, but instead of turning his attention to his tea and scone, he said, "I have an appointment with your mother. Would you tell her I'm here?"

Luna straightened. This was not part of the game.

He took a sip of his tea. "We have business to discuss."

Mr. Thin Man said no more, even though Luna stood beside him, staring at him. His nose crinkled as he pulled the lemon scone in two.

Luna walked back to the counter where Marcus stood, wiping the counter and glaring at her. Luna smiled. "Mr. Thin Man wants to talk to Mama. They have an appointment."

Marcus' chin dropped, and he stared at Mr. Thin Man.

"Marcus!" whispered Luna. "Don't stare. I'll get Mama."

The front door to the cafe opened. Jasmine LaBrere, Luna's aunt, entered, out of breath and pulling on her suit jacket. "Hey Luna,

Marcus. How's everybody doing? I swear! This heat will kill me. Marcus, your Mama in the office?"

"Yes, Ma'am. I'll let her know..."

"Got it," shouted Luna as she ran to the office door and knocked.

Marcus smiled at his aunt. "The usual, Aunt Jasmine?"

"Thanks, sweetie. Better make a fresh pot. Your mama and I have business tonight."

Marcus pulled out a clean towel and wiped down a clean coffee pot.

The office door opened, and Jackie Howard-Smythe walked out.

"Mama," started Luna. "Aunt Jasmine and a man are here,"

"I know, dear," Mama said. "I can see them both."

Luna meandered back to the coffee counter, where Marcus waited.

"What business?" Marcus whispered.

"I don't know," she answered. "I thought you would."

Luna stared at her mother's face, once so long and beautiful, now wore puffed cheeks and heavy eyelids. Luna tapped Marcus's arm, "Lipstick."

"Shit," Marcus said.

"Don't swear," said Luna, slapping Marcus' arm.

They watched their mother and aunt embrace.

"How's Frank?" Jackie asked.

"Good," replied Jasmine, rolling her eyes. "The hours a policeman has to work. If I'd known, I would never have married the man."

"He can't work more than you," laughed Jackie.

Jasmine snorted and pushed Jackie toward her office. "Now before we get started, I want go over a few things with you."

"Jasmine," Jackie said to interrupt her, but Jasmine continued.

"Now, I asked Frank to do a check on this guy. On the surface, everything looks legit, but I still have some reservations."

"Jasmine," Jackie smiled and took Jasmine by both arms. "I believe..."

The front door opened and a man wearing black jeans and a sports jacket over a black tee-shirt entered. He stopped with the door open, looking first at Jasmine and Jackie and then around the room until his gaze landed on Mr. Thin Man.

"Hey," he said, exposing bright white teeth. "I see we're all here. Great. Thought I was late."

Jasmine looked around the room, stopping at the man in the doorway before turning to see Mr. Thin Man, who stood, stepping in front of a table where one of the overhead lights covered him with dull, yellow light.

"I was trying to tell you, the Chef's already here." Jackie reached out to shake hands with the man who had just entered.

"Jackie LeBrere-Smythe," she said.

"Mike Young. Can't tell you how glad I am to finally meet you." Mike stepped forward to shake hands with Jasmine. "Jasmine, it's been a while. Good to be working with you again. Have you met Max?"

Luna stopped pretending to be busy and leaned on the pastry counter, resting her head in her hands. Her head slipped out of her hand at the voice of Mr. Thin Man. He stood in front of her mother.

"Dr. Smythe-LeBrere," Mr. Thin Man said. "Can't tell you how happy I am you decided to take up my offer."

As often as Luna had heard him, there was something different in his voice. His voice was always kind, like a favorite old song, but tonight it rang like a bell in the attic. His words were a strange mix of caution and courtesy, but not directed at her. Luna watched as their eyes met and held for too long.

A chill ran down Luna's spine as Mr. Thin Man continued. "Your *Philosophies of the Just* is still one of my favorite economic theories. I had hoped by now to read the follow-up to it. Perhaps this place will help you with it."

"Perhaps," said her mother.

Jasmine and Mike Young settled around the large table in the center of the room.

Luna didn't hear the beeping of the coffee pot.

"Fix a tray for us, kids," Jackie said, looking at her two children, "And bring it to the table."

"Yes, Ma'am" Luna and Marcus said in unison. Luna turned to

prepare the tray. "What offer?" she whispered to Marcus, as she opened the door to the pastry case.

Marcus pulled a clean towel from behind him and used it to pick up a clean tray. "No. Use this tray. She said nothing about a meeting with anyone. Things are tight, but..." Marcus's voiced trailed away as he turned his head to stare at the table where the meeting was under way.

*****

Luna polished a glass, keeping her head down but her eyes and ears focused on her mother and the meeting in the center of the cafe. Marcus stood next to her, continuing to wipe the counter.

"It's just the way you asked for it," said Mike. He sipped his coffee, crinkling his nose. "Hey kids, could you bring me some cream?"

The glass leaped out of Luna's hands as she jumped. Marcus caught it and glared at her. "What? You made the coffee," she whispered to him and opened the small refrigerator, pulling out the carton of creamer.

Marcus pinched his lips but said nothing as he watched Luna fill the server and take it to the table.

Jackie's forced smile faded. "So sorry. I asked them to make a fresh pot."

"Oh, it's not the coffee," Mike said. "Just not a big coffee drinker unless it's full of cream. I got some beans when I was in Africa. They kind of turned me off black coffee. Now, add cream and chocolate, that's another story."

"Marcus makes a fine chocolate latte," Jackie said, smiling.

Luna rolled her eyes. That's what her girlfriends said about Marcus, but she assumed they just had the hots for him.

"No trouble for me. I won't be here long. At least if Jasmine's okay with the changes we talked about."

Jasmine looked up from the contracts. She turned off the flashlight on her phone. "Everything's here," she said, shaking her head.

Mike turned to Max. "Great! Max, anything you need or want before signing?"

Max nodded, saying nothing.

"Are you certain?" Jackie asked, cradling the mug of coffee. "You've seen the financials. I can't pretend your investment isn't needed, but I can't help but feel--"

"Jackie," Jasmine placed a hand on Jackie's shoulder. "Please. Chef Max, why do you want to buy into this place? That's the root of our concern. Jackie has plans for this place, and she doesn't want it turned into any common knockoff chain."

Max leaned forward, allowing the overhead light to wash over him so everyone could see his face. "There will be nothing common about our cafe, Jackie." His voice forced all the faces in the cafe to look at him. He placed his hand on top of Jackie's.

Luna lingered, placing the cream on the table, but when she saw Max's hand on her mother's, her eyes widened.

"Thanks, kid," Mike said, winking at Luna.

Luna turned too fast, almost falling over, but Mike reached out and caught her arm. She lifted her lips in a nervous smile and saw a scar running across the man's forehead and down the left side of his face. On most men, the scare would have made him frightening, but on Mike, his skin well-tanned and wind-worn, his eyes glittering with life, the long, too-white scar fit his character. He wore it without shame or regret. It was part of him.

She whispered, "Thanks," and walked away from the table, keeping her head cocked to listen to the conversation.

Max's voice floated through the room. "You'll be bankrupt at the end of the year without an infusion of cash. There's no hiding that. You're correct about the potential for growth considering its location, but there is no potential in serving two-day-old scones and common coffees. No offense, Jasmine. I'm the best pastry chef in the country. I need to expand my talents unfettered by the confines of traditional management. You want to create a community hub, prove your economic theories. We're perfect for each other."

"Too perfect, if you ask me," said Jasmine. "I know about your awards--"

"Where do I sign?" Jackie picked up the pen in front of her and reached for contracts.

"Jackie--" started Jasmine.

"Right here," said Mike, handing the contracts to Jackie.

"It's good, Jasmine." Jackie looked into her sister's eyes. "It feels right, and not much has felt right for a long time."

Jasmine gathered the contracts and pulled her briefcase from under the table. "Looks like you don't need me anymore tonight. I hope this works out."

"It will," said Mike, springing out of his chair. "I got a nose for good deals, and it's itching like crazy tonight. Can I walk you to your car, Ms. LeBrere?"

Jasmine grunted and pushed herself out of her chair. "We're beyond that now, Mike. It's Jasmine."

Mike laughed. "Good. Then I say it's time for a celebratory drink. Have you been to the Phantom's Menace?"

"No," replied Jasmine, squinting her eyes and looking down her nose. "You buying?"

"I've already sent a text to Cesar to put a bottle on ice. You know Cesar De LaRosa, don't you?"

"We've met." Jasmine paused, gazing past Mike, and smiled. "Very pleasant, as I recall. Helped me when there was a bit of trouble catering an event up at the Mugello estate."

Mike opened the door. "I heard about that. Glad it worked out. CC really is a super nice person and was very upset you thought she was up to no-good."

Jasmine laughed as she walked out the door. "What don't you know about what happens in Austin, Mike?"

Luna watched. She knew her mouth hung open but could do nothing about it.

Marcus whispered into Luna's ear, "What?" he whispered.

"Aunt Jasmine's going to the Phantom's Menace with that Mike guy," she said, forcing her lips to close.

Mike held the door open for Jasmine. Before he left, he looked at Luna. "Be seeing you around." He winked again and left.

Luna spun to stare at her mother as Marcus mumbled, "What the hell is going on?"

"Not everyone can see this venture for what it is," Max said as he and Jackie watched their friends leave.

"I suppose," said Jackie. "Jasmine's not just my sister. She runs the most successful catering and event planning business in Austin. I never would have been able to start this without her."

"It's good to have family in the business. Now, there's a great deal I need to do. I'll go through the kitchen tonight. My sous chef will be here in the morning to start the cleaning. For the next five days, no one in the kitchen, please. That won't be a problem, will it?"

Jackie raised an eyebrow and tilted her head up. "No. We don't cook, but I think you'll find the kitchen very clean and -"

"No offence, Jackie, but you're not a chef. Assuming deliveries are on time, we'll be producing in a week."

"Deliveries?"

"I can't work with outdated equipment." Max lifted the edges of his mouth. "This is all part of the plan. Together, we'll see a profit by the end of the year. Now, if you'll excuse me, I'll get to work."

Max left Jackie sitting at the table, drinking her coffee. Luna let out a long exhale. She hadn't realized she'd been holding her breath. She watched her mother sitting alone at the table in the middle of the room.

"This is all we need," muttered Marcus, and moved toward Jackie.

Luna shook her head. "It's done, Marcus," she said, knowing he wouldn't listen to her. Looking back just once, her eyes widened. Her mother sat smiling as Marcus took her arm and whispered. His expression remained the same as it always was, grim, unhappy, disappointed. She was used to that, but seeing her mother's smile, her easy breathing as she leaned back and listed to Marcus was new. Luna cocked her head as she stared. Her mother looked almost like she did before Tony died.

Luna turned away. She'd walked over to the front door and turned off the OPEN sign. She opened the door to check the porch for stragglers, just as mama always told her to do. *Like there would ever be people waiting to come in here.*

A chill ran up her spine. She shivered and peered into the mostly empty parking lot. Across the street, standing behind a shiny, new pickup truck, an old man stood leaning on a stick. He was huge, swaying, and Luna thought he might fall over. She was about to step outside when her mother called, "Go ahead and lock up, Luna. It's time to go home."

Luna returned her gaze to the new pickup, but the man was gone. She shrugged and did as she was told.

*****

There were only two people in the dog park and fewer on the streets surrounding the park. The albino German Shepard leaped, catching its ball, and ran glowing in and out of the streetlights. It barked once as it reached the woman with the wild, red hair streaming down her back.

"That's my girl," said CC, taking the ball from the dog. She threw it with her right hand. "Go get it, Fluffy." CC slapped her thigh with her left hand. "Do the mosquitoes ever quit?"

"Fluffy. I knew she had a simple name," said Tom, squinting as his own dog, much smaller than Fluffy, ran toward him carrying a ball sloppy with spit. As Tom's dog passed Fluffy, she dropped her ball and ran after Fluffy. "Myrtle," shouted Tom, laughing. "Myrtle's usually afraid of big dogs, but she likes Fluffy."

CC grinned, pushing the red curls and sweat off the side of her face. "Fluffy has that way about her. Where's..." CC paused and lifted her index finger. "Wait. Don't tell me her name - your wife - Jane. Where's Jane tonight?"

Since taking possession of their new home, CC had taken Fluffy to the dog park every evening to let the dog run and meet her new neighbors. Sometimes James Earl, her business partner and lover, came with her. Tom and Jane, the accountants whose home/office shared the same parking lot as CC's home/office, brought their own dog to the park, too. Tonight, Tom and Myrtle were on their own.

Tom pushed his shoulders up and puffed his chest as wide as he could. "The Reverend Dr. Cairns," he said in his deepest voice and a horrible Scots brogue before laughing and pulling the golf towel from its hook on his belt loop to wipe the sweat off his face. "If James Earl hadn't researched him so well for us, we never would have taken him on as a client. You should hear him rant. I thought American evangelists were obnoxious." He pulled a small bottle from his pocket. "Here," he added. "For the mosquitos. Never leave home without it these days. And speaking of mosquitoes, don't forget the barbecue Saturday. I'll get the yard sprayed before then. We've invited everyone on the street. Afraid we invited a few clients, too. But don't worry, Cairns already refused the invitation."

"Looking forward to it, and thanks. James Earl's been dealing with him and only through email. Glad I didn't have to talk to him. He sounds like a real monster." CC sprayed her arms and legs with repellent before taking the ball from Fluffy, who sat waiting for another throw. "I told you we were vegans, right?" She tossed the ball, and Fluffy barked as she ran after it. Myrtle, having caught up with Fluffy, turned and follow Fluffy again.

"So's Carmichael and his partner, the lawyers on the corner. I think they're vegans. They may be vegetarians." Tom pointed to the single-story home at the end of the road. "They're cat people, but they like walking. If you're out in the early hours, you'll see them."

CC nodded when she felt a familiar tickle run down her spine. She lifted the red curls off her neck and turned to look behind her. "Fluffy and I like to run before the sun and heat. I'll keep an eye out for them."

CC felt the corners of her mouth perk up as the familiar tickle ran down her spine again. She looked behind her again. This time, she saw the man wearing a tall hat standing just outside the light over the gate to the park.

Fluffy ran past her, dropping the ball to whisper a growl at the man. Her lips curled up as her ears pointed straight and the line of fur running down her spine spiked. Myrtle barked once, and Tom bent to pick her up. He squinted to see the man, but Myrtle squirmed, her own fur standing on end.

"What the matter, sweetie?" asked Tom, losing his balance and almost falling as Myrtle continued to squirm.

CC grabbed Tom's forearm. "That's enough, Fluffy," she said between pursed lips. "Be nice. You okay, Tom?"

Tom's eyes returned to the gate area. "Don't know what's gotten into her." His voice shook. His eyes did not leave the man in the shadows.

CC turned to the man and put a hand on her hip while waving with the other hand. "Hi, Clay. Be with you in a minute."

"How can you see who it is?" asked Tom, not looking at CC.

CC patted Tom's shoulder, turning him away from the gate. "A bit of an eccentric, but a good guy. Don't let the undertaker gear spook you. He really is an undertaker."

"Oh," said Tom, nodding. "I should get home, see how the meeting went. We'll see you Saturday."

"Saturday," nodded CC, watching Tom, carrying Myrtle, hurry to the gate on the opposite side of the park.

CC walked toward the man in the shadows. "Damn it, Clay. You need to work on your social skills. You're a nice guy. Why do you gotta be all vampy all the time?" CC never lost the smile on her face, even as she bent over to attach the leash to Fluffy's collar.

"I cannot hide what I am. You of all people know that." Clay's voice crept through the shadows to her. He lifted his upper lip, revealing white teeth gleaming in the streetlight.

"Can it, Clay," replied CC, opening the gate. "That stopped working on me a long time ago." She stopped in front of him. "You gonna give me a hug or what?"

Clay removed his hat and bent over to reach his arms around CC. "It's always a pleasure to be with you CC. You're the only human who hugs me."

CC patted his back as he straightened and replaced his hat. She looked up into his face. "That's because I know you're not going to bite me. You could try to wear," CC paused, putting a finger to her lips, "something a little less 'Dickensian undertaker'."

"I am what I am," replied Clay, walking beside CC toward her house.

CC watched his face as they walked under the streetlight. His round, black eyes, usually deep and mellow, contained lines around their edges. His dark brown skin grayed around the edges of his thin sideburns, touched with silver. Even his usual dreadlocks hung as though discarded.

CC swallowed a lump in her throat. "This isn't a social call," she whispered.

"No," he said as they crossed the street, arriving at the walkway covered with the pink petals of Crepe Myrtles in full bloom. The turn-of-the-century house, her new place of business and home, stood silent in the darkening night. Above the doors, a window with the house numbers edged in gold and lit from the vestibule, provided the only light. Along the street, other houses had glowing windows and streetlights illuminating small yards. Only her house felt dark and unwelcoming.

"My house," she sighed, smiling despite the worry growing inside her.

Clay removed his hat and stepped over a box as he crossed the threshold. CC shrugged her shoulders. "I brought the last of the boxes over this afternoon. It'll take a few days to get situated."

"It's neater than I expected," he said with no visible sign of humor.

CC unhooked Fluffy's leash and stepped around Clay to close the curtains that hung in front of the grand garden window in the old sitting room-turned-reception room. They were heavy, blue velvet drapes and dust splashed onto her face as she closed them.

Clay arched his eyebrow as dust drifted onto him.

"Go lie down, Fluffy," she said, and pointed Clay to the next open door on the far side of the room. "My office is in better shape." She led Clay across the reception area stacked with boxes. "At least it's clean, even if it isn't organized yet."

A large wooden desk sat in the center of her office before a wall of old oak bookcases filled with books, computer monitors, cameras, boxes, and more boxes. CC flipped the light switch on the wall, and when the overhead light remained dark, stepped toward her desk. She tripped on the edge of a rug rolled up next to a box and caught herself from falling on the corner of one of two overstuff client chairs. Grunting, she reached for the desk lamp and clicked it on. It provided enough light for her to step around the other client chair and around another box to the floor lamp in front of a curved alcove filled with windows. She closed the heavy drapes that matched the drapes in the reception room.

"Some improvement," Clay said. "Your client list must be growing. These old homes are not inexpensive."

She removed a box from one of the client chairs, pointing Clay to sit in it. "Sort of. Mike Young bought the other half of the building for his office. We share the reception area. He even has a bedroom in back, but I don't think he plans to use it much."

Clay set his hat on this lap. He did not look around the room.

"What's wrong?" she asked, sitting in the chair next to him.

"Where is your young man?" Clay asked.

"Full moon," she answered.

"Yes," nodded Clay. "So much on my mind, I hadn't realized."

CC stared at the straight-faced vampire. She bit her lip, waiting for him to speak. Releasing a long sigh, she asked, "What's wrong, Clay?"

Clay stood, going to the window and peaking outside to the empty street. "I found a body," he said. "A child." His shoulders dropped as his chin fell to his chest.

CC's hand reached for her neck, remembering the warning she'd received during the summer about a killer of children coming to Austin. Her pulse increased, but she forced herself to slow her breathing. "Tell me," she whispered.

Clay turned. His eyes fixed on her hand covering her neck before looking into her eyes. "I didn't realize how damaged he was until I cleaned his body."

Clay reached out, pulling CC's hand away from her neck. Clasping her hand in his, he said, "You expected this."

CC realized she'd been holding her breath. She felt her hand on Clay's icy fingers and squeezed back. "I need to see him."

Clay nodded. "Come after eleven."

CC nodded. "I'll meet you there." She led Clay to the front door.

Clay stood at the open door. Turning, he lifted CC's chin with his hand. "She chose you to make this right, didn't she?" he said.

"What?" CC said, her eyes widening.

"Mary doesn't mark humans unless they're special."

"Marked?" CC stuttered.

Clay produced the smile of sympathy and care he was so well known for. "Humans can't see it, but I can. It's nothing to be ashamed of. It will keep you safe from those who don't follow the rules. I'm surprised you didn't know."

Clay stepped outside, placing his hat on his head as he merged into the shadows of the small yard. "Eleven o'clock," he said, and he was gone.

*****

CC slumped into the sofa, breathing in the steam from her coffee. She shivered when the air conditioner turned on to blow cold air on top of her head. There were no boxes in the living room, and it was almost comfortable. James Earl set up the enormous television screen even as the movers brought in the ugly brown sofa, coffee table, and patched recliner from their rented house. They looked squalid in front of his new, extra-large screen.

Fluffy jumped onto the sofa and put her head in CC's lap. Without thinking, CC gripped her coffee mug by the handle to scratch the dog's too-white ears. Shifting to take a sip of coffee, she watched her reflection on the shiny black screen. Fluffy glowed white in the reflection, but CC could barely see her own reflection. Only a mass of red hair, black on the screen, and black eyes in a pool of pale skin stared back at her. She stretched her neck and saw no mark.

"I can't believe she marked me," CC said, shaking her head. A wave of nausea crept through her as her coffee hit the bottom of her stomach. She put her mug on the coffee table and cradled her head in her hands. Fluffy licked her face.

CC counted breaths until she could sit up without feeling sick. Leaning back, she allowed Fluffy to lean into her, warming her with soft fur and moist breath. She thought of James Earl and the last time she'd gone with him to the vineyard. He ran that night with abandon, being the beautiful wolf he was. "But not like always," she said, closing her eyes, seeing the guest room, the moonlight spilling from the window over the bed as she closed the shutters, hearing the silence of the stately home oozing with the opulence of great wealth. "I didn't know Mary was in the house until I saw her in my room. Even you didn't know, Fluffy." CC took a deep breath. "Oh god, Fluffy," CC said, rising too fast and putting her head back between her knees. "Does James Earl see it, too? Does he know Mary marked me?"

She'd been near Mary before, at a distance, but that night Mary filled her with an overabundance of awe, fear, loathing, and want. "What happened?" she said in a whisper, not expecting an answer. Mary Midnight, for so long a voice in the air, a silhouette standing over there, beyond clear sight, stood too close, spoke of shared fears, nightmares, loves so deep they wiped away time. And she filled CC with a comfort she had always wanted. In return, Mary fed on her, taking her blood. "Did she take my soul, too? No. That's silly."

CC shivered, remembering Mary's voice. "A monster walks this earth. It walks on two legs in the day, but it fears the sun as the eye of God. It knows how to be a man but forsakes the knowledge to satiate its needs. It feeds on the young, seeking redemption in the solace of innocence. It will never know peace, only pain, bound in the corruption of words. Find it, Catherine. Find it before it destroys all we love."

That's when Mary bit her. CC remembered. She shivered, knowing at that moment Mary took more than just blood. And CC had given willingly, wanting to fill the space between them until they became one.

"Find the monster. My champion will kill it." Those were the last words Mary said before CC slipped into a sleep so deep, she didn't know if she would ever wake.

"Why mark me?" asked CC, standing. Was it, as Clay suggested, a warning to the other vamps in the city to leave her alone? Or was there something else to it?

*****

Fluffy yawned and stretched her neck out of the sidecar as CC idled her motorcycle. They were a block from Clay's funeral home.

"Stay," she said, as Fluffy set a paw on her leg. "It's well after eleven. Don't these people have to get to work tomorrow?"

Fluffy didn't reply.

CC shook her head, tapped her phone. *Too many people.* She sent the text to Clay.

"We're hardly inconspicuous," she mumbled. "And that's your fault. One more time around the block, and everyone will be pointing at us."

Clay replied, *Back gate.*

CC pulled into traffic to turn the corner to the back of the building. As she approached the rear of the funeral home, the tall brick wall surrounding it broke as a black gate slid open. The brick crematoria with their skinny chimneys filled the rear of the funeral home parking lot. The tall fence allowed the funeral workers to park securely as well as move between crematoria and labs unobserved.

CC watched Clay open the rear door for her as she parked and removed her helmet. "Stay in the yard," she told Fluffy as the dog bounded out of the sidecar to sniff the perimeter.

"Mr. Rivers was more popular than I assumed. Although, I suspect the large number of cousins has more to do with his winning the lottery last week than his passing this week. The lab staff are gone. We may work without interruption."

Most of the lights in the lab were off. Clay locked the door behind her as she pulled her phone from her hip holster and turned on the flashlight.

"I have him in the small lab. No one bothers me when I'm there," Clay said as he led her down a wide hall. Light spilled in from under the double doors leading to the funeral parlor.

CC heard hushed voices, some arguing, some laughing. At the end of the hall, Clay stopped to look behind him, then he unlocked a dark-green door. The chill of the room slapped CC in the face. The sweat still trickling from under her hair sent chills across her skin. Her light reflected off a stainless-steel table in the center of the room and stainless shelves covered with glass bottles and instruments she didn't know the names of. Clay clapped his hands twice and the overhead lights flashed on.

A white cloth draped over a body on the table. "This him?" she asked.

Clay slid to the head of the body with the quickness of a vampire, and she wondered if she would ever get used to their swift, graceful movements. He lifted the ends of the cloth, folding it three times with perfect creases to reveal the body.

CC pulled a pencil from her pocket, pushing it into her mass of red curls she knotted on her head as she bent forward to examine the body.

"I see what you mean," she said. Although she wore gloves, she kept her fingers a breath above the pale skin. Part of the neck was missing, with the esophagus half in and half out of what remained. His chest lay open to the light. One of his lungs, graying and scarred, pushed against broken ribs. The face, young and sweet, smelled of cleaner. Dark bruises covered the torso and limbs with more bruises and chafing encircling the wrists and ankles. The legs and arms, like the neck, contained holes with clean edges. CC placed her gloved finger in some holes where the white of bone reflected the overhead lights.

"Not a wolf," said CC.

"And not vampire," replied Clay. "Yet, there is no blood in him nor on the ground where I found him."

"Clothes?"

Clay pulled a black bag from under the table and set it on a tray. "Such as they are." Grayed and dirty cut-off jeans lay torn and bloodied. Tattered briefs caked with dirt and blood lay in a ball next to the jeans.

"Nothing else?" CC asked.

"A broken plastic disk. He wore the disk in his right ear."

CC lifted the body's right hand. The nails were broken and filled with dirt and dried blood. "Any tissue under the nails?" she asked.

Clay's head shook. His eyes fixed to a point beyond CC. "The boy couldn't have been over thirteen. He's malnourished. The calluses on his feet say he didn't wear shoes often. No belongings near him. I'm afraid he was discarded before this desecration."

"Any signs of sexual assault?" CC gilded her hand up the other side of the body. She stopped at his head and picked up a comb, pulling it once through a lock of dark hair. She put the comb into a plastic bag. "I don't see any sign of him fighting back. He may have been drugged. Street kids know how to put up a fight."

Clay turned his head away from CC. "No sexual assault, but..."

CC pushed on the body to turn it on its side. "More bruising and bites from this side. Clay," CC sighed, waiting for Clay to finish his sentence.

Clay pulled a handkerchief from his pocket. "No heart, CC. It's been ripped out, and there is flesh missing." Clay held his handkerchief to his mouth. "I've never seen that. How do we proceed?"

CC grimaced at the holes, but returned the body to its back, taking pictures of the boy's face before covering it with the white cloth. "First, let's see if I can find him a name."

Clay raised an eyebrow.

"If his face has been online, James Earl will find him. I'll have him clean up a picture for me to show around, too. Where did you find him?"

Clay's eyes widened as he stared at CC, and then he closed his eyes. "Outside the Long Center near the running path. He was hidden in bushes. I smelled him before I saw him. The smell," Clay paused, contemplating his words. "The smell was more than death and decay. There was something else, just a trace. Something evil."

"Lucky you found him before anyone else did and called the police.

Can you draw me a map to exactly where you found him? I'll want to check out the place before too many people walk around there."

"Let me take you. I've been doing this a long time and I've never seen anything like this - abomination. And if it's one of us..."

CC nodded her head and placed her hand on his arm. "Let's go."

*****

CC arched her back and looked up. "Anything strike you as unusual before you found the body?" She stepped over low shrubs and back onto the grass to stand next to Clay.

"No," he said. "Only that odd smell, but the smell of decay was most prevalent. He must have been here for some hours."

CC looked around. The city glowed in the night. The streetlight overhead needed replacing, but the other lights made it easy to see. "Wish the light wasn't out." She put her finger to her lips and began walking in a wide circle. "You found him early this morning?"

"Which is now yesterday morning," Clay said, eyes fixed on CC as she circled the area.

"I'll need to come back in the daylight, get a better look under the bushes. Not likely too much left, but you never know. Wish James Earl were here."

A siren and flashing red light interrupted her. She lifted her head to see the shadow of Clay slide into the darkness of the trees. Fluffy barked, jumping from the tree line to sit at her feet. Smiling, CC turned to the green SUV with the flashing red light. The driver stepped out.

She waved. "What's up, Renaldo?"

"I thought that was you, CC. What are you doing out here at this hour?"

"Exercises." CC reached out to shake Renaldo's hand. "You working or stalking me?"

"Just finished a stakeout the other side of the river. You don't look like you're exercising." Renaldo reached to pet Fluffy but pulled back as the dog bared her teeth with a quiet growl.

CC laughed. "Be nice, Fluffy. I'm training her to search. Too hot to do much in the day. Done for tonight? I was about to get some coffee. Want to join us?"

Renaldo Sanchez rubbed his hand over the stubble that made up the beginnings of a beard. "To search, huh? Sure, why not. But what about your friend?"

"Fluffy rides in the side car," CC said as both she and Fluffy walked to her motorcycle.

"No, I mean," Renaldo looked behind CC. He shook his head "Whatever."

"The place next to the station? Goggles, Fluffy." CC didn't wait for a reply from Renaldo. She placed the goggles over Fluffy's eyes and started her motorcycle.

*****

CC pushed her phone into her jean's pocket then set her feet on the low table. Renaldo handed her the hot cup.

"Thank you," she said, and held the cup to her lips. "Nothing like hot coffee at zero dark thirty. Helps to relax the mind."

"Heard you and James Earl got new digs." Renaldo sat opposite CC on the empty couch. He bent over to put a cup of water down for Fluffy.

"Almost settled in. You should stop by sometime. You'll drool over the surveillance equipment James Earl is setting up. So, what's up with you tonight? Anything exciting?"

"Nah. Our supposed drug dealer keeps nine-to-five hours." Renaldo leaned back, sipping his coffee and exploring the room. Aside from the barista reading his book behind the counter, only two women in medical scrubs sitting at the counter eating sandwiches and chatting non-stop about a birthday party for a twelve-year-old occupied the coffee house. He watched CC close her eyes. "So, what kind of stuff is Fluffy learning to search for in the park, at the height of the witching hours, when most of the city is asleep?"

"Any kind of stuff I need to find." CC laughed. "What kind of drug dealer only works days?"

"A boring one," Renaldo said, shaking his head. "Come on. You can tell me. What were you really doing? Or is it some kind of state secret?"

CC laughed. "You're too good for me. But seriously, nothing interesting. Well, right now it's not interesting enough for you, but I'll let you know if that status changes."

"Fair enough. Where's James Earl?"

"Out of town for a couple of days - always working. What about you and Anna, or was it Joanna I saw you with last time? You two still an item?"

"Naw. Dating another cop is a mistake. Our schedules keep criss-crossing, and everybody knows about it. I take it business is good. I mean, an office downtown isn't cheap."

CC leaned forward and lowered her voice. "You and me got into the wrong end of investigations. James Earl's the one making all the money. Amazing what you can find out about a person with nothing but a name and a phone number."

Renaldo laughed. The two women in medical scrubs received calls at the same time and dashed out of the coffee shop. "Someone's in the emergency room," he said as he drank his coffee.

CC watched the women leave. "Yes," she said. Her eyes followed the women as they walked in front of the windows.

Renaldo focused his eyes on CC. "Probably a kid with an earache."

Fluffy stood and barked once.

Renaldo's phone twinged. "Damn," he said, looking at the screen. "Gotta call out. Call me when you're ready to give me something interesting."

CC watched Renaldo gulp down half his coffee and head to the door. "Catch you later, Renaldo. Thanks for the coffee."

Renaldo turned and waved, but his expression said he was already on his way to the scene.

"He's too smart to lie to, Fluffy," CC said, reaching over to pet her dog. "Ready to head home?" The barista looked up from his book, sighing when he saw CC lean back into the couch.

*****

The car hit the steep curb as Marcus pulled into the parking lot between the cafe and the student co-op. Luna's head thumped against the window. She shook her head. "Seriously?" she croaked as she stretched her neck and arm. "Mama's opening up this morning. We don't need to be here."

"What the..." Marcus muttered. He turned the key off and opened the door before the engine had time to turn off.

"Marcus!" Luna grumbled as she opened her door to follow him to the back of the cafe. A full trash can held the kitchen door open. The broken table kept in the back of the kitchen for them to work on leaned against the wall near the door. Three bags of trash slumped before it, along with two buckets, mops, and her favorite broom.

Luna watched as Marcus picked up her broom and stormed into the doorway. He heard him yell, "Hey!"

Before she could reach the open door, Marcus backed out as a short, round woman with enormous breasts spreading in front of her, draped in a stained white tunic, chased him with a larger broom.

"Who the fuck are you!" the woman demanded, stopping in the doorway and squaring her shoulders to Marcus.

Luna froze. Her big brother cowered in front of the woman whose neon blue hair and thick, black lines around her eyes contrasted with cheeks hot pink with sweat.

Luna fought a giggle rising in her throat, especially when the woman looked to her and lowered the broom.

"Oh shit! You must be Marcus and Luna. Chef said I'd see you this morning. Sorry if I gave you a fright. I didn't realize the sun was already up. What a night," the woman said, pulling a bandana from her back pocket and wiping her face.

The woman turned away from Marcus and walked into the kitchen.

Luna ran into Marcus' back when he stopped in the inner doorway. Luna pushed her way past him, only to stop as her jaw dropped, but she didn't care. The old refrigerator, sink, and stove were gone. The door to the old walk-in freezer was gone. Bright new light fixtures in the ceiling shone onto sparkling countertops. A ladder stood in the center of the room. One end of a pot rack hung from a chain on the ceiling. The other end rested on top of the ladder.

The woman placed the broom on a far cabinet and reached for the ladder but stopped. She turned, looking first at Marcus and then Luna. "Oh, sorry. I'm Flo, Chef Max's sous chef. Nice to meet you. You scared the hell out of me, man. I don't like heights, they make me woozy, but wanted to get this hung before the new island comes in. You can imagine what I thought when I see two enormous arms lifting a broom running in from outside."

Luna moved her mouth to say something as Marcus wouldn't or couldn't, but she found herself tongue tied. Flo continued, "Chef wants this place cleaned out by tonight." Her pasty face blanched at Marcus' silence and turned to Luna, reaching out her hand. "Luna?"

Luna nodded, then jumped to grab Flo's hand, wincing as Flo's grip viced her fingers into one. "Nice to meet you, Flo," she said.

Marcus walked further into the kitchen. Luna watched as the lines on his face stiffened and his cheeks gray. She felt her own shoulders stiffen seeing her brother's eyes widen. An explosion was on its way, and not for the first time, she felt embarrassed that a stranger would see it. "Looking good, Flo. We just stopped by on our way to campus. Marcus' taking me to get my books. This is my first semester at UT." She reached for her brother, but it was too late. His eyes froze at the empty slot where the refrigerator had stood.

The blood vessels on Marcus' neck popped out and his lips pinched, hardly moving as he asked, "Where's all the food that was in here?"

Flo smiled, turning to reach for the ladder to climb up. "Trash. Stored wrong."

Luna stepped forward to stay between Marcus and Flo, but Marcus didn't care. Her ears ached as he shouted, "We don't throw away perfectly good food. I don't know what you think you're doing, but no way--"

Luna cringed as Flo interrupted Marcus and stepped back as Flo's gray-blue eyes turned into steel bullets. Without raising her voice, and despite being a foot shorter than Marcus, Flo towered over Marcus. "When you learn how to run a fucking kitchen, I'll listen to what you have to say."

Luna jumped when her mother's voice broke into the kitchen. "I won't have that sort of language in my establishment."

Flo looked down, fumbling with her words. "Yes, ma'am. Sorry, ma'am. Won't happen again."

Jackie nodded. "Why are you here, Marcus? You're supposed to be helping Luna get her books."

"Mama, she says the kitchen if filthy--"

"Who better than a chef to judge the state of a kitchen." Jackie's face remained impassive. Luna recognized the look and kept her mouth closed. She turned to watch the effect on Marcus.

His face faded from gray to a pale brown as his eyes softened and his shoulders fell.

Flo twisted the bandanna in her hand. Only after wiping her hands on her tunic did she offer her hand to Jackie. "I apologize for the language, Ma'am. My name is Flo - well, Florence, but everyone calls me Flo. Chef said to be sure I introduce myself to you and answer any questions. You have my word; I'll keep my language proper."

Jackie shook Flo's hand. "Pleased to meet you, Florence. Call me Jackie. Don't let us bother you. The kitchen is your domain. I'm confident you and Chef Max know what you're doing."

"Yes, Ma'am. If you'll excuse me. I'll get back to work. Time flies and all that. I'll be quiet as a mouse."

Jackie sighed. "It's not like we get many people this early. Once I get the coffee machines working, I'll be in my office. Don't worry about bothering me."

Flo grinned, showing a large gap in her front teeth. "Yes, Ma'am."

"Thank you, Florence." Jackie left the kitchen. Luna took a deep breath and looked at Marcus. His chest was puffing, and she sighed.

"Mama," Marcus called and rushed out of the kitchen, following his mother.

"Don't mind him," Luna said to Flo. "He's excitable."

Flo took two steps up the ladder. "No, shhhh - shooting around that." Flo took a deep breath before taking another step up the ladder.

Luna looked to the ceiling, noticing two eye-bolts and chains already in place for the pot rack. "Would you like some help?"

Flo turned her face to the open door to the café. Luna cringed as Marcus' voice carried into the kitchen. "How can we afford a sous chef? We can't even afford to hire wait staff."

Jackie's voice, not as loud, but firm answered, "We talked about this last night, Marcus. Chef Max bought forty-nine percent of the shop. He's in control of the kitchen from now on."

Luna moved to the far side of the ladder and climbed to the top. "Looks like you've done the hard part already. It doesn't look too heavy."

Flo's cheeks blushed as she looked up at Luna. "Thanks," she said, and stepped down the ladder one rung at a time. "Can't tell you how much I appreciate it."

"No problem." Luna lifted the end of the pot rack to connect the hooks to the chain. "Heavier than I thought, but I got it."

Flo moved to stand behind Luna. She raised her hands up as though to catch her. "I got you if you fall."

Luna laughed at the worry in Flo's eyes, but her attention turned back to the café where Marcus' voice, now pinched and stiff, said, "But mama, this is our family business."

"It still is, Marcus," replied Jackie, her voice softening. "He bought forty-nine percent. It's enough to pay the bills and more. If Chef Max hadn't come along, we'd be closing the cafe at the end of the year."

Luna attached both corners of the pot rack and climbed down, bumping into Flo who refused to move away until Luna had both feet on the floor.

Flo's cheeks, still burning red, said, "I'm going to take a smoke break."

Luna nodded but remained leaning against the ladder.

Marcus' voice croaked, "I knew things were bad. I didn't realize they were that bad. What did Aunt Jasmine mean by the contract being too good? What's the catch in all this?"

Luna leaned forward, afraid she'd miss her mother's answer. "Daddy and I always talked about opening a coffee shop and cafe, building a community, a safe place to talk and learn. It seemed right to use the insurance money on this place."

A ping of doubt filled Luna's heart. They didn't talk about Daddy. The espresso machine clanked on and the sound of steam rushing through pipes covered their voices. When the machine quieted, Marcus said, "This chef could buy us out at any time," Marcus said.

"He promised he wouldn't," said Jackie.

"Promised. But it's not in the contract?"

A flutter of hope spurred inside Luna. *If he buys us out, Mama would go back to teaching. We'd have money again. I wouldn't have to wait tables.*

"I believe him," Jackie's voice lost the sadness Luna was so used to hearing. "This feels right, Marcus. For the first time in six years, I feel like we're in a good place."

"Mama," Marcus groaned.

"It's done, Marcus." Jackie's voice told Luna that the argument had ended. "Take Luna to the bookstore."

"Yes, ma'am," replied Marcus.

Luna dashed outside, finding Flo leaning into a gap in the fence talking to someone from the student co-op. She was handing him a bag of the bread that had been in the refrigerator last night.

When Flo turned around, her face flushed bright red. "You're not going to tell your brother about that, are you?"

Luna laughed. "I ought to, just to rub it in," she said but stopped Flo's brow creased. "Not a word."

The relief on Flo's face was instant. "Thanks," she said. "I gotta keep this job. The wife and kids are depending on it."

"You have a wife?" Luna asked.

"Well," Flo stuttered and looked down. "We're not actually married, not yet. She's still in the Army - getting out in a few months, but she doesn't want to risk her benefits."

"Oh," was the only thing Luna could say. Marcus shouted her name from inside the kitchen. "It's nice to meet you, Flo. Gotta go." She rolled her eyes and continued. "Apparently, I'm not responsible enough to go get my own books."

"Luna!" shouted Marcus as he stepped out of the kitchen. "Let's go." Marcus did not look at Flo.

"Smoking is bad for you and especially your kids," Luna said as she turned to the car. "And it stinks. I like you, Flo. We're going to be good friends."

Back in the car, Marcus turned up the air conditioner to blow hard. Luna fastened her seat belt and pulled the printed copy of her classes from her backpack. "Some of the books are e-books. That will save us some money, but it'll take me a while to get used to them. Mama always used real books for my schoolwork."

Marcus leaned forward with his eyes closed. Most of the sweat on his forehead dried in the cold, blowing air.

Luna sighed. "You know, I think Daddy would be happy we have a real chef for the place. You know how he liked good food."

Marcus straightened his back and put the car in reverse. As he twisted to look behind him, he stopped long enough to look into Luna's face. "More than us."

Luna took a deep breath and turned away from Marcus. She bit her bottom lip to still the trembling. "I'm trying, Marcus."

She twisted when she felt his hand on her shoulder. "I'm sorry. I am, too."

*****

A steady stream of customers, mostly students moving into student apartments, dorms, and co-ops, flowed in and out of the cafe all afternoon. Luna sat at a table close to the front door pretending to read through her new biology textbook. She woke to find the syllabus for the class on her dresser, Marcus' attempt to prepare her for college. She sighed, tired of pretending to read, provide service with a smile, and wipe down tables.

Most of the students coming in walked straight to the coffee counter, talked with old friends and roommates, and left when Marcus handed them their drinks. There was no food in the display counter, but the aroma of yeast, flour, and sugar drifted from the kitchen and settled over everyone. Luna had no names for all the aromas, but they filled her with mouth-watering promise, hints of comfort and wonder, and they made her stomach rumble. The students walked out smiling at their coffee drinks, but their eyes lingered toward the kitchen door watering for tastes of pleasure. An old man still sat at the table near the coffee counter. When Luna offered to get him more coffee, he growled at her. She watched two girls about her age sitting in front of the stage, still filled with plants. Their voices were low, but when they giggled, the sound filled her with envy. They didn't have textbooks in front of them. *Must be nice to not have a crappy job.*

Luna didn't realize she was staring at them until she noticed one of the girls, the one with flaming gold hair, lift her frozen drink cup and point to Max while whispering to her friend. The other girl, with not so flaming gold hair and pimples, laughed out loud, causing the first girl to blush. Luna frowned, turning her attention to Max, Chef Max, according to her mother, but always Mr. Thin Man to her.

She scrunched her face, not getting it. He was old, at least in his thirties, maybe even forty. While she wouldn't call him good looking, he wasn't ugly. *Maybe it's because his face is hidden in the shadows - being all Mr. Mystery Man.* He was at the table he always sat at, the one truly dark corner even in the middle of the afternoon, silent, and reading a book. If he noticed her or the girls looking at him, he made no indication.

"You've got to take your studies seriously," Marcus said as he plopped down in the chair next to her. He picked up her biology book and flipped through the pages. "Looks like the one I used. Can't see what's new in this edition. Waste of money buying new books."

Luna pulled the book from his hands. "It's what the instructor requires," she smirked. "But you read the syllabus, so you know that. Should I be as good a student as you?" She asked her question with a smirk on her face.

Luna's shoulders deflated as the argument she expected from Marcus didn't arrive. She glared at him, only to find him staring at Max. "What is he doing? He's been sitting there all day."

"Calibrating the ovens," Luna said. "That's what he told me when I asked. You'd know that if you got off your high horse and talked rather than just making drinks and frowning." She picked up her math book. "But it looks to me like Flo's doing all the work. I haven't seen him take his nose out of that book since we got here. It's precisely a week since he said he'd be producing, and it looks like Flo's doing all the work." Luna twisted as the bell over the door rang again. "Where is everybody coming from?"

Marcus still stared at Max. "Classes start this week. It's expected-"

Luna interrupted Marcus by pointing to the kitchen door. "Here we go again," she said. Flo carried a tray from the kitchen covered with fancy looking rolls. "It's the same thing every time. He'll tell her to proof them longer, bake them longer, stir something a different way. It's just weird. He barely tastes them."

As if on cue, Max lifted his face to Flo as she placed the tray in front of him. He picked up a roll, pulled it apart, and lifted it to his nose, sniffed loud enough for Luna and Marcus to hear, and then he took another roll, pulled it apart, squished pieces between his fingers, and rolled it in his hands. He put a ball in his mouth and chewed. "Good," he said, nodding to Flo. "Make a note of the humidity. It's high today, so you'll need to make adjustments when it's lower."

"Yes, Chef," Flo replied, grinning as though someone walked up and gave her ten thousand dollars. She lifted the tray, stopping as Max pointed to the two girls Luna had been watching. She walked to them and offered them rolls. "Chef says they're good enough to eat. On the house."

The girls giggled as they grabbed the rolls. One of them even blushed.

Flo then walked to Luna and Marcus. The smile on her face beamed. Any larger, and it would break her cheeks. "They're good," she said. "Have one."

Luna reached up, taking one. Her stomach grumbled again as she moved it to her mouth. "Thanks, I didn't have breakfast this morning, and all the smells in her are making me hungry." She bit into the hot roll. A wave of warmth and comfort flowed over her. Bliss ticked her tongue. "Oh, my goh, these 'r goo," she managed to say despite the full mouth.

Flo's face glowed even more. Luna frowned at Marcus, who shook his head refusing a roll.

"Marcus." Luna kicked his leg under the table. "She's been working all day. The least you could do is pretend to like her." She watched Flo take the tray to the grumpy old man. He seemed to like Flo. He took a roll and ate it, smiling at her.

Luna felt the roll thud into her stomach as Marcus' eyes glared at her over lips pressed so tight white lines formed around his brown lips. "Do you realize how much this is costing us for her to figure out how to cook?"

Luna opened her mouth, but Max looked up from his book, catching her eye. The light above his head reflected his sea-gray eyes, sending a chill through her. He shook his head. It was slight, almost not there, and then he turned his face back to his book.

Marcus didn't notice. He turned his face to follow Flo with his eyes glaring holes into her back. The girls she'd been watching walked past her on the way out the door.

Luna rose from her chair. "I should clean that table."

Marcus said nothing, but cleared his throat before thumping toward the kitchen door. A group of students walked in with the two girls heading to the coffee counter. Marcus stopped for only a moment before turning to walk behind the coffee counter and force a smile on his face. Luna watched him as his hands twisted a towel almost to breaking as he listened to the girls discuss which drinks to order.

Luna wiped wet rings of condensation off the table before sitting across from Max. "Why are you making Flo do all the work?" she asked, leaning forward to see the title of the book he was reading. The title wasn't in English.

"She's learning," he said without looking up.

Luna leaned back in her chair, crossing her arms across her chest. "How can she be learning anything if you're just sitting here reading your book?"

Max lifted his face. As usual, she caught her breath when his eyes looked at her and through her at the same time, but then he smiled that little smile he wore that said he knew what she wanted to talk about. "She knows how to do what needs to be done. She's learning finesse."

"Sounds like a fancy way to say you're being a lazy ass," she said, smirking. "And you need to pay attention to what's around you. Those girls that just left, one of them had the hots for you."

"Florence is a talented chef, one of the best I've run into in a long while. If I were in there watching her every move, she'd believe I had no faith in her. And I noticed the young women looking at me. They thought my face very interesting, but the pimpled girl said I was too skinny."

Luna straightened. "How did you..." She bit her lip, imagining the whispered voices she couldn't hear. She looked at Max, seeing his grin take a sheepish turn. "You're making that up," she said, laughing.

"Perhaps," said Max. He turned his head, listening for something. "Marcus doesn't like me much."

Luna guffawed. "You think? But don't let it burn you. He doesn't like anyone anymore."

"Anymore?" asked Max.

Luna sighed and leaned into one arm lying on the table as the fingers of her other hand tapped the table to a beat only she heard. "He used to be fun. Always a pest and in my way, but still fun to be around. Maybe now you're here and Mom's not worried so much about money, he'll get back to his classes and chill a little. Classes start in two days, you know."

Max's lips squeezed together for a moment, then he returned his gaze to her. "You don't seem anxious about starting college."

"Are you kidding?" Luna exclaimed, sitting up "It gets me out of wiping tables and cleaning up spilled coffee. I can't wait. Besides," Luna leaned forward, lowering her voice so only Max could hear. "School's always been easy for me, especially now that Marcus all but flunked out last term. As long as I make passing grades, I've got it easy." She winked at Max.

Max nodded his head. "I've no doubt you'll go far, Luna."

"You got that right," Luna said, standing as another group of students entered and pulled tables together. "Until then, I've got to wait tables. At least I don't have to work at the museum anymore. Of course, I got paid for doing that." She sighed as she stood. "Back to work," she muttered and helped the students put the tables together.

*****

"My feet are killing me," Luna said, sitting on the bench in front of the cafe. The night air hung heavy on her shoulders as she leaned over to pull her new slipper shoe off her right foot.

Marcus huffed as he locked the door. "Should have worn your sneakers." He stopped in front of her. "Do not take those shoes off until we get to the car. You don't know what you'll step on."

Luna watched Marcus march down the walkway leading to the rear parking lot. She mimicked him under her breath, but he ignored her. Deciding he'd leave her if she didn't keep up, she slipped her shoe back on and limped to catch up. "We've never been busy on a Monday night. Glad I didn't wear my heels."

She turned into the rear lot and coughed at the wall of cigarette smoke hanging near the back door. Marcus, head bent down and swinging his backpack from his shoulder into the backseat of the car, coughed overly loud. Luna looked for the source of the smell and saw Flo leaning against the back door. She stared at the round woman, usually so confident and sure of herself, squatting down with her head bent over and a phone pressed against her ear.

"Luna," whispered Marcus, nodding at her to get into the car.

"Just get the fuck off the couch and come get me!" Luna jumped as Flo's voice echoed across the parking lot

Luna and Marcus stared at each other, and then a loud sniff hit their ears.

Marcus, to Luna's surprise, asked, "Flo, you okay?"

Flo threw her phone to the ground and turned to walk away from them. She put her hands on her hips before turning to face Marcus. "I'm cool. Thanks."

Luna watched Marcuss eyes narrow and widen. Finally, he pulled back his shoulders and nodded as Luna mouthed the words, "Offer to drive her home."

"Can we give you a ride home?" Marcus asked.

Flo picked up her phone, staring at it. "Thanks. But don't worry about me. I'll catch a bus."

Luna felt her jaw drop as Marcus said, "Come on, Flo." He lifted his voice. "You're just on the other side of the freeway, aren't you? It's no trouble."

Flo looked from her phone to the coffeehouse, and then to Marcus. "You sure? I don't want to be a bother."

"Get in," said Marcus, shaking his head and grinning.

Luna moved to open the back door and slide into the back seat. "You take the front," she yelled to Flo.

"Thanks," Flo said again as she closed the door. "I really didn't want to ask Chef for a ride home again. Nice car."

"It's mama's," said Luna, leaning forward to put her head between Marcus and Flo's. "She said whoever closes should have the safest car. But it's kind of silly when you look at how Marcus drives. He drives like an old woman. I swear, the day he speeds is the day hell will freeze over."

Marcus cleared his throat. "Language."

Flo laughed. "If I'd been half as careful, I might still have my license. I've crashed more than one car in my time."

"I don't have a license either, but then I don't want to drive. If I can't walk or ride my bike where I want to go, there's no point in going," Luna said. "Did you really lose your license?"

"Luna," said Marcus. "It's none of our business."

"I fffff-screwed up my life in more ways than I can count," said Flo, easing her back into the seat. "You name the poison, I sipped it. Jail time did me good. It's where I learned to cook. Cooked good enough to get a scholarship to culinary school. That's where Chef Max found me. He straightened me out before I flunked out of it."

Luna couldn't help a thrill singing out of her voice. "You've been in prison?"

"Yes, ma'am. And don't for a minute think I can't end up right back there. I work hard every day to stay clean and straight," Flo added, laughing.

"I've never known someone who's been in jail. What was it like?" asked Luna.

Marcus coughed and his face tightened, but he kept his eyes on the road. "Luna, Flo's life is her own business--"

"No, Marcus," interrupted Flo. "I wish someone had talked to me straight when I was a kid. The way I figure it, we all gotta look out for each other. Luna, if you want to know what it's like, I'll tell you, but not tonight. Let's sit down sometime and talk over milkshakes."

Luna grinned. "Thanks. I'd like that. Is that where you became a lesbian?"

"Luna!" Marcus yelled.

Flo laughed. "No, Luna. I was always a lesbian." Flo stopped laughing. Her face fell with a giant sigh as Marcus turned onto her street. She pointed to a broken parking lot rimmed on three sides with a two-story apartment building. "You can drop me off right there."

A too-thin woman stood smoking a cigarette on the top walkway. Flo sighed as she exited the car. "Thanks for the ride. Oh, you ah, won't tell your mom I was swearing, will you?"

Marcus nodded. A tired smile formed on his face. "We all lose our tempers, Flo."

Luna watched Flo slosh up the stairs. She jumped as Flo's voice suddenly yelled, "What's so fucking important that you couldn't pick me up this time?"

"I think we should leave," Luna squeaked and leaned back, feeling too young to be where she was.

Luna didn't like the relief that flooded Marcus's face as he pulled away. She imagined what an apartment in the brown, dingy building must look like. The doors with their peeling green paint radiated thoughtless progress into nothingness in the overbright security lights on each corner of the building. Even the cracks in the parking lot looked like endless chasms that would never fill. Perhaps she, too, was glad to be leaving the place.

A group of six men walked out of a downstairs apartment. One of them shouted to Flo and the woman standing next to her. Luna noticed two of the men watching Marcus pull away. Marcus turned his head, and Luna's eyes widened as she watched the speedometer increase until it rose above the posted speed limit. As they continued to move away from the apartment building, she couldn't help feeling eyes boring into the back of her head. She turned to look through the rear window and could no longer see the men, but she thought, for the briefest of moments, a pair of yellow eyes on the roof of the apartment building looked at her.

* * * * *

At nine years old, she was certainly old enough to play in the lot behind the apartment building whenever she wanted to. She liked playing in the dark. That nasty Jon, the six-year-old boy from next door, wasn't allowed outside when it was dark, and he was never allowed to play in the back lot like she was. *Boys are so gross.*

Ruby cradled her dolly. "You're such a bad girl. You're going to bed without any dinner."

Ruby wrapped her dolly in the little blanket and placed her in the hole between the old car that never moved and the side wall. Ruby tucked the blanket under the doll's chin. "There you are. The sooner you go to sleep, the sooner it will be morning, and if you're good, I'll find you some breakfast."

Bright light beamed through the breezeway from the front. Ruby squinted, but seeing no one walking toward her, ignored the light, until she heard, "What's so fucking important that you couldn't pick me up this time?"

Ruby ran to the edge of the building. Flo, one of Jon's moms, and Mrs. M were fighting again. If they woke up mommy, she'd be mad. Ruby held her breath. Mrs. M didn't yell back at Flo, but Ruby watched as men walked out of 7a. She was never to talk to them; that was one of the few rules mommy made. She watched only long enough to see the shiny white car pull out of the parking lot and drive away.

Ruby skipped back to dolly, sleeping soundly in her little make-believe room. She picked up her dolly and cradled it in her arms. "Something smells awful," she said. "Let's move closer to the field."

Ruby walked across the broken blacktop. The smell followed her. She stopped near an overgrown bush. Someone breathed heavily, like grandpa did when he was very sick. Ruby didn't see the shadows around her move.

Jon found Dolly the next afternoon and took her 10b, but no one answered the door. Jon brushed the dust off Dolly's dress and set it by the door. There was a new tear on the sleeve. Ruby would probably blame him for that. She was always yelling at him for something which was silly. It wasn't his fault Dolly only had one eye, and wasn't it he who found a new arm for her? He didn't mind that Dolly now had one pink arm and one brown one. Sighing, he walked back to his own apartment.

He didn't see Ruby again.

2

Shadows dance, unaware of you.
They stretch and yawn.
They hide from light, as dreams twinkle the stars.
When least expected a spark,
A twitch, a twist, and new friends emerge
Even as demons dance unseen to songs no one else will hear.
You're listening to Mary Midnight online and in your mind.
Gather your friends or dance alone.
Dance alone, and dreams fade to not.

CC turned her motorcycle off under the highway overpass. Three teens in cut-offs and t-shirts passing a cigarette to each other watched her from their position under half a tent. A fourth teen stood on the street corner with a sign and freckled mutt at his side. CC reached into the sidecar to pull out paper wrapped sandwiches from a cooler.

"Lunch?" she yelled over the roar of cars and trucks speeding through the city. The boy on the corner walked up to her as the others watched.

"Thanks," he said, grabbing the sandwiches.

CC opened the second cooler and pulled out four bottles of water. "PB&J. You'll want these to wash them down with."

The boy with the sign bit into a sandwich and nodded to the other three. They walked to CC and took the bottles and sandwiches. Each nodded.

CC handed out cards with lists of homeless shelters listed on them. "Take these if you need a safe place to sleep and a hot meal. The one on top is only a few blocks down the road."

The smallest girl with almost as many freckles as CC said, "I've seen you before, but not at any of the shelters. Saving souls?"

CC smiled at the freckled girl. "Nah. Just like to help when I can. Right now, though, I'm looking for someone." CC pulled out the photo James Earl created of the dead boy. James Earl opened the boy's eyes and added color to pallid cheeks, wiping away the death gray and filling in with golden brown. She was especially pleased with the quality of the picture, even if it took him over a week to create. While the boy's features were stiff and forced, he didn't look dead. "He's not in trouble." CC added before showing it to the teens.

The first boy took the picture. "That's Louis. Haven't seen him in a while. Thought he and his sister must have found him and gone home. You working with her?"

"Sister? No. Do you know her name?"

The other boy asked, "Why are you looking for him? What he do?"

Three weeks of searching, and these kids were the first to admit they knew the boy. Answer wrong, and they would shut their mouths, and she'd spend weeks convincing them to trust her. "He's dead," she said, lowering her eyes. "I want the bastard who did it to pay."

"Shit," the freckled girl said. "We haven't seen Maria for a while. You think she's okay?"

"They were always together," the other girl said. She spoke as though her throat hurt and with a thick Spanish accent. "I don't think they've been in Texas long. Neither spoke English. Well, Maria learned enough to work."

"Thanks," CC said. "Any idea where they flopped?"

"Try the park, near the river. They're some good spots there when the weather's warm. No one can see you from the paths," the lead boy said.

A green SUV with a flashing red light stopped near them.

"He's looking for me," said CC, turning to face Renaldo with a wide smile.

The teens strolled across the frontage road, ignoring the car horns and shouts to disappear behind an alley only a block away.

"Why do I keep running into you, CC?" Renaldo smiled as he watched the teens.

"If I didn't know better," CC said, raising her eyebrows, "I'd say you were sweet on me."

Renaldo looked into CC's face. "Come on, spill it, CC. What are you up to? One of the kids a ways back talked to me about a red head on a bike with a sidecar passing out sandwiches and asking about a kid. Maybe I can help."

CC scratched her chin and fingered the folded paper with Louis's photo on it. "Those kids were the first to give me a name." She handed the paper to Renaldo. "They called him Louis. Said he and his older sister, Maria, were always together. She takes care of him, but they haven't been around in forever."

Renaldo examined the photo. "Neither is familiar, but I'll ask around." He looked around and lowered his head close to CC's. "Election season. Mayor wants a crackdown on crime. Prostitution stings running all week. I'll keep an eye out in case we pick them up. Know what Maria looks like?"

"All I've got is this photo and now a name. Kids said Maria works the streets."

Renaldo nodded. "Not much to go on, but we're likely to pick her up with the stings. What's your angle on this?"

CC pulled a sandwich out of her side bag. "Sandwich?"

"Save it for the kids. The tall boy's checking us out. I think he's waiting for you."

CC nodded. "Thanks."

"How does this tie in with what you were doing at the park?"

"Client confidentiality," CC said as she fastened her helmet.

"Bullshit. I'll call if I pick any Marias looking for a little brother."

"Thanks, Renaldo," CC called as she drove away from Renaldo toward the alley where the oldest of teens waited.

*****

CC met Darious that evening at a food truck court near the freeway on the East side of town. He said he was eighteen, but CC doubted it.Darious devoured the tacos and two burgers CC bought for him. She bought a large box of chicken and biscuits and thumbed it while he ate.

Darious didn't look up until he had swallowed the last bite of burger and washed it down with his soda. Eyes jumping between CC's face and the box of chicken, he asked, "You going to eat that?"

"It's for your friends, but once I hand it to you, you can do whatever you want with it."

Darious nodded as he set his burger down. "I'll take it to them."

"I don't mind if you just want a good meal, but is there something you want to tell me?"

"You seem okay," he said, as he took a deep breath. He looked into CC's eyes. She could see the fear hiding behind brown eyes as easily as she saw the sickness in the yellow surrounding the brown. "Something happened to Maria."

"Tell me what you know," CC said, nodding encouragement.

"Maybe a month ago, I found her where you found us today. She was scared. I figured she was just worried about Louis. She takes good care of him - he's not right in the head, you know. Anyway, she was all jumpy and looking around her. I had picked up a couple of burgers, but she wouldn't eat."

"Did she say what was wrong?"

"It didn't make sense. She kept saying something about a mostruo sombra. Whatever that is. And diablo: I think she thought the devil was after her. I tried to take her to a shelter for girls, thinking she'd feel safe, but she wouldn't go. The later it got, the more scared she got. It was near midnight, and a sweet Mercedes drove by flashing its lights to us. She ran off. It wasn't anybody, just a guy I know slowing to show off the car he'd jumped."

CC allowed her gaze to wander from Darious to James Earl, sitting at a table surrounded by students. He shook his head without looking at her.

Darious finished his soda. He stood to leave. "You think she's dead, or you'd ask more questions."

"Louis is dead," CC said, handing him the box. "Might be a good idea if you and your friends stuck together for a while."

"We'll be alright. Thanks. I'll take this to the others."

"My cards inside. It has my cell on it."

Darious nodded and left the food truck court.

James Earl left the table with the students to sit beside her. "What are you thinking?"

CC bit her lip, staring at nothing. "I don't like it. Two kids gone, and nobody but us knows," she said, her voice low so only James Earl could hear it.

James Earl put down his water bottle. "You think it's -" He wiped the sweat dripping from his forehead with his napkin.

CC put a hand on his arm. "I think," she said, and halted. "Something is going on that you and I know nothing about. I need you to search for any mention of missing children in the area for the last three months."

James Earl stared at her. "What do you know?"

CC focused on her hands, folding and refolding a paper napkin. "I was warned something was coming to the area, a monster."

"Babe?" James Earl said, his eyes wide.

CC scanned the crowd around them and dropped her voice to a whisper. "Mary came to me a few months ago. I didn't tell you about it, because - you've been dealing with so much, and then she's so creepy. Anyway, she said something was coming, and she wanted us to find it."

James Earl closed his eyes. Letting out a long sigh, he laughed. "That's what's been bothering you. I thought I'd done something."

"Sorry. I should have told you sooner, but I don't know what we're up against or what to do if we find it."

"We know where we can get answers," James Earl said as he leaned forward and kissed her cheek. He gathered his trash. "Text Cesar." He stood, smiling at her. "Set up a meet."

CC's eyes widened. "I thought you didn't like Cesar."

"He's a good guy," he said, picking up the trash on the table.

"James Earl," she said, shaking her head. "Just the other day you were going on about how you didn't like him."

James Earl laughed. "Yes, he creeps me out, but what vamps don't? He's been good to us, and he is kind of *in charge* of the city. He'll want to know."

CC nodded. "You're right. I just figured you were uncomfortable around him."

He set his hand on her shoulder as he bent down to kiss her check. "We're good at finding bad guys. He's good at keeping them in line."

"Thanks, babe," she said, and pulled her phone out of her pocket. She hoped he didn't ask too many questions about her meeting with Mary Midnight. Even the thought of that night with Mary sent a shock of feeling making her heart beat fast. She caught her breath. *Damn! He smells good.*

*****

Scarlett, Luna's new friend from English class, beautiful with her rich brown hair cut in a bob from her perfect chin and tips dripping with burnt orange, lounged in her chair sipping her coffee. Her thin but shapely legs stretched into the aisle between tables. "God! This is sooooo boring," she said. "How did you keep yourself awake to read the whole thing?" Scarlett pushed her laptop away from her. "It's Sunday and tomorrow's a holiday. I need some fun, Luna."

Luna laughed. "Tell me about it. At least I don't have to work today. You know Mama homeschooled us. She used to set the timer. If I couldn't answer her questions to her satisfaction when the timer buzzed, I had to do it again. It was easier to just to get the boring stuff over with. I can't believe we already have an essay due. Class only met once."

Luna startled when Marcus spoke from behind her. "I told you. Night classes work fast. Stupid thing to do your first semester." He picked up the empty plates from the table.

"Thanks, Marcus," Scarlett said, moistening her bright red lips with her tongue.

Luna rolled her eyes and shook her head.

Scarlett kept her eyes focused on Marcus. "It's the fast pace I like: The need to push harder and harder until boom, everything fits together, and then you're on to something else."

Marcus shook his head and looked toward the front door as a man with long, gold curls entered the cafe. Marcus headed to the coffee bar.

"Your brother is hot," Scarlett said, watching Marcus.

"All work and no play," Luna said. "Boring with a capital B. You'll need more than a pretty smile to get his attention."

Scarlett sighed and grinned wider. "Ooh, a challenge."

Scarlett's regular bevy of beautiful friends arrived at the cafe behind the golden-haired man, laughing and waving to Scarlett and Luna.

"About time," muttered Scarlett under her breath. "Put that laptop away, Luna. You're going to end up just like your brother."

"No. Thank. You." Luna said and slammed the lid shut on her laptop after clicking save. Her essay, complete.

Luna grinned as the other girls gathered at the coffee bar where they ordered and chatted as though no one else was in the cafe. She liked her new friends. They were all gorgeous, and they all welcomed her into their little group, none more than Scarlett. Luna had sat next to Scarlett on the first night of class. There were no other chairs available. At first, Scarlett only smiled and nodded as Luna chatted excitedly about her first week of college, but when Luna mentioned she was only seventeen, Scarlett laughed. When Luna answered the professor's questions and mentioned she's already read *The Yellow Wallpaper*, Scarlett invited her out for coffee after class. When the coffee house of choice was the family cafe, Luna laughed and bought coffees for everyone. Since then, Scarlett had taken Luna under her wing.

The girls continued to chat, not noticing Marcus, but Luna noted Marcus not wearing his usual, *let-me-take-your-order* smile. The evil glare in his eyes slapped her in the face. She followed his glare. It wasn't at her new friends but on the door leading to the kitchen where the golden-haired man walked. Luna jumped out of her seat and ran behind the coffee bar.

"Idiot," she whispered in his ear before turning to smile and greet her friends. "You want everyone on campus boycotting us because our service is so bad." And then louder so the girls would hear her, "You've got to let me do this, Marcus. These are my friends. First round's on me, girls."

"Yea, Luna!" they shouted.

Marcus took a step back, closing his eyes. "Did you see the way Max just took over when that guy came in? He thinks he owns the place."

"Forty-nine percent of the place to be exact," she muttered beneath her breath while putting on the most charming of smiles she could. "Make two chocolate lattes and one white chocolate. I'll get the fraps."

Marcus blocked her path to the machine. She turned her back on the girls to stare at him. "Marcus! Get a grip!" Whipping back to the girls, she said, "Head over to the table everybody. I'll bring the drinks over when they're ready."

"Thanks, Luna," one girl said as she led the others to the table where Scarlett sat ready to hold court.

Max walked out of the kitchen with the golden-haired man. Luna did a double take when he winked at her with the clearest, most sparkling blue eyes she'd ever seen. The two went to Jackie's office and walked in after only a courtesy knock. Marcus put his hands on the espresso machine but did nothing except stare at the office door until it opened again.

The man with the blond curls walked out laughing with Jackie. Max walked behind them, his face neutral.

"Kids," said Jackie with her hand on the blond man's shoulder. "I want you to meet Tomas." Jackie lifted her hand before the blond man could interrupt. "I mean, Tommy. He's our new night manager."

The cup Luna was filling poured over with coffee. "Shoot!" she exclaimed, pulling a towel from a stack under the counter. She wiped her hand with it and reached to soak up the spilled coffee. "Hi, Tommy. I'm Luna. Mr. Grim here is Marcus. Nice to meet you."

Tommy walked behind the bar, picking up a cup and saucer. "Let me help, Marcus. Looks like you have your hands full."

Luna grinned to see Tommy's face glowing in the steam and overhead lights. His grin, framed with pouty pink lips, begged to be kissed. With one hand, he poured coffee while he used his other hand to pull a golden curl behind his ear.

"What am I making, Luna?" he asked.

Luna had never heard a voice like his before sweet, mellow, and enticing. Her heart skipped a beat, and she felt a tug in her gut she didn't recognize. "Um," she began.

"Two chocolate, one white chocolate latte, three coffees, and two fraps," Marcus growled. "I've got this." He moved to stand between Tommy and the espresso machine, but Tommy glided in front of him.

"No sweat," Tommy said. "Let me get a feel for the place while it's not too busy." He winked at Luna, who set a tray on the counter.

"Mama," Marcus said, trying to whisper but failing.

Max said, "Excuse me, I hear the oven timer." Luna heard no timer but watched Max nod his head at Tommy. It almost wasn't a nod, and she might have missed it if the tone in Max's voice had not said, *Told you Marcus was a problem.*

Luna wanted to laugh. Max knew when to make an exit. "Coward," she whispered under her breath.

Max looked back to Luna and winked before disappearing into the kitchen.

Tommy's hands danced behind the coffee machines, syrup bottles, and cups as though he'd been doing it all his life. "Go on Luna," Tommy said, grinning to show a slip of teeth whiter than Luna had ever seen.

"Jackie said you were here *studying* with friends tonight. Let me wait on you."

Luna couldn't help herself. The giggle poured out of her mouth. "Thanks."

"And Marcus," Tommy continued. Luna spun around staring into Tommy's eyes and shaking her head just enough to shout no, when she saw Marcus' face, frozen with lips pinched, eyes narrowed and wrinkling to a point near his scalp. He didn't move.

"Light crowd and almost closing," Tommy said, turning to Marcus, his hands still moving. "Why don't you take an early night?"

And then, as though the earth shook and dropped her into its bowels, Marcus's shoulders dropped, along with his chin and face. He nodded. "Sure," he said and walked to the office, saying nothing.

*****

Despite James Earl messaging her neck, the tension between CC's shoulders grew. She sat on the couch in Cesar's office, waiting. The thumping of the music from the bar provided a soft but steady thump, which increased her tension.

"Sure you don't want something, babe?" James Earl asked. His deep voice, soft and caring in her ear, made her smile.

"No, but thanks," she replied too fast, as the familiar twinge that meant Cesar's presence ran along her spine. She rolled her shoulder for him to stop.

The music blared as Cesar opened the door carrying a stack of papers. CC's hand lifted to the front of her neck. Cesar paused, looking at CC and raising an eyebrow. Heat rushed across her face as she wondered if Cesar knew about the mark Mary Midnight had made. *Please don't say anything about a mark.*

"Sorry you had to wait," said Cesar, sitting behind his desk and placing the papers in a folder. "How's the new place?"

"Great," said James Earl, sitting next to CC and stretching out his legs. "How's your security system running since I fixed those bugs?"

"Perfect." Cesar nodded his head and turned his attention to CC. "You're not here to talk to me about the security system."

CC pulled her back up straight. "Clay found the body of a kid a few days ago. It's bad. And I believe his sister is dead, too."

Cesar leaned back in his chair. His dark eyes stared into CC's. She stared back, watching her reflection in their darkness, hoping to see the mark Mary made but dreading she would. Before losing herself in his eyes, she cleared her throat. "Mary told me a monster was coming to town."

Cesar leaned forward. His eyes, so dark, turned to storms. His eyebrows furrowed and his jaw tightened. "Vamp? Wer?"

CC took a deep breath before answering. "Neither."

Cesar's face blanched, if that was the right word for a face already pale. "From out-of-town then," said Cesar, leaning back and templed his fingers in front of his face.

James Earl stopped rubbing CC's neck.

"Clay didn't realize anything was wrong until he cleaned the body. There were bite marks all over the boy, but not ones I recognized, flesh cut away, his chest ripped open, and his heart ripped out. Clay doesn't know what killed him."

"Clay would know if it was one of us, and he would have told me himself," said Cesar. He walked to the wall of windows overlooking the nightclub with its Labor Day weekend crowd. He pushed a button under the windows, closing a screen that muffled the thumping of the music until it was only a whisper. "Can you tell me what else Mary said?" He went behind the bar and placed a bottle of wine on the bar.

CC leaned back and sighed. "Only that a monster was coming, and I needed to find it before it killed more children."

Cesar poured three glasses of wine and moved to sit on a chair across from CC, handing her one glass. "More children? So, this is an ongoing fight. Did she say what it was or how to kill it?"

CC took the glass. "She said she was sending a champion to do the killing." CC took a sip of wine.

James Earl took the offered glass of wine. "What is it, Cesar? I know

I'm new, but I thought I understood vamps and wers enough to get by. If neither killed the boy, what did?"

Cesar shrugged his shoulders. "The champion part is straightforward. He's already in town. I'll arrange introductions. As for what the monster is-" Cesar sipped his wine. His eyes stared into the glass. When he spoke, his voice was low, soft, almost dreaming. "Rumors. All sorts of different names; Monsters, Demons, Inbetweeners, Charmers. They're thought to be humans on the edge of being unhuman but never actually changing."

James Earl interrupted, "I kept fighting the change. It almost tore me apart. You think I could have become one of these things?"

Cesar shrugged. "I don't know. Max will know more. He's been around for a very long time."

James Earl put his hand on CC's knee. She put her hand on his. "Why does Mary want CC tracking this thing?"

CC felt her face warm again as she looked at Cesar. "Nobody knows why Mary does anything, kid. I thought you would have figured out that much by now."

James Earl straightened his shoulders. "Guess it's a vamp thing," he said.

"Babe," CC scolded, but Cesar laughed.

"We're all bound to each other whether or not we want to be. And CC has a gift for finding those she hunts for, and for spotting us." He stood and went to his desk. "I hate paperwork," he said as he sat. "I'll set up a meeting with Max. He needs to make himself known soon, anyway. An old guy like him shows up in town and folks get antsy, worried about power plays. Don't mention his name to anybody."

"Is he an Eldest?" James Earl asked.

"No, but he is old. Been around a hell of a lot longer than I have. That makes him dangerous."

James Earl's shoulders raised. "How dangerous?"

"Dangerous enough for *you* to leave alone. He'll cut you slack since you're so new, but piss him off and you're toast. Give me a couple of days. In the meantime--"

"In the meantime," interrupted CC standing. "We'll keep looking, and I have a house guest arriving in a few hours."

Cesar moved to open the door for CC. "Thanks for that, by the way. I wasn't sure where to put her."

"Glad to help," said CC. "Think she'll be able to help with finding this thing?"

"Hope so," said Cesar, shrugging his shoulders. "She's supposed to be a good tracker. Be careful until we have a better idea what this thing is and how we kill it. If you think you find the monster, don't go after it alone."

James Earl pushed his way in front of Cesar and out the door, reaching for CC's hand as she followed. "I'll take care of us," he said.

*****

The bus lumbered into slot eight. Passengers stood, stretched their backs, and whispered as people do at three in the morning. Those without companions looked out the windows, hoping no one would notice them leaving the bus, but at three in the morning, it wasn't likely they would blend into a crowd. The crowd from Las Vegas didn't want to be seen by anyone after a holiday weekend of gambling and debauchery.

Eugene waited for the other passengers to shuffle off the bus in the slow stupor that passengers have after a long, uncomfortable but cheap ride. Her leg bounced up and down, up and down.

"Austin, Texas," she breathed more than said as the last passenger stepped off the bus. "Take it easy. Seline," she said to the driver. "Thanks for the ride."

"You take care, hon," said Seline, not looking up from her phone.

Eugene jumped the last step of the bus to the platform, stretching her arms out wide and breathing in. "Smelled worse bus stations," she said and followed the last of the passengers into the terminal.

Rows of black wire benches sat empty except for a man sleeping in the middle of the room, his head resting on a backpack, his arm wrapped through the handle of a new suitcase, and his jacket tucked under his chin. Two women and a man wearing blue uniforms stood behind the ticket counter chatting as the man typed at a computer. One woman sat up and waved to a couple walking up to the counter with tickets in their hands. Most of Eugene's fellow passengers trudged to the exit door, more asleep than awake, but Eugene was more interested in the few heading for an opening in the wall under a mural.

As no one stood in the station waiting for her, Eugene made her way to the mural and the restrooms. She slowed as she caught sight of a man sitting on the floor next to the opening until she saw the cord of his phone plugged into the wall and ear buds in his ears.

In the restroom, she pulled off her backpack and jacket. A woman with gray hair looked up from washing her hands to watch Eugene in the mirror. Eugene couldn't help but grin at the woman. "Hot, isn't it? Big difference from the AC in the bus."

The woman nodded and looked down at her hands, but Eugene saw the woman's eyes stare and her nose crinkle as Eugene's long arms stretch to reveal the floral ink flowing from her fingers to her neck. Eugene straightened her back, tugging her black vest down in front to reveal the green vines, red, pink, and yellow roses growing from her cleavage. The woman said nothing but stood near the door waiting for someone in a stall.

Eugene pushed the door open, delaying putting her backpack back on to allow the woman to see the lotus flower growing over the edge of her skinny jeans. It would give the woman something to talk about for the rest of the night.

The man with his phone plugged into the wall, the man sleeping, and the employees were where Eugene left them. She scanned the room for her contact. Seeing no one, she turned to look at the mural. Caballeros dancing next to a couple with a donkey and long robes, walking away from two Dia De Los Muertos characters, started back at her. Her lips pursed as her eyes fixed on the individual characters. The musicians in the mural weren't mariachis, although she supposed their graphic shirts and big belts made them Texans. The dancers wore cowboy hats, and the Dia De Las Muertos cats were cool, especially the one in the old time Zoot suit.

"Rather like this one, but wish it wasn't over to the restrooms," a male voice said.

Eugene jumped, spinning a hundred and eighty degrees, her fist raised. "Mr. Tittler," she said, opening her fist.

"Your daddy said to look for the tall, skinny, white kid covered in tats. This way." The middle-aged man turned, leading Eugene to the exit. "I have to admit, I assumed I was picking up a boy."

Eugene slowed her pace to keep pace with her much shorter companion. "Yeah. I get that a lot. I think my folks were stoned when they named me and my brother. Mama always laughs when folks ask her about our names. It's all in the pronunciation, she tells them. Same name, spelled the same, just said it different: I'm Eugeneii, and he's Eugene without the double 'ii' sound, but everyone calls him Phin."

Mr. Tittler shook his head and opened a car door. "Never mind. You'll be staying downtown close to campus with friends of mine. I expect you to help with daily chores. When the semester is over, we'll see. I know you're tired from your trip, but if you hustle in the morning, you can get to campus for late registration."

"Classes?" Eugene squeezed her lips.

"UT has a fine MFA program. I made a few phone calls. You're already admitted."

"I appreciate your help, Mr. Tittler, but you see-"

"You're to stay out of trouble. Your folks agree this is a good idea."

Eugene bit the inside of her cheek as hard as she could. This mild-looking civil servant, with his middle age pouch, gray temples, and deep brown eyes, could rip her throat out, or so she'd been told. As he sat straight, driving his economy wagon at the posted speed, she had her doubts. "With all respect, sir," she said, pausing. "I don't think jumping right back into my Masters is the best option for me, seeing as I just got here. Thought about getting to know-"

"It was Mrs. Smith's wish, too," Mr. Tittler said, signaling to turn a block before his turn. "I'm not asking why you did what you did. It's not my business. My job is to keep you off the radar. That means out of trouble and out of my way."

Eugene opened her mouth, but Mr. Tittler turned his head. His eyes flashed red and a growl crawled out of his throat. "Do not make this hard for both of us, Eugene Elizabeth Plumb. I don't want to be your jailer, but if you make trouble, I will be."

Eugene folded her arms across her chest. "It wasn't my fault," she muttered as her chin hit her chest.

They rode in silence for another ten minutes. Mr. Tittler stopped on a quiet street with old houses. "You'll bunk here. They're our kind of people."

Eugene stood next to the car, staring at the old house. Light spilled out of the windows from behind heavy curtains. Sweet, floral notes tinged with the heavy damp of humidity filled her nose. She inhaled, enjoying the flowers until the smells of the city followed the flora scents. Mildew, trash, rubber, oil, people - lots and lots of people, and wolf. Not Mr. Tittler, someone else, very close. "Our kind of people," Eugene replied. "I didn't know there were many of us here."

"They're good people," Mr. Tittler said, standing next to her. He put his hands in the pockets of his gray slacks and stared at the ground. "Eugene," he said after a moment. "I didn't want to get off on the wrong foot. We should be friends. Not many wolves in Austin. And your daddy said you had a good heart. Mrs. Smith said that, too. Call me Ezra." He held his hand out to her.

Eugene's shoulders relaxed, and she shook Ezra's hand. "Yes, sir - I mean Ezra. Sorry, I know they put you on the spot. I only wanted to do the right thing."

Ezra stepped onto the walkway as the front door opened. Light spilled out, revealing a woman in shorts and tank top and long, red hair. "That's all we strive to do, Eugene."

A white German Shepherd barked and raced down the path to meet Ezra.

*****

Two large offices and a waiting room covered most of the first floor. An antique looking stairwell divided the larger of the offices and the waiting room from the smaller office. Behind the stairs, a door let to a long room divided into a galley kitchen and living room. As Eugene sat on the sofa, she took in the old walls, old floor, old curtains, and new high-definition television screen. The old sofa wrapped around her, comforting tired bones and filling her lungs with the scents of CC, James Earl and his very sexy cologne, Fluffy, Ezra, and *vamps*. CC sat crossed legged next to her, cradling a cup of coffee in one hand and petting Fluffy, curled up and leaning against her with the other hand.

"You're not at all what I imagined," CC said. "From the pictures James Earl showed me--"

"Oh, my God!" Eugene interrupted. "Is there anyone who hasn't seen those pictures?"

James Earl, sitting on the arm of the sofa behind CC, laughed. "Doubt it. No less than three casinos have claimed a wolf running down the strip as their publicity stunt and are reenacting it nightly."

Eugene buried her face in Fluffy's fur. "I'm never going to be allowed back to Vegas, am I?" She looked up, directing the question to Ezra, sitting in the recliner near her.

"Not for a while," he said. "If the situation were different, I'm not sure Mrs. Smith would have allowed you to leave."

Eugene put her coffee cup down on the table. Her stomach turned, and the coffee turned to mud in her mouth.

"Ezra," said CC. "Give her a break. She knows she messed up. I'm sure there's a very good reason. Besides, the timing couldn't have been better." CC reached over Fluffy to place her hand on Eugene's shoulder. "Just breathe. You're safe here. I'll keep the grouchy old wolf off your back."

Eugene lifted her eyes to stare at CC. The woman wasn't wer. She wasn't a vamp or anything else. She was only human, yet the vibe she emanated said more than human. *Touched?* She shifted her gaze to Ezra.

"I knew Mrs. Smith was pissed. I didn't think she was that pissed, I mean-"

Ezra nodded to CC before smiling at Eugene. "It's good now. Mary intervened. Said you she needed you here. But don't go back to Vegas until Mrs. Smith says it's okay."

"Mary?" asked Eugene.

Ezra cleared his throat. "Vamp. Very, very old."

"Oh," said Eugene. She pushed her tongue to the roof of her mouth to not ask more about Mary. Ezra didn't want to talk about her, and CC's face, turning scarlet and sweaty, told her Mary was not a topic for casual conversation. Even Fluffy turned her back on Eugene to lick CC's face.

Eugene changed the subject. "Why do I need to be here?"

"That thing you were running after on the Strip is here in Austin," James Earl said. He leaned forward, rubbing his hand along CC's back. "He killed a street kid. Ripped out his heart."

"He's the only one we know for certain. There are probably others," added CC.

Ezra sat up and looked at CC. "You think they're more bodies out there."

CC sighed and her normal color returned. "I'm working on the assumption that Maria, Louis' sister, is also dead."

"Police will get involved soon," snorted James Earl. "They'll screw things up for us."

Ezra leaned forward. "CC, should I send my kids out of town?"

Eugene watched CC's face twist in thought. "I don't know, Ezra. I don't know what this thing is looking for."

"But you have a theory?" asked Eugene. "I saw this thing leaning over a dead kid and flipped. I didn't think to look at the kid, and by the time I realized I'd been spotted, got home, changed. Well, Mrs. Smith's vamps were at my door. I didn't have a chance to go back for the body-"

Ezra cleared his throat. "A hotel security guard found the body, one of us. Mrs. Smith's people cleaned it up. If they find anything on the body, they'll let me know."

CC nodded. "Good. Until then, we hunt. James Earl is gathering data on missing kids in the Austin area."

Eugene bit her thumbnail. Her mind whirled with questions. "Are we sure it's only going after kids?"

"That's what Mary told CC," said James Earl. He smiled at CC, continuing to rub her neck. "I went to the spot where Clay found Louis. There was an odd scent there, but it was several days old. I couldn't tell what it was.

"But then you're still new to all of this," said Ezra, standing. "You should have called me to go with you." He shook his head. "CC, I need to get home, talk to Sally. See what she wants to do about the kids. Eugene, I'm leaving you in good hands. Call me if you need me. Don't forget to be at the cafe by six."

James Earl rose. The relaxed smile on his face shifted to a straight line. He followed Ezra out of the living room.

"You look tired, Eugene," said CC. "Let's get you settled."

CC lead Eugene up the stairs as Ezra and James Earl walked out to the offices and toward the front door. "Haven't had time to do much more than put a bed in one of the spare bedrooms. We'll go shopping this weekend. You can help me decorate. Ezra said you're an artist."

Eugene stopped at the top of the stairs, surprised at the large eyebrow window at the end of a wide hall with two doors on each side. CC opened one of two doors on the left side of the passage. The room was spare with old, faded floral paper peeling in the corners, but the bed was new. Eugene smelled the fresh bedding. "This is great," she said. "Mostly, I work with glass," she began, but stopped as James Earl's voice echoed through the house.

"That's bullshit!"

Ezra's voice followed, not as loud, but with authority and finality. "You're too new to this, James Earl. Stop taking it personally. Eugene and her brother turned when they were fourteen."

"You turned when you were fourteen?" asked CC, looking up at Eugene.

"Yeah. Mom and Pops said it was the coolest thing they'd ever seen.

Well, once they figured out we weren't going to rip them apart, they thought it was cool."

CC nodded. "Awesome. I was pretty shaken when we realized what James Earl was." The smile left her face, and she stared at the wall as though she could see through it. "James Earl changed last year. He's still getting used to everything."

"Thought so," said Eugene. "Newbies are always edgy."

*****

Eugene's cup clanked into the saucer on the table, the last drop of coffee splashing over the edge and onto her sketchbook. "Argh," she grumbled, picking up a napkin to clean off the spot. "That's my assignment. And where the hell is Ezra."

The Thursday crowd washed in and out, and still she waited. Ezra set the meeting for five o'clock, after Eugene's last class, but the sun was full out. Eugene shook her head.

The server bumped into her table as a crowd of jocks pushed between tables on their way out. Eugene grabbed her cup as it tipped off the saucer. She looked up. The girl's eyes squeezed shut and her lips clinched, but she said nothing. When the jocks left, she took in a deep breath and forced the corners of her mouth to turn up.

Eugene's chin dropped. "You're gorgeous," she said, and pointed to the chair opposite her. "Sit."

The server cocked her hips and crossed her arms. "You and me, we don't play on the same team. You want more coffee or not?"

Eugene opened her sketch pad. Not looking at the server, she puffed air out of her cheeks. "Homeschooled?"

The server opened her mouth but said nothing.

"Sorry," Eugene said, looking up. "Most of the homeschooled kids I run across have pretty narrow world views. I want your face, not your body. Please?" Eugene studied the server's face and grinned as she saw her nametag. "Luna," she added. "I need a face for my class. You're gorgeous, and your eyes are the most interesting I've seen all day. I promise - I'm not into girls."

Luna reached for her nametag and then turned her head to the coffee counter. "Sure, but if you see my brother come out of the office, shout. I don't want to get reamed for not working."

"Brothers!" laughed Eugene. "Gotta love'em - even when they're a pain in the ass. My twin, only three minutes older, and he thinks he knows everything. He's hiking the Wilderness these days. Me," Eugene put her pencil under Luna's chin, pointing her face for the best light. "I'm not into roughing it so much. I mean, I love living off the land, but give me a coffee and pastry, and I'm out of there. You don't look like much of a camper. What's your bother look like, so I can warn you?"

Luna laughed. "I like my meals hot and working toilets. He's taller than me and always looks pissed off."

"Got it. Not much into serving, are you?" Eugene's eyes jumped between her sketch pad and Luna's face.

"God no!" Luna said, slouching until Eugene tapped the table with her pencil. "This is my mom's place. She used to be a professor, but now she's following her dream of running a coffee shop." Luna rolled her eyes and smirked.

Eugene stopped sketching to look into Luna's eyes. She squinted, as though focusing on something other than Luna's eyes. "Seems like business is booming."

Luna looked behind her, to the left and right. "Mama got a chef for a partner. Before him, this place was dead."

"Yeah?" Eugene said. The hairs on the back of her neck came to attention. Under the scent of coffee, she smelled the night and blood that was vampire, but had yet to see one. "So, this chef any good?"

"I've gained three pounds since he started." Luna rolled her eyes and pushed her chair back. "Look, my brother or Mama's going to come out soon. I gotta make like I'm working."

"How about bringing me another coffee, black, and something from your chef? I got enough to work on for now."

"Sure." Luna nodded and walked to another table to take the order.

Eugene watched Luna move around the room before returning her attention to her sketch, indignation over having to wait for a vampire, temporarily forgotten. Her pencil glided from line to line and shade to shade. The fingers of her other hand followed, brushing and pushing; her attention was focused on her sketch.

Luna brought a pot of coffee, filled Eugene's cup, and set an eclair in front of her. Eugene nodded and held her pencil up for three seconds before nodding to let Luna move away.

"You're good," a man's voice said behind Eugene's head. She leapt out of her chair, dropping her sketch pad and a stack of pencils on the floor, squatting and ready to fight.

A golden-haired cherub stood in front of her. She rose to her full height as the cherub's face laughed. "Chill," he said, bending down to pick up the sketchpad. "Austin's a friendly place. The sketch is good, but you don't have her eyes. Close, but not quite there."

Eugene squinted as she took the sketchpad from the outstretched hand. She breathed in, recognizing the scent of vamp, but not the one she smelled earlier. "I'm just getting started. It'll be good."

The man pulled out the chair Eugene. "Tommy," he said, mocking a bow. "And you're Eugene. I was told to keep an eye out for you."

Eugene remained standing until Tommy sat in the chair next to her. "What's up? If you're not who I'm supposed to be meeting, where is this v-guy? I got better things to do than sit around waiting."

"You're here for Max. He's the chef and the reason we're both here. A royal pain in the ass, has been since we met." Tommy folded his arms and used his right hand to rest his chin on. "Can't remember when we first met. Been ages. Only older than me by a few decades but acts like an Eldest already." Tommy's eyes turned to Eugene's arm. He leaned close to Eugene, reached out, hovering his hand over Eugene's arm as his eyes widened. "Love the ink."

"My mom's work," replied Eugene, stretching and twisting her arm under the overhead light to show off her tattoos. "Who's this Max? Ezra told me I needed to be here tonight, but he didn't say why. And where is Ezra? He said he'd be here, too."

Tommy remained fixed on Eugene's tattoos. "The monster you chased down the Vegas Strip is here - in Austin."

Eugene rolled her eyes as her shoulders slumped. "Does everybody know about Vegas?"

Tommy laughed rolling his head back. "Babe, pictures of you running down the Strip under the full moon are still trending."

Eugene snarled, as Tommy continued laughing. "First, I'm Eugene, not Babe. Second, it was extenuating circumstances. I would have had the son of a bitch if the crowd hadn't gathered to see that stupid volcano. It killed a kid. I saw it, and -"

Tommy stopped laughing. His perfect pink lips straightened as his clear blue eyes shot into Eugene's face. "He's killed here. More than once, and you're the closest anyone's gotten to him in years. We've got to kill the freak of nature before he kills again."

Eugene sat up. "Then I need to talk to Max."

"No." Tommy's voice hardened and his hand gripped her wrist. "You've met Luna. Her brother Marcus is behind the counter. The monster killed their younger brother years ago."

Eugene nodded, staring at Marcus and Luna. "And you think the monster is after one of them now?"

Tommy leaned back in his chair, rubbing his chin with his hand. He cocked his head to one side. "That's the running theory."

From behind the coffee bar, a young man with such an angry countenance he had to be Luna's brother called out, "Tommy! We're getting busy."

"That's Marcus," Tommy said, waving to the young man. "Owner's son, huge chip on his shoulder and heading for a nervous breakdown if he can't let it go. Luna's seventeen going on twenty-seven with no clue what's beyond that front door. Our job is to make sure all stay here and safe."

Eugene squinted, studying the faces of Marcus to Luna. Both unique. She turned her gaze back to Tommy. "They're adopted."

Tommy grinned, letting the front legs of his chair hit the concrete floor. "You see it! Good. I thought you had to be smarter than you look." He laughed and stood.

Eugene watched Tommy walk behind the coffee bar. His pink lips and dimples gleamed in the overhead lights, causing the young women in line to giggle and flirt. Tommy said something to Luna as she picked up a tray of cups and pointed to Eugene.

Eugene bit her bottom lip and pulled her pencils out before returning to the sketch. Luna walked by, setting a mug of something dark, frothy, and incredibly sweet smelling in front of her. "Tommy says you'll be working here. Why didn't you say so? I'll show you around the place when it slows down."

Eugene held up her hand. "Didn't know 'til just now that I would be. I take it the angry guy up there is your brother."

Luna snorted. "Yup, but don't let him scare you. Tommy's a good guy, but a bit clingy. How he knows what's going on when this place is crazy is beyond me. Talk to you later."

Eugene watched Luna, Marcus, and Tommy work. Luna and Marcus didn't speak to each other. They snapped snippets of necessary information back and forth. Tommy laughed and flirted with all the men and women at the bar. Eugene returned to her sketch. "Something about her eyes," she muttered, and then straightened her back.

She looked back up to Tommy, who was flirting with three pretty women at the bar, but somehow knew Eugene was looking at him. He winked at her. The light shining above him reflected the clear oceans of blue in eyes.

Eugene watched Luna sitting at a table near the office door. Marcus called to Luna, who looked up with the smirk of disgust. As she stood, she looked over the room, and for the smallest of moments, an overhead light glittered gold in her eyes and reflected into Luna's eyes. "I'll be damned," Eugene whispered.

*****

Luna took one last deep breath before crossing the threshold into

The Phantom's Menace, following Scarlett and her regular bevy of beauties. Luna flushed to think she was among them. She fisted her hands to not giggle and stare at everyone around her until her fingernails cut into her palms. She would not embarrass herself or her new friends. Not all Scarlett's friends were twenty-one, but they all had identification saying they were. Scarlett provided Luna with a driver's license, and with the white halter top Scarlett loaned her and the make-up, she supposed she passed as Rose Baker from Virginia, even though she didn't fill her halter like the photo of Rose did.

The bouncer looked bored as they entered. He slouched on a stool scanning the identification Luna and anyone gave him with the most cursory of glances. Scarlett told her to be sure to smile and wink at the bouncer. She did, but he only stared at the back of a man standing on the far side of the door. The man turned and waved to the bouncer. The other man was Mike Young, the lawyer she met the night mama signed the contract with Max. Luna watched the bouncer's sad eyes perk up and the faintest of smiles appear on his face. And then Luna read the sign above his head. "Smile, You're on Camera." She shrugged her shoulders and hoped there was no facial recognition software running. "I'll die if I get caught and they call mama," she muttered.

Luna's new friends knew how to move through the crowd. The bright lights, roving lasers, and flashing videos screamed into her eyes as the music forced its fast beat through her until her heart mimicked the beat. Around her were more people than she imagined could fit into one place. She hadn't seen this many people in one place since the last time she attended public school. Since then, she was always at home, at the cafe, or maybe Aunt Jasmine's. She breathed in the sweat, the perfumes, the beer, and... *fruit juice?*

Scarlett grabbed her hand, pulling her close to yell into her ear. "Know what you want?"

Luna leaned into Scarlett. "Whatever you're having."

Scarlett nodded, the glitter in her hair escaping, creating a halo around her face. "We're going to see if we can get a table over there."

She pointed to the far side of the bar under the second story overhang. "First one who makes it claims it for the group."

Nodding, Luna wove through the dancefloor. The heat from the bodies bumping and rubbing against her sent shivers of excitement through her. Her face ached from the smile bursting the corners of her mouth up. A man taller than everyone on the dancefloor spun around as she approached and he smiled down on her with the prettiest hazel eyes she'd ever seen. His broad shoulders shook to the music, and he bent his head to her ear. "You're new," he yelled and grinned, flashing a dimpled chin.

Luna felt her face flush and hoped he'd think it was the heat. "First time here," she said.

He bent his face to her ear, placing a hand on her shoulder. "There's a first time for everything."

The heat of his breath on her neck and his hand sliding from her shoulder down her back tickled her skin. Sweat formed on her upper lip. She breathed in the scent of his breath. It shuddered its way to her groin. Someone in the crowd bumped into her side as the song changed, and the crowd pushed her away from the tall man. She shivered, then followed Scarlett.

A waitress was clearing a table next to the dancefloor as Luna approached. Scarlett slid to a stop at the table, plopping her handbag in the middle of the table before a couple moving toward the table could reach it. Luna watched the waitress lean into Scarlett and write out the drinks order. At one point the waitress looked up from the tray with its order pad toward Luna. Luna looked away. The song changed, the DJ said something Luna didn't understand, and the lights dimmed as lasers flashed throughout the club. The waitress's eyes danced with the lasers, almost as though they reflected the lights, but then the lasers moved on, and blue eyes, clear like a sunny day, smiled at her.

"What do you think?" Scarlett screamed in her ear. "Not here ten minutes and already catching attention."

Luna cleared her throat and turned to the dancefloor to hide the flush rising in her face. "I didn't get his name," she said.

Scarlett laughed. "I keep forgetting you're only a freshman. That's Thad, first string point guard on the basketball team. Good work."

The other girls leaned into the table and Luna lost the track of conversations over the noise of the music as she watched the people around her. The table provided a great spot to watch the dancers. A bar ran all around the dance floor in the shape of a horseshoe, covered by a second-floor bar and tables overlooking the dance floor. Other groups stood around tables, but Luna decided she was at the best table. Upstairs would give a better view, but from this table, she only had a step down to be on the dancefloor.

Scarlett pulled on her arm and Luna followed her to the dancefloor with the other girls as a group of very handsome men in identical fraternity shirts waited for them. The man Luna danced with was her height, as she was wearing her tallest heels, and she was sure he told her his name, but she couldn't hear it. He took her hand, and they bumped a few times before Luna pulled herself as far away as she could on the crowded floor. She maneuvered space between them. Looking up, she followed a mirrored wall running along one side of the horseshoe between the ceiling and the top of the bar. She allowed her eyes to follow the mirrors to its end over the entrance and the black staircase curving to it along the black wall.

The man she danced with pointed to the mirrors. "Only by special invite," he said. "You special enough to get one?"

Luna focused on his face, almost lost in the flashing lights of the room. He had a nice smile, and she realized the girls had paired her with him because he was younger than his fraternity brothers, but then he bumped into her again and she felt a hard lump against her thigh. She decided he was what Marcus had told her to watch out for: *One of those men who only want sex.* She couldn't help but smile at him. *Might be worth it.*

Scarlett bumped into her and nodded her head in approval. Luna decided this boy might be fun to be around. Another dancer bumped into her back, and she fell forward in her partner's arms. He laughed. As he helped her gather her balance, his hand squeezed her right breast.

Luna jumped and backed away. Before her partner could reach out to her, another couple merged between them.

Luna walked back to the table, unsure whether she should try to find her dance partner or blow him off. One of the other girls arrived with her. The music changed. The server was placing cold glasses of beer on the table, and the other girls pulled out credit cards. Luna didn't realize until she saw the sweating glasses how thirsty she was, but as she reached for a glass, the server reached forward, slapping a red plastic wristband around her wrist. The server smiled and tightened the band before handing her a tall, thin glass. "On the house," she said and walked away.

"Busted!" one of the other girls barked before drinking half her beer in one gulp.

Luna scrunched her eyebrows and put the glass to her lips. "Orange juice," she said. The other girls continued to laugh and pointed to the wristband on Luna's wrist. Only then did Luna see *No Alcohol* etched in the band.

Scarlett returned to the table, and seeing the wrist band, shrugged her shoulders. "At least you'll drink for free."

Luna took another sip of her juice: it was the best orange juice she'd ever tasted. She joined the other girls in laughing about the wristband and as she relaxed, being the butt of the joke; she noticed a light behind the mirrors above her and someone standing, staring at the dancefloor. A woman with red hair stood next to a man. And then they were gone, hidden as something like a screen moved across the mirror.

*****

Luna's eyes widened and the grin on her face stretched so wide, Eugene thought her face might break. Eugene recognized the vamp on the stool checking ID's and laughed as he ignored Luna's ID. Luna's obvious relief at passing into the Phantom's Menace would have been comical if not for her quick change into enthralled fascination with the place.

"Come on," said Tommy, walking across the street. "We'll lose her in there, no telling where she'll end up."

Eugene stepped out of the alley to follow. "What's the big deal? This has gotta be one of the safest places for her."

"From the monster, sure. But from herself?" asked Tommy.

Eugene nodded as Tommy reached a hand out and pulled Eugene to the curb. "Max is coming out tonight. I want to see this." A car honked its horn and skidded to miss them both as Tommy led them across the street.

Eugene stifled a growl, but more than a grunt emerged from her throat. She pulled her hand out of Tommy's. "I'm perfectly able to cross a street," she snapped, harder than she intended.

"Touchy," Tommy laughed. "But then it is that time of the month."

"Asshole," Eugene retorted. She twisted her neck and rounded her shoulders to loosen the tension building in them. She didn't need to see the moon to know it was almost full. "Let's see how nice you are when you're hungry and I've got the key to the larder."

Tommy turned to face her, causing the flow of people on the sidewalk to bump into each other. "Eugene," he said, looking up into her face and wearing the slightest and slyest of smiles. "You are a tease. I can't wait for you to hold my keys."

Eugene flushed and pushed him into the crowd, gathering and hoping for admittance into the nightclub. "Will you get inside?"

Eugene lost sight of Tommy's golden head in the crowd, but the sudden giggle of the woman next to her and the sultry "dude," from a man ahead of her, made it easy to follow him.

She found Tommy standing next to Stanly. "What took you so long?" he asked, still wearing that grin she so wanted to wipe off his face.

Before she could answer, Mike stepped out from behind Stanly. "Eugene," he said. His eyes darted, searching behind and around her. "Didn't think this was your type of place."

A lump fell from her throat into her stomach. She'd met Mike Young last week, here at the club, when Ezra brought her to meet Cesar. He'd gone out of his way to be nice to her and calmed her before her meeting with Cesar, who turned out not to be not as scary as she'd expected him to be. Cesar and Mike both told her to come whenever she wanted. She opened her mouth, but nothing came out.

Stanly reached his arm out and pulled her close. He grumbled. "Ignore him, kid. Big meeting tonight. It's got everyone all -you know." Stanly put a finger to his head and shot.

"Oh," Eugene said. "The Max thing is-"

"Hey," Mike said, and put his finger to his lips. "I saw Luna come in. Shirley will keep her sober."

Stanly harrumphed. "Another stupid kid to keep an eye on."

Mike put his arm around Stanly's shoulders and squeezed. "I got this, love. It'll all good." Mike nodded to Eugene. "Keep a low profile if you can. Tensions will run tight tonight."

"Gotcha," nodded Eugene, and followed the crowd into the club. Tommy hadn't waited for her.

It wasn't hard to locate Luna and her friends. They were the troupe of beauties others watched. Tommy swayed, bumped, and slithered through the dance floor like a fish in the sea. His smile, his flashing eyes, and his dimples turned heads. Everyone wanted to dance with Tommy, and he spread himself among the masses as though doing them all a favor.

Eugene put her hands in her pockets. Mike was right: This wasn't her type of place, but she sighed and caught the eye of a server passing her with a tray full of drinks. Even with all the sweat and cologne drenching the room with pheromones and sex, Eugene smelled night and blood on the server.

"Hey," she said.

The server stopped in front of her. Dark blue, penetrating eyes as transparent as they were dark, narrowed and looked up into Eugene's face. A sneer rose on the right side of her face, but before it could form, her eyes widened and she smiled. "Eugene?" she asked.

"Yeah?" said Eugene, wishing she could sound confident and not so much like a little girl.

"Boss said you might be around tonight. I'm Shirley. Give me a shout if you need anything."

Eugene nodded and Shirley stepped away from her. And then Eugene remembered her purpose for being in the nightclub. "I'm shadowing one of the chicks at the table across from here," she said, using her head to point to Luna's table. "The shortest one's a minor."

"Already on it," said Shirley, smiling and using her nose to point to a red wristband on her tray. "There's good watching upstairs at the long bar. Your girl won't notice you there."

"Thanks, Shirley." Eugene nodded and followed Shirley's gaze.

The bar looked different at night, filled with bodies both human and not. She caught the eye of Tommy, still on the dance floor and looking refreshed, with a pink glow to his cheeks. She nodded to the second floor and checking that Luna and her friends were on the dancefloor, she went upstairs.

There were just as many people upstairs, but the bartender pointed her to an end spot where the wait staff gathered to pick up orders. She sat on a stool and realized she could see everything on the floor except the bar immediately beneath her. Luna and her friends still danced. The bartender set a sweating glass of ice water in front of her. She smiled and drank, not realizing how thirsty she was. She set it down, and he laughed.

"Not used to the heat here," she said.

"It's September. It'll get better," he said and filled her glass.

"Shirley was right. I can see everything from up here, Fred," said Eugene, having noticed the bartender's name tag. His aftershave and the surrounding alcohol did not hide his vamp scent, and when he smiled at her, his beautiful vampire eyes reflected the lights.

"Yup," he muttered, leaning over the bar. "Everything."

Eugene returned her attention to the dance floor. Luna's dance partner, tall, dark, and far too handsome, loomed over her. Eugene saw one of his hands moving, sliding along her breast. Without thinking about it, Eugene growled. And then someone bumped into Luna and the two separated. Eugene followed the path of bodies bumping into each other, back to the source. Tommy looked up at her and winked.

"Watch the growling," Fred said, and moved to take an order.

"Don't be stupid, Eugene," she said to herself. She stretched her neck, breathing deep to release tension. "Do not screw up your first full moon in town."

Eugene jumped off the bar stool as Shirley's voice, soft and seductive, whispered in her ear. "Good advice to give yourself."

"Shirley!" Eugene's hand went to her chest. Her heart pounded fast against her rib cage, but then Shirley giggled, and Eugene laughed. "You caught me. I talk to myself."

"Won't tell a soul," Shirley said and sat on the bar stool next to Eugene's. "I'm on break. Thought I'd see how you were doing."

"I look desperate?" asked Eugene.

"Nah," said Shirley, leaning back and spreading her arms along the bar.

Eugene looked back to the table where Luna and her friends stood talking about everyone they saw. Shirley's bustier, especially as she stretched out with her back to the bar, revealed so much bust that no one could not stare at her. "Saw you put the band on Luna. Very swift."

"Practice," nodded Shirley. "Boss is strict about minors. Bartenders need to know for sure and so do we. Stanly says you're from Vegas."

"Ya," said Eugene as she leaned back herself, partly to be comfortable, and partly so she didn't have to look down at Shirley's breasts pushing their way out of her bustier. "I started off working on my MA at UNLV, but then I got this job with a glass artist. It was awesome, but then-"

Eugene stopped, realizing she wasn't supposed to talk about why she had to leave Vegas, but instead of needing an excuse to stop talking, Shirley stood and leaned against the railing pulling Eugene with her.

"Look at that," Shirley said and pointed to a tall, thin man entering. No matter where he stepped, people moved out of the way. Even the lights flashing and strobing through the crowd seemed to miss him. He stopped at the apex of the entrance. When he looked up, his eyes reflected the lights. Eugene gasped.

"I've heard rumors he was in town," Shirley said.

Eugene raised her eyebrows as Shirley looked at her.

"An old guy, tight with some of the Eldest. Goes by Max these days, so my sources say, and my sources are the best."

"Max," Eugene said, realizing this was the vamp calling the shots for the hunt she was now on. Eugene looked down and saw Luna still laughing and talking to her friends, but then she turned her head toward the entry.

"Mike's taking him up."

Shirley's voice grabbed Eugene's attention, and she returned her gaze to Max and Mike.

"Come on," Shirley said, and lead Eugene downstairs to the bar opposite Mike's office. Fred followed them.

At the downstairs bar, Eugene noticed Shirley and Fred's eyes glued to the windows. She stepped back into the shadow and opened her wolf eyes. Cesar stood in the center of the windows. CC sat in a chair at his desk with Fluffy under her chair. Max entered, and the two men embraced. Then the show was over. The blinds closed.

"Wicked," Shirley said.

"Trouble," Fred said.

"Back to work, kids," said Stanly.

Eugene hadn't noticed him arriving. She shook her head and closed her eyes. When she opened them, her human eyes looked down on Stanly, who didn't look at her. He looked lost, staring at nothing.

Shrugged his shoulders, asking, "Another war? Mike won't tell me anything."

"I don't think so," Eugene said.

"But you're not going to say either," said Stanly with a shrug. "I gotta get back to work." Stanly walked away without waiting for a reply.

"Oh, man," Eugene grumbled and jumped off her seat to follow Stanly when Fred tapped her shoulder.

"Boss wants to see you," he said.

"Huh?" Eugene turned to look at him.

Fred tapped the earpiece in his ear. "Cesar says he wants to see you. Use the stairs." He pointed to the stairs in the corner.

*****

CC allowed her head to fall back on the couch to stare at the ceiling. When she closed her eyes, she saw Maria laying on the slab with an enormous hole in her chest.

Fluffy's muzzle brushed CC's neck with a faint whine. "I'm okay, Fluffy," she said, scratching his ears. "I'm just tired."

The thumping of bass and drums vibrated through the floor and walls of Cesar's office. She watched through the wall-sized window The Phantom's Menace. Like rivers driving to the sea, bodies flowed on and off the dancefloor, swirled and ebbed along the banks of the bars surrounding the dance floor and rippled up and down the steps to swirl around the tables and bars on the second-floor balcony where onlookers watched the dancefloor and drank. Hard to believe it had been less than a year since Hunters crashed into the bar to kill vampires and the innocents that got in the way. The resulting fire terrified the people of Austin as rumors of terrorists and drug cartels spread on the wind. People panicked and then they got angry. Law enforcement sealed the city until they caught the villains.

CC shuddered. "We were wrong to think we were better than them," she whispered. Too many innocents died. After a city-wide funeral for the victims of the fire, peace returned. The club reopened, and the city celebrated being weird.

Cesar opened the door. The music from downstairs slammed into CC's head, making her sit up. He carried a bowl in one hand and a bag in the other. Fluffy jumped off the couch and barked once before sitting in front of CC.

"Fluffy," said Cesar, smiling. "Is that how you treat your friends?" Cesar set the bowl on the floor in front of the large window. He pulled a treat out of the box.

"Long day?" he asked, petting Fluffy.

"Oh yeah," replied CC. "I like the view from here."

"I open the blinds to impress guests. Where's your young man?"

CC settled back and closed her eyes before answering. She'd wanted James Earl here, but with the full moon tomorrow, he was too irritable. He didn't want to meet another vampire, especially one Mike had warned him not to tick off. CC didn't want to talk about James Earl with Cesar. "You sound like an old man and make me sound like a cougar."

"I've got strings of cougars coming in most nights. Want me to introduce you? You can compare -"

CC grabbed a pillow next to her and threw it at him.

Cesar caught the pillow without looking up from pouring water into Fluffy's water bowl. "Sorry," he said. "Wine?"

"Yes," CC sighed. "I thought Max would be here by now."

Cesar opened a bottle of wine and poured two glasses. "The old guys keep their own timetables." He handed CC a glass and his shoulders sagged. "Besides, he needs to make an entrance. He'll wait until he feels as many as possible are here. Tonight's as good a time as any to let everyone know he's in town."

CC lifted her head and eyebrows in question.

"Someone his age showing up in town raises questions. It's important everyone knows he's not making a power play. There are enough vamps tonight here to spread the word. Another reason to keep the blinds open."

"It's a one-way mirror," began CC, then nodded her head as a smile of understanding spread across her face. "Which vamps can see through."

Cesar nodded, adjusting his tie with his free hand before moving to his desk and pulling out a mirror to smooth his thick, dark curls slicked back and perfectly in place.

CC leaned forward. "Just how worried do I need to be tonight?"

"You? Not at all," Cesar said, picking up his wineglass and sitting in the chair across from her. He placed his glass on the coffee table. "Mary's made sure of that."

CC's hand wrapped around the front of her neck before she thought about it. "Is it so obvious?" she asked.

Cesar smiled. "Humans can't see it."

CC forced her hand away from her neck and wrapped both hands around her wine glass. "What about other unhumans?" she said, staring at her wine.

Cesar cocked his head, almost closing his eyes as he looked at her. "I don't know. You'll have to ask one."

CC nodded and sipped her wine, avoiding his gaze. "Good wine. From the vineyard?"

"Vintner sends me a case every month. I keep it for meetings. Too good for kids down there."

The constant thud of the base wound its way up CC's spine. She shifted, enjoying the steady rhythm. "James Earl is seven years younger than me. If I were a man, you wouldn't think twice about our seven-year difference, and you certainly wouldn't call me a cougar."

"Sorry about the cougar remark," said Cesar. He looked down and lifted the corners of his mouth. "I meant no offense." He stood at the window, but CC felt his eyes on her in his reflection.

CC took another sip of wine. Silence with Cesar was usual and comfortable. "Don't worry about it. All you vamps seem ancient to me. I guess it's got me kind of sensitive talking about age these days."

Cesar turned and fixed his eyes on CC's. "Most vamps turn and burn. They can't handle the change. And those that don't burn right away have maybe forty, fifty years - can't handle everyone they know dying."

"I hadn't thought about it like that," said CC. "It must be lonely. How old are you?"

"Too old for cougars," said Cesar, sipping his wine. "I had help staying alive."

CC stood to look over the bar with him. Stanly, the bouncer, Irma and Jason, bartenders, looked up at them. "They see us. Funny I hadn't noticed until you told me." She knew those three were vampires. She watched the faces of others on the dance floor. This was where vamps came to feed. They moved through the club sipping from the young and healthy - never hurting, never killing.

Cesar watched over human and vampire. He rebuilt after the attack faster than most expected. CC understood the necessity of the place. Vampires needed a place to move about freely and live normal lives. Humans relaxed and blew off steam with all the free juice they could drink. It didn't hurt that the alcohol was cheap and brewed locally. "Harry helped you," she said.

"Yes, and I miss him," Cesar said. He said nothing but watched until, "I know Max from way back," Cesar said in more than a whisper, as though he was remembering. "He's alright. He's fair and practical. Easy to piss off, like most old guys. Might be good that James Earl isn't here." Cesar lifted his hand to stop CC from speaking. "Sorry. I know he's still adjusting."

CC realized her hand lifted to cover her neck and pushed it down. "Cesar. About being marked-"

Cesar's hand went to her shoulder. "He's here."

CC followed Cesar's gaze to the entrance, where a tall man stood in the center of the rivers of people. His hair was long. Even from this distance, CC saw firm muscles rippling through his tight black tee-shirt. His presence was undeniable, and more than a few heads turned to look at him.

Mike Young swam through the crowd to stand beside him. He looked small next to Max. Max leaned over Mike as though listening to him. Mike pointed to their right. Together they walked under the stairs to go behind the bar and ride the elevator up to Cesar's office.

*****

Cesar motioned CC to a chair in front of his desk at the ding of the elevator arriving and the sound of the doors swishing open while he moved to the center of the window wall. He made a final adjustment to his tie as his face changed from the open friend she knew to the sophisticated gangster he pretended to be.

CC felt Max before she saw him. The tingle along her spine, the slight dread in her chest she felt when she'd been close to Harry and Mary was there, but this was subtle, like a shadow slipping into her vision from around a corner, a hair tickling the back of her neck, a fear but also a calmness. She had nothing to fear from this man. Max stepped into the office. She relaxed her shoulders, easing herself into the comfort of the plush cushions. He stopped as he crossed the threshold. His eyes swept the room, stopping briefly when CC caught his gaze. Her heart skipped a beat at the brief gaze of those clear eyes, ageless and as haunting as haunted.

"Max," bellowed Cesar, opening his arms wide in welcome. "Good to see an old friend. It's been too long."

CC watched Max's long legs glide more than walk the ten feet needed to be in front of Cesar. The corners of his mouth pointed up in a small - all show - smile.

Max opened his arms and the two men embraced, kissing each other's cheeks.

"Good to see you, too, old friend."

A deep, low growl issued from Fluffy sitting next to CC. She put her hand out. "Quiet, Fluffy."

Max turned to look first at Fluffy, who stopped growling and lay back down under CC's chair, and then to CC.

Mike squeezed her shoulder, pushing her down as she moved her feet to stand. "This is Catherine Carson. I told you about her."

"Ms. Carson," Max's voice, deep and melodious, floated through the air to her ears.

"Call me CC," she said, lifting her hand to his.

He glided in front of her and took her hand. His fingers were cold and firm. He bent low, hovering his lips just above her fingers. CC shuddered as a chill shot through her arm.

"Playing it up, aren't we?" she breathed out, giving him a wink.

"All in the game," he whispered back.

When CC turned back to the desk, Cesar was already sitting behind it. Max stood a moment longer in front of the window before turning to take the chair next to her. Mike moved to stand near the entrance, hitting the button to close the blinds. As they closed, the noise of the bar faded to the softest of whispers.

Cesar sat back in his chair as Max stretched out his long legs in front of him and slouched, steepling his fingers in front of him. Neither man said anything until the blinds closed.

At the click of the blinds, Cesar and Max both loosened a tightness in their shoulders CC hadn't noticed until it was gone. She smiled, more to herself than the others. Mike, to her surprise, didn't relax. He remained standing at the entrance to the office, his hands in front of him, and his face serious.

"How's it going at the cafe?" asked Cesar.

"Good," replied Max. "Since I started baking, business is booming."

CC raised her eyebrows, wondering what type of code baking was for vampires.

Max turned his head. "I am a Pastry Chef," he said. "A damn good one."

CC flushed.

"I've bought into a family-run coffee shop here in town," he continued. "I need to be where I'm seen, but also where I can see what's happening around me."

CC nodded, not knowing what to say. This vampire who could crush her as easily as she could crush a spider, but he relaxed in front of her, remaining as cordial as an old friend.

"You have information for me?" he asked, dropping the gaze of his clear, silver eyes from hers. "Mike tells me you think there are two missing children."

Cesar grumbled. "How many more are we going to find?"

"The police didn't see Louis. Clay found him and called me when he realized this wasn't a usual killing or anyone's accident. I don't need a special education to see this was no human killing – there were blood and flesh missing."

Max nodded his head, waiting for more. When she remained silent, he added, "And?"

"The flesh was torn off, and his heart was ripped out of his chest."

"You suspect a sibling is missing," Max stated more than asked.

CC furrowed her brow. "His sister. You've seen this before?"

"No," replied Max. "Maybe. Your partner is a Wer, yes? Did he smell anything odd about or around the body?"

"Yes," CC nodded. "He didn't see the body, but he went where it was found. Said something smelled strange in the area."

"I need to see the body."

Mike cleared his throat, his voice carrying a seriousness CC didn't recognize from him. "Clay has the boy, but he's been dead at least a week. I'll set up the meet."

"No," said Max, shaking his head. "Clay knows me. I'll call him."

CC realized she was holding her breath when Cesar said. "You suspect something, or is it a someone?"

"Mary said a monster was coming to town," said CC. All the suspicions and innuendo turned her fear into anxiety and an anger over the death of two children boiled inside her. "What exactly are we looking for?"

*****

"It's very rare," said Max. He looked at CC, his face showing no emotion. "Some say, when an unhuman refuses to change, they become something between human and unhuman. Eldest are always on the lookout for someone changing, but sometimes, very rarely, the change begins and there is no one to provide guidance. These poor souls become something entirely different, unknowable, because they don't know what they are."

CC squinted, waiting for more.

"If you don't know, you're not a demon," continued Max. "You behave like one."

Cesar snorted. "Hardest thing I ever did was accept I wasn't a demon or cursed by Satan, but then I was young and civil war waged around me. I killed loyalists without thought until Harry found me."

CC stared at Cesar, opening her mouth to ask when this was. Before she could ask, he smiled at her, "1938, Spain. It was a bloody time."

"Without guidance," continued Max, "Any one of us can end up a killing machine - neither aware of what we are nor what we could be."

"And you think whoever killed these kids believes he's a demon?" CC asked.

Max nodded. "It's a theory. He's left a trail, hard to follow, but it's there if you know what you're looking for. I ran into him once before, here in Austin, back in '85."

CC closed her eyes, searching through her research into Austin. Max added, "1885. I thought the killer of a little girl was someone else. I let my bias cloud my judgement and missed the chance to kill the monster."

"Servant Girl Murders," CC said. "I read about them. That was a vamp?"

"No," Max answered. "A human killed the women. An unhuman monster killed the little girl. I'm sure Mary sent me here back then to catch the monster. She's still pissed I let him get away. That's why I'm back."

CC noticed the shudder in Max's shoulders. It was subtle, almost not there, but she saw it. She felt her own fear increase, realizing this vampire feared Mary Midnight more than she did.

"So how do we find this monster or not-fully unhuman being?" CC asked.

CC watched as Max's lips pressed together. His eyes stared into the distance for a moment. Cesar leaned over his desk. "Trust her, Max" he said. "She knows what she's doing."

CC jerked her head to look at Cesar. Her eyes widened with the confidence in Cesar's voice and excitement to be trusted by him.

Max turned to her. "One thing I know for certain about this thing: He chooses children who carry the vampire genome and those related to them."

CC felt her mouth drop. Before she could speak, Mike broke in. "No way."

Max nodded. "I told you I ran into him before. I was here to check on a little girl. She was on the edge of puberty, with signs of the change emerging. She was such a beautiful little girl, full of promise and great things, despite the prejudice of the times. She was going to make the world a better place for being part of it."

Max's voice carried regret and heartache. CC rubbed her chin as she digested information from a hundred-year-old murder. "How did you know she was going to be a vamp?"

"I didn't know. But there were signs," replied Max. "Just because someone has the genome doesn't mean they'll change. I only knew for certain she was something not entirely human. She may have never turned. She saw things humans couldn't or wouldn't. Told you, she was sharp. She knew what I was the first time she saw me, but she said nothing to her mother or grandparents. Perhaps I should have taken her away then, but she was so young. A girl that age needs her mother." Max stopped speaking and sat up. "Five years ago, a boy, Valentino LaBrere, was taken. It's his family that owns the coffee shop I bought into."

"You think this monster will come for one of the siblings," CC said. She took out her phone and typed Valentino's name into a text. "I'll have James Earl pull up the police file. Was the body found?"

"Yes, about three weeks after his disappearance. Not much left, according to the papers. Anything you can get would help."

CC looked up from her cell phone. "I have good contacts with the local police. Let me see what I can get."

"I, too, have collected information over the years. I'll send what I have to you. Mostly newspaper clippings and such." He closed his eyes and shook his head. When he opened his eyes, he said. "It's time other eyes looked for the pattern I cannot see."

Cesar cleared his throat. "Be careful with the police. If they get involved, we'll have a hard time keeping this quiet."

"I know," CC nodded. She turned back to Max. "Can you determine if the sister is a vampire in waiting? What about Maria or Louis?"

"There's no guarantee I'd be able to tell," replied Max. "I don't want you hunting for this thing on your own." He lifted his hand as CC grimaced and opened her mouth to object. "Cesar says you're a good hunter. I believe him, but this thing has the strength of a vampire. You cannot kill him on your own."

"From what you've said, and from what Mary said, I have no intention of facing this thing without you."

"Good. I understand your partner is newly turned. It will be dangerous for him, too."

"If we're all working together, we'll get this thing. Besides, I've got Eugene here now. She was close to it. We'll find it, you kill it." CC set both her feet on the floor, but she resisted standing.

Max leaned back in his chair. "I wish I had known you the first time I ran into this thing."

CC closed her eyes, breathing deep. When she opened her eyes, she saw pain written across Max's face.

"He only kills children." Max's voice whispered like a breath. "Any child who might turn vamp and any child in contact with his prey."

"Whether or not they can turn," CC finished as the fear of her word sank in.

"Yes," Max said.

Silence filled the room, drowning out the dull thump of the bass and drums of the dancefloor below them.

"Max," Cesar said, breaking the tension in the room. "If you let me tell the others, we might be able to stop..."

CC's phone beeped. She tapped her screen and looked up, dividing her gaze between Max and Cesar. "My contact with the police," she said, looking up at Max. "He found a body and say I should see it. It might be Maria. Mike, can you drive me?"

Mike nodded. "Sure."

CC nodded but kept her eyes on Max. "If I go now, he'll let me on the scene."

"I'll drive you," Cesar said, pulling his keys out of his pocket. "Mike, keep an eye on the place. Find Eugene. She's the only one to be close to this thing. She can help."

CC stared at Cesar, and then Mike. She stood, not sure what to say, but Max put his hand on her arm. "Don't go after the thing, CC. It will kill you."

CC nodded agreement and followed Cesar out the door.

*****

CC resettled herself, trying to not turn and look through the rear window. Fluffy shuffled her paws until she could lean her head against CC's head. As CC starred in the side mirror, she lifted her hand to scratch Fluffy's nose, jumping when Cesar barked a small laugh.

"What?" she asked.

"Max. I think he's testing how good you are," he replied with a smirk.

Eugene, sitting in the back seat, snorted. "Typical vamp."

"Testing me?" CC said and jerked to look behind her again. Fluffy barked once, then curled into the seat and closed her eyes.

"It's him you're feeling, isn't it?" Cesar said so matter of fact, CC could only nod. "He's an apex hunter, CC, if you'll pardon the expression. He's not going to sit around doing nothing while you're gathering information." Cesar stopped the car as a mass of bodies strolled across the street. "And then there's me vouching for your excellent hunting skills. He doesn't believe me - completely."

CC opened her mouth but closed it as she took in a breath to think. She'd once labeled herself a hunter, a hunter of the undead - vampires. And then she met James Earl, struggling with the change from ordinary human fugitive to werewolf. Everything she thought she knew about unhumans changed. She, the Rev, Reverend Brown, who led the hunter group, knew about James Earl and that somehow, he realized the group was wrong.

CC jumped when she felt Cesar's hand on hers. "No one holds it against you, CC. You're still a hunter. You're just more discerning than you were. Everyone knows that."

"God!" CC said, shaking her head. "You were on our hit list. How can you be so accepting of me, James Earl, all of this?"

Eugene pushed her head next to Fluffy's. "You went after Cesar?" she said, her grin as wide as her eyes. "You've got more guts than I thought."

Cesar squeezed her hand once before letting go. "If it makes you feel any better, I was watching you, too."

"No. That doesn't make me feel any better. I thought you were going to kill me the night you found me spying in the house."

Cesar laughed. "It did kind of piss me off, but I already knew about James Earl. As you were with him, you were off limits. It took guts to do what you did. I admire your - skills."

"CC," Eugene said, sitting back as her face became grim. "You are good. I wouldn't have tried to break into Cesar's house."

"It wasn't my house at the time," Cesar said. "But I was in charge of security. If you had broken in, I would have had you for dinner."

"Assuming you could catch me, old man," scoffed Eugene.

Flashing red and blue lights flooded the car, and Cesar turned to park on a side street. "I'll stay here with Fluffy. The invitation was for you. Eugene, can you blend into the crowd without showing up on the late news?"

"It wasn't my fault!" shouted Eugene.

"Ignore him, Eugene," said CC, opening the door. "He's just jealous he can't walk onto the crime scene."

"No," Cesar said, raising his voice to be heard over the gathering crowd and music from the nearby ice house. "I enjoy sitting in the car with Fluffy." Cesar raised his hand as CC opened her mouth Cesar continued. "I want details. Max doesn't talk that much."

CC smiled as she nodded and closed the door. She watched Eugene exit the back door and immediately blend in with the crowd. Watching Eugene reminded of her the way James Earl could move through a crowd. Her body twisted and turned, molding its way through the sea of bodies until it disappeared. Unless Eugene purposely pushed on someone, no one noticed the long, lean body slithering by.

*****

It was ladies' night at the icehouse. The band on the stage was a local favorite, and the crowd spilled onto the street surrounding it. CC slid through the crowd with practiced ease, smiling and turning down propositions. The prickle on her skin reminded her of Eugene's presence, near but not too close, sliding with the crowd, flowing through it with refined skill. And somewhere, the faint tickle on the back of her neck was Max, but she didn't see him. The closer she got to the icehouse, the harder it was to see where she was going, but the flashing police lights guided her around to the street behind. A single uniformed officer leaned against a cruiser, clipboard in hand, and eyes glued to the crowd behind CC.

As she handed him a business card, his expression changed from condescending to acceptance. "Sanchez said you were coming. Come on in. They're in the alley on the right, behind the warehouse."

"Thanks," she said and walked under the yellow tape.

Straightening, she tugged at her blouse and re-tucked it into her jeans. The green, button-down blouse wasn't unprofessional, but she hadn't expected to be in working mode tonight. She buttoned the top three buttons of her blouse.

A man wearing a cowboy hat walked out from between two patrol cars on her right. CC stopped before bumping into him. "Frank," she said, smiling and reaching her hand to take his. "Good to see you."

"CC," the big man grinned even as his eyes narrowed. "Renaldo said he called you. What's your connection?"

CC liked Frank Jarvis, the senior police detective. She'd met him last year and decided the gray on his chin was thicker now, as was the bulge in his middle. "Looking for a street kid. Her brother was found dead a few weeks ago. You look like married life is treating you well."

Frank nodded his head, and lead CC down the alley and around the officers gathering evidence. He patted his belly. "That's what I get for marrying a caterer. Jasmine's not only a fine cook, she brings home leftovers and samples. Sanchez," he shouted and waved his hand. "I'm stuck with that damn sweep. Just stopped to check in on things."

"Sure," CC said but stopped as Frank bent to her ear.

"I got a feeling there's more here than we can see," Frank said, lowering his voice. "Can we meet tomorrow?"

CC forced her face to stay neutral. "Sure," she said.

Frank nodded. "That new place, Coffee Philosophy, two o'clock." He turned away as Renaldo approached. "Wrap it up as soon as you can, Renaldo. I'll see you at the office." He touched his hand to his hat. "CC."

Renaldo, face blue in the light of his phone, stopped tapping and put his phone in his pocket as he stood in front of CC. "He'll be in a bad mood until these sweeps are over. Politics," Renaldo spat. "That's all they are."

CC nodded. "I know about politics. Where's the body?"

Renaldo led her into the alley. Away from the night breeze, the stink of dumpsters and urine in the hot, heavy air hit her in the face. Her nose crinkled as the stench stuck in her nose and throat. Renaldo pulled a handkerchief from his pocket and handed it to her.

"I've never smelled death like this," CC said. "How long has she been dead?"

Renaldo shook his head. "You're not smelling the body I called you about. She's over here." Renaldo pointed to a line of brown trash cans to the side of the giant brown dumpsters. Two were knocked down, their contents spilled across the alley. A white sheet lay across a stack of trash behind the downed cans.

Renaldo stepped on his toes to get over the trash, indicating CC stay where she was. He squatted down and pulled a corner of the sheet back, revealing a girl's face. Despite her mouth fixed open in a scream, with teeth missing and broken, her right eye smashed inward, enough of her face remained for CC to see it wasn't Maria.

She closed her eyes and took a deep breath through the handkerchief. She opened her eyes, looking up, hoping Max could see. "What happened to her," she whispered as Renaldo lowered the sheet.

"No details yet," Renaldo said, shaking his head. "More was broken than her face, but until the autopsy, nothing's certain. Well," Renaldo paused, looking around him. "No heart. Torn out of her chest."

CC squeezed the handkerchief to her face to breathe, but the alley's stench slugged her in the stomach. "You said she wasn't what I was smelling."

Renaldo stood and motioned to the dumpster they'd passed on their way to Darius. Men and women in white overalls stood inside it. CC watched as a pair of gloved hands lifted an evidence bag to a waiting technician outside the dumpster.

"Body parts, juvenile. It's going to take a while to get through it all." Renaldo's voice cracked as he looked at his phone to read the notes he'd taken. "The kid in the dumpster's been here at least a week. The property manager said they're due to pick up trash tomorrow. Homeless man found the girl's body and called it in. The responding officer looked around to find the source of the smell and found the remains of the kid. Only luck we got here in time."

CC watched as the tech inside the dumpster rose with another bag. "I need air." She turned her nose to the girl's body. "I'm pretty sure that body's Maria." CC said and turned to walk away.

Renaldo joined her. "Me, too. I'd like you to come by after the autopsy. Think you can get your witness to identify her."

CC handed the handkerchief back to Renaldo. She stopped as they entered the street and the breeze, taking in the fresh air and sounds from the ice-house. "Sure. Tomorrow evening?" she said, staring ahead of her. She thought someone leaned against a light pole at the end of the road. She squinted, realizing it was only a small tree struggling to survive in compact earth and city pollution.

"You've got that look again," Renaldo said. His eyes focused on hers as his face tightened in anger. "Don't shit with me, CC."

CC jerked her head around to face Renaldo. "I'm not," she said, forcing her voice to remain low and controlled. "You saw the picture of Maria. That girl looks like her, but I never met her."

"There's nothing ordinary with that girl's death."

CC straightened, realizing she's been holding her stomach with her hands. "Let's talk tomorrow," she said, scanning the surrounding area.

Renaldo rolled his eyes. "And your witness?"

CC pushed herself to her full height and put her face inches in front of him. "Street kid. You met him the other day when you found me. I'll have to look for him." She took a breath as her stomach settled and she turned to walk away. "I'll call you as soon as I find him."

"CC," shouted Renaldo, stepping forward to follow her. "Don't leave me hanging."

CC didn't turn to look at it. "We'll talk tomorrow."

CC tripped but caught herself. The icehouse crowd thinned. Ahead of her, she saw Cesar standing outside the car with a cup of coffee in his hand. "This is bad," she said loud enough that anyone passing her would think she was talking to herself, but Cesar shook his head.

*****

Once through the crowd, Eugene breezed between the apartment complex behind the icehouse and followed the fence between it and the street. She kept CC within easy scent and listened to her banter with the old man with the cowboy hat. Eugene didn't need the other officer to point her to the body. Death poured out of the alley between restaurants. It rose above the burgers, steaks, and beer, oozed its way along the ground to find whoever passed by, and slapped them in the face. And just above the sweet reek of death, him. There was no doubt. The stench of the killer they hunted floated on the breeze. It rose above all the other smells.

Eugene put her hand on her stomach as it turned with remembrance. Walking home from a long day of bending, blowing, and forming glass, the desert breeze flew over the streets filled with bodies, murmurs, laughter, yelling, screaming. All the sounds the tourists in Vegas made drifted over the sounds of music, bells, ringing, and money. And then the one quiet turn between massive parking garages. She would walk through the lot and find herself three blocks off the Strip and at the bar she would work. Money was tight, and they guys begged her to come help. That's the only reason she went that night, but it changed everything.

The blind corner where no cameras turned, and there *it* was. She smelled it before she saw it. Maybe if she'd been listening and watching, she could have saved that kid, but her mind wandered with fatigue, hunger, and wondering if she'd make enough to pay by morning for the rent. It was huge and gray; man or beast? She still didn't know.

It lumbered over something. A hand like an anvil lifted over its head. Its voice howled in the wind. "Where's the others?"

A scream more like a whimper answered and the anvil-like hand slammed down, landing with a squish and a plop. Blood, flesh, and brains filled Eugene's nose, and she froze.

CC's voice interrupted her memory. "I'll call you as soon as I find him."

Eugene realized she was holding her breath. She took a long breath in. Letting out a growl gurgled out her throat.

"Are you okay?" Max asked.

Eugene turned her head. She didn't realize the vamp was so close, but he didn't surprise her. His was the familiar scent from the cafe.

She took in another slow breath, closed her eyes, and relaxed her face. "I smell him," she said. She rolled her shoulders back and straightened her back. "I'll never forget that smell or what he did to that kid."

"Good," said Max. "Can you track him?"

Eugene looked into his face. His square jaw and deep eyes returned her stare.

Despite trying to relax her face, her teeth clenched. She recognized the same expression on his face. "It would be easier." She paused, but he made no sign of understanding. "It's easier to track when I'm wolf," she said.

"Can you do it and not be seen?" he asked.

He didn't raise an eyebrow. His face remained unremarkable and in no way condescending.

Eugene smiled. "Yah. But if it gets out-"

Max interrupted her. "I'll follow. You should know my scent well enough. It won't get in your way?"

Eugene's mouth fell open. Never had anyone asked her that before. "No."

"Good," Max said.

They heard CC say, "This is bad."

"It's very bad," Max said. "I'll run interference. Give me your clothes."

Max pulled a backpack off her shoulder, and Eugene removed her clothes. A moment later, she shifted to the wolf. The scent of their prey burned her snout, and she growled.

Max nodded. "Let's go."

Eugene leaped down the road, careful to stay in the shadows and away from the vamp trailing her. She would find the monster and she would rip its throat to shreds.

*****

Her eyes opened. Something wet and sticky moved in her hand.

"Bean!" muttered Joslyn as she shook the little brown chihuahua away from her. "Ugh! What have you been eating?"

The little dog barked once and ran the circumference of the pool as Joslyn stretched her arms and put her feet to the cool concrete. The skin of her back itched where the vinyl of the lounge chair had pressed into her. Before she stood, Bean leaped onto the chair and onto her lap.

"Silly old dog," said Joclyn, scratching the ears of her dog. "At least some friends don't let you down."

She stood, carrying Bean, and went to the outdoor refrigerator to pull out two bottles of water. The first she opened and drank half before stopping to take a breath. Setting Bean on the granite bar, she opened the other and washed Bean's paws and mouth.

"Can you believe that Roberta?" Joslyn asked Bean. "We go through all this planning to have a real grownup weekend, and then she chickens out. No way she wanted to go to the weekend lock-in at church. She hates Mrs. Cambell. She's just a chicken. All that planning. Well! I don't need Roberta to enjoy a weekend in the house all by myself. Well, with you Bean. Glad I told Mom Roberta's mom didn't mind Bean staying with her."

With a harrumph, she put Bean on the ground and looked around.

She kept the pool lights off in case Mom and Dad told the neighbors they'd be gone for the weekend. Besides, she liked sitting by the pool at night. The moon was full and twinkled in the black water. Streetlight and those little safety lights dad put in between the stairs last summer provided more than enough light for her to make her way up and down the hill to the house.

Joslyn stretched and walked to the far edge of the pool deck. If she stretched her neck, she could just see Town Lake. "Must be late," she said. "Park lights are off." She was sure there was some sort of festival going on at the park this weekend. She'd walk over and have a good time. Maybe she'd message Andy and see if he wanted to go. Boys weren't allowed in the house when Mom and Dad weren't home, but if she met him there, she'd still be following the rules. "Just in case Mom and Dad find out I'm not spending the weekend with Roberta."

Bean growled, his tiny "I'm scared," growl. Joslyn put her hands on her hips. She squinted her eyes and peered into the shadows of the trees and rocks around her yard. She'd heard a lot of sirens early in the evening. When she checked the neighborhood watch app, she'd discovered the police were raiding the Lower East Side, whatever that meant. Jocyln liked the East Side. She loved strolling through the art studios and eating at the taquerias.

"No one's going to bother us," she whispered as she bent down to pick up Bean. That's when she noticed how quiet it was. She heard the cars on the freeway mixing with the rustling of the leaves and lapping of water from the lake, but she heard no birds flying above her. The owls didn't screech. The crickets didn't sing.

A drop of sweat ran down her back, chilling her skin. She hugged Bean close to her chest. Bean whined and hid his nose in Joslyn's neck. A car drove down the street and stopped nearby. Someone opened one door and slammed it closed. Someone opened the door to a house. "You made it," a man's voice said. "Tough shift?"

"I'm exhausted," a woman's voice answered.

"Your tea's ready. I'll heat your dinner."

Jocyln shrugged her shoulders and walked up the steps to the house.

The air hung stale and flat against her skin. A stink worse than garbage drifted into her nose. She held Bean a little tighter. The steps turned onto a landing, the only place in the yard where trees and bushes hid both pool and house. A chorus of barks and howls filled her ears. Bean barked and barked as her little paws pushed and scraped to push away from Jocyln.

With an "ow!" Joslyn lost her grip on Bean. The dog dashed down the steps, away from Joslyn and to the house. Joslyn followed, running down two steps at a time. She reached the pool and stopped on one foot. Bean squealed once and fell silent. A faint splash, and Joslyn watched a dark spot floating away from her.

Cold gripped her like claws. She couldn't breathe as the stink engulfed her. Darkness filled her mind until she heard the voice like Mr. Cambel made when he told stories of the Devil.

"Where's the other?" the voice asked.

Joclyn didn't answer. In the cold, the stink she smelled poured over her face along with hot, wet breath, and Joclyn vomited her fear. She knew nothing else.

3

Walk in the night, unafraid,
And shiver as the shadows take you.
Walk in the night with the conscious of a friend,
And dance in the shadows of the moon.
I'm Mary Midnight, online and in your mind.
Be careful who you walk with.
The dance is long but brief for mortal touch.
But a touch so soft will light the path that shadows take.
Even as they bend to will, to want, to waste.

Eugene ran with the constant gait of the hunter on an easy trail. The trail did not meander. It headed east. She stayed in the shadows, sprinting to cross streets, but she remained out of sight. From time to time, she stopped and turned her head. Max kept up with her, always just out of sight but always upwind of her. She stopped in the shrubs near the frontage road and waited. The intersection was well lit and busy despite the lateness. If she crossed the intersection, someone would see her. It was time to see how good Max was at running interference.

She sat on her haunches and watched as a homeless man and his dog crossed the intersection toward her. The dog's ears honed in on Eugene's breath. The hair on its haunches lifted as its nose raised and lowered. Eugene stood, ready to frighten the dog away, when Max walked up to the man.

"Looks like you need a meal," Max said, handing the man some bills.

"Bless you," the man said with practiced mechanics. And then the man's eyes saw the bills. His eyes widened and his mouth opened wide.

Max bent over and petted the dog, which responded with a happy yap. "And don't forget my new friend here."

"We'll both have a good meal tonight. Thank you," the man said. He walked away, his limp forgotten.

A moment later, Max sat at Eugene's side. Eugene nodded, satisfied that Max was okay - for a vamp.

"I assume," Max said. "The scent is still good."

Eugene nodded.

"CC found that boy somewhere around here," Max said as he stroked his chin with his fingers. "Perhaps tomorrow afternoon, you two can check out the encampment they talked about."

Eugene gave a quick growl. The scent was good, but the wind was picking up. It could fade if they delayed chatting.

"You're right," he said. "Rude of me to talk when you can't talk back. Let's get to the other side." Max stood but remained hidden from onlookers by the shrubs. "Be ready and stay close to me."

Eugene stood, lowered her head, and sniffed the air. The change, when it came, was subtle. The smell of darkness and light mingled over her head, and then the light was gone. She felt Max step forward and followed, relying on her connection to his scent more than her eyes. They walked across the southbound frontage road. Under the interstate five men and one woman sat in front of a tent talking in hushed voices over the noise of the traffic, across the northbound access road, and behind a service station.

The smell of dark and light mingled again, and Eugene could see the trees and businesses in front of her. It only took a moment, and she caught the scent of her prey. Without looking at Max, she leaped forward toward her prey.

On this side of the freeway, drawing close to the river, the smell of water settled over everything but did not hide the scent. She followed it past the multiple businesses and past crowds lingering outside of bars. She followed it through neighborhoods weaving in and out parked cars and snarling at neighborhood dogs growling at her. She followed until the scent changed.

At the edge of the river in a park, she stopped. The scent changed, and then a small dog issued the shortest of howls before it yapped and stopped. Max stepped out from behind a tree as the neighborhood dogs answered with panic, angry, sorrowful songs. In the songs they sang; Eugene heard what she needed. She barked once to Max and dashed up the hill, running as fast as she could. *Max will have to keep up.*

She ran across a road and up a hill, through backyards and over fences. As she reached the side of a dark pool, she stopped. Blood filled her senses: small dog, girl. The neighborhood dogs sang again in anger and vengeance.

Eugene sniffed the wind and followed a trail upstairs. He stood there, over a body, lifeless and pale. Blood poured from his mouth, dripping down a beard, long and matted. Yellow eyes glared at her. White teeth--or were they fangs?--glistened red and white in the moonlight. It leaped toward her. Eugene crouched to attack, but Max threw himself against the man/monster. It howled - screamed and tossed Max off as easily as if he were a mosquito.

Max landed on his feet, squatting. The man/monster was between him and Eugene. Eugene's eyes fixed on the creature's neck; a pulse pushed against the skin that pushed the scraggly hair. *Rip. Tear. Let the teeth sink in. Hold.* But before she leaped, it ran through the bushes and trees, disappearing into shadows within shadows. The neighborhood dogs growled and howled as it passed. Eugene turned to follow, but Max's voice stilled her.

"No, Eugene." If he breathed, Eugene would have said he was out of breath. She turned, ready to growl at him, but blood streamed down his neck from great gaps, caused by teeth? Claws?

Blood from the girl and the chihuahua filled her snout, her tongue, saliva poured down her lips pooling on the ground beneath her. A growl rose in the throat. Her hair rose along her spine as head lowered. Muscles tensed in her joints, ready to pounce.

Max stood to his full height. He stared at Eugene, raising his hand, showing her his palm. His other hand gripped his throat as more blood poured from between his fingers and with it night, blood, and death mingled in her mouth.

Eugene shook her head, and then a small bark followed by a high-pitched whimper startled her. She turned. The chihuahua climbed the step crawling on its belly toward the hand of the girl. Max took a step toward the small dog. Eugene turned her gaze back to Max and growled, baring her fangs, still dripping with saliva.

Max coughed. "I'm not that hungry," he said and walked past the dog back to the pool.

Before Eugene's touched the small dog to lick away blood, Max returned with a towel wrapped around his neck. He squatted, wrapping the small dog in the towel. "Your backpack got ripped off my back. It's in that bush over there."

Eugene remained where she was, her eyes darting between Max and the small dog.

Max rose, cradling the small dog wrapped in the towel. He closed his eyes and tilted his head. "I need you on two legs, Eugene. Please,"

Eugene leaped into the bush, gripping a torn strap in her teeth. Behind the bush, she pictured her human side and transformed. "Hang on, Max," she said, just above a whisper as she pulled on her jeans. "I just bought this backpack," she muttered, pulling out her vest.

"Sorry," said Max. His voice cracked.

Eugene stopped buttoning her vest and stepped in front of the bush. "You sound like shit," she said.

Max stepped forward, handing her the wrapped-up dog. "I have to go. Call CC to pick you up. Let her call the police." A breeze rustled the leaves above her, and Max was gone.

"Hang on, kid," Eugene said. The chihuahua stopped whining as Eugene held it close with one hand while sliding on her shoes one at a time.

*****

CC walked into the living room, stretching and pulling a t-shirt over her head, then she stopped. "Eugene! Come get your dog off my couch."

"Not fair," shouted Eugene from her bedroom. "Fluffy can sit on the couch."

Bean, the tiny Chihuahua, sat up and whimpered. The sound echoed off the plastic cone wrapped around his head.

"Oh well," CC mumbled, bending over to pick up the little dog. She held him close to her chest, careful not to touch the cast wrapped around his tiny arm. "Guess it's hard for you to get around, isn't it little guy?"

Fluffy barked and jumped on the couch.

"I see the wet spot, Fluffy. I know you didn't do it."

Bean whined.

"Not your fault, little guy," replied CC, pushing Fluffy off the couch and walking to the dryer at the end of the kitchen, under James Earl's stairs to search for a towel.

She had just set the towel on the cushion when Eugene entered. "You left him on the couch: You clean it."

Eugene cringed but began cleaning. "Sorry," she said. "Didn't want him in the bed with me. Afraid I'd roll over and hurt the little guy."

CC went back to the kitchen and turned on the coffeemaker, still holding the little dog. "You need to take him home?" She asked.

Before Eugene could answer, James Earl entered and took over making the coffee. "You can't take him back to someone who'd name a boy dog Bean."

"He's a tough little guy," Eugene said.

"No," said CC. "We are not keeping him."

James Earl handed her a cup of coffee. "He'll have to stay a few days, at least until the parents return."

"Just because they weren't home last night doesn't mean they aren't home now," Eugene said, throwing the towel in the washing machine and pulling another clean one from the dryer.

"It's what Frank said when he called me," said CC between sips of coffee. When Eugene raised her eyebrows, she added, "He's the one I called after I picked you up last night. Looks like Joslyn stayed home while her parents went away for the weekend."

"She couldn't have been more than fourteen," replied Eugene.

"Said told her parents she was staying the weekend with a friend at some sort of church thing," said CC. "He spoke to the parents on the phone. They're in Cozumel and will be back later today. They tracking down the friend and her parents to get the full story. By the way, babe, don't forget we're meeting Frank this afternoon."

"What does he want?" asked James Earl.

"I'll be there," Eugene added. "Gotta work this afternoon."

"Good," James Earl replied. "See what you think about this guy. Not sure I trust him."

"Frank's a good guy," CC said. "I'm going to do some more research. Max sent me the files he's collected over the years. We're missing something, I know it."

"Nevertheless," added James Earl. "Eugene, keep an eye out for anyone coming in just before or after Frank."

Eugene nodded. "Sure, do you want me to..." she trailed off and watched as CC, carrying Bean and her coffee, left the living room.

*****

"That's Luna," said Eugene, setting a cup of coffee in front of CC. "Behind the counter is Marcus. Their mom, Jackie, is out today."

James Earl took his cup from Eugene. "They have any idea what's going on?"

Eugene snickered. "Totally cool with their mums partnering with a vamp to save the family business and a werewolf serving customers."

CC rolled her eyes. "Inside voice, Eugene. That's why you're in Austin."

Eugene's cheeks blushed pale pink. "I'm never going to live that down."

"No," smirked James Earl. "You're not."

"Ignore him, Eugene," said CC, hiding her own grin behind her coffee mug. "It'll get better." She set her cup down and waved to an older man with a cowboy hat walking in the front door. "It's Frank. He doesn't want to know about you."

Eugene set the third cup on the table and walked away.

James Earl put his hand on CC's. "What does he want?"

CC stared at James Earl. His golden eyes glowed in the low light of the coffee shop. They focused on her face. As he squeezed her hand, the tension in her shoulders melted. She straightened her back and took in a deep breath enjoying his smell mixing with his new cologne. "We can trust Frank. He knows how to not ask certain questions," she said.

James Earl smiled. "No harm in making sure." He tapped his phone.

CC recognized the lines running across the screen as James Earl scanned the room for listening devices. He winked at her.

When Frank arrived at the table, she produced her friendliest of smiles.

"Good to see you, Frank," she said.

Frank Jarvis nodded. "You're both looking good. Seems like every time I run into CC here, you're off somewhere else, James Earl. Glad you're both here, actually. Is that cup for me?"

James Earl slid the cup in front of Frank. "No sugar, half-n-half, none of that low fat shit," he said with a grin. "I remember."

Frank chuckled and took a sip.

CC recognized the look of bliss that comes with the first sip of good coffee. "So," she said. "What's up, Frank?"

"To the point, as usual," Frank answered, nodding his head. He took another sip and looked over her shoulder out the window. "Renaldo tells me there was something familiar about the body he found last night and the death of young Joslyn, the one you called me about last night. He also tells me you were holding back."

"Frank," started CC, but Frank held up his hand to stop her.

"It seems to me," his thick Texas drawl lingered as though remembering a well-rehearsed line, "there could be some similarities between the killing of those kids last night and the murder of a kid about five years ago."

James Earl leaned back in his chair. CC watched as s his breath quickened, his eyes focused on Frank, and his ears quivered.

The crash of porcelain shattering filled the room, followed by a deep voice rising in volume. "Will you pay attention to what you're doing!"

CC breathed in the moment of silence in the cafe before muffled giggles and unrepentant laughter filled the room along with the usual comments, "Someone's in trouble," "Poor thing," and "That was a hell of a crash."

James Earl sat up and stared as Marcus threw a towel on the floor in front of Luna. "If you paid a lick of attention-"

"I got it," said Luna, shrugging her shoulders and standing in front of Marcus.

Marcus's voice increased in volume. "She dropped the plates on purpose. She can clean it up!"

"I did not," said Luna, yelling and stretching to stand in front of Marcus.

"Luna," said Eugene, lifting a hand to Luna's shoulder.

Luna pushed Eugene's hand off her shoulder. "I'm tired of him telling me what to do."

Marcus reached his hand to Eugene who twisted, grabbed his hand, and pulled herself so close to Marcus, she bent her head to stare down at him.

James Earl said, "I think I can help." He stood and walked to the coffee counter. "Hey, can I get a top-off?"

"He's all right," Frank said, turning his attention to CC.

CC watched Marcus force himself to face James Earl. "Sure," he said. Eugene guided Luna away from the coffee counter.

"Yes, he is," replied CC. "So, there's a similarity to the murders?"

Frank nodded. "Yes. And this is one of those you-don't-get-out-of-your-head cases, even if I hadn't married into the family." Frank sipped his coffee and pulled a thick roll of papers wrapped in a rubber band out from the breast pocket of his jacket. He kept his hand around it, while tapping it on the table.

CC waited. Her gaze focused on nothing as her brain made

connections. "Your wife's sister," she said, nodding her head. "That's why you wanted to meet here."

Frank lifted his head and grinned. "Yup. My nephew and niece made that scene over there. Not that they like admitting I'm their uncle. And from your knowledge of who's who in this case, we are looking at the same killer."

CC rolled her eyes as her cheeks burned. "You caught me in a rookie mistake," she said. "Yes, I know about Valentino. Until this moment, I didn't connect your wife's name with the case, even though I've read through all the reports."

Frank lost the grin on his face. He looked into her eyes. "If you take a broad look at the murders, there are connections between Valentino's case, the girl from last night, that body at crime scene I met you at, and then the bloodless bodies we found last year. You helped us out with those. They're still listed as unsolved, and I don't reckon I'll ever see their murderers in jail. But this one," Frank looked at the roll of papers before offering it to CC. "This one needs to be solved, not just because I want it solved. The family needs closure. They're not doing well, but you know that, or James Earl wouldn't have been so quick to jump up and help those two." He turned to watch James Earl talk to Marcus.

CC opened the roll. The first page was a copy of the police report on the disappearance and murder of Valentino LeBrere, the younger brother of Marcus and Luna, followed by copies of news reports. The boy, Valentino a.k.a Tony, disappeared along with his friend walking home from school. His friend was found wandering the streets of the warehouse district three days later, alone, confused, beaten, and dehydrated. Valentino's body was found two weeks later. The last page was a copy of the report and coroner's note on Joslyn Bridges, the body found the last night.

CC looked at Frank. "Valentino's body looked like-"- she stopped, catching herself before saying Louis. "It wasn't all there," she said.

Frank nodded. "What kind of monster rips out the hearts of children, CC? Can't be many."

CC cleared her throat. "Does Renaldo know you're giving this to me?"

"No," Frank replied. "He's too good at putting two and two together. But you and I know this isn't the type of case the police will solve."

CC nodded. "Like it or not, Renaldo's involved. He knows something *unusual* is going on."

Frank took a long sip from his coffee. "I know. Do what you can. This family needs the case closed." He looked back to watch Marcus behind the coffee counter. "They're good kids but strung so tight it won't take much for either to break." Frank stood to leave. "Thanks for the coffee. I'll talk to Renaldo. Be careful."

CC watched him leave the coffee shop as five high school students walked in, their new uniforms and hair sticking to their sweaty bodies. They were laughing and talking as they made their way to the coffee counter where Luna greeted them with a smile.

*****

Eugene felt the hair on the back of her neck rise and a growl roll from her throat, only stopping at the back of her lips at the last minute. She stared into Marcus's eyes: dark, brown pools rimmed with pink instead of white. Puffed sockets lined almost black against his dark skin. Sweat beaded on his forehead. His breath quickened.

Eugene heard James Earl before she saw him. She took in a deep breath, lowering her arm and letting go of Marcus's arm.

"Hey, can I get a top-off?" James Earl asked, setting his empty cup on the counter.

Marcus turned to the counter. "Sure," he said.

Eugene guided Luna through the kitchen door and sat her at the small table where Florence sat writing in her notebook. Florence nodded and pulled her phone out of her pocket. "Gotta make a call," she said, and went to the back door.

"Sit," Eugene said to Luna.

Luna sat, folding her arms. "I didn't do it on purpose," she muttered.

Eugene sat next to Luna and leaned back against the wall. "Okay," she said and rested her head on the wall separating the kitchen and coffee shop. From this spot, she could hear the voices in the cafe and James Earl talking to Marcus.

Luna's bottom lip pouted, and she stared straight ahead. "Why does he have to get so hot and bothered all the time and at me! I'm not doing anything wrong. Why don't you ask him what's wrong," said Luna. She sighed, waiting for something. She just wasn't sure what.

James Earl changed his mind about a coffee and asked for a latte. "I like them, but so full of sugar," he said. "They can make me jumpy."

Marcus' voice shook but answered, "Yeah. It makes me jumpy, too –" he coughed. Luna heard the gravel in his voice grate against his chest. She focused on his breath. "Excuse me. Too much sugar, and I can hardly hold a cup let alone mix the drink."

Luna's voice started low, but her volume inched up. "I tried that. It's always the same thing: we need this place to work, stop being such a kid, grow up. He's pissed off, he's stuck working here just like me. He just won't admit it."

Eugene lifted her hand. "Easy there, Luna. What makes you so sure he doesn't want to work here. Seems to me, he's pretty good at his job. Most people who don't like their jobs aren't good at it."

Luna stamped her foot and would have stood if Eugene hadn't taken her hand. "Look at me, Luna. Do I look like a server?"

Luna laughed. "Not really,"

Eugene listened as James Earl said, "My kid sisters used to drive me nuts, too. For all their trouble, they were good kids."

Eugene waited, wanting to hear Marcus answer. Once again, she heard his breathing and realized the gravel she'd heard earlier came from his chest, not his throat. "Some kids have to grow up a little faster than others," he said. "Anything else?"

"I got it," said James Earl. "Thanks."

"So," asked Luna. "If you don't like waiting tables, why are you doing it?"

"Money," said Eugene. "Grad school is expensive. I can't ask my folks to pay for it and send me an allowance. That wouldn't be right."

"I thought you got a scholarship?"

Eugene laughed this time. "You think it pays for meals? Clothes? Insurance? No, it pays for my classes and books, but the rest I gotta pay for. Besides, there are worse jobs than waiting tables."

"I can't imagine one," sighed Luna, sinking low in the chair. "I hate working here."

Eugene sat up. "I don't know why. This place is hot. Everybody wants in. This is the place to see and be seen."

Luna wrinkled her nose and scratched her chin. "I suppose it is pretty hot these days. It's not an empty store like it used to be."

"You and me are the only females here with an excuse to talk to every hunk of man who walks in here." Eugene nodded and stood. "Speaking of, a line is forming. I'm getting back to work."

Luna stood with Eugene. "You really think he likes working here?"

"Watch him. He's a natural with customers, and other than a few weird cleanliness qualms, he knows what he's doing."

Luna nodded. "I suppose."

Before Eugene stepped out of the kitchen, she leaned forward to speak into her ear. "Maybe cut him a bit of slack. He's about worn out."

*****

CC watched Darious. His eyes darted around him, untrusting, but too curious to look away. Mike stood behind Darius, hand on his shoulder, whispering in his ear. James Earl stood next to her. He heard what Mike said. He heard everything, but CC knew the words, comforting, soothing, easing the shock about to come. Renaldo and the coroner's technician watched Darious, waiting with what CC considered remarkable kindness and patience.

It took most of the evening to convince Darius to identify Maria, even though CC knew it was her. The description was too perfect. It hadn't been hard to find Darious. As soon as he saw her, his face had paled. His hands shook, but he finally agreed to come tonight. Mike was along to make sure Darious said nothing Renaldo shouldn't hear, and Max was nearby.

It was well past midnight. Renaldo made no objection when she suggested the late hour, and CC suspected Frank had talked to him about unusual cases.

Darious lifted his head nodding to Mike then looked at Renaldo, "I'm ready," he said, his voice holding the faintest of tremors.

The technician pulled back the cover. CC couldn't prevent the gasp from her lips. The girl's face, and she was too young to be called a woman, looked remarkable in its unremarkableness and so alike her brother that she thought for a moment it was Louis. Her dark skin paled to almost white over high cheekbones before it faded to blue along the hairline. Long, thick eyelashes clumped and spread, forming perfect sickle moons below what must have been huge, round eyes like Louis'. Plump lips lay chapped and broken beneath a nose perfectly placed, if not for the flattened right side and blue-black color. Strands of hair, darker than brown but not black, lay across her forehead. One hair rested over her right eye, where a dark ring oozed its way to her temple. Only the long hair made her unique from Louis.

CC resisted the urge to push that loose hair away from Maria's eye. She watched Darious's hand lift then resettle rigidly along his side. The tears forming in his eyes told her they were looking at Maria's body.

Renaldo took in a breath. "Darious, is this Maria?" he asked, his voice low but authoritative. CC admired his ability to command the attention of Darious while respecting the young man's grief.

"All you have to say is yes or no," Mike said.

Darious lifted his head and looked to CC. "Yes," he said, and turned away.

CC watched Darious's face as his skin turned green and gray around his ears. Mike put a hand on Darious' back to move him away, but before Mike could lead him to the door, Darious ran out of the room. Mike turned to Renaldo with a shrug, then followed Darious out of the room.

The technician stood back as Renaldo pulled the cover off of Maria.

James Earl turned away, groaning. "Son of a bitch!"

CC shook her head. "You can say that again." Even as dread oozed through her, she reached out to put on a pair of gloves and leaned in to examine the chunks of missing flesh from Maria's hips and thighs, ligature marks around her wrists and ankles, obvious bites scattered up and down her body, and a gaping hole rested between her breasts.

"Any ideas?" Renaldo asked, watching CC examine the body.

CC shook her head. "No," was all she could say. She couldn't tell him about a monster, but she also needed to make sure the marks on Maria's body were the same as she had seen on Louis' body.

Mike returned to the exam room. "Darius is outside," he said. "Sorry, Sanchez. He won't come back in."

CC looked up, seeing sweat running down Mike's face and his shirt sticking to his chest. "I'll get him to come talk to you, Renaldo," she said.

"I can handle the kid," Renaldo said. His eyes fixed on James Earl. "You okay, James Earl?"

CC jerked her head up to look at James Earl. He stood wide eyed, staring at CC. "The smell," he said. He nodded his head, and she returned her attention to the damage done to Maria. She sniffed, but the only thing she could smell was James Earl's new aftershave. It mingled with masculine scent and complemented what she assumed was the hint of wolf on his skin.

"Any sign of her brother?" Renaldo asked CC.

Mike coughed. CC rolled her eyes as she looked at him. "No," she said. "I still have feelers out."

James Earl stepped away from the body as Mike stepped forward. Renaldo raised an eyebrow. "But you think he's dead," he said.

"My client thinks he is," Mike said.

"Client?" Renaldo asked, darting his eyes between Mike and CC.

"Darious," Mike said. "He said Maria took care of her brother and when he went missing, she was sure someone had taken him. He's been missing for over a month now. My client believes, well - we're working on the assumption he's dead."

"And you're here to make sure I don't beat a confession out of him," Renaldo said with only enough sarcasm to keep it from being an accusation.

Mike beamed his toothiest smile. "Something like that."

"I've seen all I can handle," CC said. "Will you let me see the coroner's report when you're done with it?"

Renaldo's shoulders dropped as he sighed. "You know I can't let you see it, but-" he lifted his hand to stop her from interrupting. "I'll let you know if there's anything significant - if I can."

James Earl cleared is throat.

"Thanks," CC said before James Earl said more. "I'll let you know if I find out more about Louis."

An awkward silence filled the room until Mike clapped his hands. "Glad that's done. Don't mean to sound insensitive, but I'm ready for breakfast. Guys, if we get in the car now, we can catch up to Darious. Renaldo, I'll bring him to talk to you later today."

CC nodded and followed Mike and James Earl out the door. Renaldo stood by the door and put his hand on her arm as she walked out. "What are you not saying?"

CC jumped when she felt his hand on her arm, and he removed his hand. "Lot to think about, and I'm telling you everything I can." She turned her head to see Mike and James Earl waiting for her. "I promise. We both want the same thing, Renaldo, to stop a monster from killing children."

"I get the feeling when you say monster," Renaldo twisted his neck to not look at Mike and James Earl. "I assume you mean someone crazy."

CC nodded her head. "You talked to Frank? Then you know when I say monster, I mean monster."

Renaldo took a deep breath and whispered. "Louis is dead?"

James Earl called out, "Babe. We gotta go."

"We'll talk later," she said and walked away from Renaldo nodding her head.

*****

Darius wouldn't eat, but he drank some coffee and left, promising he wouldn't stray from his regular group of friends, and that he'd contact CC or Mike if he heard about any other disappearances. CC watched him walking out of the coffee shop. His shoulders slumped even as he drank his coffee. He wouldn't take any food.

"I don't like him being on his own," CC said as she set her own mug on the table.

"He knows how to take care of himself," said Mike with a mouth full of breakfast sandwich. "You going to eat that?"

Mike grabbed the container of avocado spread from the center of the table and opened it.

James Earl watched Darius walking away. "If he was a target, he'd already be missing."

"We can't be sure," CC answered, turning her attention to him but not focusing on him. "Can you? I mean, can you see if he's -" she stopped speaking to look around her and lower her voice. "Can you tell if he's not 100% human?"

"That's hard to tell," said Mike before James Earl could answer. "I've known young vamps walk right past another vamp and not bat an eye."

James Earl snarled. "I'd be able to tell. There was something odd about Maria."

"I'm not doubting you. I'm just saying," Mike paused, swallowing. "You're new to all of this. Maybe we should get someone else to make sure. Speaking of, why aren't Eugene or Ezra here?"

James Earl scoffed. "Renaldo would've loved to see them."

CC reached her hand over the table to rest on James Earl's. "What's different about Maria's smell from mine or Mike's?"

James Earl closed his eyes as though remembering something. "It was subtle. I smelled death, but there was something else there, just under that sweet reek. Cold, wet, foreign, not human. I can't place it. It was on her, but not her."

Mike put his sandwich down and took a sip of coffee. "Did Clay mention an unusual smell?" he asked CC.

"At the dump site, he said he smelled something odd." CC sipped her coffee. "Max was at the coroner's office. He might know what it was."

"Until Max speaks, you're stuck with me," snorted James Earl.

Before he could say more, Mike added, "How certain is Eugene that she'd recognize this not-quite-unhuman?"

CC closed her eyes, pressing her lips together, but James Earl slapped his hand on the table. "I've got this," he said.

CC placed her hand on James Earl's hand.

James Earl pulled his hand away from CC and stood. "Whatever. I want to get back to my search for Maria and Louis' real names. They may have family looking for them. Darius' friend says she thought they were from Panama. I'm going to narrow my search to there. And I'm still looking for the old preacher's lost kids. You coming home or staying?"

CC stared at James Earl. Her eyes widened, and then she picked up her napkin and wiped her mouth. "When I'm done."

"Whatever. I gotta piss." James Earl turned and walked away.

"Sorry," Mike said. "Did I say something?"

CC watched James Earl's back as his feet stomped across the coffee shop and down the hall leading to the bathrooms. "He's still adjusting," she said.

Mike chuckled. "You think?" He emptied his cup of juice. "Sorry. I can't imagine how hard it is for him right now."

"Ezra's helping all he can, but he's a family man, and his oldest is reaching *that* age," CC said.

Mike shuddered. "I wouldn't want to go through puberty again, and if she takes after her dad, he won't be much help to us or James Earl for a while."

"Wolves inherit?" CC asked. "I mean, I know with vamps, there's never any family, so no one knows for sure, except maybe Mary."

"Some wolves do," Mike began, and pointed to the last croissant on the plate. "You going to eat that? Remember, Ezra's mother was a one hell of a wolf in her day, but his sister isn't."

CC nodded. She stared at nothing, thinking of all she'd learned about vamps and wers and realized she still had much to learn.

"Want me to talk to Ezra?" Mike asked.

"Huh?" CC said. "Sorry, in another world. I want as much info as I can. I need to let Cesar know we found Maria."

Mike nodded. "He's as eager to catch this thing as Max."

CC said nothing until Mike touched her shoulder. "Maybe you shouldn't go out hunting for this thing. Let Max do it."

CC opened her mouth to speak, but Mike held up his hand and looked at James Earl. "It's going to be dangerous for more than you, especially if he can't control-"

James Earl's voice echoed over the coffee shop from the door. "Ready to go?"

She picked up their to-go cups. "We know the general areas where the bodies were dumped. It's time to find this thing before he kills again." She followed James Earl to the car. She looked back at Mike. "Tonight."

* * * * *

Eugene banged on the bedroom door. "Wake up!" she shouted.

"What?" replied James Earl.

Eugene raised her eyebrows and scowled when she heard a low growl from James Earl's throat. Then she laughed, hearing CC mumble, "Will you calm down? She's our guest."

Now I know who the boss is. "It's the news," shouted Eugene, pushing the door open. She took two steps into the room, then plopped onto the bed between CC and James Earl's feet. She handed the tablet to CC. "You gotta see this - missing kid. It's got to be our guy."

CC pulled the bed sheet up to her neck with one hand as she grabbed the tablet with the other hand.

"Damn it, Eugene," huffed James Earl twisted his feet to the floor while keeping a blanket tight to his midsection. "You can't tell from a news article it's our monster. Kids go missing every day."

"It's him," exclaimed Eugene. "I know it. He's a foster kid, last seen close to home, just after dark."

CC scrolled down the page. "This says nothing about him being a foster kid."

"Look at him." Eugene took the table and swiped to another page. "Now, look at the parents. They're white. He's black."

"That doesn't mean," began James Earl, but he stopped and looked at CC, whose face paled. "What is it, babe?"

"Renaldo said they were sweeping last night right next to the family's neighborhood," CC replied.

Eugene watched CC. The bedsheet dropped, revealing a scar running from her shoulder, down her arm, and disappearing under the sheet. CC handed the tablet to James Earl. He took it and pulled the sheet up to CC's neck.

CC let the sheet fall. "Let's assume this kid, Lamond, was taken by our monster." CC pushed her feet out of the covers and onto the floor. "What time is it?"

"A little after noon," said Eugene, turning her back on CC.

"Go to class," CC said, walking into the bathroom. "James Earl, find out all you can about Lamond and his family. I'll call Max as soon as I've cleaned up." She closed the door but opened it almost at once. "He's not likely to be up yet. I'll leave a message with Cesar. Eugene, head to the cafe as soon as class is over. If they haven't found Lamond by then, we'll assume our monster has him. This narrows our search tonight."

The door closed. Eugene sighed and folded her arms. "Gotta work there today anyway," she muttered.

A pillow hit her on the back of her head. "Will you go?" asked James Earl. "I'd like to get out of bed."

"I didn't take you for the bashful type," said Eugene, standing up.

"Go to class," CC yelled from the bathroom.

Eugene rolled her eyes. "Yes, ma'am," she muttered.

"Get used to it," James Earl said. "She's kind of bossy when she's planning."

Eugene turned to look at James Earl. His back was to her as he stretched. Eugene admired his firm buttocks, slim waist, and muscular back, but the tightness in his shoulders and slump in his neck told her he was not the confident man he pretended to be.

"Go!" shouted James Earl, throwing another pillow toward her.

Eugene closed the door and heard the pillow hit the floor. "Babe," she heard him call. "Is she always going to walk into our bedroom?"

*****

Ezra arrived first. He rushed in, breathing heavily and wiping sweat from his brow. "Long day," he said, sitting next to James Earl. "Thought the mayor was going to talk my ear off. Between the council's planning meeting and that missing kid, it's a mad-house at city hall."

"Oh," CC said, grinning and pretending her finger burned as she touched his shoulder. "Talking with the mayor. You are important."

Ezra opened his mouth, then closed it, chuckling. "It did come out like that, didn't it?" He looked up as Eugene shouted his name and waved from behind the coffee counter. He waved back. "Eugene, get me some ice tea, will you?"

Ezra's face straightened as he returned his gaze to CC. "You're sure our monster took little Lamond?"

James Earl nodded. "We didn't see him do it, but we might as well have. Before coming here, we drove out to where he was last seen. I found the same smell I got from Maria's body."

Ezra rubbed the stubble on his chin. "Same smell?"

CC put her hand over James Earl's. "We also did some digging. Lamond's adopted, found abandoned as an infant. Nothing on biological parents. He's athletic, never gets sick; his mom says he doesn't sleep well at night."

"Sounds like me when I was growing up," Eugene said, setting a glass in front of Ezra.

"Me, too," James Earl said. "There's always a chance Lamond just wandered off, but we can't risk it."

"Agreed," said Ezra and CC at the same time.

"I tracked him once," said Eugene. "I can track him again."

"No," said CC. "I want you here keeping an eye on things."

They all looked across the cafe to Marcus at the counter and Luna sitting at a table with her books.

"Out!" shouted Florence from the kitchen. Tommy walked into the cafe from the kitchen door. Even with his western hat and shades, he looked like Tommy.

"What's he done now?" breathed CC.

He sat at the table. "Really want to know what I've been doing?" he asked and picked up her hand to kiss it.

"Do not cause trouble," CC said, smiling, and then yanked her hand away from his lips.

"I listen and obey you in all things, my sweet Catherine." Tommy removed his hat and bowed low. "You're looking ravishing, Eugene."

Eugene raised her hand. "Don't start. We need a plan to catch this monster before it kills Lamond."

Ezra cleared his throat. "Perhaps we should meet-"

James Earl interrupted him. "Who's going to hear us here? Besides, we need Max. If he's right about this thing-"

"He's always right about these things," sighed Tommy, sitting in the chair next to CC. "One of the many things annoying about him."

"Eugene," shouted Marcus from the counter. A line of customers stood chatting in front of him. "A little help, please. And Tommy, if you're not too busy to work." Marcus' sarcasm escaped no one, and two of the young women in line looked toward Tommy and giggled.

"The price of fame," said Tommy, standing. "Max is on his way. For an old man, he moves awfully slow in the daylight."

Ezra set his glass down and lowered his head. "I'm taking Sally and the kids to the vineyard this weekend. They'll stay there until we get this thing."

CC nodded. "Good. I wouldn't want to worry about them, and with you and James Earl there this weekend, we know they'll be safe."

"I'm not going," said James Earl.

CC caught her breath. "But babe, tomorrow night-"

James Earl reached over and took CC's hand. "Full moon. I can handle it. I'm needed here." He looked at Ezra. "I can control the change."

Ezra pinched his lips and scratched at his stubble. Nodding, he said, "Ordinarily, I'd be glad you were here, helping, but someone needs to be there keeping an eye on things. I was planning on that someone being you."

James Earl opened his mouth to speak but said nothing. CC felt his frustration. She, like James Earl, expected Ezra to disagree. She counted on him to disagree with James Earl. The stress of dealing with the anomaly showed especially on him with his quick moods swing. The low growls he assumed she didn't notice, even the quivering ears when he was excited. "You've always said you thought Millie was a wolf," CC said, speaking so only they could hear. "It would be prudent to keep an eye on her."

"If she's changing, I'll be no help to her," said James Earl to Ezra. "I've just learned to master myself. Besides, she's a kid. It'll be awkward being naked in front of her."

Ezra twisted in his chair. "I'll trust the safe room up there. We all need to work together to catch this killer."

CC felt the sudden chill down her spine and Max joined them at the table. "I couldn't agree more," he said. "But first, tell me what you've learned about this missing child in the news."

*****

"I don't know," Luna said to Tommy as steam from the coffee machine filled the space between them. "I mean, he's just weird."

Tommy poured the steamed milk from the pitcher to the waiting cup. "Looks weird," he said, placing the cup on the tray in front of Luna before placing another pitcher of milk in the machine and pulling the lever to send more steam between them. "You know the saying, 'Never trust a skinny chef.'"

Luna laughed. "Yeah, how *does* a baker stay skinny? And thinking about it, I never see him eat anything."

"That alone makes me suspicious." Tommy grinned and placed another mug on the tray. "Order's ready."

"Hope it slows down soon. I have *another* essay due for my English class - like almost every week. It's not fair."

"The life of the overworked student," Tommy said, wiping down the coffee machine. He stretched his neck over the machines to look around him. "We're slow enough, why don't you pull your books out. I'll shout if I need help."

Luna turned, keeping the tray of cups steady. "You don't mind? Thanks," she said and delivered the drinks to the couple holding hands at a table near the stage.

An hour later, the light from her laptop dimmed as it slipped into low-power mode. Luna jerked up as the muscles in her neck screamed like an ice pick were piercing them. She straightened her back and rubbed her neck, twisting to untwist from the precarious slouch at the table closest to the front door.

The couple near the stage still ogled each other. A young man in a Longhorn jersey sipped coffee and read a book at a table near the door, and Eugene sat at a table with Tommy playing cards. The emptiness and quiet shook Luna awake.

"Gin," shouted Tommy, slapping his cards on the table.

Eugene scratched her chin, eyeing Tommy over her cards. "You cheat," she said.

Luna sighed and closed her laptop.

"Pay up, pup!" Tommy proclaimed. "You lose again."

Luna heard Eugene snort. She looked at the tattooed woman and wondered what kind of person she was. Artist, waitress, hunter. When she picked up her book, she looked at a sketch of her own face. She pulled it close and under the overhead light to examine it. The face in front of her was pretty, delicate, and very, very young. Even though it was a pencil sketch, the eyes glittered from an overhead light, causing them to dance as they stared at something.

Above her face, the words, "Server, 17, Daydreaming," flowed with the precision of practiced loops and curves. In contrast to the fine script of the title, the signature, "Eugene Plumb" lay flat and scratched.

Luna looked to Eugene to thank her, but at that moment, Eugene stood scraping her chair across the concrete floor. She threw her cards on the table and stomped to the closet next to Jackie's office, pulling out the broom all the while glaring at Tommy.

Tommy leaned back in his chair, putting his feet on the table. "Don't look at me like that unless you have something to say. I won. You sweep." He stuck his tongue out. Eugene did the same and then dragged the broom to the back of the cafe where she lifted chairs onto a table before sweeping.

Luna glared at Tommy, but he only smiled and put his hands behind his head. She put her laptop in her backpack and walked to Eugene, reaching for the broom.

"Let me sweep," Luna said. "You've been working harder than me."

"Thanks, but I can't prove he cheats," Eugene said, still glaring at Tommy. "But when I do..."

Luna turned away and headed to her mother's office. She watched Tommy leap out of his chair and ring the bell over the coffee counter. "We close in fifteen, folks." His voice carried through the quiet room without shouting, but then he had a voice people wanted to listen to. "Who wants one for the road?"

The man in the jersey closed his book and waved to Tommy. "Double espresso, light, please," he called out.

The woman ogling her man stood but kept her hands inside her man's hand. "Cocoa with extra cream," she said.

"You cheat at cards," Luna said, passing Tommy.

Tommy, turning his cupid lips into a snarky grin, said, "Of course I do. It's no fun losing."

"I'll be out in a sec. I want to sync my files on mama's Wi-Fi, not the cafe's Wi-Fi," Luna said and pushed open the door to Jackie's office.

Luna stood with her back to the door, allowing her eyes to adjust to the darkness. The parking lot between the cafe and student co-op lit the office through the window with shadows from the old live oak darting around the room in the night's breeze. Boxes stacked two and three high filled the normally tidy office. Even the old couch along the right wall held boxes, but the lids were off of these boxes. The whites and manillas of their contents reflected the streetlights.

"Weird you not being here, mama," Luna whispered. "But that's why Tommy's here: A night manager."

She flipped on the light and skirted the boxes to sit at the one open space on the couch. The only chair in Jackie's office was behind the desk, and that was mama's desk. No one sat at mama's desk except mama. As her computer lit up, her curiosity rose. She knew the boxes contained Jackie's research from her days at the University. She picked a folder resting on top of the box next to her. Papers fell, scattering over and under the couch and covering the floor with graphs and charts in multiple colors.

She grunted and kneeled to pick up the pages. *Economic impact blah blah blah blah* "Spare me," she said turning the first page one way then another trying to make sense of the numbers and graphs. She gave up and gathered more pages, hoping she stacked them in the correct order. She stopped when she noticed her mother's handwriting on the back of one graphs. The ink color matched the blue mama always used at the office and not the black on any of the other pages she'd seen. "Profit/ loss statistics, shift in rate of arrest for vagrancies, prostitution? Drug possession? Urban revitalization.Yuck!"

"Mama's thinking again." Luna took the lid off another box. It, too, was full of folders tagged with fresh sticky notes and scribbles. She remembered seeing similar files in Jackie's office on campus that day when everything changed. It was Bring Your Child to Work Day. She was supposed to spend it with daddy, but they called him in for an emergency surgery. Mama had a full day of lectures, leaving Luna to fend for herself in the office bored wishing she was at school. A tear trickled down her cheek. She wiped it away.

Standing, Luna placed the lid back on the box to make it look like she hadn't been going through her mother's things. The overhead light blinked and went out.

"Just what I need," she muttered and turned for the door. The light from the cafe streamed in under the door. "You better not be trying to spook me, Tommy." She waited a moment, then took in a breath. "Eugene?" she whispered.

From behind her, she heard a scratching on the window. The blinds were open, as usual. The parking lot light was out. There was just enough light from the streetlight to make shadows darker and stretch further into the office. The scratching started up again. Luna cleared her throat and threw her shoulders back. "Grow up. Be a woman," she muttered.

She felt around the desk and boxes as she moved to the window. She found the cord for the blinds and pulled. No one stood in the parking lot. The Co-op next door was dark except for a few emergency lights along the stairs. "Talk about your partial power outage."

A squirrel dashed across the parking lot and leaped from the top of a pickup truck to the fence between the parking lot and co-op before running to a low branch of the old Live Oak. Luna laughed. "Run, run, stupid, fuzzy-tailed rat."

She took a deep breath, relaxing her shoulders when a ripple of energy traveled down her spine landing with a thud in her stomach. From behind a car on the far side of the lot, a pair of yellow eyes glared. They glowed from a roundish, shadowed head swaying as though caught in a breeze, unblinking. Luna's breath stopped. Her heart pounded once in her chest and then it, too, stopped. A growl, long, low, guttural, floated through the silence. From where she couldn't say. The yellow eyes inched in her direction. The face that held them only shadow.

Luna's left hand reached behind her for the desk as her knees crumbled. "Ow!" she exclaimed as her hand clasped an open box cutter, slicing her palm. The pain shook her fear away, and like a gale through a window, she coughed. Air poured into her lungs. Her heart pounded again, filling her ears with the rush of blood through her veins.

The office door burst open, the light from the cafe spilling in. Luna looked behind her, blinded by the light and the figure of Tommy standing in the doorway.

"Move!" he shouted, pushing Luna away from the window and onto the couch.

"Tommy," she cried out. She opened her mouth to say more but stopped as his shoulders relaxed and he closed the blinds.

"Are you okay?" he said, not looking at her. "I heard you call out."

"I cut my hand. It's no big deal," she said, not sure why she felt the need to calm him down.

Tommy's head shifted his right ear toward his shoulder. His blond curls shook. Without looking at her, he tossed the towel from his belt to her. "Wrap your hand tight to stop the bleeding."

Luna didn't notice Eugene until Eugene picked up her hand and wrapped the towel around it. "Where's the first aid kit?" Eugene asked, wrapping the towel around Luna's hand. "Let me help."

Tommy turned, walking out of the office as though it were on fire. "I'll get it."

"It's nothing," said Luna.

Eugene smiled. "Don't think you'll need stitches, but it's going to hurt like hell. I doubt you'll be much use serving for a while."

Luna caught her breath as Eugene added pressure to the cloth. "Ow! If it means I get out of serving for the next week, it's a good thing."

Luna wanted to look out the window and see if the eyes were still there, but not with Eugene here. She opened her mouth to laugh, but only words came out. "Who'd have thought Tommy would be so squeamish over a little blood?"

*****

James Earl leaned against the side of the newest brick office building on the block and pulled a bandana out of his pocket. "Damn! It's hot."

CC gulped the last of the water from her bottle. The heavy air beat down on her. No one walked the streets. The police raid a block over ended two hours ago. Not even a patrol car remained in sight. Only the most desperate ventured out now, and CC and James Earl were desperate. They needed the monster to show himself, so they could maybe save Lamond. CC looked at the clouds blanketing the sky, growing thick and heavy. She felt a curl brush the back of her neck and turned around. "A breeze. The storm will start soon."

"Call it a night?" James Earl asked.

"A little while longer." CC taped her phone. The map blared into her eyes. "We're in the area where the kids last saw Louis and only three blocks away from where Lamond disappeared." A drop of rain hit her screen. She lifted her head and looked across the street at a mostly empty three-story parking garage. The lights from the lot glowed around the building, making the rest of the area all the darker. "But maybe we hang there 'til the rain stops."

A burst of wind blew down the road, wiping the last of the sweat from her body as they jogged into the protection of the garage. A public parking sign hung over the entrance of the first floor. An orange security arm blocked cars from driving up the ramp. As soon as CC and James Earl stepped under the threshold of the garage, stopping in front of the ticketing machine, thunder cracked and rain poured from the sky, following the wind. Sheets of rain blinded the lights from the street. The yellow lights of the garage glowed against painted white parallel lines and a half dozen cars scattered on the first floor. The bright light over the ticketing machine flickered, but the lights remained on.

CC pulled her phone out and sent a text. It beeped in reply. "Max says it's raining all over. He's on his way to pick us up."

James Earl walked up the ramp, away from the light. The structure provided parking for those who worked in the office building across the street. Few chose to overnight their car on the public level. He cocked his head as though listening. CC followed him up the ramp. Two cars ten spaces apart were parked on the ramp, and she could only see one on the second level.

"What is it, babe?" CC asked. She watched him disappear and reappear in the flickering fluorescent lights on the ceiling. A tingle ran up her spine. She recognized the feeling and turned to see the cherub faced vampire standing behind her.

"Tommy!" she hissed. "What are you doing here?"

The golden-haired vampire lifted his hands in surrender, smiling wide enough to show his dimple. "Surprise," he said. "I missed you, CC. And while your boyfriend can defend himself, you don't stand a chance. I want to help."

"If I need a big brave vampire to come to my aid," CC said, putting her hand on her hips. "I'll call for Cesar."

Tommy's cheeks glowed as his lips formed into his perfect pout. "I'm hurt, CC. Can't I worry about you?"

"You are supposed to be watching-"

A growl echoed through the garage, interrupting her. CC froze, her hand reaching for the gun on her hip.

Tommy moved to stand next to CC. "It's here," she said.

"That wasn't James Earl?" Tommy asked.

Another growl echoed.

"That one was," said CC. "But the first growl wasn't."

Another growl echoed down on them. "He has it under control," CC whispered, more to herself than Tommy. She felt the shaking in her voice.

"Stay here. Text Max. Let him know it's here," Tommy said, and vanished before CC could answer. Thunder rolled down the street and through the garage. She held the phone tight and sent a text. She put it in her back pocket as she heard the intake of a breath, deep and choking. A shadow of a man that must be the monster stood in the rain outside the lights of the garage, silhouetted by lightning. He was huge, with shoulders broad and looming. The figure took a step forward, almost into the light of the garage entrance. CC saw deep, round yellow eyes reflecting the yellow lights of the garage. They reminded her of pools of urine in the alleys behind bars. The head craned as though listening.

Pointed ears stood proud of thick hair drooping under the flow of rain. It took another step forward. Light reflected white, sharp teeth glistening with a wetness she hoped was rain from inside the thick coarse hair of a beard that hung long past where a chin should be. An arm reached out a hand at least as large as her head and pointed a finger at her. The tip of a long, yellow nail caught the light, surrounded with dripping gray hair. It made a noise like a deep asthmatic breath. "We are one," it said.

Cold sweat beaded on her skin. The creature took another step toward the garage. She pulled her gun from its holster, aimed, and shot in one breath.

Rage poured from the mouth of the beast as it flew back into the shadows, its roar drowning the sound of the gunshot. From her right, another growl preceded a large brown wolf leaping toward the figure. It smashed into the creature, which roared again, pushing the wolf away. The wolf flew past CC's head and slid along the wet concrete floor until it stopped with a thump against a car.

Tommy appeared behind the creature, lifting him at the waist despite being half its size. CC aimed her gun, but Tommy and the creature squirmed into one image.

Tommy yelled, "Shoot it!"

CC hesitated. The creature yelled, swinging its massive body into a turn and roll. Tommy leaped off the creature with a loud plop and splash into a muddy pool. CC shot, but the creature ran into the storm, disappearing into the darkness.

CC grabbed her knees, gasping as she closed her eyes. She no longer heard the creature, only thunder and a loud car speeding up and getting close to them. "Max," she hoped.

She put her gun in its holster as she stepped out of the cover of the garage to reach a hand to help Tommy, but Tommy jumped up and pushed her into a puddle as the wolf ran into him, knocking him to the ground. The wolf bit into Tommy's shoulder, tearing out a chunk of flesh. Tommy didn't scream but rolled to his side. His fangs flared white as his eyes reflected the light and he lunged to bite into the wolf. The wolf howled.

Tommy lifted his face to look at CC. Blood ran down his chin. "Run!" he shouted.

CC pushed herself up and ran up the ramp leading to the second floor, as far from the entrance as she could get. The wolf leaped faster than she could run. She froze, seeing him standing in front of her, rain, mud, and blood dripping from his fur and fangs. She raised her left palm to him as her right hand surrounded the hilt of her gun. "Babe, you know it's me. I need you to take a step back. Remember me."

The wolf answered with a growl. She gazed at his eyes, their usual red glow burning a sickly orange in the yellow lights.

"James Earl," she said, forcing her voice to remain soft despite the roaring of a car engine racing in the driveway and thunder pounding in her ears. "I know you're there, babe. See me."

The horn of a car blared in answer as tires squealed to a stop behind her.

The wolf leaped. CC fell and rolled as Tommy pulled her down and under him. The wolf's claw swiped at her wrist as her arm pulled away from Tommy. Instead of the wolf landing near her, she heard the wolf howl, but this time in pain. Tommy lifted them up and she turned to see Max holding the wolf in his arms, squeezing. The wolf yelped. CC looked into his eyes and saw the brown eyes she recognized.

"Don't kill him!" she yelled, trying to pull away from Tommy, but his hands held her back like steel clamps.

The wolf fell to the ground.

Tommy released his grip, and CC rushed to the head of the wolf. He lay in front of her, panting until she picked up his head and put it in her lap. She closed her eyes to breathe. When she opened them, James Earl lay unconscious in her lap.

*****

CC sat on the couch in Cesar's office. She leaned back, allowing her eyes to close and soak in the silence. The storm had long passed, and the rain danced on the roof in soft, large drops. Her wrist throbbed, but Cesar had cleaned and bound the scratch running across her wrist. It hurt, but it no longer burned.

"Shit! Shit! Shit!" Cesar mumbled as he paced back and forth in front of the strongroom door hidden behind the private bar in his office. He poured himself another cup of coffee, took a sip, and turned to pace again.

James Earl sat in the armchair in the far corner of the room with a blanket wrapped around his shoulders.

CC opened her eyes. "Will you please sit down?" she said. "You're driving me nuts with all the pacing."

"I'm driving you nuts," exclaimed Cesar. "I told you. You couldn't kill that thing. Leave the fighting to Max, but no, you had to go hunting, and now I've got a vamp who'll be waking up really hungry soon."

"Max is taking care of him." CC rubbed her forehead. "Aspirin? I've got a headache."

Cesar stopped pacing and sighed. He looked at CC and nodded before pulling a bottle of aspirin from his desk drawer. He took a wine bottle from the refrigerator and poured a glass. "How about you, kid?"

James Earl did not look up. "I'm fine."

"You sure, babe?" CC asked. "You got a hell of a squeeze out there."

James Earl shook his head. "I'll heal."

Cesar harrumphed. "Of course you will, but that doesn't mean you don't need aspirin."

James Earl leaped to his feet, throwing the blanket on the floor. The oversized gray sweats hung off his limbs like old skin. "Don't you get it?" he growled. "I almost killed her!"

"But you didn't," Cesar said, his voice dropping in volume until it was just above a whisper.

"Stop acting like you know what you're talking about. You don't know shit!"

CC opened her mouth, but James Earl's eyes reflected the desk light back at her. She felt the hair on her neck rising. Before she could say anything, Cesar replied to James Earl, "I know if you don't keep your temper, you'll try to hurt her again."

James Earl jumped backward, his jaw dropping. "I'm sorry," he said, looking at her. He walked out of Cesar's office.

CC stood to follow, but Cesar put his hand on her shoulder. "Let him go. He'll figure this out on his own. He's smarter than most of us."

CC spun, wanting to shout, but seeing no pity in Cesar's eyes, she slumped back to the couch. "Thanks," she said. She straightened her back but closed her eyes. When she opened her eyes, Cesar still stood staring at her.

Max walked into the office from the strongroom, closing the door behind him. "Tommy will sleep till the sun goes down," he said.

CC nodded. Seeing Max's paler-than-usual face told her Tommy would heal because Max fed him. If he had recrimination for James Earl, he hid it. "It's time to evaluate what we learned tonight, but first, I need breakfast and that aspirin," said CC.

Max sat across from her. "You were right about where he'd attack. That's more than I've been able to do."

CC stared at Max. His previous over-friendliness even haughtiness gone.

CC nodded and pursed her lips. "Do we know this is a he?"

"Smelled male," Max replied.

"Great," Cesar grumbled. "That only narrows the suspect list down to half of Austin."

"No," Max said. "He doesn't stay in one place long enough to be noticed by natives. I suspect he's killed more than the three we know of."

"You think Lamond's dead," whispered CC.

Max nodded.

"I do, too," said CC. She looked to the door James Earl had walked through, hoping he would be there, but he wasn't. She sighed. "We learned something very important tonight that should narrow our search."

Max and Cesar looked at her. Max raised his eyebrow. CC wanted to laugh and tell him he looked like Mr. Spock. But it stuck in her throat. James Earl, the Treckie, wouldn't appreciate it.

"He spoke to me," she said. "He said we were one."

"Well," said Max, leaning back and tenting his fingers.

CC tried not to laugh.

"What does that mean?" asked Cesar.

"Maybe," Max started but stopped and studied CC's face. "You've met him, perhaps during the day."

Cesar nodded. "You sense us better than any human I've ever known, CC. You sensed him before you saw him, didn't you?"

"Yes," said CC. "I even knew what direction to look."

CC jumped out of her chair. "Oh my God! The kids. Tommy was supposed to watch them."

Max grabbed her arm, stopping her from walking out. "They're good," he said. "Eugene's with them. The creature was outside the cafe tonight. Luna saw it before it moved on to find you."

CC sat. Cesar whistled. "Well, that's a development."

"Eugene will try to get Luna to talk about it tomorrow," Max said. "Tommy let me know that much before he went to sleep."

"In the meantime," said CC. "I'll ask my cop friends to see if they can get some extra patrols near the coffee shop."

"Renaldo Sanchez?" asked Cesar.

CC nodded.

"Good man. Just be careful. He's sharp."

"I know," CC said. "But we need his help." CC stood again. "Guys, I'm hungry and tired. Cesar, drive me home?"

Cesar nodded, but Max stood raising his hand. "I'll take you home. Time I get to my kitchen. Cesar, I'll be back before Tomas wakes."

Cesar sat back at his desk. A harumph and narrowing of his eyes told CC he wasn't happy, but whether it was because he had to watch Tommy or not drive her home, she couldn't tell.

*****

"Mary Ramey, eleven years old, died in August 1885." CC read the information on a webpage she'd found on the Servant Girl Annihilator murders. If this was the same monster, then he was old, older than many of the vamps she knew. *Not older than Max or Tommy.* Sighing, CC leaned back in her chair, putting her feet up on her desk. Vamps didn't live the long lives of myth. Thirty or forty years, everyone you knew was dead. *Everyone needs someone to love.*

The text on the page blurred and CC slammed her feet to the floor. "Focus, woman!" She rubbed her eyes as the smell of coffee drifted into the room and into her nose. Her eyes widened. She smiled.

Renaldo stood at the open door to her office, holding a carrier with three large cups of coffee. "For a security consultant, your security sucks. I walked right in and you didn't even know it."

"Is one of those for me?" CC asked. She reached out her right arm until she saw the bandage and twisted to stand and reach with her left arm.

"Looks like you need it. Late night?" Renaldo handed her a cup. "I've got one for James Earl, too."

"He's upstairs, and I'm sure he knows you're here. He's got cameras everywhere."

As if on cue, a bell pinged from the intercom on her desk, and James Earl's laugh entered the room. "Thanks for the coffee, Renaldo. Be down in a sec."

"I figured after the night you had, you'd need some," Renaldo said sitting in one of the client chairs opposite CC.

CC looked at him over the edge of her cup, tugging her right sleeve, glad she was wearing a long-sleeved blouse. She savored the coffee, feeling the heat and caffeine relax and awaken her. "We were up late," she said.

Renaldo nodded, drinking from his own cup. "There were reports of gunshots from the parking garage on the East Side about three o'clock this morning. Close to our raid last night, the one I told you about."

"Really?" CC said, gathering the papers Max had sent her and putting them into folders. "I'd have thought you'd be too busy with paperwork after your raid to answer calls about gunshots."

"A uniform took the call. They found a few blood stains, rain washed too much away for good samples." Renaldo pointed to CC's computer monitor. "Not enough to do?"

"Learning all about my new hometown," CC said, looking him in the eye. "It's important to know the good and the bad."

James Earl walked into the office. He picked up the coffee cup Renaldo offered. "Thanks. I need this. What's this about gunshots?"

Renaldo looked from James Earl to CC. "In a parking garage, in an area you were at last night."

"Don't look at me," James Earl said. "I don't like guns."

CC said nothing. She hated lying to Renaldo, but if she admitted to firing her weapon, he'd have to know why, and then he'd make a report. His name, connected to a woman known for dealing with strange cases, would be mud.

Renaldo shook his head. "You were out there looking for someone because you told me you would be. I helped you, now you help me."

CC cringed. Guilt filled her, but James Earl stepped too close to Renaldo.

"Back off, Renaldo," he shouted. "I owe you nothing."

"Hey!" CC shouted and pounded her hand on her desk and grimaced as pain shot through her arm and up her shoulder. "Back down, babe. Renaldo's doing his job." CC turned her glare to Renaldo, whose expression turned from smug to chastised. "And you know me better than that. If I had anything I could tell you, I would. If we had been there, and I had fired my gun, it wouldn't have been for target practice. You'd need a warrant to check my gun, by the way. And if I had shot at something and grazed it, it might have bled, but the rain would have washed the blood away. Even if it didn't, the blood sample wouldn't help you. And in the end, little Lamond would still be missing, even if we're still all looking for him."

Renaldo took a breath and sat down. Not looking at James Earl, he nodded his head. "You'd tell me if someone was hurt?"

"Damn right I would," CC said, forcing herself to lean back in her chair. She thought about the files from Frank's case. "You been reading up on some of Frank's old cases?"

James Earl shook his head and stomped out of the room. "I hate double talk."

CC watched him. Worry tugged at her. She wished he would change his mind and go to the vineyard.

"Yes," Renaldo said, his eyes fixed on her desk and the large calendar laying on it. "Why?"

Resolve trickled down her spine. She respected Renaldo and she needed his help. "It's about Louis and Maria," she said. Renaldo leaned back in his chair, crossing his right leg over his left knee. "Frank talked to me the other day about an old case. There's a lot of similarities between his old case and this one." CC stopped and held up her hand as Renaldo harrumphed and opened his mouth ready to complain. "He knows there is nothing official either of you can do. I did some checking. He took a lot of heat for keeping the case going as long as he did."

Renaldo nodded, the muscles on his face relaxed. "I'm not Frank. I want justice."

"Don't think for a minute Frank doesn't, too. You caught Maria's case. We can work together to find her killer. We can get justice, but you may never close the case. Are there any kids other than Lamond Duncan missing?"

Renaldo sipped his coffee. She watched him as he stared at the window. The longer he thought, the more she knew she was doing the right thing.

Renaldo stood and smiled at her. "What am I looking for in the missing kid files?"

"Adolescents adopted, fostered, or living on the streets." CC cringed when she said it, but it might narrow down the search, even if there was no one to report some of these kids missing.

"I'll get on it. Call you when I get something." He turned to leave but stopped at the door. "And the garage last night never happened?"

"I didn't say that," CC said, returning his smile.

"You're still a Fed, CC: obnoxious as ever." Renaldo shouted over his shoulder as he made his way to the front door.

CC picked up the folder from Max and leaned back in her chair. She focused her eyes on the folder in front of her, but her eyes kept looking up at the people walking past her window. It was almost five o'clock and people were in a hurry. The aroma of the coffee drifted in and out of her lungs, teasing her. She fought her eyelids to stay open.

*****

Fluffy's tongue in her hand made her sit up. "Caught me," CC said, scratching Fluffy's head. "I could use a nap, but no rest for weary, or is it wicked?" She stood and stretched. "Give me a sec, and I'll take you out." People still hurried past her window with their own cares and worries. Eugene rode her bicycle past the window. CC leaned forward to see Eugene turn into the driveway. "Come on, Fluffy." CC closed the curtains.

Fluffy followed CC down the narrow hall to the kitchen and curled up next to the back door. Fluffy didn't go into James Earl's workroom. CC knocked on the door. Hearing nothing, she opened the door and walked up the steep stairs.

He decided before moving in that the small attic room would be his workroom. Previous occupants used it as storage. When the house was built, it was a servant's room. It had no connection to the upstairs bedrooms. Only one small window under pointed eaves allowed natural light in. A single lightbulb had hung in the center of the room when they moved in, looking as though it broke multiple fire and safety codes, but James Earl rewired the room stringing lights along the angled eaves. He filled the wall with the window with computer monitors blocking the sunlight. A long desk ran the width of the room, holding his computer towers, laptops, and gaming equipment. The wood floor already held grooves from James Earl's ergonomic office chair rolling back and forth as he gamed and worked.

"Hey," she said, seeing James Earl absorbed reading the information on his monitors. On one monitor, Renaldo got into his SUV and pulled away. On another, Eugene pulled and twisted the padlock on the oversized storage shed/garage where they stored the bicycles, their motorcycles, and Ted and Jane parked their tiny electric car. She kicked the door, twisted the lock again, and this time it opened. "We should get a new lock for the shed," CC said.

James Earl turned to face her. His eyes were narrow and his brow was furrowed with deep lines.

"What's the matter, babe?" she asked.

"I don't like Renaldo knowing what we're doing," he said and turned back to his monitors.

CC pulled the small chair he kept in the corner for her next to him and leaned into his side. "I don't either, but we're going to need his help. And he's a good guy. Why are you growling at him?"

James Earl said nothing. He typed into his keyboard without looking at any of the screens. "I'm not growling at anyone. I've got to get this information printed out for that Cairnes guy."

CC squeezed his arm. "Arguing with those who are trying to help us will -"

James Earl slammed his hand on the desk and turned to look at her. "I almost killed you last night. Don't you get it? I'm a danger to everyone around me."

CC gazed into his eyes. The golds and browns danced in the glittering of red and green reflections from the computers and their monitors. "You won't kill me," she said, touching his face when he tried to turn away. "Look at me. I trust you. It was too much excitement. Let's both go to the vineyard tonight. We'll stay the weekend and clear our heads."

James Earl sighed. His head dropped as his spine curved down. "Last night was a mistake. It won't happen again."

CC watched her man return his hands to his keyboard. She watched numbers and symbols flash across screens. "I know, babe," she said "This is so new for both of us. The stress of running into this...this... monster, or whatever it is, is getting to both of us. Maybe you *should* go alone."

She stood to leave, but James Ear reached out, taking her hand in his. He kissed her fingers before looking up into her eyes. "I love you, CC. Never forget that, please. I'll work on the control thing, promise. As soon as I'm done with this, I'm going to the vineyard. I promised

Jane I'd drop these reports off to the client before the weekend was done. Won't take another minute."

CC kissed his lips and went downstairs. She picked up her forgotten coffee and went out the back door where Eugene sat on the step talking to Fluffy as the dog sniffed the edge of the shed.

Eugene leaned forward. "Want me to take you to the park, Fluffy?" she asked.

CC answered. "Wait an hour. It will be dark then and easier on her eyes."

Eugene nodded. "Got it. Didn't think about sunscreen or shades for a dog until I met Fluffy." Fluffy put her paws on Eugene's shirt. "You can wait an hour. Can't you Fluffy?"

Fluffy barked as James Earl came out the door.

"I'm going," he said, stopping only to give CC a kiss on the cheek. CC hugged him, breathing in his spice and life, enjoying the touch of his skin against hers, and the mingling of his body heat with hers.

With a last kiss on the lips, he pushed away from her. He strapped his backpack to the seat of his motorcycle. Before starting the engine, he said, "You two be careful this weekend. Don't go running around after dark without backup."

CC didn't say goodbye. She waved and forced a smile on her lips. She never liked him going to the vineyard without her, but she disliked her not wanting to go with him more.

As the sound of his motorcycle faded, Eugene said, "I'm serious. I'll take Fluffy to the park; they won't need me at the cafe for a couple of hours. Max is there, so the kids are safe."

"Max is already there?" CC looked at the blue sky and sunshine. "That's odd. I'll go with you to the cafe," CC said, surprised she wanted to go. "We need to go over the details of your encounter with the creature. We're missing something."

CC closed the front door behind Eugene and Fluffy and went into James Earl's workroom. Sitting in his chair, she breathed in his scent. The wall of monitors showed every room in the house and multiple angles outside the house. She watched Eugene walking Fluffy into the dog park. On the smallest monitor, the image remained frozen on Renaldo entering CC's office.

*****

Eugene stretched her legs and twisted as she got out of the sidecar of CC's motorcycle.

"You know," Eugene said. "It's kind of comfy. Wouldn't want to take a long trip in it, but short ones are okay."

"Fluffy thinks so," said CC tying the helmets on bike's seat. "She's going to be pissed you got to ride and she had to stay home."

Eugene twisted to look at the back of her legs. "Revenge done," she said, wiping away the white dog hairs covering the back of her pants.

"Sorry," CC said. She didn't offer to help wipe off the fur, and she tried to not smile.

The coffee house was full as students, commuters, and daters sauntering in and out. Many ordered and left. Others ordered and sat. The line at the coffee counter stood at least twenty deep. CC scanned the dining section and was surprised to see Max stand and wave to her from a table on the far side of the cafe near the stage. It was the only table with no ceiling light above it. Being furthest from the windows, it was always dark.

"Damn," muttered Eugene. "Busy night. Better get to work."

Eugene disappeared into the kitchen door behind the coffee bar while CC weaved through the tables to reach Max. Mike sat at the table, too. She swung her backpack into a chair. Mike took it, setting it on the ground between the chairs. "Are you nuts?" he whispered with a harshness she'd never heard him use. "You know James Earl can't control himself. What were you thinking going out with him last night?"

CC bit the side of her mouth and took in a long breath before answering. "You don't know what James Earl can or cannot do. Nobody got killed, did they?"

"Tommy-"

"A scratch," CC said louder than she intended, to interrupt Mike.

She smiled at the bronze god of an athlete sitting at the table closest to them, who looked up at her. "It was only a little nip," she whispered back. "Ezra said James Earl's been doing well - besides, he knew me."

"I wouldn't swear to it," Max said. "But then I didn't have to use much force before he yielded."

Mike harrumphed. "I don't like it." Mike raised his hand as CC opened her mouth to argue with him. "I'm sorry. It's just he's unpredictable. I still remember the night of the funerals. The way he killed. It took a lot of talking to get him back to human form."

A shudder ran through CC. The night of the funerals. Was it a year ago when the vamps gathered to cremate the dead and the Hunters attacked? James Earl didn't even know he could change at will then. It had been all CC could do not to run and hide as the vamps and wers tore the attackers apart. The visions from that night still haunted her, but since then she'd seen the beauty in the wolf that James Earl was. His grace and power mesmerized her as much as it terrorized her.

CC reached out and put her hand on Mike's. "I remember, too," she said. "Maybe his control isn't what it will be, but he's getting there."

"On the other hand," said Max, staring up at the ceiling. "If he hadn't been wolf, our prey might have taken you, CC."

Eugene set a sandwich and a cup of coffee in front of CC. "That's what Tommy thinks," she said.

CC squinted in Max's direction. "What *was* he looking for?"

"You were there. Don't you know?" asked Max before looking up at Eugene. "Has Florence left yet, Eugene?"

"Just did," said Eugene, still standing next to CC.

"Good. She works too hard. Now, CC. What makes you so special?"

CC picked up the sandwich. "Nothing," she said. "I'd think it has more to do with both James Earl and Tommy being there." Her phone vibrated, jerking her to attention. She pulled it out and read.

"That could be it," nodded Max, frowning. "But he talked to you, even reached out his hand."

"If you ask me," began Eugene, but she stopped when CC's phone dinged.

"It's Renaldo," she said, looking up from her phone. "Report of a body, a kid. He's on his way to check it out. He'll let me know if it's like the others."

Mike whistled. "The killings are speeding up."

"Might not be our guy," said Eugene. "But I'm not holding my breath. I gotta work, guys. Don't leave me in the cold this time."

"Tommy thinks the creature came here the other night for Luna," said Max. CC followed his gaze to Luna standing at the table where Jackie sat talking to two men.

Max waved to her as he leaned close to CC. "We know what's special about her. See if you can gain her trust. If she's on the verge of change, she needs someone to help her."

CC straightened her back. "Me? Shouldn't that be you or Tommy?"

"Eugene's tried but lacks experience weeding out truths and lies. Tommy makes friends too easily to gain trust, and Luna thinks I'm weird. If she is on the verge of change and this creature is after her..." Max faded off as Luna reached the table.

CC gave a silent sigh, realizing Max was right. She put her sandwich down and smiled her widest smile. "So, you're the famous Luna."

*****

Flo passed Luna with a tray of croissants. "Here you go," she said.

Luna picked up a glass, filled it with ice and tea. "Here," she said to Flo. "Take a break. You look beat."

Flo took the glass and pressed it to her sweaty brow. "Thanks," she said. "I am beat. Chef was here when I got in at five. Looks like he'd been cooking for hours."

"Miss?" asked a man with gray in his beard and no hair on his head. "Two coffees, one black, one white, and I'll take a couple of those croissants if they're as fresh as they smell."

Luna pushed the corners of her mouth up. "Yes, sir. Have a seat. I'll bring it right out."

Luna turned, rolling her eyes. "It's been this way all afternoon. I'm tired and want to go home."

Flo drank the glass of tea in one swallow and stretched around Luna to refill it with tea. "I hear ya. Wish I knew what was up with Chef. Did I do something wrong?"

Flo arranged a tray with two plates and croissants to sit next to two cups of coffee. "Flo," she said, lifting the tray. "There's nothing you can do that's wrong. He's been back there at that table all afternoon with that lawyer, Mike Somethingorother, and now that red-headed woman. She came in with Eugene. They're plotting something, I know it. I just need to get close enough to hear them."

"Let me know what you find out," said Flo. "Chef told me to go home as soon as I got these out. See you tomorrow?"

Luna nodded, picking up the tray and moving away from the coffee counter as Marcus returned to the coffee bar.

The man with the gray beard and no hair sat as far away from Max as possible. Luna grimaced as she eyed the cafe for a practical way to maneuver close enough to hear what they were saying. "Here you go," she said, placing the cups and croissants on the table.

"You're not Jackie's little Luna, are you?" asked the man.

Luna froze and studied the man. The gray beard, the balk head, the laughing brown eyes were familiar.

The man laughed. "Now I feel like an old man. You won't remember me, I'm sure. Doug Hansel. Your mother and I used to work together. You remember Luna, don't you, Brad?"

Luna studied the plump man with roses for cheeks. There was something familiar about the thick, red hair flying about his face.

"No way!" exclaimed Brad. "I remember walking into your mom's office and seeing you sitting in her chair, your feet dangling off the edge. And look at you now, all grown up. I would not have known you." Brad reached out his hand to Luna. "Bradford Dank. Thanks to your mom, Dr. Dank now."

Danky Brad is what mama called him. Luna couldn't help the smile forming on her face. She felt her cheeks burn, and she looked down at Dr. Hansel. "I remember both of you," she said. "It's good to see you again."

"I hear you started taking classes this term," said Doug. "Good for you. If you're anything like your mother, you'll soon rule the school."

Luna nodded, unsure whether she should continue talking to these men she didn't really know or get back to work. Her mother saved her from deciding when she sat at the table.

"Doug, Brad," Jackie said. "I'm so glad to see you again. Luna, would you bring me my mug?"

"Yes, ma'am," said Luna as she backed away, her curiosity for why her mother was meeting old colleagues overtaking her desire to get away from them. She bumped into a table where an old man sat alone. Luna's eyes widened. "Sorry," she said. The man was huge. Gray hair flew around his face and hung low on his shoulders. Thick facial hair hid the features of his face except for his eyes. Dark, black penetrating eyes stared back at her with a fierceness that made her heart skip a beat.

"Mind yourself," the man's gruff voice growled at her with a brogue; at least she assumed it was a brogue.

"Sorry," she said again, and hurried to the coffee bar.

"Mama wants her mug," she said to Marcus.

Marcus looked up from the croissants he continued to arrange in the display case. "Really?" he asked. He looked at the table where Jackie sat. "Good."

"Good?" whispered Luna, afraid she was going to scream. "Why is this good?"

"It means mama is living again," Marcus said. His face remained calm and expressionless. "Maybe it's time we all did." He handed her Jackie's mug.

Luna set the mug on the tray, squinting as she looked at her brother. "That'll be the day," she muttered.

"Luna," Marcus said, but then he closed his mouth and shook his head. "Nothing," he added and went back to work.

Luna shrugged her shoulders and took her mother's mug to her.

"He's been very enthusiastic about it. He's even named it Midnight Bites," her mother said.

"Would mean a lot more work, but if he's run the numbers and says it'll be profitable, why not," said Danky Brad.

"Mama," Luna said, setting the mug in front of her mother.

"Thank you, dear," her mother said. Jackie returned her face to Doug. "I'd always imaged a real community gathering. The cafe is working now, and a safe, late-night spot to gather is exciting."

The men laughed. "I remember when you first told me you wanted to open a coffee shop. Thought you were off your rocker."

"I just love the aroma of coffee. It just makes you feel good. Perfect for study and talking philosophy, and now a little music, too," said Jackie then turned to look up at Luna, still standing next to her. "That's all, dear. Thank you."

Luna nodded, trying not to let the sound of her teeth grinding drown out the conversations in the cafe. She looked around, noticing Max looking at her.

"Luna," he said with that tiny smile he used that always looked like he was up to something. "I don't think you've met my friend, CC."

"So, you're the famous Luna," CC said, holding out her hand. "Nice to meet you."

"Yeah," nodded Luna. "Ah, hi."

"How's it going, Luna?" Mike asked with a wink.

Luna was about to reply when CC's grin stopped her. CC had a nice face, way too many freckles to be pretty, but shining despite the lack of light, and her clear, kind eyes bright and filled with honesty - that can't be faked, but at that moment, her grin twisted at the ends and her eyes gaze a sudden sparkle as she looked from Mike to Luna.

"Luna," CC said, still wearing that wicked grin. "Mike and I have just opened up a joint office a few blocks from here, and we're looking for a receptionist. We can't pay much and it's not full time, but Max said you might be interested as you won't be working here for much longer."

Luna bit her lip before yes slipped out of her mouth. There was something behind this offer. Max couldn't know she didn't want to wait tables. Mike barely knew her. Why had CC referred to her as famous? But a job in an office, answering the phone. Not serving coffee or cleaning tables. "Sure," burst from her lips. "But I'll have to talk to Mama first."

She watched the smile on CC's face relax. She looked happy again. "It will be a few weeks before we're ready for you. Here's my card. Stop by and check out the place when you can. We'll talk then about we need and you can do."

Mike cleared his throat. The color of his face changed. It had been pink and flustered when she arrived. Now, his lips pursed as he forced a smile. "Sounds good, assuming your mom says it's okay."

Luna looked behind her. Her mother was still chatting and laughing with her colleagues, and Marcus was busy at the coffee machine. She leaned over the table and lowered her voice. "My classes are all at night, so my days are free, except Tuesday and Thursday mornings when I have my KINE class."

"Good," CC said and picked up her sandwich. "Welcome to the family. As long as you're still working here, would you bring me one of your brother's chocolate lattes? They are the best."

Max looked up at Luna. "You'll like working with CC and Mike. They're good guys."

Luna hated it when he turned his clear, gray eyes on her, looking into her soul. "Okay, I'll be back with your drink," she said, and walked away before he read her mind.

A voice from one of the large tables where a group of writers sat with their laptops glowing and heads down called for her. Two of the group ordered refills. As she passed the table where her mother sat, she heard her mother's voice. "We'll call it Midnight Bites. Clever, don't you think? We'll start doing a couple of nights a week and see where it goes. Chef Max thought of the name. I think it's clever."

The men at the table nodded their agreement.

Luna shook her head. "Can this night get any weirder?"

*****

Eugene walked through the kitchen to the alcove separating the kitchen from the back door and put on her apron. Tommy sat on the bench where the others set their backpacks and purses.

"You're looking rather pink for a man who nearly bought the farm," she said.

Tommy yawned. "Hardly worth the trouble to talk about. Besides, I woke up at Cesar's wonderful smorgasbord on a Friday night."

Eugene grunted at his grin. "Pig," she said. "This place is crowded. You going to sit back here and lick your bruised pride all night or work?"

"Bruised pride. Posh!" scoffed Tommy, standing and tying his apron on. "I got closer to that monster than you did."

"True," she said with a straight face. "But I didn't get my ass kicked by a wer." She left him to sulk on his own, knowing he would have to have the last word.

"I was holding back for CC's sake. She is in love with the beast, although I can't see why. He's so moody and whiney. A woman like that can have any man she wants, and she chooses some adolescent pup not worth the price of his pride."

Eugene stopped before entering the cafe. "You like her."

"Of course I like her. I'm working with her, aren't I? Besides, that thing was after her last night. I need to figure out why." Tommy pushed past her through the doorway. "Marcus, I'm here now. Why don't you take your dinner break?"

Marcus shrugged his shoulders. "As soon as things lighten up."

"Tommy," said Eugene, picking up a tray filled with cups and glasses and reading the ticket on it. "You sly dog. I never would have thought you'd go soft for a woman," she said mouthing the last words. *"I mean a human woman."*

Before turning to take an order, Tommy said, "Will you get out of my way, please?"

Eugene lifted the tray over their heads. "I'm not standing in your way," she said. "I prefer boys."

Tommy rolled his eyes. "Keep an eye on Luna, will you? I heard her on the phone with that friend of hers. She plans on sneaking out to a party later tonight."

Eugene stepped away from the coffee bar. The familiar ring of the bell on the door caught her attention and she looked up as a large old man stepped outside. She stared wondering why he was familiar, but then she heard Max talking to Luna and returned to her job.

*****

Lamond thought about his mother. He missed the days when he could curl in her lap and fall asleep, feeling her chest rise and fall, hear her heart keeping time to her humming, and the smell of tea and sugar from her breath drift. On cold nights, she'd wrap a blanket around them both, leaving the smallest of holes for him to look through so he could watch the letters on her book form into words as he drifted to sleep. If he could have anything in the world right now, he'd be wrapped in his mother's arms.

The concrete he lay on sent waves of cold through him with each breath. His back ached from lying on his side. His arms ached from being tied together. He tried to wiggle his fingers, but they wouldn't move. If they did, he didn't feel them. Even his feet, which were always hot, felt like popsicles in his shoes.

He lost count of the days he'd been here. He didn't know if his mother was looking for him. "She's going to ground me for sure when she finds me," he whispered aloud. Tears once again traced their way down his face.

The strange man who had taken him off the street didn't talk much. He'd made all sorts of noises as though dragging something heavy when they first arrived wherever they were, but as darkness descended and the cold crept in, the man left.

"Please, God," Lamond prayed. "I promise to be good if you help Mama find me. I promise not to go to the store again without asking again." Lamond sniffled. "I only wanted a candy bar."

From somewhere around him, for sound echoed strangely around him, a door opened. Lamond tried to sit up, but he was too cold and he hurt too much.

"Where're the others?" The voice of the strange man scratched its way into Lemond's ears.

"What others?" Lemond asked. He no longer held back his fear. He couldn't. It hurt too much.

Something hard and cold hit his face. He heard a crack, and pain shot from his right cheek through his head and down his spine.

"What others?" shouted Lamond, with only half his mouth. "I'll tell you whatever -"

Again pain broke across his face and head, but this time lightning bolts flashed across his eyes. Lemond tried to curl into a ball, but his bound feet and hands would not move. They were tied to something.

"Where are the others?" The voice cracked again, neither with speed nor impatience.

Lamond tasted blood in his mouth. His body shook, and warmth filled his lower body as his bladder emptied. Tears no longer fled from his eyes. He couldn't see anything or even feel his eyes. He opened his mouth to say something, but he could think of nothing to say that wouldn't make the man angry. A sob spilled off his tongue.

The same icy fingers that took him off the street squeezed his right shoulder. "Where are the others?" the voice asked. This time it whispered into his ear.

4

Eugene insisted on coming. She and Fluffy sat in the sidecar grinning as the wind swept through their hair. CC laughed to see them with their heads raised and nostrils flaring, but as they turned onto Sixth Street, a river of partygoers halted their progress. The motorcycle idled as they waited for the lights to change.

"Aren't we close to where Maria's body was found?" asked Eugene.

CC looked at the street sign. "Just a few blocks that way," she said pointing with her nose east.

"Hmm," Eugene hummed, nodding her head.

The light changed, the river ceased crossing the road, and CC drove on. She drove past the icehouse and around a row of restaurants, turning into an ally between a new condo building and an old apartment complex.

"This is it," said CC. "We'll wait for the others before looking around. Stay close, Fluffy."

Fluffy jumped out of the sidecar as soon as Eugene removed her goggles.

CC watched Fluffy stretch her back and sniff the ground around the motorcycle. Outside the circle of the streetlight, Fluffy's hair glowed like a beacon in the darkness. CC smiled, glad for the dog's company. The crowd from a nearby club roared as the strings of a steel guitar mixed with drums, guitar, and fiddle.

"Pops loves country music," said Eugene, leaning against the streetlight. "Especially fiddle. I don't think he'd like this though, too electric."

CC nodded, listening to the music and shrugging her shoulders. "Not my thing, either."

Eugene leaned against the corner of the building. "You know," she said, "Max is okay."

CC looked at Eugene. Eugene's wide, clear eyes and calming smile gave her a face open to all emotions. It didn't surprise CC that Eugene wanted to talk about Max, but that she wanted to do it now, while they were waiting for him, surprised her. "I think so, too, but he's holding back. He knows something he's not telling us."

"Agreed," replied Eugene, nodding. "Haven't met many vamps who don't hold their cards close to their chests. I don't suppose he's any better than the rest. Still, could have knocked me down when he stood up for James Earl."

"I don't know that he stood up for him." CC bent to one knee, petting fluffy. "Better to say he gave him the benefit of the doubt."

Eugene folded her arms across her chest and grimaced. The slightest of growls preceded her words. "More than anyone's given me."

CC couldn't help but grin. "James Earl showed me the pictures. You're a fine-looking wolf."

Eugene nodded her head. "Yeah, well, the pictures aren't that great, but thanks."

"You want to talk about it? The boys are taking their time getting here," said CC, looking down the street.

"Tommy was giving Max a hard time. He wants in on the action as much as I do, and he's kind of pissed Cesar is coming. Max and Tommy don't like each other very much." Eugene pushed herself away from the streetlight to stand close to CC and Fluffy.

"Cesar says they're both old. They're very different characters," said CC. "You sure you're okay? You look wired."

"It's the moon," said Eugene, kicking a rock away from her foot. "I don't have to change, but it always feels unnatural not to when the moon is full. Besides, I need to be here with you right now." She kicked another rock. "You should know about what happened in Vegas. I mean, maybe there's something there that will help you find this thing." Eugene looked up gazing at the moon. At last, she spoke. "I worked late to finish a project. I showed you the pics of my neon work. That's why I was in Vegas. You should see the workshop there. It's the best. The glass shop here on campus is nice, but this place was the bean. Anyway, sometimes I filled in bartending at the place off the strip. The guys there were busy and told me to come in if I wanted. I was walking--I walk everywhere unless I bicycle--and was between two garages when I heard this whimper and thud. I smelled the blood and headed in that direction. That's when I saw it, bending over this tiny body. It was so small, CC." Eugene turned away from CC, her hand wiping her eyes. "The thing growled at me, and he changed, CC. It was so weird. He didn't change to wolf or a man. He was something in between. And then he ran away. I didn't think. I ran after him."

CC nodded but said nothing. Even Fluffy stared up at Eugene.

Eugene turned back to face CC and Fluffy. "You know, I don't even remember shifting. I just did it. The kid was so small. I've never been so angry."

CC squeezed Eugene's shoulder. "No one can blame you for reacting that way. I might have done the same if I were a wolf. When it came toward me the other night - If I were a wolf, I'd have changed and gone after it. My bullet pissed it off, hurt it, maybe, but it didn't stop it."

Eugene sniffed. "I'll kill it when I find it." She wiped her nose before pointing at a car pulling into a spot down the road. "Guys are here."

*****

Cesar pulled up in his new sports car, revving the engine as it glided to a halt next to her motorcycle.

Before CC could raise a hand to wave, Max stood beside her. She rolled her eyes. "Show off." She pointed to a line of police tape wrapped around a fence post where the chain link had fallen away. "There it is."

Eugene wrinkled her nose. "Still stinks like death."

"Renaldo says it wasn't pretty, but it was Darious. He still had his heart, but...." CC took a breath as though calming herself. "Renaldo says it must be the same killer, though. Aside from the beating, Darious' eyes were missing."

Max placed a hand on CC's shoulder. Ice raced down her spine. "I'm sorry, CC. I forgot you knew the boy. You don't have to be here."

"It's okay," CC said. "I want to be."

When CC looked back to the crime tape, Max was already standing in front of them. Before she took a step forward, Eugene cleared her throat.

"All that moving around so quick still freaks me out, too," Eugene said. "Would you mind staying here with Fluffy?"

CC scrunched her eyebrows. "Maybe I can't smell a blood trail-"

"No offence," Eugene interrupted. She shrugged her shoulders. "You're a walking bag of blood."

CC nodded. "Got it," she said. Behind her, Cesar stood outside his car and waved to her. She waved back. "Just going to walk a little way down. Come on, Fluffy."

Cesar nodded but remained where he was. "I'm leaving the hunting to the better hunters. At least being here means I don't have to wait for info. Stay close and call if you find something."

CC nodded and walked down the road. The music was just as loud as the cars and people on Sixth Street, but a block away on this side street, it was quiet. She didn't bother watching Max and Eugene but meandered toward the dead end of the street.

Fluffy stayed at her side, bumping into her leg. "Take it easy, Fluffy. Nobody's going to bother us." Looking to her left, she saw the corner of the large fence surrounding Clay's Funeral Home. She pulled her phone from her pocket and opened her map. She stood only two blocks away from the icehouse crime scene. The parking lot where they saw the creature last night was only one block up the next street.

"How did we miss this?" she muttered and put her phone in her pocket. The light above her sputtered and went out. She looked up once and turned to walk back toward the others.

She slowed as her ears caught the faintest, guttural growl. Fluffy answered the growl with one of her own, almost imperceptible under the other. She continued to walk but now backwards, focusing her ears on the sound as it moved, flowed around her. Close. Squinting into the darkness, she searched the deepest shadows for movement. Fluffy stopped, lowered her head, hackles raised, bared her teeth. CC stood under the branch of a live oak arching over the street between her and the alley. The hairs on her neck rose as a chill drifted over her. From the parking lot on her right, the click, click, click of claws on gravel stopped. Fluffy's eyes reflected the full moon above them.

Breathing in, she waited. The sensations in her body were familiar. The creature, this monster, this bringer of death, steeled her resolve. She waited. Two squirrels dashed from the tree's center, across a limb, jumped onto the roof of an old car with no tires parked beneath it, and ran up the downspout of the back of a building.

The smell of decay enveloped her and then the slightest hint of - cologne? The air in her lungs pushed against her ribs. She opened her mouth, surprising herself when her voice didn't shake. "Who are you?"

"You know me," wheezed the voice from last night.

CC squinted, but she saw nothing in the shadow of the tree other than more shadow. Fluffy's muscles tensed against her own leg. "Stay here," she said to Fluffy.

The tension in Fluffy's muscles transferred to CC's leg and wove with her own tension, giving CC confidence.

"We hunt," the voice fluttered as the leaves in the tree rustled in the night breeze. "We are one."

"I'm nothing like you," spat CC. "You kill children."

"We must stop them before they grow. Come, before they take you."

CC let the rage she'd bottled up since seeing that first body, young Louis, boil inside her. The rage straightened her back. "Max," she said, soft but commanding. "Eugene. Cesar. He's here."

She felt Max at her side before he formed in her peripheral vision. She neither heard nor saw him arrive, but his presence stilled her growing rage. And then Cesar stood beside her. A breath hissed and echoed around them. She heard footsteps, light and fast, along with quick breaths. Eugene neared, a growl rolling out of her on her next breath.

CC raised her hand breathing in deeply through her nose. The cologne, familiar. "Wait," she said.

The streetlights flashed and burned to brightness. As the street filled with their humming, Max said, "He's gone."

Eugene cracked her neck. Fluffy sat, looking up at CC. CC scratched Fluffy's ears and looked at Eugene. The wolf glowed in Eugene's eyes, but as her breath slowed, her eyes, like Fluffy's, only reflected the moon.

"You okay?" she asked Eugene

"I'm good," Eugene said, forcing a smile.

CC looked into Eugene's face. "The same one you chased in Vegas?"

"Yes," Eugene said, nodding, but then she bit her lip and shook her head. "But different. I'm going to burst."

"I'll follow, but I'm already losing his trail," Max said and disappeared in the shadows.

"Hang on," CC said to Eugene. "Get in the sidecar. I'll take you to the park. Cesar, I'll meet you at the club."

*****

If she didn't shift soon, she was going to sink her teeth into someone and rip. In one breath, Eugene heard CC shout, "Pick you up by five." The next moment she leaped down the hill and into the trees. She skidded and rolled, sending leaves and mold and dirt up and all around her. The smell of earth in her nose sent shivers along her spine, tickling her ears and her toes. Her tail wagged with delightful abandon. She stopped rolling, enjoying the taste of the river air on her tongue. *Did I answer CC? Pretty sure I did.*

A splash in the river and the smell of fish pulled her to the edge of the river. Two men, long gone, stood at this spot as the sun hit its zenith. Their feet trampled bramble and grass as they made a path before wading into the river. Eugene sniffed where their cooler sat on a rock in the shade as the sun warmed the surrounding rocks. She sniffed until she found the fish heads and entrails. The wolf ate with delight.

She ran. She smelled. She chased squirrels. She caught one and ate. The last of her fears and anger washed away as she rolled in the cool water splashing on the shore. The mud oozed between fur and skin, cooling, smoothing, calming. Only the music blaring from speakers on the water disturbed her. The music tried to drown out the voices and machines of the city. She stood, shaking her fur dry, when she heard a familiar laugh. Standing still, aiming her ears in the laugh's direction. So familiar. Lifting her nose, she smelled the breeze flowing off the water. Grass, trees, river, squirrel, trash, a snake, rats, people, beer, popcorn, Luna.

Head low and tail stretched behind her, Eugene criss-crossed through brush and rock up the hills, following the river and the music. A path followed the top of the hills. She kept low to avoid the lovers meandering and not taking in the view. Houses emerged following the edge of the river, each with boat docks jutting over the water. Some had pools built into the side of the hill. The hillside, while rocky, was easy for Eugene the wolf to traverse. Not so much for the few humans who tried to climb down it. Twice, she stopped and waited in the shadows as teens and no longer teens skidded and laughed at themselves for falling down the rocks. Turning her head up, she saw moss covered granite engraved with Mt. Bonnell. *Damn, Didn't think I'd walked that far.*

At last, she reached a rock jutting over a large house with lights burning brightly over the water and music pouring out of speakers hanging from the lights. The trees and brush hid her from those on the path above. She lay flat to peer over the edge of the rock. Orange and white streamers fluttered in the river breezes while college students danced, ate, drank, and smoked. Eugene stared until she saw Luna, bright red cup in her hand, leaning against the far side of the boathouse, out of view of the partygoers. A young man leaned near her, stroking her face and hair. His white tee shirt sparkled in the moonlight, accentuating massive arms rippling with muscles and a wide, firm back.

Eugene fought to keep from growling, but the hackles on her back rose. Her lips curled and danced near her snout. The moist air of the river dripped along her white teeth.

And then a familiar voice spoke from above her. "She's old enough to take care of herself."

Eugene turned, fangs bared and head low. Tommy sat on a rock five feet above her, his feet dangling in the air. He shook his head as he looked down at her. "She's not as dipsy as she pretends to be. I've been watching her since she snuck out of the house an hour ago. Her stealth skills confirm my suspicions: she's smart, and she's snuck out many times before tonight; however, I suspect this is her first college party." Tommy slid down, landing a foot in front of Eugene. "Isn't she supposed to be exploring boundaries at her age?"

Eugene relaxed her muscles, turning her back to Tommy and resuming her watch on Luna. The man with Luna continued to stroke her as his head bent low to her neck. Eugene heard Luna say, "Oh, Thad," and see her hands press into his back.

"Too classy for this group. I hope she realizes that before it's too late," said Tommy, sitting down and folding his legs beneath him. "We can only hope Luna doesn't lower herself to their idea of sophistication."

Eugene snapped at Tommy's hand as he reached it out to touch her side.

"No offense," he said, pulling his hand away. "The way your ink shows in your fur is amazing." Tommy's eyes were wide as they scanned every inch of her back and side.

Eugene stretched her neck and turned so he could admire all of her coat. Ever since her mother told her how her tattoos wove through her fur, she'd loved showing them off. Distinct facsimiles of the tattoos rose from her undercoat flowing with the natural nap of her outer coat creating fascinating images. Eugene was always proud to show off her mother's work. Her mother was famous in the tattoo industry, but there were very few she could show off the work in her wolf form.

"But I digress," Tommy said, pulling his eyes away from Eugene and back to the party below. "I gather from your current state and CC closeting herself with Cesar that something happened." He sighed, shoulders lowering. "Damn it! I need to know what's going on. I've paid for my mistakes. It's time for someone to trust me."

Eugene sat next to him, realizing how much they had in common. If Tommy were another wolf, she wouldn't think twice about turning human to talk to him, but Tommy was - well, Tommy was Tommy. He wasn't unlikable, but his directness and scheming left her in doubt of his true motivations. She studied his face. His crystal eyes reflected the stars above and the lights below. His pink, pouty lips formed a line so straight she thought his face might break. But most surprising were the worry lines sprouting from the corners of his eyes along the smooth, perfect skin of his face.

From below, she heard Luna say, "Yes."

Eugene changed and remained sitting next to Tommy under the overhanging rock. "I need to talk about it with someone," she said.

Tommy reclined on the rock without looking at her. "I'm a good listener."

"The police were gone by the time we got to the crime scene, just like CC said they would be. Me and Max were checking things out. CC had walked down the street, and...." Eugene pinched her eyebrows together and stared away visualizing the scene. "Well, it just showed up and started talking to CC."

"Again?" Tommy whistled. "Curious, not good, but curious in an interesting way."

"I know," exclaimed Eugene, forcing her voice to remain low. "Max and I were close, but we didn't hear it until she called out."

They sat in silence, listening to the party and a couple walking along the path above them dreaming of building a house bigger, grander than the ones below them - one day.

"Did CC tell you what it said?" Tommy asked.

Eugene hugged her knees tight to her. "He wanted her to hunt with him," she said. She bit her lip, shaking her head, and then asked. "Is it true she used to be a Hunter?"

"Yes," Tommy said. He sat up and looked her in the eye. "She's a good person, Eugene. I trust her with my life."

"When I met her, I could tell right away she was special. I had to ask, just to make sure." Eugene stretched her neck out to look for Luna. "She smells different."

"You want me to find you some clothes," asked Tommy. "I don't mind, as long as one of us keeps an eye on Luna."

"No, I want to run some more. I was so pissed that neither Max nor CC would let me charge that thing. I mean, we were right there. Why are you so worried about Luna?"

Tommy stood and looked down at Eugene. "Why?"

"Nobody tells me anything."

Tommy stood. He gazed first down at Luna and the party and then at the trail above them, but Eugene didn't think he was looking at anything. "This is important, Eugene. Was it the same creature you saw in Vegas?"

"Huh," Eugene mumbled, and closed her eyes, seeing every detail of her hunt in Vegas. "Yes and no," she said. "The same, but not the same. Familiar and not. I don't get it. I was sure it was the same, but now-"

Tommy interrupted, moving to sit in front of her. "The smell. The same or different?"

Eugene pushed all the air out of her lungs, breathed in a long, slow breath. Her nostrils flared. "It's too wet here," said Eugene. "But I get what you're saying. The same, but different. It's changing - same creature but different."

"He must be dead," Tommy whispered, and sank his head into his hands.

Eugene stared at Tommy. "Who's dead?"

Tommy lifted his face. His pale white face whiter, his eyes rounding. If Eugene didn't know better, she'd have said he was tearing up. He asked, "Do you know if Ezra took his family to the vineyard today?"

Eugene's breath quickened. An agitation, not directed at Tommy but at herself for missing something, said, "Yes. What does that -"

Tommy stood. "This monster or whatever will come for Luna soon. Will you watch her the rest of the night?"

"She's its target," Eugene said, filling with a sorrow she didn't understand. She risked another look over the rock to the party. "I don't know; I didn't see it before."

"We can't let that thing force her into a decision or kill her before she has a chance to choose."

Eugene stood, head tilting as though listening. "She's leaving with her new friends. Sports car."

Tommy's mouth twisted with indecision.

"I'll follow and make sure she gets home," said Eugene. Tommy raised a hand to her, but she stopped him from saying anything. "I know how to stay out of sight, despite my escapade in Vegas. Text CC so she doesn't come out to pick me up in the morning. I hope whoever you think is dead, isn't."

"Thanks," he said, and looked at the trail above.

Eugene stood, but before she leaped off the rock, she heard Tommy say, "By the way, nice ass."

She barked a laugh and ran to the path overlooking the river. She'd risk being seen to catch up with the car. *Who's dead?*

*****

Eugene looked as though her fur would burst through her skin, so CC dropped her off at Barton Springs. "Stay in the trees, and don't let anyone see you," she said. "I'll pick you up here at five."

"You're a peach, CC," said Eugene, pulling her underwear off. CC turned to place Eugene's clothes in her saddlebag. When she looked up, a long tan wolf ran down the hill into the trees along the river. For the briefest of moments, the full light of the moon bounced off her fur. CC's jaw dropped in awe as the swirls of color and shapes rolled over the fur. She remembered seeing the Star Trek insignia on the side of James Earl's wolf back when he had it shaved into his head.

"Damn," she said. "You'd think her mom knew the tattoos would show on her fur."

Fluffy barked once before curling into her seat.

CC drove back toward downtown and The Phantom's Menace. Too much was happening, too fast. She needed answers, but she needed to talk them through with someone. Max was holding something back, she was sure of it, and Eugene was Eugene, but Cesar was always there to listen.

Closing time for the bars meant the streets were full of people wandering up and down the roads looking for something to do. As she sat at a light watching people staring at her and Fluffy, she considered what she knew. The monster wasn't the usual madman bent only on killing. He was too careful, too methodical, too knowing. Had she surprised him as he planned to take someone else tonight or last night, or had he been watching for her or for them?

She reached over to pet Fluffy without thinking about it. "What do you think, Fluffy," she whispered. Fluffy licked CC's fingers. "There's more to this thing than we know."

Sighing, she turned the corner away from The Phantom's Menace to the garage behind the club. Cesar had given her a key code to park and enter the club at the private entrance. The first three floors of the garage were public parking. Once she entered the code to cross the ramp onto the fourth level, darkness covered her. Minimal light sources guided her to the far side of the garage, near the private walkway. She stared into the shadows made by her headlight between cars and around corners. Fluffy jumped out of the sidecar as soon as CC removed her goggles and unbuckled her. CC set her helmet on the seat. "Must be nice to have lots of money," she said, then stopped as a flash of light caught her eye. Far to the west, barely seen between buildings, lightning flashed.

She smiled, hoping it would bring rain, until she remembered Eugene in the park.

Shaking her head, she muttered, "Too far away." She made her way across the gated bridge to a single metal door. The back light of the keypad provided just enough light for CC to see Fluffy sitting at the door, her tongue hanging out of her mouth and her eyes on CC.

CC tapped in her code, wondering if someone had purposely used her birthdate as the pass code. She never could remember numbers, but until tonight, didn't think to ask. Opening the door, she waved to the camera over the door. Most of the employees knew her and if not her, they knew Fluffy.

The thumping of drums and bass hit her in the face like the cold, air-conditioned air. She closed the door and stood until her eyes adjusted to the dim light of the narrow hall. She faced a window running the length of the hallway. To her left, the elevator door gleamed in the ambient light. Next to it, another steel door kept out unwanted guests who made it up the stairs from the dancefloor. Below her, the lights of the club flashed and strobed over a crowded dance floor filled with bodies jumping, spinning, and sweating. Fluffy stood leaning her paws on the window as though examining the room below with CC.

Laughing, CC said, "You wouldn't like it down there, Fluffy. Too many people." They turned to their right to walk the five feet to Cesar's office. She didn't knock, knowing if he hadn't seen her on the camera, someone had and told him she was there.

The door opened to the left of Cesar's desk. CC liked Cesar's office. The massive wooden desk looked old fashioned from the front, but from this angle, she could see multiple touch screens, buttons, and sliding doors holding everything from notepads to automatic weapons to wooden stakes. She walked past the massive one-way window, looking over the club to the back of the office where a wet bar/kitchenette waited. A white ceramic bowl with Fluffy's name painted in red lettering sat on the bar. CC filled it with water as Fluffy jumped onto a bar stool and splashed and licked until satiated. CC wiped the bar top with a towel conveniently placed next to the bowl.

She pulled a bottle of water out of the small refrigerator and made her way to the sofa, allowing the stuffed cushions to wrap around her. Fluffy jumped onto the couch to curl up next to her.

The sound of the music filled the room, then diminished back to a soft thudding as the door to the office opened and closed. CC opened her eyes as Cesar walked to his desk.

"Hey," she said. "Hope you don't mind. I've made myself at home."

"You're always welcome," Cesar said, wearing his usual smile, genuine, she knew, when she visited. "You want to know something."

CC sat up. "Do you trust Max?"

Cesar looked at her. "Yes," he said. "That doesn't mean I don't keep him in my sights."

CC finished her bottle of water. Cesar got up and moved to the bar. "Wine?" he asked, opening a bottle before she could answer. "The old guys don't survive without secrets."

"What about you?" she asked as Cesar handed her a glass of wine.

"Everyone has secrets, CC. Talk to me." He sat on the chair across from her.

She looked at him, realizing he always stayed a few feet away from her. "This thing we're hunting isn't some out-of-control lunatic. He knows what he's doing."

Cesar sipped from his glass, not looking at her. "We already know that," he said, turning back to her. He peered into her eyes. "No way he would have survived this long if he was an ordinary killer. What gives?"

CC closed her eyes, selecting the right words. "Something's wrong. He knows me, and I know him, but I don't know how."

Cesar said nothing. He leaned back in the overstuffed chair, watching CC.

She looked at him and then looked away to pet Fluffy. "He said I was like him."

Cesar shook his head. "You're nothing like him."

"But," she said, and stopped to think about her words before continuing. "What if I am? The Hunters I was with killed-"

Cesar leaned forward and took one of her hands in his. "You're a good person. You are not like this--whatever he is--nor are you like your old friends. That's why they're not your friends anymore."

CC squeezed his hand before sitting up. "Then what is Max holding back? He must suspect a connection."

"Ask him," Cesar said. He continued to hold her hand.

"If he's using me to get at this thing, and he thinks I'm working with-"

Before she could catch her breath, Cesar was sitting next to her, his arm around her. "You're one of the best humans I know, and I've known a lot of them. No one thinks you're anything like this monster. You never were. You never will be."

CC raised her eyebrow. She wanted to laugh. "You can't promise that."

"I can," Cesar said. The muscles in his eyes tightened and jaw squared as he looked at her. "Nobody kills in my city unless I say so."

"Unless Mary says--"

"You have her protection," interrupted Cesar. As quickly as he had sat next to her, he stood at the window, looking over the crowd. "She wouldn't protect a killer."

The anxiety building in CC fizzled away. Her shoulders relaxed as Fluffy sat up and leaned into her, pushing her snout onto CC's neck. She wondered how far Cesar would go to keep his word to her.

*****

After almost breaking her ankle for the second time, Luna kicked off her blinged-out three-inch spikes with their sparkling red heart-shaped padlocks and danced in her bare feet. Her feet felt better, but now Dwain, her current dance partner, stood an extra three inches taller than her. He laughed when he looked down at her.

He leaned forward to talk into her ear. "You still look hot, Luna, especially in that dress."

She looked good. The white dress Scarlett loaned her hugged her as though made for her. It was, Luna admitted, perhaps a bit tight across the bust, but that just made not wearing a bra feel that much better.

Not that she had large breasts. Scarlett said she should flaunt what she had. Mama might have said she was showing too much cleavage, but mama was at home, and Luna loved the plump flesh oozing out of the dress. She also enjoyed the looks Dwain and the others made when they danced. Scarlett even showed her how to glue a glittering orange star to one of her breasts, almost hidden but peeking out from between her cleavage. Dwain, in particular, must have seen it. His eyes never left her chest.

Whenever one song ended, Scarlett brought Luna another beer and introduced her to someone else. By the third beer, Luna decided she liked the drink, especially the hotter she got. She panicked once when someone tripped and spilled a beer down the front of the white dress, but Scarlett laughed it off. "That's what washing machines are for," she told Luna.

"But the dress is kind of see-through wet, isn't it?" asked Luna, still trying to wipe off the excess beer.

"Nonsense," said Scarlett. "It enhances your mystique."

She saw Thad, the very handsome and very tall man she'd danced with for two minutes at the club last week, when she came out of the restroom in the boathouse. Still damp with the beer and sweat, the dress clung to her. She felt a heat she'd never felt before rise from inside her chest. He stood close to the house, talking to Scarlett. They both waved and smiled when Luna looked at them. When the song ended, he brought her a beer. The music was slow, and he held her tight against him. The heat of his body pressing against her burned, but she would not push away. The burn tingled sending waves of heat through her spine, lightening her head and tingling her toes. She leaned her ear against his chest. The constant pounding of his heart in her ear echoed the growing thumping between her legs.

She lost herself in the feelings swelling inside her as she felt him pressing against her. His body swelled. As his hands rubbed her back and slipped down to her buttocks, she fought the urge to react to the moistness forming between her legs. She kept her eyes closed, enjoying the feeling.

She opened her eyes as the music faded. Thad had moved them to the far side of the boathouse, just out of the lights and crowd of the party. The walkway on this side of the boathouse was narrow, but Thad pressed her into the cool wood of the boathouse. With him in front of her, she had no fear of falling into the water. Thad's right hand stroked the side of her face. His left hand rubbed her arm until it reached her thigh. Her breathing grew deep and fast as his body pressed into hers. Her head swam with want, but her stomach turned, and without warning, she belched. Her face burned.

Thad laughed. "Girl, you're something else."

Luna worried she'd turned him off her, but his left hand crept under her dress, squeezing her buttocks. She breathed in, "Oh, Thad."

Thad's head bent down to her neck. He kissed it again and again. At last he stopped and breathed into her ear, "You are so hot. I gotta have you. Say, yes. Please, Luna."

Thad's left hand continued to squeeze. His right hand reached down, pushing the hem of her dress to her waist. His tongue licked the sweat from her neck. His teeth bit the top of her breasts.

"Thad," she breathed out. "Yes." She wanted to say more, but at that moment his hand reached between her legs. His fingers probed, and her heart skipped.

Thad's mouth reached her cleavage and his tongue delved deep. Next, his teeth slid along her breasts. And still his fingers probed. She saw lights dancing in her eyes with colors she'd never seen before, and for a moment, she thought she saw two eyes glowing from the hillside above her.

And then it was over. Thad pulled down her dress and lifted his face to hers. He grinned ear to ear and opened his mouth. The orange crystal star lay on his tongue. He lifted it from his tongue with his hand, then licked his fingers. "Lovely Luna," he said. "You're a prize any day of the week." And he walked away.

Luna remained leaning against the boathouse, catching her breath. Looking down, she realized the once white dress was a mess. The yellow of the beer looked like piss. It crinkled with sweat. She tugged at the hem. Until now, she hadn't realized how short it was. Then she lifted the top, pulling it over her nipples. It only just covered them. Her hands went to her head to straighten her hair. As she removed her hand from her head, she saw it shaking. She clutched them together as Scarlett peered around the corner of the boathouse.

Scarlett smiled. "There's my girl!" Scarlett walked around the corner with two red cups in her hands. "Here you go, Luna. Cool off before you head back to the party."

The beer tasted different. Something sweet mixed with the bitterness of the beer, but it was cold. Luna drank it all in one gulp. "Thanks," she said.

Scarlett pulled lipstick from her pocket. "Better fix your lips. You're a bit smudged." Scarlett winked and Luna did as she was told before following Scarlett back to the party.

No more music blared. Half the people were gone, and the rest were leaving. "Neighbors complained and called the cops," Scarlett said. "Let's find someplace else to go."

Scarlett picked up another red cup from a table, but before handing it to Luna, she poured something from a flask into it. "This makes it better."

Luna drank again in one gulp. Her thirst demanded it. By the time Scarlett gathered the other girls, Luna drank two more red cups with beer and something else in it. Inside the car, the girls complained Luna stank and made her lay down in the back of the hatchback. But when Luna felt her stomach turn and belched, Scarlett stopped the car, helped Luna to the side of the road, and sat her down before driving away with the other girls.

Luna watched them drive away, unsure what to do. The ground shifted, reminding her of the time she'd been on a boat in the Gulf to look for dolphins. With barely enough warning to bend over, her stomach vomited all the liquor and anxiety she'd consumed, and she fell asleep where she lay. The last thing she remembered before falling asleep was a large dog licking her face.

*****

"Why are you still wearing that?" CC asked as Eugene filled her coffee cup.

"I kind of like it," Eugene said. Eugene looked down and the long, full skirt and t-shirt with its blinged red heart. Neither was anything she'd ever purchase.

CC leaned forward to whisper. "You stole them."

"Did you expect me to pull Luna off the street and find a payphone to call you while naked?" said Eugene, nodding her head. "Please, CC, give me some credit. I've had to do this before." She set the plate of hot croissants in front of CC. "Not pull drunk teenagers off the street. I mean steal clothes. Not that I've had to do it often. I'm very careful, but sometimes things happen. It's not like what got me kicked out of Vegas happens often."

CC shook her head before lifting her cup to her lips. "I get it," she mumbled before Eugene opened her mouth to say more. "It's just, so..." she paused and wrinkled her nose. "Not you."

Eugene laughed loud enough the people standing in line turned to look at her. "You're telling me. Still," she added. "It's comfortable." She bent over to whisper. "I always take the clothes I have to steal back clean and ready to wear. Gotta get back to work. Marcus just gave me *the glare*." She winked to CC and turned to take the order of the couple behind her.

The Saturday afternoon crowd ebbed, allowing Eugene to return to CC's table with more coffee at regular intervals to keep her awake. As the first of the lunch crowd arrived, Eugene heard Luna shifting and muttering to herself in Jackie's office.

"Marcus," said Eugene, walking behind the coffee bar and setting a tray with coffee and muffins in front of him. "Why don't you take this to Luna. She's awake."

Marcus lifted his head out of the steam of the espresso machine. "How do you know she's awake?"

"Heard her," said Eugene, not looking at Marcus. "I would take it in, but you could use a break." She handed the tray to Marcus. "I remember the first time I got shit-faced. So embarrassing. I couldn't look anybody in the eye for like - an entire day."

Marcus opened his mouth but closed it without commenting. "Shout if you need me." He added two bottles of water to the tray.

Eugene watched Marcus enter the office and turned to make sure CC saw it, too. CC nodded to Eugene, and Eugene noticed the stress around CC's eyes made prominent by dark circles. With the overhead lights beaming in her face, the puffed cheeks of weariness, but at the same time, the firm jaw of determination she hadn't noticed before. Her shoulders squared, and in her eyes, behind the weariness, stress, and worry, a light showed. With each breath, determination, like that light, grew.

"Excuse me," said an older man at the counter. "I'd like an Americano, light."

Eugene jumped and turned.

Manny, the new weekend barista said, "Got it. Take a break, Eugene. You're a thousand miles away. And what are you wearing?"

Eugene snickered and picked up a bottle of water as she headed for the kitchen.

Eugene sat at the chef's table, leaning against the wall between the kitchen and cafe. Flo looked from behind a cloud of flour, nodding to Eugene, but did not stop kneading.

Marcus' voice, louder than it had been, but low enough that only she could hear, asked, "What did he do to you?"

"Nothing I didn't want," Luna replied. Eugene released a long sigh. Luna's voice might be coarse and scratched from alcohol, vomit, and fatigue, but it was also confident with the just right amount of recalcitrance.

Eugene stood, stretched, and drank her water in one long gulp. She'd let CC know Luna was awake and no worse for wear when her phone buzzed. As she reached for her back pocket, she laughed, realizing she wasn't wearing jeans. She pulled her phone out from its clip under her shirt. Seeing the number, her eyes widened.

*****

Luna's head ached. Her body ached. She set her feet on the floor and felt cuts and scratches like needles pushing into her bones. "Ow," she said.

"Don't stand up," Marcus said.

Luna searched the room, finding Marcus sitting in one of mama's visitor's chairs. She was on the couch, covered with an old quilt, and wearing a man's ugly plaid shirt. She winced as Marcus lifted her feet, setting them back on the couch before turning on the desk lap.

"You walked through some glass," Marcus said. Eugene and CC cleaned the cuts. They said it was better to let them heal in the air until you were ready to get up. I'm going to wrap them up now so you can walk. You'll have to wear my socks, but they're thick and will help cushion your feet."

Luna watched her brother place cotton pads on one foot and wrap it with gauze before sliding on a thick sock and doing the same with her other foot.

"Oh, here," said Marcus, stopping long enough to hand her a bottle of water. "Drink."

Luna took the bottle. Her mouth tasted like cotton and throw-up, but she couldn't bring herself to drink anything.

"Drink," he said, setting down her other foot. "I know you don't want to, but it will make you feel better. You need to get yourself together before mama gets here."

"Mama?" asked Luna. The air left her lungs, and she leaned forward. "Mama's going to kill me."

"No, she's not," said Marcus.

There was something different about Marcus's voice. There was no scolding or mumbling about incompetence. The calm, soft voice speaking to her now reminded her of his old voice, the one he had before everything changed.

"I'm not going to tell Mama you snuck out of the house, went to a party, and got so drunk your so-called *friends* left you on the side of the road."

Luna drank the water. It landed in her stomach like a rock, but it stayed where it was. She drank more, but the cotton in her mouth wouldn't clear. "How did I get here?" she asked after drinking half the bottle.

Marcus pulled the paper off a muffin and handed it to her. "Blueberry. You're favorite. Flo made them just for you when she saw us bringing you in. She put in extra blueberries."

Luna took the muffin in her hand and stared. "Who's 'us'?"

"Eugene, her friend, CC, and me. Eugene found you. She's weird, isn't she? All those tattoos. And she never stops talking." Marcus stopped and poured coffee into a cup. "This will give you a little energy. I know you've started drinking coffee - to impress your new friends."

Luna nodded and then put her hand to her head, regretting nodding. "Thank you." She bit into the muffin, allowing the flavor to melt on her tongue. Flo made wonderful blueberry muffins. She swallowed, and it felt good going down. "How did Eugene find me? I remember getting into the car to come home and then a dog licking my face. I remember Thad." She couldn't help the smile forming on her face.

Marcus' voice took on an edge Luna had never heard before. "What did he do to you?"

"Nothing I didn't want," she said. She forced herself to sound as honest as she felt, even though a momentary doubt passed over her. She took a sip of coffee and another bite of muffin. "You were going to tell me how Eugene found me and I ended up here and not at home."

Marcus stared at her. The familiar hard lines of his anger softened. The face of the big brother she remembered helping her roller skate and walking to school smiled at her. "Eugene said it was chance. She went to Mt. Bonnell. Not sure I believe her about that. Who goes sight-seeing at night? Anyway, she didn't have a car, so she called her friend CC. I've seen her in the cafe a lot. She, Eugene, and Max seem to be friends. Odd looking group. Anyway, they took you to their place, cleaned you up, and called me. I came in early to help set up for the day."

"And mama?" asked Luna.

"She's with Aunt Jasmine and Uncle Frank," said Marcus, topping off Luna's coffee cup.

"Really?" asked Luna, closing her eyes at the volume of her voice sending knives of pain and colors across her eyes. "I didn't think she liked Uncle Frank."

"No." Marcus shook his head. "You and I don't like Uncle Frank." Marcus stood, went to the front of the desk, and pulled a bottle of aspirin from the top drawer. "Here." He set the bottle on the tray. "Take these when you finish your muffin. Take your time. I brought some clothes. Afraid you'll need my old sneakers with your feet wrapped up like that. I told mama you came in with me to get some extra hours in. She won't believe you want to learn the business, but she'll believe you wanted more hours for the money."

Luna watched Marcus open the door. "Marcus," she said. "Thank you."

"No. I don't deserve your thanks. I'm sorry I've pushed you to grow up so fast. If I was a good big brother, I wouldn't have let fear overtake how much I love you. Enjoy being a kid as long as you can. I'll take care of mama and business."

Before Marcus closed the door, Luna shouted, "I love you, too. Sorry I'm such a pain."

When the door closed, she said to herself, "Well, that went better than it could have. Maybe I'm growing up." She pulled the quilt off her shoulders and saw the slacks and blouse Marcus brought for her. "He has no fashion sense. I hope none of my friends come in today."

*****

CC rubbed her neck and stretched her back. The sound of Eugene's voice rose above the murmur of the lunch crowd. "It's about damn time you called me back!"

The grin on Eugene's face widened as she weaved through the tables with her phone pressed to her ear.

CC stared at her computer screen. The city map and her crime scene notes stared back at her, flat and untelling until Eugene pulled the wooden chair opposite her dragging the legs and making them scrape against the concrete floor. "Don't give me that old, 'I've been in the wilderness,' bullshit. You know when I need you."

CC jumped in alarm until she saw Eugene's eyes widen and her teeth glimmer under a smile so genuinely happy, CC couldn't help but smile back.

"It wasn't my fault!" Eugene pouted, folding her arms across her chest and frowning.

CC laughed, having heard Eugene say it so many times.

"When will you get here?" Eugene asked. "Cool. How's mums and pops? Good. Love."

Eugene ended her call. Still grinning, she said. "Luna's awake. Having a nice talk with Marcus."

CC raised her eyebrows and Luna nodded. "No, really. They're not yelling at all. He seems genuinely concerned about her - oh, and that their their mom not find out Luna was out drinking."

"Not surprising," said CC. "He cares for her. Who's coming?"

"My brother," said Eugene, her eyes wide and glistening. "The shithead's been doing the whole *Wilderness thing*. I can't believe him sometimes."

Eugene stopped talking as CC's eyelids lowered halfway before widening.

CC shook her head and sat up. "Sorry," she said. "Tired."

"Go home," Eugene said. "You got, what, an hours' sleep before I called you? I'm here to keep an eye on the place. Tommy and Max will be here when they wake up. It's overcast, so I won't be surprised if they show up early."

CC stared at the screen in front of her. The lines and street names blurred. She closed her eyes and sighed. "You're right. I know there's something here-" Her own phone buzzed and bounced on the table next to her hand.

She picked up the phone, recognizing Jane's phone number. Before could say hello, Jane asked, "Where the hell is James Earl? He promised he have those reports for me this weekend."

CC rubbed her forehead but lifted her head before replying. "He told me he was wrapping up some research before he left on Friday."

"Before he left?" Jane's voice cracked from fierceness to a long moan. "CC, what am I going to do? I'm supposed to meet with the client later today. If I don't have that information..." she left the rest unsaid.

"Calm down, Jane. If he said he'd have something for you this weekend, then he will. Have you checked all your emails? Spam folders? I'll see if I can reach him, but I expect he's on his way home now. If not, I'll get on his computer and find his report for you."

Jane sighed. "You're too sweet. Thanks. I'm sure you're right. It's just that this guy is so - irritating. He's driving me and Tom nuts. For an old bible thumper, this guy is anything but a humble practitioner of good vibes. Sorry to call fussing, but if you talk to your man, please tell him to call me."

"I will," said CC, and put her phone into her back pocket. "That does it for me, Eugene. I'm going home to sleep."

"Good idea." Eugene stood and looked over her shoulder. "Luna's looking none the worse for wear. I better help her out."

*****

Luna smiled at each customer saying "please" and "thank you" and "come again." She cleaned tables without complaint. She even waited until the other servers finished their breaks before taking one herself. Eugene worried.

As she wiped a cup before filling it, she leaned close to Marcus. "Are you sure she's alright?"

Marcus' eye squinted as he searched the cafe for Luna. "Why? Does she look sick?"

Eugene put the cup down. "She's being so - quiet."

"Enjoy while you can," said Marcus, sighing. "Don't you have work to do?"

Eugene put her hand on her hip and mocked him. "Don't you have work to do? Dude, I carried her home last night. She was so pissed, completely oblivious to everything. Why are you the one acting like you've got a hangover?"

Marcus looked toward his mother sitting at a table, talking with graduate students. "Shh," he said in a hurried whisper. "It'll kill mama if she finds out Luna got drunk."

Eugene studied Marcus' face. As he always wore a serious face, the hints of panic in his widening eyes and the tick forming at the corner of his mouth glared. "Chill, Marcus," she said. "She won't hear it from me. But the two of you better have your stories straight. Moms always know when their kids do something stupid. It's their job." Eugene picked up the tub of dirty dishes. "Now me, I learned the hard way to tell to my mums everything. Made living a lot easier without worrying about what she *might* find out. Then again, I didn't go to school that much. We lived kind of in the middle of nowhere. That doesn't mean I didn't knock around stupid plenty of times."

"Eugene," said Marcus. He paused, staring at nothing. "Alcohol killed our dad."

Eugene nodded her head. "That's why Luna's working so hard."

Marcus shook his head, but Eugene continued before he could say more. "Dude. I get it. Your mom won't hear about last night from me, but you and Luna should have a long talk."

Marcus kept his head down, cleaning the countertop. "Luna doesn't care," he said.

"Bullshit," Eugene spat out. "Look at her. It's killing her keeping up that façade. She cares more than you think."

Eugene carried the tub of dirty dishes to the kitchen. She stopped to look behind her when she heard the door open and the familiar pattern of Ezra rushed through her senses. Putting the tub down, she pushed back the kitchen door to the cafe to greet him, only to find him staring at her wide-eyed and stern as sweat poured down his forehead.

Instead of his usual business attire, he wore khaki pants and a collared pullover buttoned to the neck. He stood out from most of the crowd with his graying stubble and fatherhood Old Spice scent. He walked to the coffee counter, ignoring Marcus to speak with Eugene. "Would you mind getting me some coffee, Eugene?"

Eugene's eyes narrowed. She watched him walk to a table in the far corner of the cafe. Stress oozed through his usual steady, confident stride and out the flap of neck choked by his shirt collar. Fear and anxiety filled her nose.

"Who's he?" Marcus asked. "I've seen you talking to him before."

Eugene poured the coffee. "My uncle," she said, not looking at Marcus.

"Uncle?" Marcus said and smirked.

Eugene straightened to her full height to look down her nose at Marcus. "You gotta get out of the house more often, dude."

She watched Ezra not watch her walk to his table. His usual calm brown eyes flashed red from the afternoon sun flying through the large front windows as he shifted in his chair. The hairs on the back of her neck stood straight. Her heart pounded in her chest. She took a deep breath to steady herself, and then he looked up at her, and the red disappeared. Once again, cool, dark, but exhausted eyes looked at her.

"Can you sit for a minute?" he asked.

Eugene pulled a chair to sit next to him. "What's wrong?" she asked.

Ezra's hand shook as he lifted the cup to his lips. Eugene reached for his other hand and held it in hers.

Ezra's stoic face melted. Dark bags sagged beneath his eyes. Worry lines tempered with age creased long and hard from each eye, disappearing into his scant hairline. Sweat beaded on his forehead "Do you know where CC is?"

"Home," replied Eugene. "She was here 'til just after noon, but she was dead on her feet, so went home to sleep. It was a hell of night here. Have you heard-"

Ezra's rattled breath interrupted her. "James Earl didn't show at the vineyard. His phone goes straight to voicemail."

"I heard him say he was going," said Eugene. "Late Friday, but he said he was dropping off some papers and heading up there. He seems like the type to change his mind, although I think he'd at least tell CC if he had, unless you think-".

"He called Friday to tell me he was on his way." Ezra sipped his cup. "I couldn't come back here to check on him. Sally's worried too much about the girls. Lucy's eleven. Signs are there, Eugene. She's wolf."

Eugene nodded. "I understand."

"That's just it," said Ezra, shaking his head. "James Earl is like one of my own. He had a rough time changing, and he's still having trouble. Lately, he's been so--I don't know. It's just not like him. And he's so angry."

"Shit," Eugene said under her breath. "CC got a call from some woman. I think it was the accountant next door to them. He's doing some work for her. She called CC, looking for James Earl. He didn't deliver reports or something."

Ezra sipped his coffee. "James Earl always takes care of business."

*****

Eugene pushed the door of Cesar's car open. Her mouth watered as the soup sloshed in their cups as she balanced them in the holder with the coffee cups.

"Let me," said Cesar, standing in front of her.

"Damn," Eugene said. "I hate it when you guys move so fast."

"So I've been told. The sun," he pointed up as he took the carrier from her. "I'd like to get inside."

"Fair enough," answered Eugene. She looked to the upstairs of the house and tilted her head. "She's up."

"I think she heard the car." Cesar stood at the door with his hand on the knob.

Eugene waited. Her heart ached. She hadn't expected it to. She didn't like James Earl all that much, but she liked CC. After a deep sigh, she said, "I'll tell her."

"No," answered Cesar, without waiting for more. "Let me. Mrs. Smith told me your tracking skills included phone searches."

Eugene nodded. "Yeah," she nodded. "Good idea. I'll get right on it." She took a sandwich and cup of coffee and pushed her way into the house and up the stairs to her room and tablet.

"I hope some of that's for me," CC yelled from the living room. "Oh." She stood and tightened the belt of her shabby gray robe. "I heard Eugene. Didn't realize you were here, too."

"I figured you'd be up soon." Cesar looked up and smiled as he handed her a cup of coffee. "Also brought dinner."

Eugene stopped before closing her door. Cesar's voice was softer than she'd heard before. "You heard from James Earl?"

Eugene closed the door, opened her table, then took a bite from her sandwich. "Now where are you, James Earl?" she asked as her fingers began dancing across the keyboard.

*****

"You heard from James Earl?" asked Cesar.

CC pulled her back a little straighter. Worry lines shot out of Cesar's eyes. His shoulders slumped forward. His usual commanding presence drooped before her. "No," she said. "Why?"

Cesar led them to the sofa and sat down, motioning CC to do the same. He handed CC a bowl of soup. "You're running on empty. Eat." He leaned back and waited for CC to take a sip. When she set the cup down and looked back at him, he said, "He didn't go to the vineyard."

"Seriously!" she shouted and pulled her back straight to look Cesar in the eye. "You're checking up on him?"

"No," replied Cesar, shaking his head. He looked down, his eyes drooping. "Ezra called me. He's worried. James Earl told him he'd meet him up there."

Neither spoke as CC's rage fizzled and froze to a knot of worry and dread. "It's not like him," she said at last.

"I know," said Cesar.

"He didn't get a report over to Jane - the accountant next door -

before he left." CC picked up a coffee mug, squeezing it in her hands to prevent them from shaking.

Cesar reached over and took the cup from CC's hands. "Can he control the change when the moon is full?"

"He says he can," CC mumbled. "Cesar, has there been an-"

"No," Cesar interrupted. "No reports of a wolf attack."

CC's shoulders slumped, and she leaned her head over her lap to rest in her hands. "Good," she whispered.

"CC," said Cesar. He spoke as though choosing his words. "I know you two have been arguing. Is it possible he went away?"

CC looked up and smiled. She took his offered hand and squeezed. "Anything's possible," she said. "But I don't think so."

"There could be Hunters in town," Cesar said.

"There's one Hunter we know of - besides me," CC nodded. "The thing knew me. It makes sense he'd know James Earl, too."

"We'll find him," Cesar said and slid close to CC and put his arm around her.

"I know," she said, leaning into him. Fear and anger battered her chest. She closed her eyes and forced her breathing to slow and took the offered strength from Cesar's hard but cold body.

She wiped a tear sneaking out of one eye. "I know there's a pattern. I can almost see it."

"You're exhausted," said Cesar. "The last few days have been tough for all of us, but you need sleep. We'll monitor things. Eugene's trying to track James Earl's phone now. By the time you're awake, she should know something.

CC yawned and pushed Cesar away. "Don't you start vamping me-"

"I wouldn't do that," Cesar said, his voice still soft. "Even if I didn't already know you don't fall for it."

CC slumped. Fluffy walked in from the kitchen and put her head on CC's lap. "Sorry," she said to Cesar. "But I can't sleep. I've got to find the pattern." She paused as she stood, once again tightening her belt.

Cesar leaned back on the couch. "I'm not going anywhere, CC."

CC nodded, reached for the remote to turn on the large screen, and then turned on her laptop.

*****

Sylvia turned her head toward her house on hearing her mother's voice yelling in the backyard. She sighed and spoke to Nikki, her best friend. "Here it comes. The twit is late again, and guess who's going to go look for him."

Sylvia's mother opened the front door and stood on the stoop, her arms crossed the way she did when she was angry. "Matias!" she yelled, looking up and down the street. Her face stopped looking as her eyes fell on Sylvia sitting on the curb watching the neighborhood boys playing football on the street. "Sylvia, go find your brother. It's late. And you better be back in here before it gets dark." Sylvia's mother turned and walked back inside the house, letting the screen door slam shut.

"Yes, mama," Sylvia yelled across the lawn. She turned back to Nikki. "What did I tell you?" Sylvia shrugged her shoulders. "Brothers are such a pain. You're lucky yours are grown up and out of the house." She stood, wiping the lawn off the back of her jeans.

"Want me to come with?" Nikki asked as she stared at Angelo throwing the football.

"Naw. Faster on my own. If he's not at Charlie's, then they're playing on the swings in the park. Won't take me long. Keep my place warm."

She walked away from the game, but not before noticing Jesus watching her walk away. She slowed her pace, putting her hands in her back pockets to highlight her curvaceous backside.

Charlie's house was over one street and at the end of the block on the other side of the park. She stopped walking and looked at the park. "I'll check here first," she said under her breath. She heard the buzzing of the streetlight above her yawning awake and felt a wave of gnats pass by her face. The wind shifted. The first autumn chill of the season. Her watch vibrated.

Sylvia smiled at her birthday present from her mother. Her new smart watch gleamed in the streetlight as the text flashed across the screen. The band was cheap but bedazzled with enough hot pink crystals to please her. She read the text from Nikki: *Going for pizza. Jesus says he'll wait for you. :)*

Sylvia giggled, replying with a happy face.

Stepping off the street into the park, she said, "Matias!" she yelled. "I know you're here. Mama says to come home right now." *Don't make me miss pizza with Jesus.* She opened her mouth to yell again but stopped when a voice tore through the wooded area next to the swing sets. "Keep running," it said.

"Matias!" she yelled. She opened her mouth, afraid to call out, but the sound of running feet, breaking branches, and the birds scattering out of the trees caught her voice. She hesitated only a moment then stepped forward, calling out, "Matias?"

Charlie, Matias's friend, ran out of the woods slamming into her. "Where's Matias?" she yelled as she grabbed his shoulders.

Charlie, pale and wet from running, opened his mouth. He gulped in air, then pushed away from Sylvia. "Run! Matias run -" A crash of branches echoed from the wood. He turned to look, then ran away from her.

"Charlie," Sylvia called after the boy. "Where's Matias?" Sylvia felt her breath catch. She'd never seen Charlie afraid, and the long shadows in the woods seemed to grow longer as she stood in front of them. She breathed in the fresh breeze. "Nobody messes with my little brother." She stepped into the trees, waiting just long enough for her eyes to adjust to the sudden dusk. She filled her lungs to call out, "Matias," but before she could finish his name, a hard push on her back sent her falling to the ground.

Her hands hit twigs and rocks. As she pushed forward to lift herself, cold steel hands lifted her backwards. One hand clamped her over her mouth and nose. She couldn't breathe. She wanted to fill her lungs and scream, but the grip on her was too tight. A second arm grabbed her waist. Ice ran through her. She kicked her legs, but the more she kicked, the more the fingers pinched her nose and mouth. She looked up as the purple sky poking between dark leaves faded to blackness.

5

The pains of time ravage the unweary
Even as life flows along its banks.
Swim in the stream,
Glide along the waves,
Flow in harmony,
Or dissovle on the rocks broken on your journey.
You're listening to Mary Midnight online and in your mind.
Even the strong crumble in the war of time.
Only those who flow with the current survive the Fall.

Eugene pushed CC's bedroom door open. "Hey," she said, and stopped. No one was in the bed. A whiff of coffee tickled her nose and she leaped down the stairs to the living room and found CC, feet stretched in front of her on the coffee table, slumped back on the couch, asleep. The enormous television screen rotated through pictures of Austin. Eugene stepped forward on her toes, hitting the board that squeaked. CC sat up and shook her head.

Eugene cringed. "Sorry. Didn't mean to wake you."

Eugene jumped when Cesar spoke from behind her. "Just made a fresh pot," he said, and handed her a cup. He sat in the chair next to the couch after handing CC the other cup.

Eugene pursed her lips. "You two been doing this all night?"

"I fell asleep a few times," said CC. "I'm just not finding the pattern."

"Maybe there's not one," offered Cesar.

"Madmen do things for a reason. Just because we don't understand it doesn't mean it's not there." CC pulled a keyboard onto her lap. "And this monster is no madman."

"Unfortunately," said Eugene, moving Fluffy aside and sitting next to CC. "I have more data for you. Body of a nine-year girl was found last night outside her apartment complex. No details in the news, but there's something familiar about the address." She handed her tablet to CC.

CC returned it and typed the address into her own computer. The television, with its scrolling photos of Austin, changed to a map of Austin. She added a blue dot marking the latest body. "Does the story say whether the girl lived in the building?"

"She went missing over three weeks ago," said Eugene. "Might be worth checking out, seeing why it took so long to report her missing."

"I'll call Renaldo," said CC. "Where's my phone?"

Eugene jumped off the couch, resisting the urge to cringe even as she felt her shoulders shrink and her cheeks burn. "Oh, sorry. I've got it upstairs. Needed it to hack into James Earl's phone records. I'll go get it."

Cesar asked, "Have you found anything?"

"Maybe," Eugene said, shrugging her shoulders. "Maybe not. Let me get the phone. I'll show you."

As Eugene turned to walk out, she stopped at the sound of Mike entering from the back door. Stanly, from the bar, was with him, and Mike was on the phone. "I don't know," he was saying. "Her cars here. Yes," he stopped and looked at CC. "She's here. Come on over."

"Who's coming?" asked CC.

"Renaldo," said Mike. "He says he's been trying to reach you for two hours, but your voice mail won't pick up."

"Eugene," shouted CC.

"On it," shouted Eugene, and leaped up the stairs, keeping her ears open to what the others were saying.

"I just heard about another body," CC said.

"That's what he's coming here about," answered Mike.

CC mumbled. "Damn. There's got to be a pattern in here."

"I'll help, but first I gotta get to bed. I'm beat," Stanly said.

"Be right with you, hon," said Mike. "As soon as we heard about the body in the news. Stanly headed to the scene to find out what he could. Too crowded even for him to get close, but he saw Max's cook. Guess she lives there."

Eugene hit her head with her hand. "That's why the address was familiar," she said to no one. "You are so dense, Eugene. Details, Pops always said I don't pay attention to details."

Reaching for her phone, she noticed the sunlight filtering through a crack in the drapes. Without thinking, she reached over and pulled the blackout blinds down behind them. "Like blackout blinds, idiot," she mumbled. "Vamps in a house means you gotta have these."

"Take the room next to Eugene's," CC said from the stairwell. "I'll get dressed."

Eugene stepped into the hall just as Cesar closed the door of the bedroom next to hers. CC stood facing her.

"You have my phone?" CC asked, holding out her hand.

*****

Sitting in a dark room in the early morning with a vampire was just weird, but Cesar was a nice guy, even if he kept shushing her. She supposed she'd been in weirder situations. Eugene leaned back in the rocking chair next to the door left open just enough for a sliver of morning light from the hall window to enter Cesar's room and the sounds of CC talking to Renaldo and Frank. She could even hear Mike telling Stanly to shush. He was listening from his room, too.

"Thanks again for breakfast," CC said with a mouthful of food.

Renaldo harrumphed, but Frank prevented him from saying anything. "We are waking you up. It's the neighborly thing to do."

"Unless you're trying to bribe me," said CC with a mock laugh. "You still think I'm holding something back, don't you, Renaldo?"

Renaldo choked on his coffee. "CC." He coughed and shook his head. "I know you wouldn't hold out on purpose, but I don't want to see the body of another dead kid. If there's any way we can pool our resources, we need to do it now."

"He's right, CC. Maybe it's time I stepped back a little. I've been harping on him not working with you because, well because you have sources that could be dangerous to know about." came Frank's reply.

Eugene whispered, "I like Frank. Resonate voice. You can hear-"

"Do you mind?" snapped Cesar. He sat opposite Eugene in the corner of the room away from the light.

"Sorr-ry" glibbed Eugene and crunched on one of the breakfast taco's CC had given her before telling her to go upstairs so she could talk business.

Cesar's face turned away from her and she shivered as his eyes reflected the little light in the room.

CC's voice interrupted her crunching. "I've been working on this all night. Look." CC's fingers tapped on her keyboard, pounding them as though to force them to give her answers. "Here's a map of every re-ported missing child in the Austin area for the past six months. Here it is with the locations of Darius, Maria, Joslyn, and now Ruby, assuming her death was by the same killer."

Frank answered, "Heart was ripped out. Signs of a hell-of-a-beating. It's the same killer."

Renaldo's voice came next. "The bodies are clumped in the immedi-ate downtown area. What's that blue dot?"

"Based on what Darius told me, that's the intersection where Maria was last seen," said CC. "The other blue circles are where our victims lived. What can you tell me about Ruby?"

"Sad," said Frank. Eugene stopped chewing and tilted her head to hear the details. Frank's voice lowered as a harshness caught in his throat. "Nine years old, and mother didn't realize she was missing."

"Then who reported missing?" asked CC.

"Here's the initial report," said Renaldo. "A neighbor reported her missing on the 29th of August. Ruby was a friend of one of her sons and got concerned since he saw the mother but not the child."

"Did she see or hear anything relating to Ruby going missing?" CC asked.

Renaldo continued. "Only that the place wasn't fit for children and cops were doing nothing to make it better."

"You okay with me going over there and looking around." Eugene smiled, noting how CC didn't ask.

Frank laughed. "Rather hoping you would. Witness didn't give us much, but then she's got history. Maybe she'll open up to you."

Fingers tapped on glass followed a ding on CC's phone. "There's her info," said Renaldo. "Florence Laurent. I don't think she's keeping anything back, but with a record, she's cautious when talking to cops."

"Name's familiar," said CC.

Eugene whispered, "Cesar!"

Cesar glared at her in response.

Eugene answered the glare with a glare even as she bounced in her chair. "That's Max's sous chef - from the coffee shop."

Cesar put his hands in front of his face. He closed his eyes.

"Cesar," Eugene whispered again. "You can't go to sleep now."

Cesar lifted a finger and opened his eyes. "You're working today?"

"Not 'til this afternoon."

"Go to the cafe now. See if you can get Flo to talk to you about it."

Eugene leapt to her feet with a thud.

Cesar shook his head. "Wait."

Renaldo hissed. "I've got another blue dot for you. Lamond Duncan disappeared from his backyard. You mentioned his name to me. Also found his body last night. Here's where we found him. Here's where he lived."

"Big family bar-b-que going on, too. A party for Lamond, his formal adoption day," said Frank.

Eugene whistled and said, "He's getting bolder, speeding up his killings."

Cesar said nothing. Eugene watched as his jaw tightened and the muscles in his neck turned into knots. "In my city," he muttered. "Go," he added. "I need to talk to Max."

Eugene filled her backpack with books and swung it over her arm. Below her, Frank and Renaldo were saying goodbye. She waited for them to leave before stepping out of the room. A glance back into the guest room before closing the door revealed Cesar pacing, his face blue in the light of his phone.

She jumped and turned, hearing CC's voice echo through the house. "Eugene, still here?"

*****

Flo brought out a tray of fresh pastries. Luna leaned over the counter, deciding which one she wanted. "I'm starving," she whispered.

Flo offered her a sandwich. "Pimento and cheese."

Luna grabbed the sandwich. "Thanks," she muttered through her mouth full of sandwich. "Marcus dragged me out of bed early this morning. Payback for yesterday." She turned around to find Marcus ignoring her. He sat at a table with his laptop in front of him, but his fingers did not type. He stared ahead, his eyes not blinking.

The late Sunday lull was in full swing as the evening crowd strolled out and students mingled in study until closing. She reflected that in only a few weeks, the cafe changed from an empty building to a hotspot. The menu continued to expand. Chef Max even talked about keeping the cafe open for twenty-four hours.

She didn't notice her mother approaching. "You look a thousand miles away," said Jackie pouring hot water into a cup for tea.

"Just thinking," Luna said, swallowing the last bit of sandwich.

"What did you think of Flo's crepes? I love them, and the ROI is amazing."

Luna laughed.

"Are you making fun of your old mother?" Jackie asked with a wink.

"Nah, It's just...." Luna looked at her mother. The worry lines were still there, but camouflaged by cosmetics, something she hadn't worn in a long time. Her eyes still looked tired, but there was a gleam in them she recognized from before all the troubles started.

Jackie leaned over the counter, stirring her tea.

"It's happening so fast."

"It doesn't feel real, does it?" Jackie nodded. "It's hard for me to wrap my head around it, too. If Chef Max hadn't come along, I'm not sure where we'd be."

"He's not a gangster, is he?" asked Luna. It sounded stupid the moment it came out of her mouth, but she was tired, Max was weird, and it'd been a long time since she chatted with her mother without being angry.

"Luna." Jackie's eyes rounded and she leaned forward. "Don't be silly. Chef Max is like any other artist seeking validation: eccentric, but he wants to succeed here as much as we do."

Luna stared at the food displayed on the counter. She pulled a clean towel and wiped away the crumbs she'd made while eating.

Jackie put her hand out and covered her daughter's hand. "What's bothering you? Does it have something to do with school, your new friends? I know I've kept you close since - well, you're growing up so fast these days."

"Classes are fine," Luna said, watching a group of students take a seat around one of the large round tables. They opened backpacks and pulled out computers, books, and notebooks. One of the women sneered at a table of younger students. "Graduate students," sighed Luna. Three of them came to the counter to order.

One, a tall woman with long blond hair, cleared her throat as the other two placed their orders. "Excuse me," she asked with a thick West Texas drawl. "Are you Dr. Howard-Smithers?"

Jackie looked up smiling. "Yes, I am. How can I help you?"

"I told them it was you!" The girl grinned, showing bright white teeth. "I'm citing your book so much in my thesis, I feel I know you. May I buy you a coffee and pick your brain?"

Luna's chin dropped as her mother's face brightened, stress lines melting away.

"Sounds a lovely way to end the day," she said. "Are you okay, Luna?"

Luna nodded, unable to say anything, and fixed the drinks.

When she delivered the drinks to the table where her mother was talking economics, Luna frowned to see her mother smiling and talking statistics and graphs. She stopped in front of Marcus, who sat staring at their mother. The blinking light on his monitor flashed *battery low,* but he didn't notice.

"I knew you weren't studying," she said.

Marcus blinked his eyes and closed his laptop. "Great," he mumbled. "I hope it saved what I had. And like you would know what it's like to study. If you want to succeed in school, you have to take your classes seriously. Even Eugene is here most of the afternoon studying, and she's just taking art classes."

Laughter erupted from their mother's group.

Marcus smiled even as his eyes drooped. "It's good to see her laughing again."

Luna leaned on her arm. She was tired and didn't see what was so special about her mother laughing.

"Why?" she asked.

Marcus closed his laptop and placed his book on top of it, perfectly centered. "We've been so unhappy for so long; do you really not see what it means to laugh?" Marcus put his laptop and book in his briefcase. "I'm going to plug this in and make sure my work saved." He walked to the office without giving Luna another look.

Luna's breath caught in her throat as her heart pounded in her chest. Her lungs froze, neither breathing in nor breathing out. She felt blood rush to her face, and her fingernails cut into her palms as she squeezed her hands into fists. Everything was changing so fast, too fast, just like it did when Tony died.

She didn't see Tommy enter the cafe or sit next to her until she heard his voice and felt a cold hand on her forearm. "You look like crap."

Luna let out the breath she hadn't realized she was holding. The lights from the ceiling glared in her eyes as they bounced off Tommy's golden curls. His more-clear-than-blue eyes reflected her face, and she realized she did look like crap. "Hi, Tommy," she managed to say as her heart and lungs once again moved in unison. "I've been working all weekend. What are you doing here? I thought you were off tonight."

He wrinkled his nose and waved his fingers in the direction of her head. "What's that thing on your head?"

Blood rushed to Luna's cheeks as her hand reached up and tugged at the red bandana Eugene gave her to cover her matted curls. "I didn't have time to do my hair this morning. Eugene let me borrow it."

Tommy nodded. "Speaking of, where is the tall, tattooed wonder?"

Luna laughed, releasing tension she wasn't aware she had been holding onto. "Left a while ago. Came in on her day off to study. How weird is that?"

"Not so weird. She's new in town. We're probably the only people she knows," said Tommy, standing and straightening the cuff of his sleeve. "Unlike me. I have places to go."

Luna drew her eyebrows together. "I hadn't thought of that."

Marcus stepped out of the office and folded his arms across his chest.

"Marcus is glaring," Luna said. "He's my ride home. Joy."

Tommy frowned at Luna, then at Marcus. Rolling his eyes, he said with a snarl, "Children."

*****

Eugene jumped at the sound of shattering glass in the kitchen, followed by CC yelling, "Damn it, Max! I knew you were here. Now stop popping up behind me like that."

Eugene finished buttoning her favorite old leather vest and bit her tongue to not laugh out loud. The dryer buzzed in the kitchen, and she made her way downstairs and through the kitchen to find Max standing at the door with his hands on his hips.

His upper lip crept up in the mildest of sneers. "Is this your kitchen?" he asked.

CC's cheeks flushed. "It's all we need. We don't cook."

Eugene leaped over the broken glass and CC stooped, picking up a large piece of glass as Max said, "I'll clean up. I made you spill it."

Eugene pulled her jeans out of the dryer as Tommy walked into the kitchen from the back door carrying two pizza boxes. Eugene looked up to catch his eye, but it was too late. "Are we having a party?" laughed Tommy

CC snarled, pulling a mug out of a cabinet and filling it with coffee.

"You didn't cut yourself, did you?" Tommy poured on his charm.

"Can it, Cupid," CC snapped, and pushed past Max toward the living room.

"Yeah, Cupid," laughed Eugene. "It's about time you got here. I'm starving."

Tommy handed Eugene one of the pizza boxes. "The works with extra cheese, Tatt girl," he said before following CC out of the kitchen.

Eugene rolled a slice of pizza and ate half of it in one bite as she watched Max. He moved with the grace and care she'd expected of vamps, but Max was old. His movements followed a practiced order and efficiency she'd never seen before. Even his face, so calm and so restive, flowed with his movements. But his eyes - his eyes took in everything. She shuddered, thinking of what it would be like to sneak up on him. Even Tommy, who she knew was just as old as Max, didn't have a dark suspicion guiding his gaze.

"Are you going to put pants on?" asked Max, without looking at Eugene.

"Oh," she mumbled and pulled her jeans on put them on. When she turned around, Max leaned against the kitchen counter, his arms folded over his chest and his dark eyes glittering in the overhead light. "What?" she asked. "You've never seen a woman put her jeans on before?"

Max laughed. Eugene couldn't help but laugh with him. Few laughs were as joyful as the one she heard now, but perhaps it was because it was from such an unusual source. Max's face remained suspicious, the line of his mouth solid, his eyes hidden behind a large brow, and his teeth whiter and wetter and then teeth ought to be. "You're not afraid of me, are you, wolf?" he said.

Eugene shook her head. "I'm scared shitless, old man," Eugene replied. "Ezra told me I'd be I'd be stupid not to be."

Max nodded his head. "Ezra's a good man."

Eugene turned her head, hearing Ezra enter the house. When she returned her attention to Max, he too was listening. She spoke, "Hey, Max?"

Max turned his attention back to Eugene.

"Do you think Flo will be okay? I mean, this whatever-it-is, that thing is getting close to us. You don't think he'd, well you know...." She didn't finish her thoughts.

"I've taken steps to ensure her safety and those of her children," Max answer but stopped before saying more.

Ezra's voice was clear and weary. "James Earl is missing."

"I know," replied CC. "And police found two more dead children last night. I'm sure James Earl is fine."

Eugene heard the momentary choke in CC's voice.

Max straightened and turned to face Eugene. "I need you to find James Earl," he said. He shook his head. "Please," he added. "Ezra says you're an excellent tracker."

"That's my brother," Eugene said. "He's the expert tracker."

Eugene only blinked when Cesar entered the room. She wasn't sure from where.

"According to Mrs. Smith," he said, knotting his tie, "Your brother is one of the best in the Wilderness, but this is the city, your domain."

Eugene folded the stolen skirt and blouse. She breathed in the soap, the water, her sweat, the owner's perfume - jasmine and musk, and the oak and grasses of Austin. "I'm good," she said. "But three days; he left on his bike Thursday afternoon. I saw him." She shook her head. "I don't know if I'm that good. On the other hand, I have a good idea of his general direction after hacking into his phone's GPS."

Cesar smiled. "Mrs. Smith's exact words were, 'Eugene can find the rat that farted in the rain on your sidewalk three days ago'."

Eugene studied the vampires. Secrets rested safely in those faces, but each also contained a casual honesty, too. "I'll try," she said. "Where do you think he is?"

Max wasn't listening to her. Her attention turned to CC reviewing the news about the latest missing child.

A shiver ran down Eugene's spine when Max's eyes returned to her. Darkness leached out of the room and into those too clear, dark eyes. His voice dropped low so only she would hear him. "If he's lucky, he's already dead."

*****

"Are we certain our monster killed Ruby?" asked Tommy. He sat on the arm of the couch next to CC.

"Renaldo confirmed it. Beaten, heart ripped out. And will you please not hover over me?" said CC, pushing Tommy away from her.

Tommy leaned down to CC's ear and whispered, "But I enjoy being next to you, Catherine."

CC stopped pretending and shoved him off the couch. "Down!" she yelled.

Fluffy sat up and barked once at Tommy.

Tommy fell to his feet. "You are such a flirt." He winked at Fluffy.

"Tomas," said Max, entering the living room. "Time for grown-up business. According to the news, the child's body was found in a public space and near her home. Our monster is changing tactics."

"Can the dark and spooky, Max," shot Tommy. "You're not the only one here who knows what he's doing."

Fluffy returned to CC's side on the couch and rested her head on CC's lap and tail on Cesar's. CC picked up the tablet from the coffee table and tapped until the television screen displayed the map she'd created earlier in the day. Her hand stopped long enough to rub her temple where fatigue and stress jack hammered in her temples. "Look at this," she said, ignoring Tommy as he sat on the floor at her feet. "Where's Eugene?" she asked, looking around her.

"On an errand for me," said Max, not looking at CC.

When Max said nothing else, she circled Clay's Funeral Home on the screen. "Here's Clay's. And here are the locations of the other bodies, and here are bodies found over the last three months by the police."

Cesar leaned forward, examining the map. "He knows about Clay. This is a different map than the one you showed Frank and Renaldo?"

"Duh," replied CC, rolling her eyes then stopped. "When did you change clothes? I thought you were sleeping upstairs."

"I went home to change," Cesar said, shrugging his shoulders.

Max cleared his throat and stood in front of the large screen pointing. "We're also in the center of the circle whether we're in the cafe or in your house."

CC highlighted her own house. "We already know he's aware of me. Safe bet he knows about all of us," she said.

"Did he leave the bodies here for you to find," said Max, "or did he find you after leaving the bodies? How much does he know about any of us?"

"Maybe he left them for Clay?" said Cesar. He leaned back, stroking Fluffy's back.

"It's not like New Year '85," said Tommy. "And it's just like '85." He leaned his head against the couch but kept his eyes on the screen. "He hid a killing in plain sight for us then. The detectives, such as they were, assumed it was the same as the other Servant Girl Annihilator killings."

"So many bodies," said CC. "We'll have to concentrate on the ones we know he did. Are you both certain we're after the same killer from a hundred years ago?"

"Do we know *where* the children were taken from?" asked Max.

CC tapped on her keyboard.

"We know the general location of Maria's and Darious' abductions," replied Cesar.

"We know he took Lamond from his backyard, here," CC said. Fluffy eased her snout close to CC's face, and CC scratched the dog's ears. "It's difficult to move a body, even a child's. Austin is a twenty-four-hour city. He's got to be very careful not to be seen."

"We know he's careful, and yes, I'm sure we're looking for the same killer as '85." Tommy said scratching his chin. "What does he know about us?" Tommy's eyes narrowed as he looked between Max and CC.

Max kept his eyes on the screen. He pointed to the parking garage where they first encountered the creature. "After the other night, he knows a lot more about us than we do about him."

No one spoke. Each focused on the map in front of them. Clay's Funeral Home, the cafe, and the house they were sitting in burned like beacons in the center of the map. The silence broke when CC took in a deep breath. "He wants me to help him," she said. "Let's see how badly he wants to talk to me."

"No!" shouted Tommy. "It's too dangerous."

CC rubbed her temple as pain stabbed her temples. "We know what to expect. We'll be ready for him, and if it means we can prevent another child being murdered, it's worth the risk."

"CC," began Cesar.

Max shook his head stopping Cesar. Almost as though to himself, he said, "You know she's right," he said to Cesar. "Tomas and I will stay close to CC. Cesar, keep up appearances. I don't want any of your people spooking this monster."

"They won't," Cesar said. "But questions are being asked. We won't be able to keep it hidden for much longer."

CC stood. The others followed. "Sun is down. He's out on the streets somewhere. We'll start circling the area, widening it as the night progresses. We need to let Clay know what we're doing." Max raised an eyebrow, but CC lifted her hand to stop him from speaking. "He already knows something's going on."

Cesar grunted. "I will be at the club, keeping up appearances."

Tommy snorted out loud.

Cesar stepped in front of him. He snickered. "Out of the way, Cupid. Eat your pizza, CC. It's still warm."

"Oh." CC put her hands over her stomach as it grumbled. "Thanks. I'm starving. Vegan?"

"Of course," muttered Cesar, walking out the front door.

*****

Eugene realized James Earl had been at each body dump site. His phone's GPS told her that, and his scent, although faint, lingered at each one. "He had the same idea as Max," she said to no one. She got off of her bicycle and walked it around the apartment building. It surprised her to see Flo, but then then this was her home.

Flo leaned over the railing on the second floor. She held a cigarette in one hand and the hand of a small boy with the other. "Yo, Eugene," she shouted. "What are you doing out here?"

Eugene waved. "Just riding around."

"This time of night?" Flo turned to a sour-faced, skinny woman with black, stringy hair. "Take him. I'm going down to talk to a friend."

"What kind of friend?" the sour faced woman asked. "You're always telling me you don't have friends. That's why I have to drop everything I'm doing every time you need a ride home."

"Shut it," murmured Flo, and walked down the steps to Eugene.

"Sorry," said Eugene as Flo approached her. "Didn't mean to upset anyone."

Flo squinted once at the sour-faced woman. "No problem. You shouldn't be out here by yourself. What are you really doing?"

"Just riding. Still trying to figure out how to get around in the city. And then when I realized I was near your apartment building, I thought I'd come over and see where that body was found. You know, I'd have thought I'd have more excitement in Vegas, but it turns out Austin is a mystery haven."

Eugene stopped to take a breath. Flo raised her arms, laughing. "Okay, okay. I get it. Come on. I'll show you, but then you should head home. This area's not all that safe." She beckoned Eugene to follow, and Eugene leaned her bike against the wall of the building. "Don't leave your bike. Geez! You want it stolen?"

Eugene followed Flo to the back of the building. The smell of death hit Eugene in the face. Her eyes watered.

Flo shook her head. "Stinks," she said. "I know. Cops kicked up all the trash piled up back here looking for clues, I guess. Anyway, manager said the city was coming to pick up the trash, but don't shit waiting for that to happen." Flo lead Eugene past an overflowing dumpster and around two piles of trash. "There." She pointed with the cigarette to an empty spot just off the pavement of the parking lot. "Only clean spot around here. Well, it is now. Cops cleaned out the spot, moving the body. She was nine, and a friend of Jon's. That's the oldest, the one you saw me with."

Eugene watched Flo, surprised at the mournful quality in her voice. "Just a little girl," said Eugene.

"Her foster mom never paid her much attention." Flo tossed her cigarette on the ground. "Only kept her around to collect a check from the state."

"You didn't smoke much of it." Eugene noticed more than half the cigarette was unsmoked.

Flo's face remained sad, but when she looked up at Eugene, she forced a smile. "Been trying to quit, and it stinks so much back here already. You seen enough? It's really not safe for you out here."

"What makes it safe for you and not for me?" asked Eugene. She breathed in deep, taking in all the smells. Under the trash and smoke of Flo's cigarette, and underneath the stink of decay, she caught a whiff of James Earl--sweat, fatigue, fear, cologne. She wanted to stay and search, but she couldn't with Flo at her side.

"The guys around here don't fff-mess with me," Flo said.

Eugene wanted to laugh, but the earnestness with which Flo spoke told Eugene that they had tried. "I'm pretty good at taking care of my-self," she said, keeping her voice low. She searched over Flo's head, into the shadows surrounding them. A new scent tickled her nose.

"Maybe," Flo nodded. "It's just that," she paused and looked down as though thinking of the right words. "Something else is going on. I mean, the guys around here are tough, but even they've been staying in."

Eugene sniffed. The scent of fear. It oozed out of the building. From Flo, only a little, and not the fear of the unknown, the fear of worry, the fear of hope slipping away. But from the apartment building, the fear of the men and women inside it crept out of the doors and windows and slid along the ground until it oozed up Eugene's legs to her nose. "Why do you stay here?" she asked. She needed to find the source of that fear. Had James Earl found it?

"You saw the boy," said Flo. "He's one of two. My wife's kids. The old bitch is their grandmother. If I go, they have no one to keep them safe until Malia gets back."

Eugene nodded. "You're tougher than I thought. To stay here, I mean, when you don't have to."

Laughter burst from Flo's lips, but Eugene saw the fear in her eyes. "I've had to be. They shouldn't have to."

"Flo," shouted a small voice from the breezeway of the apartment building.

Eugene turned to see a little boy. At first, she thought he was the same one she saw on the landing, but this one's hair had a touch of blond at the tips. His frame widened at the chest, and he stood with more of a slump than his brother. Like his brother, he wore faded shorts and no shoes.

"Flo," he shouted again. "Grandma's going out."

"Stupid cow!" muttered Flo. "I told her not to go out tonight."

"Why not tonight?" asked Eugene.

Flo pulled back her shoulders. "She's been going out every night. Look, I gotta take care of the kids. You should go."

Eugene nodded her head. "Right behind you." She followed Flo to the breezeway but turned back to the parking lot when Flo took the boy inside their apartment.

She walked around the field, stopping to lean close to the ground. At other times she stopped to listen to the voices in the apartment building. Flo yelled. The voice of the sour-faced woman yelled back. Fear continued to ooze from the building.

Stepping off the blacktop, she walked behind a thick, prickly bush, removed her clothes, and changed to wolf. Her senses sharpened. The fear, the hate, and the anger of the inhabitants, all flew into her. She stood, taking it in, filtering out the obvious. One silent step forward, and then another; she eased herself closer to the remnants of police tape.

There. The scent of James Earl, but not just his sweat and fear. She smelled his blood on the ground, and along with James Earl, she recognized the monster she'd encountered in Vegas. Its scent collided with James Earl's in this spot. James Earl lost.

A final lap around the field, but traces of the monster and James Earl faded to nothing. She yawned, licking her snout with her tongue, seeking any minute traces of either. Men's voices, laughter, and footsteps warned her to lower her head. She peered through the brush and trash of the lot. Three men walked toward the apartment building. One pushed her bicycle. One wore her favorite vest.

*****

"Come on, Fluffy," called CC into the shadows of the parking lot at Clay's Funeral Home. "Time to ride."

Clay placed his hand on CC's shoulder. "I don't like it, CC."

She looked into Clay's face from her motorcycle. His eyes, always so dark, glowed as they reflected the constant ambient light of the city's night. Crease lines rolled across at his usual smooth, tall forehead, as his lips pressed tight. She put her hand on his. "I'm okay, Clay. Promise. I've got two vamps at my back. Besides," she added, petting Fluffy as she leaped into the motorcycle's sidecar and reached to lick CC's fingers. "Fluffy's with me."

Clay placed his hand on Fluffy's head. His eyes widened. "Jenny chose well for you," he said. "Take care of her."

Fluffy barked as CC pulled the doggie goggles over her ears.

CC started the motorcycle. "You be careful, too, Clay. He knows you're here."

Clay nodded his head. "Why wouldn't he place the dead near me?"

CC nodded. "Makes sense in a weird dead/undead sort of way." She drove towards the gate. Before she turned away from the funeral home, she looked back in time to watch Clay disappear into the surrounding shadows. "How much we've changed, Fluffy."

Her plan for the hunt was simple. The only surprise was Max's quick adoption of it. She would drive through the streets of downtown, steadily shifting to the warehouse district. Sharon McKinsy, the child abducted from her backyard about eight o'clock that morning, lived in the Terrytown area. They assumed the creature wouldn't remain there, and CC believed the warehouse district provided plenty of space for the creature to work uninterrupted. Cesar returned to the Phantom's Menace to maintain a semblance of normalcy, but he did so under protest even after Max and Tommy assured him they would keep her safe.

She stopped at a red light and looked around her. I35 loomed bright over her head with the steady traffic expected for three in the morning. Even the homeless were asleep in their tents under the overpass. Across the freeway, the east side waited for her. She hadn't planned on driving east, but there was no sign of the monster anywhere in town. That sensation, which turned into a tickle on her neck, let her know Max was near. She turned her head only slightly to the right and felt the other tickle that was Tommy. He was ahead of her. Fluffy barked. The light turned green, and she drove forward.

Even on the east side of town, the city was quiet for those few hours between the closing of clubs and the switch to the day shifts when offices opened. Red and blue lights flashed in front of her as she neared the State Cemetery. She turned onto a darkened residential street. Loosening Fluffy's seat belt, she let the dog jump out of the side car, and she stood to stretch her legs. Max came to her side first, and Tommy a moment later.

"Did you see what was going on?" she asked.

Tommy answered. "Three patrol cars in front of a house a few blocks over. Frantic couple outside talking to them. Their teenage girl is missing."

"Are they thinking runaway?" asked Max.

"No," Tommy answered.

"Not with Sharon being taken just this morning," said CC. "This shit is too busy killing kids to talk to me tonight."

Max put his hand on CC's shoulder. His cold hand sent a chill through her, but it relaxed her shoulders. CC sighed as the taste of stale coffee filled her mouth, and she coughed to clear her throat. Fluffy sat next to her and leaned into her leg. "It's nearly dawn," said CC. "Let's get some sleep."

Before either man could answer, a siren wailed behind them. CC turned and waved to the patrol car, knowing Max and Tommy were no longer beside her.

✱✱✱✱✱

"You look like crap," Renaldo said, handing CC a bottle of water. "And since when do you not want coffee?"

"Fluffy doesn't like coffee," said CC, grinning. She bent over and poured water into a paper cup and set it in front of Fluffy. "Besides, you make terrible coffee."

CC closed her eyes on straightening as her stomach did a quick flip and a hammer beat inside her skull. "So," she said, forcing a smile on her lips. "You going to tell me about the missing teen?"

"I thought you might tell me something," replied Renaldo. "You were the one driving around the neighborhood."

CC watched Renaldo's eyes squint and bite his tongue. "I only just got to that neighborhood."

"What were you looking for?"

"A monster that steals children," she said, looking him in the eye.

Renaldo shook his head. "Anyone else tell me that, I'd throw him in the cells for being a smartass, but you probably were looking for a monster."

"Who's looking for a monster?" asked Frank Jarvis, entering the office. He stopped and looked down at CC, sitting at his desk.

"What else do you call someone who takes children?" asked CC, standing.

"Oh," said Frank. His brows eased, but his eye bounced between CC and Renaldo. "So you think Sylvia Catan was taken?"

"That's the running theory," Renaldo answered.

CC added, speaking to Frank, "It's what I'm going with."

Frank removed his holster, checked the safety on his gun, and put it in his desk drawer. He locked the drawer, studying his keys before looking back at CC and Renaldo. "I was afraid of that."

Renaldo tapped a pen on his desk. "He's openly admitting there's more going on than we can image."

Frank's nose twitched as he stared at CC.

CC tried to smile as she rubbed her temples. "That's the first sign of acceptance."

Renaldo leaned forward and lowered his voice. "Why were you driving around with only Fluffy at your side if you think can find the killer?"

Frank closed the door to the office. "Slow down," he said to Renaldo. "Certain cases shouldn't be talked about in the office."

"And this is one of them," snarled Renaldo. "I know, but we're talking kids here. We agreed yesterday to talk to each other."

Frank shook his head. But before he could reply, CC spoke. "I wasn't alone, and I'm pretty sure this killer wants to talk to me."

Renaldo whistled. "No shit? What makes you think that?"

Before CC could answer him, her stomach turned cartwheels, and her vision blurred. For a moment, she saw the bloodied face of a girl, her teeth gritted as she pushed her body forward. The concrete beneath her was covered with dirt and dust, and stained with dark spots. A sprinkling of sunlight amidst vast shadows rose and fell around the girl. The smell of urine and blood filled CC's nose. She gagged. The vision changed. Sunlight snuck out from shadows over the concrete floor. White parallel lines pointed to a mound, familiar but broken. A wave of sorrow enveloped her.

"What's wrong?" Renaldo asked pushing himself to standing.

"You okay, CC?" asked Frank.

Fluffy barked once, her eyes staring at CC.

"Tired," CC said.

"Let me get you a ride home," said Frank.

"Mike's coming to get me," she said. "Your officers made me leave my bike on the street. Hope they haven't impounded it."

"I'll take care of it." Renaldo picked up the phone "You sure you're okay?"

CC sniffed, forced herself to concentrate, to move her muscles. Frank offered his hand to her. She shook it and whispered, "I'll be okay. Just give me a minute. And let Renaldo decide what he can handle."

"Once he knows, he can't unknow." Frank walked with CC down the hall and out the front entrance.

Cesar's favorite sports car, with its tinted windows, waited on the curb in the building's shadow.

Frank opened the passenger door. "Cesar," he nodded. "Be careful, CC. I know just enough to be scared shitless, but if you need me, call."

CC nodded. "Thanks." CC looked up, seeing the blue of the sky growing brighter. Then she saw the reflection of a pale, tired face in Cesar's dark glasses.

Cesar pulled away from the curb. Neither spoke until the car pulled into the parking spot behind the house.

CC turned to Cesar, who did not look at her. "James Earl's dead," she said.

"I know," replied Cesar. "I found his body in the club's garage an hour ago."

CC pulled her keys out of her bag and stepped onto the back stoop. Her foot slipped and a loud crack broke into the early morning sounds of a city preparing for a Monday morning. "Who left a dish on out here?" She said without thinking and opened the back door. She dropped her backpack on the table. Eugene, stretching out on the sofa in the living room, stoop up.

"What's up?" Eugene asked.

"We took his remains to Clay's," said Cesar, taking off his shades.

Eugene stood. "Who's dead?"

Cesar's voice, calm and low, answered, "James Earl."

CC's stomach no longer did cartwheels, but a wave of nausea swept through her. Eugene sat slumped, sitting on the couch, lit only by the creeping sunlight inching in through thick drapes. Behind her or glowing from her, a wolf rose like fog over a still lake. Blood dripped from its teeth. Massive claws reached out and through Eugene to CC. She closed her eyes. The nausea enveloped her. She bent over, grabbing her stomach as her vision filled with darkness. The last she remembered was Cesar's hand on her arm and back and being lifted into his arms.

*****

Eugene paced back and forth in front of the couch, where CC lay pale and unmoving. Fluffy paced with her. Cesar sat in the chair near her head. He leaned back, his fingers templed in front of his face, his eyes closed.

Eugene stopped pacing and looked at Cesar. "Shouldn't we call someone?"

"Again," Cesar answered, keeping his eyes closes. "No. She fainted. She'll be fine."

As if on cue, CC sat up with a loud gasp. "What the hell?"

Fluffy jumped onto the couch and licked her face. Eugene fell to sitting on the edge of the couch. Cesar opened his eyes, but otherwise didn't move.

"You okay?" asked Eugene, taking CC's hand in hers. "You passed out. Scared me to death. You're freezing. Cesar, get that blanket from the dryer, will ya?"

"The wolf," CC said, but stopped and closed her eyes.

Eugene looked to Cesar. He shook his head just enough for Eugene to see it shake.

CC took in a deep breath and let it out. "I saw a wolf. It was huge."

Cesar spoke, without moving. "Was it Eugene?"

CC looked between the two of them. "I've seen Eugene's wolf. This one was huge."

Eugene stood, backing away from CC. "I'm sorry," she said. Her heart raced, unsure what to do.

CC pushed her legs to the floor and pushed her hands against the seat. Eugene rushed to her side, seeing her eyes glaze over. Cesar stood. "You saw her wolf in the park. Now you've seen her inner wolf, her werewolf. The one she keeps under wraps." he said. "We all have inner demons, CC. You are a seer of those demons. I thought you might be."

"Cool!" said Eugene. "So, that's how you always know when I'm around." She picked up a glass from the coffee table and handed it to CC. "Here, drink some juice. It will make you feel better."

She cupped her hands around CC's hands shook.

CC drank and pushed the glass away. "I hate apple juice. And what are you talking about?"

Cesar leaned forward. "You always know when we're near, don't you?"

"You told me once that was just hunting skills." She reached for the glass and drank more juice, cringing as it hit her tongue, but color returned to her face.

"That's what I thought," said Cesar with a shrug. "Max said you were different, and considering his age, he may have met others like you, even if you are a rarity."

"Isn't CC kind of old to just be figuring this out?" Eugene asked. She watched a sneer form on CC's lips. "Not that you 're old," Eugene added.

"Your wolf showed itself when you were fourteen," said Cesar. "When it did, you were surrounded by people that loved and accepted you as you. The rest of us were alone and scared. Some of us turned out bad. Some of us didn't survive the change. CC's always had this ability, but she didn't need it 'til now."

CC leaned back. Her eyes stared at the ceiling. "And now that I'm surrounded by unhumans, my mind has learned how to use it."

"That's my theory," said Cesar. "You're shivering. I'll get the blanket. Keep drinking the juice."

"It's cool," said Eugene. She bit her lip and stood. "Hungry? Luna and Marcus stopped by before you got home and dropped off a tray of pastries. Making sure I don't tell their mum about Luna's little outing, I think."

CC's lips curled up. "Sounds good. I am hungry. And would you make coffee? I can't drink any more of this crap."

Cesar returned and tucked the blanket around CC and then went back to the chair.

Eugene stood at the sink, filling the coffee pot, and closed her eyes. No one had ever seen her inner wolf, except maybe mums. Water ran over her fingers, and she shook her head to clear her thoughts.

She measured coffee into the filter, making certain the level was perfect and clicked the buttons to start the brew. She forced her breathing to slow, remembering her mother tracing the design of the new tattoo on her arm. Eugene's eyes followed the lines of the vines, roses, buds, lilies, and leaves running from her wrist to her elbow. It was the first tattoo her mother gave her. The soft pinks and reds, the shades of green and blue, the shadows and light melded into a calm retreat beneath which the wolf walked.

The wolf was always with her. Her mother drew the wolf, hidden behind the vines and flowers, waiting. The wolf watched as she stood in the kitchen. It whispered, "Run, hunt, rip, tear. Eat the flesh." But today, the invitation lacked the enticement of joy. Today, the invitation tore through her like rage in a storm.

"Not today, wolf," she whispered.

"What's that?" yelled CC.

Eugene shook herself and opened the refrigerator. "Want me to heat these up?" Eugene called out.

Eugene returned to the couch with a plate full of pastries and a hot mug of coffee. Fluffy lifted her head, sniffing the platter. "No, Fluffy," Eugene said. She cleared her throat and wrung her hands, unsure which words to use.

CC lifted a pastry to her lips without looking at Eugene. Before biting into it, she said, "I've always known your wolf, Eugene. I'd just never seen it. We're still friends."

Eugene let out a breath she'd been holding. "Good. Now, if you're feeling better, we should get back to work."

"Give her a little time, Eugene," said Cesar. "Her world has just changed."

"Oh, yeah, sorry. You rest." Eugene moved to the side of the couch, close to Cesar's chair. "I hacked his phone and traced his steps based on that-"

"Whose phone did you hack?" CC asked with a mouthful of pastry.

"Oh, ah, James Earl's. I told you I was doing it." Eugene bit her lip and looked at Cesar.

He only shrugged.

CC leaned back and sipped her coffee. Her gaze got lost on the ceiling and her nose twitched. "Tell me everything you've been up to."

"Well," Eugene started, but stopped. She looked again at Cesar, afraid CC would be angry for using CC's phone to hack James Earl's account. "Cesar asked me to do a little hacking. That's why I had your phone, remember? I told you. I used it to get into your account. Once there, it was easy to find James Earl's information. From there--"

CC raised her hand without looking at Eugene. "I don't need the details of how you did the hacking." CC took Eugene's hand in hers and squeezed. "James Earl always wanted to give me details, too. Took a while to break him of that. Results are what I'm interested in."

Eugene giggled. "Sure. Well, I traced his steps starting the day he left here. I saw him leave, if you remember. Anyway, he made a couple of stops. I supposed those were to drop off whatever papers he had to for his client, and then it got weird. He went to every place the police reported bodies of children found, ending up at the last body dump - the apartment complex where Flo lives."

Eugene turned to Cesar. "We should get Flo and her family out of that place. It's bad. The fear there isn't natural. I know it's a bad neighborhood and all, but-"

Cesar nodded. "Max is on it."

"That's what he told me," continued Eugene. She pictured Flo leaning against the railing with the little boy's hand in hers. "I like Flo, and those boys need her. You know they're not her kids? Their grandmother doesn't like Flo. Not sure she'd let Flo take the kids somewhere else, not that she's that concerned what happens to them."

CC stood. "Eugene, just how good a hacker are you?"

"Good enough. My brother and I had to hack into systems when we were kids. I told you, grew up in the middle of nowhere. Since mums and pops didn't like television or internet, we had to learn to build our own equipment and hack neighbors - such as they were out in the middle of nowhere. Phin's smarter at that kind of stuff than me, but I can-"

CC leaped off the couch, followed by Fluffy. "Come," she said, heading for the kitchen. "I've got all the passwords. We can get into everything now."

"Now?" asked Eugene. She tripped over Fluffy, who snapped at her. Cesar followed.

Fluffy curled up on her bed near the back door as CC dashed up the steps to James Earl's workroom. She clicked on the overhead lights. "I'm counting on you," CC said, pulling Eugene's arm toward James Earl's chair. "First, run the case numbers for the missing children's files I got from Renaldo and Frank the other day. Compare the autopsy reports with-"

"CC," interrupted Eugene. "This is James Earl's set up. I'm good, but he's better. There's no way I can use his systems."

"Listen to CC," Cesar said.

Eugene turned, not realizing he had followed them into the room.

He moved his head, following all the monitor and wires. "Impressive setup."

CC pushed Eugene into the chair. Before looking Eugene in the eye, she brushed away a tear before it fell out of her eye. She pulled a notebook out of her robe pocket and ripped a piece of paper from it. She started writing. "I've got all the passwords. He had me memorize them every time he changed them. He said I needed access to everything just in case he wasn't around."

Eugene took the piece of paper and lay it onto the table in front of her. Simple passwords, all related to CC - variations of her name, her birthday, their address, her body measurements. He made sure she had access to everything. "Okay," Eugene said. "I'll get to work, but it will take time."

Fluffy barked from the kitchen. Cesar said, "Tommy's here."

"Don't stop," CC said, patting Eugene's shoulder. "We need to know everything he was working on. He wouldn't have visited the dump sites unless he was looking for something specific."

"What are you thinking?" Cesar asked. "He could have been doing the same thing we've been doing, looking for any clue the police couldn't see."

CC shook her head. "No. Like me, he's been looking for patterns. He must have thought he found something." She looked down at her robe. "I can't see anyone right now. I'm going to take a shower and lay down. Eugene, shout when you find something."

Eugene watched CC turn and nearly fall. Her body shook, and her breaths came quick and short. Cesar picked her up again and took her down the stairs. The next thing she knew, Tommy stood beside her, and she heard CC's bedroom door close as sobs echoed through the floorboards.

*****

Luna lay on her bed, not sleeping. "Why can't I sleep?" she said to the ceiling. "Bugger! I'm worn out all afternoon, but the moment I get to bed, bam! Awake."

Sighing, she put her feet on the floor and reached for her running pants. Fumbling under her bed, she found her sports bra and favorite running shirt. The business card with CC's phone number sat on her bedside table. She picked it up and put it in her pocket, not sure why she was doing it.

In the bathroom, she washed her face. The puffiness under her eyes was gone. The whites of her eyes reflected the aliveness she felt. Smiling, she opened the bathroom door.

Marcus stood in front of her, arms crossed over his chest, and wearing his best, 'Oh no, you don't face.' "Where do you think you're going?" he asked.

Luna pushed past him. "For a run," she said, walking toward the stairs.

His arm reached out and grabbed her shoulder, forcing her to face him. "Luna, it's late. Please. Stay in."

Luna stopped herself from snarling. "You've never *asked* me not to do something."

Marcus shrugged. "You're not a little kid anymore. Mama's out with her old friends from the college. She won't know, but I worry about you."

Luna turned and walked down the stairs. As she twisted the deadbolts on the front door, she said. "I have to run, Marcus. I can't explain it. I just have to. I won't be more than thirty minutes. I promise." She jogged out the door without waiting for an answer, turned the corner on the sidewalk, and ran. She filled her lungs with the cool night air as clouds wove into a blanket beneath the stars.

*****

CC stopped walking down the stairs as she heard Cesar ask, "Is that what you've been holding back?"

"No," replied Tommy. "Mary said she was special. That's all I knew, but after meeting her, I saw she was special."

CC turned the corner into the kitchen and poured herself another mug of coffee. "But you're holding something back, Tommy. Stop playing around and talk to me."

Tommy sat in the overstuffed chair, nodding when CC entered the living room. "Guilt, perhaps," he said.

CC sat next to Fluffy on the couch as she leaned against Cesar. "Guilt?"

"I should have stopped him back in '85. I was here. I knew something was wrong, but I let my dislike of Max get in my way. If I hadn't, we wouldn't be in this situation."

"You don't know that," CC said.

"I do," Tomas said.

CC sipped her coffee then cradled its warmth in her hands as Fluffy leaped off the couch and curled into sleep on the floor between her and Tommy. "Tell us about '85."

"I intended just to pass through Austin, but I was hungry and bored, and Austin was full of young men and politicians full of life, so I stayed a while. Max was already here. He found me and informed me that I was not welcome. You know me well enough to know I ignored him. And them little Mary was murdered. I'd never seen Max so angry - swore I did it."

Tommy looked CC in the eye. "I've done a lot in my time I'm not proud of, but I never murdered a child."

CC nodded. "I believe you."

"Good," replied Tommy with a nod. "Max didn't, then. He pulled me off the street the night after the murder. We were at it claw and fang. I'd like to say I got the better of him, but a group of ne'er-do-wells stumbled into the alley where we were fighting. They stank of gin and beer but were sober enough to tell something was going on. Max got out before anyone could see him. It was safer for me to stay with them.

"I offered to buy a round of beer for old friends. They assumed I was an old friend, and we headed to a bar on Pecan Street. I kept them drinking long enough to get my fill and repair the scars from my fight with Max. One lad said he could get us into a brothel on the other end of Pecan. We headed out.

"We hadn't gone far when I caught sight of man across the street. Keep in mind, there were no electric lights along the streets back then. It was late. He was huge, more like a man-shaped shadow than a person, but the shape had yellow eyes. He watched us or maybe me. I don't know. I remember a stench that grew and grew. It made me afraid. It made one lad vomit. He almost fell into his own vomit, but I caught him. He vomited again, and it splattered on my pants. 'Jesus! Turn your head,' another said.

"When I looked up again, the shadow-man moved toward us. I wanted to run. I'd only been afraid like that one other time. But then a door opened. Piano music and laughter spilled out just ahead of us. 'Come on, friends,' I said. 'I see a place for us. Let me provide us with entertainment for the rest of the night.'

"They followed me in. A large man at the door scowled until I handed him a roll of bills. I told you I hadn't ever been afraid like that. I felt that way again the other night at the parking lot. It's the same killer."

Cesar leaned forward. "What did you do after that night?"

"Ran," said Tommy. "I didn't know what it was, and I didn't want to know. I think Max must have run into him, because he didn't chase me when I left town."

"We need to talk to him about it," said CC. She shivered as cool air slipped down her spine. Fluffy barked and ran to the door. "Seriously? Now?"

CC stood and followed Fluffy to the front door. As she put her hand on the knob, the chill on her spine turned to ice. She no longer saw the door. The dog park spread out before her. Someone was running through it, away from her. The runner fell, twisted, and turned her head. "Luna," gasped CC. She opened the door, and Fluffy charged outside and across the street. CC saw through her own eyes now. She was running toward Luna. A scream, and then a cry - pain, shock, anger followed, but not from Luna.

She opened the gate to the park. Cesar sat beside Luna, lifted to a seating position. Fluffy stood beside them, her hackles raised, growling, blood dripping from her mouth. CC fell to her knees, taking Luna's face in her hands forcing her to look into her eyes. "Luna, look at me. You're okay."

*****

According to her watch, she'd run two-and-a-half miles. She leaned against a fence and stretched her legs. The university stretched out ahead of her. Further down the road, the sounds of Sixth Street echoed through the buildings, calling her. "No," she said to herself. "I want water." She pulled the bottom edge of her shirt up, wiping away the sweat on her forehead, and turned to walk toward home, but she didn't want to go home. She wanted to run more, but she promised Marcus half an hour. She was late.

"At least mama's not home to worry," she muttered. As soon as she heard her own words, she laughed. When mama said she was going to a dinner party with old university friends, Luna was angry. "Silly being angry all the time. Why shouldn't mama go out and have some fun? It's what I want to do."

Smiling, she reached to her backside. "Forgot my phone." She slapped her buttocks. "Son of b! Marcus will say, 'I told you so'." She felt again and realized she'd put CC's card in her pocket. Pulling it out, she read the address and looked up at the next street sign. "Closer than home," she said, nodding her head. "Worth a shot." One more stretch of her hamstrings, and she turned right down the next street at a jog.

Jogging, allowing her mind to drift wherever her thoughts wanted to go, she didn't realize something was wrong until the darkness of the street made her miss her footing and stumble. Her left foot caught in a pot-hole and she fell forward. Realizing she was falling, she lifted her hands in front of her, catching her fall on the back bumper of a parked pickup truck but not before her nose banged into the top edge of the tailgate. She shook her head and straightened as stars flashed in front of her eyes. She put her hand to her nose as warm, sticky blood pooled into her fingers. Pain swam up the bridge of her nose and behind her eyes.

She sat on the curb between the pickup and a compact sedan and closed her eyes. Her fingers followed the contours of her nose up the bridge between her eyes. "Ow! I hope it's not broken," she muttered. "This sucks." A chill hit the back of her neck.

Above her, the streetlight glared down at her with darkness. All the streetlights were out. The houses did not have their porch lights on. Even the windows were dark. Her watch said twelve forty-five. Then she felt that familiar, disturbing prickle of hairs rising on her neck. Someone was watching her. She stood, leaning against the pickup for strength. No one was on the street. Not even a neighborhood cat walked down the street. The breeze picked up, chilling the sweat on her back. Somewhere in the breeze, a growl. A soft, moving, almost imperceptible growl flowed on the breeze, drowning the steady thud from Sixth Street.

Luna saw no one. She walked down the street looking for house numbers to see where to turn. She would go to CC's house and bang on the door until someone answered.

The growl moved closer. Luna looked behind her. Behind the pickup where she had messaged her nose, a pair of yellow eyes - the yellow eyes from her nightmares- stared back at her. She quickened her pace. Despite the darkness of the street, the yellow eyes glowed, moved closer to her, but now they rested in a darker shade of night, round like a head, a great round head, and the head moved faster than she walked.

Luna's chest ached. She kept her mouth open, unable to breathe through her nose, gulping in air as her walk became a jog and then a run. She turned left, knowing she was near CC's house. The dog park on her right sat empty but glowing in the radiant light of the city. On the other side of that was CC's house. Luna pushed through the gate and across the lawn.

She slipped on the grass, but she didn't fall. A stink rose around her despite the blood clogging her nose. It wasn't the dog poop she was expecting but a stink that choked her throat. The stink tasted like rotten water. The stink froze her lungs. She fell. Pushing her torso up from the grass, she twisted to see the yellow eyes wrapped in the shadows of a man leap over the fence into the park.

A man, but an enormous man, an oddly-shaped man. Was it a man? Two legs walked. They didn't run toward her. Two arms swung at the sides of the man shape. She closed her eyes, opening her mouth to scream. And then she heard a growl, not the corrosive growl from earlier, but a dog. A scream followed the next growl - so angry. The scream tore loud and coarse through her throat.

Luna opened her eyes. A massive white dog stood next to her, its fangs dripping blood down into fluffy, white fur. A man she didn't know sat behind her. His hands were cold, like stone. They didn't move from her arms. She turned to look at his face and shivered as eyes gleamed back at her just like the dog's eyes did now. The dog lifted its head and barked.

She had to run. She pushed away but warm hands grabbed her face, soft, gentle, but firm. CC sat close to her. They were her hands.

"Luna, look at me. You're okay," said CC. Her pale face suddenly the most beautiful face Luna had ever seen.

Luna had to laugh. She like she never laughed before. She laughed until the tears streamed down her face. "I was coming to see you."

*****

Eugene heard Fluffy's call. By the time she'd reached the bottom stair, her wolf had taken over. She ran to the front door, but Tommy stood in her way. "Hang on, Eugene. Danger's over."

Eugene growled. She smelled blood, she smelled the fear so close to her she could taste it, she smelled the stink of the creature they were hunting. Her hackles rose. She lowered her head, ready to charge Tommy.

Tommy's eyes widened. He lifted both his hands, palms to her. "Easy, Eugene. CC said to keep you here."

Eugene lifted her head, adjusting her ears to hear the barks and howls of the neighborhood dogs as the danger fled the area. Two sets of footsteps, two beating hearts moved toward the house. Fear, relief, anger wafted in, and Eugene sat down.

Tommy opened the door and Cesar entered leading Luna. CC followed.

"Couch," CC said to Cesar. "Tommy, there's a first aid kit in the hall bathroom upstairs. Would you get that for me?" CC stopped before following Cesar into the living room only long enough to look down at Eugene. "Thanks for not going after it. I need you here. Make sure Fluffy's okay, will you?"

Eugene barked once and walked to Fluffy, who trotted into the living room just ahead of them.

*****

Eugene helped Fluffy clean the blood off her fur and now they both sat in the doorway between the living room and the kitchen. There was something about the taste of the monster's blood that lingered on her tongue, between her teeth, in her throat, in her snout, and in her mind. It wasn't right, human but not human, familiar and strange, innocent and damned. Cesar leaned on the threshold near her, watching Luna stretched out on the couch. The heat of Luna's body radiated red, the smell of her fear eked out of her pores, and mingled with fear and anger burning, twisting, enveloping her. Eugene twisted her head and tuned her ears. Luna's heart beat as it should, her blood flowed as it should, whetting Eugene's appetite, but the fear and anger bubbled beneath the surface of her skin, ready to burst.

Eugene looked up at Cesar. He looked down at her, nodding.

"Do you three mind?" CC said from behind Eugene. Fluffy nudged Eugene forward, and dog and wolf moved to the coffee table. Each lay beneath it, looking up at Luna. Eugene looked at CC's face. It was always peachy-white beneath countless freckles, but tonight it glowed whiter than white in the bright light from the ceiling fan.

"Ow!" said Luna, jumping as CC placed an ice pack on Luna's nose, already turning dark as blood pooled under the surface of her skin.

"Best thing for now," CC said.

Eugene lifted her head. CC's voice held more anger than she'd ever heard from CC. She choked on her words, forcing the anger down.

"I know," Luna, rolling her eyes. "It's just... It's just I'm so stupid!"

CC's heart pounded against her chest, its echo resounding in

Eugene's ears. Her heat flamed redder than her hair. Her fist clenched and her eyes closed.

"Perhaps," said Cesar, still leaning against the far wall. "You should call your mother to come get you."

The mellowness of Cesar's voice covered the room like a warm blanket. The flames of CC's heat lowered. Even Luna eased back against the pillow behind her. Fluffy, however, issued a tiny whine. Eugene lay her head on Fluffy's back. *Vamp voice won't calm these two down.*

"Mama's not home. She's going to kill me for running late at night." Luna said.

"We'll call Marcus," CC said and picked up her phone from the coffee table. "Damn it! Eugene, where's my phone?"

Eugene lifted her head and barked once.

Cesar smiled, holding out his own phone. "Use mine. It'll save time."

"I'm not in the mood for smirks," CC said, looking down at Eugene.

Eugene put her head down on her paws. It was Fluffy's turn to lay her head on Eugene's back.

"Marcus is going to be so angry," said Luna. "And we were just starting to get along again."

Both Eugene and Fluffy lifted their heads to look at Luna.

"I promised to be home in half an hour," said Luna, her skin around her eyes tightening. She slapped her left thigh. "He's going say told you so when he finds out I was chased by our old monster."

Eugene barked and hit her head on the coffee table as she tried to stand, but the growl she heard didn't come from her or Fluffy or even Cesar, who remained leaning against the wall between the kitchen and living room. It came from CC.

"Luna," said CC between teeth clinched and a jaw so stiff Eugene was surprised CC could make any sound at all.

Fluffy pushed her head on Eugene's back and pushed her down.

CC stared down at Luna, her shoulders square to the prone girl and her feet glued to the floor. "You're too smart for this. You knew the monster was looking for you, but you went out alone anyway. You want to grow up, but you want to be treating like a kid. You can't have it both ways. So you got drunk and made an ass of yourself. It happens. You learn and move on, but tonight - you almost died. Don't think for one minute that thing chasing you didn't intend to rip you apart."

Luna's eyes narrowed. Her lips pressed together and curled up.

Before Luna could say anything, CC bent over her, not whispering, but speaking low, allowing the syllables of her words to resonate through the room. "It was the same monster that killed your little brother."

Luna's eyes turned to globes. Her breath quickened. She didn't look at anyone. "You, you," she hesitated, gasping to breathe. "You believe me." Eugene saw acceptance fall over Luna as her eyes widened and her lips quivered.

"It was the same monster," said CC, softening but keeping her eyes locked on Luna's face. "I've been hunting him since he returned to Austin. He wants you."

"I know," shouted Luna. Her body shook. She gasped to breathe. Tears fell from her face. "I didn't want to spend the day with mama at work. I was supposed to spend the day with daddy. We would have picked Tony up from school if I had, or I could have walked him home. Tony would be alive if I hadn't gone to work with mama."

Fluffy nudged Eugene to back away from their couch. They turned, keeping their heads low, and walked toward the kitchen. Cesar followed them.

As she crossed the threshold, Eugene looked back. CC sat next to Luna, who lay cradled in her arms crying. Luna kept repeating, "It was my fault."

It wasn't, but the responsibility for what might have been poured out of Luna with each tear, and Eugene knew just how Luna felt.

*****

Her body shuddered as she felt his hands poking and squeezing every part of her. Nothing was left untouched. It was so dark; she couldn't see whose hands pinched and pulled. She didn't want to see him. His breath crawled on her skin, and she thought of death. She remembered the time the squirrel died in the attic when they were on vacation. They came home to a house reeking and making everyone puke. She shivered as much from the smell as from the concrete oozing cold through her jeans onto her butt. Her hands wouldn't move. She wasn't sure she could feel her fingers.

The hands stopped probing. *He knows I'm awake.* A scream hung in her throat. She wanted to kick away at the person near her, but she had to stay still. A shudder rippled through her as his breath, cold and putrid, breathed into her ear.

"Where's the other?" his voice hissed.

"Qué?" she answered.

His icy hand slapped her face, sending her toppling off her bottom. She tried to move her arm before it hit the concrete, but it didn't move. *Hands tied. That's why I can't feel my fingers. What about my legs?* She scrambled her legs to right herself, but his steel grip pushed her legs down and the touch of something hard wrapped around her ankles tightening, squeezing until she couldn't move her feet.

"Donde está el otro?" he asked again.

"What other?" she replied. *Damn. He speaks Spanish.*

A fist pounded into the right side of her face.

"Where's the other?" The hissing didn't change. It was calm, quiet, direct, despite the fierceness of the punch.

"I don't know what -" she attempted to answer, but the fist crashed into the right side of her face. She heard a crack, and stars filled her vision.

"Where's the other?"

She whimpered, unable to answer from the pain shooting through her face.

A boot slammed into her stomach. She gulped and spit as she struggled to take in a breath.

"Where's the -" the voice stopped.

Sylvia listened, waiting for the rest of the question and another blow. Then she heard the small voice.

"Mommy," the voice, so small, hopeless, wanting, drifted into her ear.

The boot kicked her stomach again, slamming her back against a rough wooden surface. "You'll tell me," the voice said.

She lay still, listening as heavy feet walked away from her. Tears rolled down her face. Fear and pain froze her. Again, she heard the tiny voice, and she thought of Matias.

The tiny voice whimpered, "I don't know. Please, I'll be good," it said.

The sound of skin slapping skin echoed through the room. Sylvia vomited.

"Where's the other?" The monster's voice asked.

The tiny voice begged. "I don't know."

"No," she spat out, but not loud enough to be heard over the screaming of the tiny voice or the echoing flesh hitting flesh, punching, or kicking. "Matias, please be at home." More tears fell, mixing with blood and vomit as the cold from her own urine seeped into her bones.

6

Moons wane, Moons wax.
Shadows shift.
The wicked thrive on cause
Until voices fail and hearts stop.
Dance with the beat of Death and the Joy of Being.
Let the Dance overflow its banks.
Rejoice with the dancers' dreams.
I'm Mary Midnight online and in your mind.
Souls lost are souls that do not dance.
Offer your hand and dance.

Luna never liked hot tea but sitting on CC's couch with her feet on the coffee table, a cold pack on her nose, a blanket around her shoulders, and CC sitting next to her, she decided it wasn't that bad. It didn't punch her in the stomach like coffee, which she still didn't like, and it didn't need a ton of sugar or cream to make it palatable. No. Hot tea, she decided, was good for sitting, sipping, and thinking. She wrapped her hands around the large mug. They stopped shaking after she ate a sandwich and stared into the clear muddy liquid, trying to breathe in the steam and failing.

CC said nothing. She sat next to Luna, drinking coffee and petting Fluffy. The large white dog sat next to CC, resting her head on CC's lap. Luna wasn't sure what to think about the man sitting in the chair with them. He said nothing, and he helped her into the house, but he had scary eyes.

"I'm a lot of trouble for you," said Luna, lifting her gaze from her cup but still not looking at CC. "I'm sorry."

"Yes, you are," said CC after a long sigh. "But that doesn't mean you're a bother."

"No?" asked Luna. "I'm a bother to just about everybody I know. I can't seem to do anything right anymore."

CC laughed. The tinkling laugh released tension on Luna's shoulders. She took her first, good, deep breath since her run.

"It's not funny," Luna murmured.

CC lay a cool hand on Luna's arm. "Luna," she said. "You're seventeen. You're not supposed to know where you belong yet. When I was seventeen, I had the world at my feet. But as soon as I thought I was where I wanted to be, my life came crashing down." CC halted, looked into Fluffy's face. Fluffy licked CC's fingers. "When my world shattered, it whirled me through a blender and dumped my in the middle of 'where the hell am I.' I didn't think I'd ever breathe, eat, sleep, or even walk again like a real person. The same thing's happening to you now. You're forgiven for being very human."

"What happened to you?" asked Luna.

CC eased back, letting the cushions swallow her. "I was an FBI agent. A monster killed my partner, and no one believed me."

Luna scrunched her face. Before she could ask what kind of monster, CC continued. "My mistake was believing there was only one answer to questions. Things were right or wrong, good or bad. No compromise, nothing in between. Once I figured out that right doesn't always mean good, and good doesn't always mean right, I learned to live again. I walked under the sun and moon and discovered a whole world around me I never knew existed. A lot of it is good, and a lot of it is bad."

Luna scratched her chin. CC didn't look old, but she sounded old. She wasn't sure a talk about right or wrong had anything to do with the creature that chased her only an hour ago. "CC," she said. "Are you going to tell me what was chasing me? How do you know it's the same thing that killed Tony?"

Luna startled when the man with strange eyes cleared his throat. "My name's Cesar," he said in answer to the question on her face. His voice was low, sweet, mellow. There was something dreaming about his voice that reminded her of something, but she couldn't remember what.

"Do I know you?" asked Luna.

CC answered. "He owns The Phantom's Menace. You might have seen him there. He's one of those guys that shows up when you're not looking for him."

Cesar leaned his head forward just enough for Luna to see a smile on his lips. Maybe a snark. His eyes were dark but reflected the light of the floor lamp. Deep, dark eyes glowed for a moment, and then he leaned back. "Just ignore me," he said. A lovely voice, deep, euphonious, rhythmic, without trying. The voice reminded her of Max's; not the same, yet surprisingly familiar if haunting can be familiar.

CC nodded to him and turned back to Luna. "He's helping me find the thing that chased you tonight."

"There's no such thing as monsters. It was just a man," Luna said. She set her mug on the coffee table before leaning back and letting the cushions of the couch wrap around her. "Shouldn't I call the police?"

"Can you describe the man?" asked Cesar.

Cesar had such a marvelous voice. Luna yawned. "Not really," she said. "But I've seen him looking at me before tonight."

CC tilted her head to look into Luna's face. "Before tonight? Where?"

"How do you know it was the same man?" asked Cesar.

Lune turned her head away from CC to find Cesar standing next to her. She didn't notice him leaving the chair to stand next to her. A chill, like an ice cube, ran up her spine.

CC pulled a pillow from a basket next to the couch and placed it next to Luna. "Take you time, Luna," she said. "Try to remember every time you've seen this creature. Think back to when Tony disappeared. Did you see them then?"

"Mama said it was just the police keeping an eye on the house.

Daddy said it was damn reporters, but I knew someone was on the roof next door looking into my window. Marcus saw him, too." Luna's eyes closed. All her dolls and stuffed animals were in the bed with her. She'd tucked them in with her because they were afraid. Marcus sat on the bed with her, cuddling her from the top of the blankets. She wouldn't come out from her safe place, even when he turned the lights on. He checked the windows, made sure her Bo Peep lamp glowed, and he stayed with her all night. They walked through the house every night after that, checking the locks on every window and door.

"I'd forgotten about the yellow eyes until I saw them at the cafe," Luna mumbled. She wanted to tell them how much she appreciated them talking to her. "But then I saw them again when we took Flo home. I got scared, like when I was a kid. It was just my imagination."

"Sleep, Luna," said Cesar with his beautiful voice, like a love song drifting on the breeze and tickling her ear. All she could think of was sleep. She sunk further into the cushions and tipped her head into the so soft pillow at her side.

Before she lost herself, she heard CC ask, "Eugene? Tommy?"

"Tommy headed out to the house as soon as we saw what was happening. Eugene just left to check on him. She'll bring them here." Cesar's voice answered. She wanted to hear him speak more, but at last, she gave up, and dove into dreams where there were no monsters with yellow eyes or white dogs dripping blood from their fangs.

*****

Eugene sat between two cars on the curb watching Tommy, who sat in the tree in the center of the yard. His eyes remained fixed on the house, but his mouth twitched and his eyebrows arched up then down, then crunched together. Otherwise, his stillness was complete, so complete she wasn't surprised that when she blinked, he was gone.

"What?" he asked from behind her. He stood with his hands on his hips. "I can't be trusted even to keep a kid safe?"

Eugene sat up and stared at his face. His voice forced an angry whisper, but his top lip curved under even as his bottom lip puffed out and his eyebrows arched down. She changed back to human, remaining sitting between the two cars. "Chill, will you?" she whispered

"Is Luna all right?" asked Tommy.

"She's fine," said Eugene, and looked back to the house before biting her lip and sighing. "No one's checking on you."

Tommy shrugged his shoulders, forcing a half smile. "Sorry."

"Cesar says you should bring Marcus to the house."

Tommy sat on the ground next to Eugene. "The creature isn't after just Luna."

Eugene shrugged. "Luna said both of them saw and knew about the thing after it took their brother. It could want Marcus, too. In a way-"

Tommy lifted his hand, stopping Eugene. "Listen," he said.

Eugene turned her ears to the house. Marcus opened the front door and walked to the front gate. Before Eugene could scrunch herself closer to the ground, a cold hand touched her shoulder. It sent a shiver down her back. The clear night grew dark around her as Tommy blew a shhhhh into her ear. Just like the night she hunted with Max, the shadows of the cars they sat between slid around them, engulfing them. She looked up as the streetlights dimmed, as though she wore dark glasses. Even the clouds floating in on the breeze darkened.

Marcus looked up and down the street, looked at his phone, shook his head, and went back inside. As the door closed, the surrounding shadows drifted away, returning to their rightful places.

"That is so cool," Eugene whispered. "Max did that the other night. I always wondered how you guys moved around without being noticed."

Tommy's chest puffed out. "Max lacks finesse. It's a subtle art."

"Can I learn to do that?" Eugene grinned.

Tommy scratched his chin. "I don't know. We'll have to try it sometime. You'd find it useful when you need to talk at night and don't want anyone to see all your tattoos." He stood and turned his pink lips up, exposing his perfect white teeth. "They are gorgeous. Wish I had more time to exam them."

Eugene harrumphed as a wave of heat flushed her face. "Business," she growled and changed back to wolf.

Tommy nodded and wiped the dirt from his pants. "I'll get Marcus to the house. Take point?"

Tommy called out before she left him. "Eugene, I think James Earl was on to something. There's got to be something in his files."

Eugene barked once, nodding, before circling the house and then the block. By the time she returned to the street, Marcus followed Tommy out of the house.

*****

Sylvia opened her left eye. The smallest ray of sunlight blinded her. As her eye adjusted from darkness to brightness, she followed the light up. It beamed from between boards high above somewhere on walls too tall to be a house. Her body shivered as sweat beaded on her back and head slid down to the concrete floor covered with dirt and dust. She coughed. Rust and spit filled her mouth. Her chest contracted, resisting the pain of expansion that came with breath. She wanted to swear, but nothing came out of her parched throat.

She pushed her head toward the golden light, only to freeze with pain. Her hands and feet felt nothing. "Hog-tied." She thought of watching the old westerns with Papa. He'd explained what hog-tied meant. "Oh, Mama," she said. "It's daylight. Mama's looking for me." Her left eye twitched, wanting to fill with tears, but her mouth forbade tears. Her mouth ached for water. She'd cried enough last night, and it didn't stop the man from beating the small voice until it didn't cry anymore, and it didn't stop the man from pounding his fist into her face again and again and again and asking that same question again and again and again.

With a shudder, she clenched her jaw. It ached, and she was sure more than one tooth was missing. "Think, you stupid cow!" Sylvia said to herself. "Don't feel sorry for yourself. Don't wait for rescue. That's in the movies. Mama says there are no handsome princes. Think for yourself."

She lay on her right side, so cold she felt nothing on that side of her. The more she focused on the light above her, the more her left eye hurt. The sounds from last night had faded. Somewhere behind her, she heard scratching - faint - little claws. "Rats!" she said, and a shock of fear raced through her. She caught her breath and laughed. "That's using your head. You don't like rats but know what the noise is. They won't beat me."

Despite the pain of moving and the numbness of her right side, she twisted her head and forced her body to follow. "I hit something wood last night. Post? Wall? It's something to hold me up." She pushed her hips to push her legs. The top of her head hit wood. Sylvia smiled. Still pushing her body, she tried to sit, but her bindings prevented her. "Shit!" pushed from her lips. "No." She shook her head. "Mama says don't swear. Think. Don't swear."

She couldn't sit, but she could roll her body almost onto her back. Her left eye focused above her. Great blocks of shadows shifted into crates stacked so high she couldn't see the top. Above the crates, more shadows turned into beams and boarded windows. Sylvia smiled. "That's where the light is. Daylight is coming in the cracks of windows." A moan passed from her lips as she realized, "They're so high up."

She rolled to her stomach and inch-wormed her way to the wall of crates behind her. As she studied the images filtering into her left eye, she realized the blocky shadows were crates. They surrounded her. As she stopped to catch her breath, closed her left eye. Nothing but darkness filtered in from her right eye. She took a deep breath. "Worry about that later."

Stacked crates surrounded her, but as slivers of light from above traveled through clouds of dust and spider webs, gaps between crates emerged. She pushed forward. Something white shone in a spot of light. Twisting her head to the right, her left eye focused on it. Two teeth lay surrounded by red and black spots lay on the floor. Sylvia turned her head away to inch forward, even as her tongue glided across her own teeth. More than two of her teeth were missing.

A high-pitched squeal echoed through the building, followed by the softest of whimpers, "Mommy!"

Sylvia arched her body to twist in the voice's direction. Pain shot through her like knives across glass. She didn't know where the sound came from, but she had to find it. Each push and pull sent rivers of pain roaring through her. Ignoring the pain, she twisted on her right arm until her left eye found a three-inch gap between crates on the floor. A glimmer of sunlight and spiders worked their way toward her, and then a shadow from the other side of the gab moved. She stopped to cough and spit out more blood from her mouth, but at last she forced her left eye close to the opening. Two pink hands, bound like her own, pulsed and squirmed on the other side.

"Hello?" Sylvia whispered as loud as she dared. "Hello? I heard you scream at the rats. My name is Sylvia. What's yours?"

The whimpering silenced, but sobs continued.

"I think he's gone," Sylvia said. "At least I haven't heard him for a while. He must have gone away."

The voice, cracking and slurred, said, "The scary man is gone?"

"Yes. How long have you been here?"

"I don't know. I woke up here."

Sylvia grimaced. Last night, the same question over and over that she couldn't answer caused her more pain than she ever thought she could stand. And then there was that tiny voice screaming until it screamed no more. This voice, so very young and afraid, wasn't the voice she'd heard last night.

Sylvia slowed her breath. "Think," she whispered to herself. "How many of us are here?"

Taking in a slow breath, Sylvia said, "My name's Sylvia. What's yours?"

"Sharon."

"Hi Sharon. We have to be brave, Sharon. Someone will come to help us. Have you seen any other boys or girls?"

"No. I don't like it here."

A tear filled Sharon's left eye. She hoped Matias wasn't in the warehouse. It wasn't his voice screaming last night. *Was it?*

"Can we go home now? I want my mommy." Sharon's voice ached inside Sylvia's ears. Sylvia wanted to reach out and wrap the little girl in her arms but she couldn't move. "Go to sleep, Sharon. I'll find us a way out of here."

"You won't leave me here? I'll be good. I promise! I'll be good."

"It's okay, Sharon. We're both good girls, and we're going to go home soon."

That she had to endure this was bad enough, but for Sharon and whoever she heard screaming - until he didn't scream anymore-. Sylvia shivered with a cold she never knew one person could feel.

*****

Sharon's soft sobs trailed off to a faint snore.

"Think, Sylvia," Sylvia whispered to herself. "What does Mama do when she's stuck. Think. Think. Think."

With a deep inhale, she forced her bound and sore body to roll over. Her breath caught in her lungs, sending knives and stones through her ribs and spine. Concrete stones and dirt bit through her t-shirt and bra. She clinched her mouth, closed her eyes, and forced herself onto her right side.

The pain from moving was almost as bad as the pain from the torture, but she did it. Blood rushed through her, allowing a momentary heat wave. She allowed her head to drop to the floor. Pain shot through the right side of her face, but the concrete cooled the sweat on her forehead.

"There," she said. "I can do whatever I want. I just need a moment's rest."

She closed her left eye but shook her head and opened it. "No. No sleep. No time. I have to get Sharon out of here."

A rat dashed across the top of the crates separating her and Sharon. She laughed. "In the cartoon, I'd find peanut butter for the ties and the rats would chew us free." She stopped laughing as each chuckle hurt her lungs and side 'til she coughed. Even in the telltale light, she noticed the dark spots hitting the ground as they flew from her mouth.

She gritted her teeth. "I will not die here. Where there're wooden crates, there are splinters, nails, tools. I need a tool."

Sylvia took in as much breath as she could. "My arms aren't numb. I'll find - Ouch!"

Something scratched the flesh of her upper arm. She took another breath and inch-wormed her body until she realized the sharp pain moved up her arm. She inch-wormed her body in the opposite direction. The sharp object scratched her elbow and followed her arm till it caught, got stuck.

"No," she cried. She tugged her arms again. A pop, like bursting a zipper. She tugged again. Another pop. Her breath quickened. "Slow down." Another tug, another pop. "Patience." Again, she tugged, again the popping until she heard her watch drop from her wrist onto the floor.

A smile broke across her face. "It's an old man," she said. "Another old fart who knows shit about tech."

Slowing her breath, she pushed herself onto her stomach. Each stone that bit into her flesh gave her courage. She inch-wormed to twist and slide until her watch was in sight. "Oh, Mama. I'm so glad you didn't spend the money on a good watch band. I'm never going to complain again."

She moved her face as close to the watch face as she could. She tried to touch it with her nose, but blood squeezed out of her nostrils and the screen did not turn on. "Ggr," she said, and tried to reach the screen with her chin. Instead of hitting the screen, it fell onto the concrete, shooting pain through her face and down her neck.

She kept her head down. The watch vibrated. Lifting her head, she stared at the watch. The screen glowed.

"Hey, Siri," she called out. Her voice cracked. The parchment in the back of her throat wanted out. She called again.

"How can I help you?"

Sylvia laughed. "Call 9-1-1."

"Dialing 9-1-1."

"9-1-1 operator. What service do you need?"

"Help us!" Sylvia yelled as loud as she could. It forced her to cough, but she yelled again. "Help us! I don't know when he'll be back."

She yelled loud enough to walk Sharon, who screamed.

"It's going to be okay, Sharon!" Sylvia yelled to Sharon. "Please help us. I don't know where we are. We're tied up. I'm Sylvia Caton. Sharon is here, too. Please help us."

"Stay on the line, Sylvia. I'm dispatching the police to you now. We've been looking for you. Do you see or hear your attacker?"

"No. It's so quiet. Please hurry. I don't know when he'll be back."

"Help is on the way, Sylvia. I want you to stay on the phone with me. You don't have to talk, just don't hang up. I'm reading your GPS coordinates now."

Sylvia didn't know how long it took before she heard sirens. They grew louder and louder. They were so loud; she was sure they were outside the building when they stopped. Shouts and barks filled the silence of the building.

Sylvia's body shook. Tears once again filled her left eye. "Yell, Sharon. Yell, so they hear us."

Both girls yelled. A shaft of sunlight blinded Sylvia, and a figure ran toward her. She screamed till her lungs burst.

"Over here," she heard a woman yell. "Paramedics!"

A man's voice yelled, "Paramedics! I've got another one."

Sylvia allowed the pain and darkness to wash over her. Before she lost consciousness she heard, "Over here." This voice was quiet. "Call the coroner."

Before her eye closed, she saw a face looking down on her. "The handsome prince is a girl," she giggled.

*****

"Marcus?" Luna asked as wakefulness forced itself on her. She couldn't breathe through her nose and her voice scratched, but then familiar hands took her by the shoulders before arms wrapped around her. She hugged back with renewed strength. The familiar heat of Marcus warmed her, and even though the memories of being chased flooded her mind, the fear dwindled to a flutter.

As she pulled away from Marcus and opened her eyes, the dim light from the kitchen was enough to see tears running down Marcus' face.

"I'm so sorry, Marcus," she said. "I didn't mean to run so long. Really, I just meant to run for thirty minutes. I don't know-"

Marcus smiled at her and put his forehead to hers, bumping her nose.

"Ow!" she exclaimed before she could stop herself.

"Sorry," Marcus said, pushing away.

Luna pulled him back to her. "No, it's okay. I'm such a pain."

Marcus twisted to sit next to her. "Yes, you are." He put his arm around her and she leaned into him. "But little sisters are supposed to be a pain."

Luna sighed, enjoying leaning into her big brother, just like she did when she was scared of the monster outside the window. Remembering the monster, she broke their comfortable silence. "He's back, Marcus. The monster has come for me."

"I know," Marcus answered.

Luna listened to his heartbeat, thudding steady and strong in her ear. Even the faint rasping in his lungs she sometimes heard continued slow and steady. She allowed his strong, steady presence to flow over her, taking strength in his strength.

When CC's voice spoke, she jumped. "How long have you known, Marcus?"

"A couple of weeks, I suppose. No. I suspected for a while. It was just a feeling until I saw the news about that girl killed in her own yard while her parents were out of town. Her heart was ripped out. That convinced me."

"That's why you've been so pissed off at me?" Luna asked, pushing away from Marcus to look him in the eyes. "You've been worried about me."

"Yea, I didn't want to tell you I was afraid of our childhood monster. But be real, you've been a royal pain in the toosh lately."

"I have not!" Luna tried to shout, but instead pulled closer to Marcus and hugged him tighter.

Marcus returned her hug before continuing. "And then, there's you Ms. Carson."

Luna sat up as a lamp was turned on next to CC, sitting in the chair next to the couch. CC nodded and gave them a small smile, even as Cesar returned to a dark corner of the room.

"I don't doubt Chef Max wants to make the place work, but no smart businessman, and he is a smart businessman, would spend so much money to buy into our little business and keep Mama in control. There had to be something else. Then Tommy, Eugene, even you. You all hang around the place too much."

"Told you he was too smart to fool," CC said, turning her head toward Cesar.

Luna twisted her head to see not only Cesar standing in the far corner. He nodded his head but said nothing.

Marcus continued. "When Luna showed me your business card and told me of your job offer, that cinched it. You had to be looking for the monster that killed Tony. I have to admit, I didn't expect to see you talking to Uncle Frank."

"Frank's a good guy," said CC. "He's been hunting for this monster, too."

Marcus took in a deep breath and looked into Luna's face. "We've given him a hard time. I think it's time we make nice."

Luna nodded, "He'd like that. So would Aunt Jasmine."

Luna straightened but kept hold of Marcus' hand as CC cleared her throat. Her smile faded as her eyes focused on both Marcus and Luna. Even in the dim light, fine lines tightened around CC's eyes and mouth.

"Since I don't have to convince you of the danger," said CC. "We need to decide how to proceed. What does your mother know?"

"She believes," said Marcus after checking into Luna's face, "that we created a monster, it resided in our brains as a direct result of the trauma over our brother being killed. She and daddy did everything they could to make us feel safe: new alarm system, safety lights around the house, keeping us within their sights all the time. Eventually, I think even I believed the yellow eyes I saw outside our windows was our imagination. Just before Tony's body was found, the eyes disappeared."

"I always believed in the monster," said Luna. She shivered with cold, remembering the eyes. "But maybe I also decided it was imagination."

"Now you know it was real," said CC. "You'll need to convince her it was real."

From the corner of the room, Cesar cleared his throat.

"But later," CC said, nodding her head. "For now, I need the two of you to work together to both stay safe and keep your mother safe."

"What!" exclaimed Luna, pushing herself up to sitting.

At the same time, Marcus's body shook. "You think it'll go after her?"

"Not directly," said CC. "Take a breath. Each of you knows this thing is dangerous. As far as we know, he hasn't gone after any parents. It's you it wants."

CC leaned forward, squinted at each of them, and finally sat back. "I'm not sure which of you he really wants."

"But why?" asked Marcus. "Why would he want to kill either of us? Wasn't killing our brother enough? He almost tore our family apart."

Fluffy barked once and entered the room. CC looked up at the small window on the far wall. "Sunrise already," she said. "Won't your mom miss you when she sees you're not in bed?"

"On no," moaned Luna. "We should call mama."

"Left her note," said Marcus. "Tommy thought about it. I was so worried about you, I didn't. Told her you fell and cracked your nose and were at a clinic getting it checked."

"Good," CC said, standing. "If you have to lie, always put some truth in it. You probably should get it checked, Luna. Don't think it's broken, but it wouldn't hurt."

"Oh," mumbled Luna. "I hate going to the doctor."

*****

"Eugene?" asked the voice on the phone. "I need to talk to CC."

"Dead asleep, man," said Eugene. She recognized Renaldo's voice but enjoyed listening to him get frustrated. It was kind of sexy. Bean pushed his snout under Eugene's other hand, demanding to be petted. "It was a long night."

The nameless voice cleared its throat. "Look. I need to talk to CC. Tell her Renaldo Sanchez is on the line."

"No can do, Renaldo. No way I'm going up there to wake her up. That's why I've got her phone."

"Eugene!" CC's voice echoed across the hall from CC's bedroom. Fluffy barked, Bean answered. Eugene cringed.

"Great! You woke her up." Eugene leaped out of bed, cradling Bean under her arm. She opened the door to find CC reaching for the doorknob. "It's your cop friend, Renaldo."

CC snatched the phone. "We're going to talk about taking my phone," CC grumbled. "Renaldo. What's up?"

Eugene stood at the door petting Bean, watching CC. Even her freckles were pale in the morning light, streaming in from the small window at the end of the hall. Her voice grated like a lion's roar, and fluffy, pink lids surrounded her eyes.

"And you're sure it's our guy?" CC asked.

Eugene bent her bottom lip and stared at Bean. "Mums is going to kill me, Bean. How many times has she told me about not listening in on other people's conversations?" She turned her back on CC but remained in the doorway, tilting her head until she could hear Renaldo's voice.

"It's got to be our guy," Renaldo said. "The older sister went out looking for the brother just before sunset. Neighbors heard shouting in the little park a few blocks away. I think the younger brother knows something but is too afraid to talk about it."

"Does Frank know you're talking to me?" Asked CC.

"He says you're good with kids," Renaldo answered. "I can be there in ten."

Eugene cringed as CC put her hand on her shoulder and turned her around. "I need an hour. Sorry, but like Eugene said, we had a hell of a night."

Eugene didn't hear Renaldo's response. She pulled Bean up on her arm so he could reach his snout to her chin to lick.

"See you then," CC said, ending the call.

Eugene studied the floor, but when CC spoke, the lion was gone from her voice. A mellow, lonely voice said, "Thanks for trying to take care of me, Eugene, but I'm not stopping until we kill this monster."

Eugene looked up. The soft lines around CC's eyes and mouth disappeared as her lips, such a pale pink they almost disappeared, lifted and her eyes inward. "Take Bean and Fluffy out, will you? I need to shower and put myself together."

"CC," said Eugene. "Don't you think you should-"

"Not now, Eugene," CC said and went into her bedroom. Before the door closed, she added, "Don't skip class."

*****

Bean hobbled behind Fluffy in the shade of the carport between CC's house and the accountant's house. Eugene sat on the door stoop, watching them. A small terrier dashed out of the accountant's house. Bean barked.

"Hey," she grumbled, and the little dog came up to her and sniffed her toes once, then trotted beside the stoop to sniff the pieces of broken saucer. Eugene reached down to pick them up.

"Sorry if she's bothering you," came a familiar voice.

Eugene looked up to see Jane, the accountant, next door. This was the first time Eugene saw her close enough to examine.

Jane was a tall, thin woman with brown hair splattered with gray, wound tight in a bun on top of her head. Her brown eyes, narrow and long, rested on a thin face with a nose that pointed to a bulb. Her makeup was as neat and perfect as her hair and her brown slacks and white blouse.

"She's not bothering me," Eugene said. She felt her shoulders relax and a smile form on her face.

"I haven't seen the chihuahua before. Is it yours?" Jane asked, squatting down and holding out her hand. Fluffy walked up, sniffing her hand. Bean followed.

Eugene cringed. "In a way. At least I'm taking care of him for a while. It's a long story. His name's Bean."

"Like a coffee bean," laughed Jane, as Bean licked her fingers.

"You're right," said Eugene, nodding as she threw the broken dish into the trash. "I hadn't thought of that, but he is the color of a coffee bean, isn't he? I like that. He's a spunky little guy, despite the cast."

"Poor thing," said Jane, standing. "Oh, is James Earl here? I may have another client for him."

Eugene's breath caught in her throat. She took her time fastening the lid on the trash can. "No," she said. She looked at the house and heard the CC's hair dryer. "Look," she said, and turned to face Jane.

At that moment, a woman about Eugene's age opened the back door of Jane's house and yelled. "You have a call, Jane. Sorry. He sounds panicky."

"On my way," Jane called. "Gotta go. Nice to meet you and Bean."

"Names Eugene."

Jane called for Myrtle, who dashed to follow, and they disappeared into her house.

Bean barked and Eugene picked her up. Fluffy scratched at the door, and Eugene heard a car park in front of the house and two men getting out. She smelled fresh coffee, too. She reached for the door but stopped. CC was walking down the stairs.

"What do I tell people?" she asked Fluffy, who sat at Eugene's feet looking into her face.

Eugene heard Renaldo's voice and the voice of an older man exchange greetings with CC.

"Eugene," shouted CC from the front door. "I'll be back when I'm back. If anyone asks, you know where I am."

Eugene pulled her phone out of her pocket and ordered a ride. Next, she sent a text to Cesar. He took the kids to the local twenty-four-hour clinic. "CC with cops, interviewing family. Will follow."

Setting Bean in his new basket, she waited for her ride. She knew where CC was going. She hoped she had enough money on her card to pay for it.

*****

Mrs. Catan's shoulders shook. Fresh tears ran down her cheeks.

Mr. Catan put his arm around her. "We've been over this a hundred times with the other officers."

"It's okay, Saul," Mrs. Catan said, patting a hand on her husband's knee.

Frank fixed his eyes on Mr. Catan. "You'd be surprised what we can learn hearing a story again. Little things come to you that don't seem important in one telling but seem of use in another." CC admired how Frank allowed his slow drawl to play out as he lowered the volume of his voice. "It's these little things that may give us what we need to find your daughter."

CC turned her attention to Mrs. Catan. "Sylvia was sitting on the curb with her friend?"

"Nikki," Mr. Catan added.

"Yes," Mrs. Catan said. "The boys were playing football in the street. She likes one of the boys. You know how girls are at that age."

CC smiled. "I remember being fifteen."

Mr. Catan's voice jumped in. "She's never given us reason to worry. She's always responsible and courteous."

"She sounds like she is," said CC.

CC tugged on Renaldo's jacket and nodded her head toward Matias. He sat on the far edge of the sofa. His feet hung over the edge of the cushion, swinging in the air. Matias said nothing and looked at no one.

Wide brown eyes surrounded by dark rings stared far away. Dirty knees didn't hide a large scab forming on his right knee.

Renaldo closed his notebook. "Matias," Renaldo said. "Why don't we go out to the porch and get some air?"

CC sat up. "Is that okay with you, Mr. and Mrs. Catan?"

"Of course," Mrs. Catan said as she wiped the tear off her face with another tissue.

"I should have thought-" said Mr. Catan.

Matias slid off the couch and followed Renaldo outside. They sat on the porch swing. CC followed them to the porch and stood near the door behind them.

"I'm Detective Sanchez but call me Renaldo. Your parents call you Matias. Is that what your friends call you?"

"Yes," Matias answered, not looking at Renaldo.

Renaldo guided the swing back and forth, allowing the cool afternoon to still around them. CC leaned against the house, listening. If Matias knew anything, he'd tell Renaldo. Down the street, a small SUV parallel parked. Frank reviewed what the Catans knew. The waiting paid off.

"Sometimes my sister calls me brat."

Renaldo's face relaxed, and a smile lifted his face. "My sisters called me worse names than that."

"Are they mean to you?"

"All the time, but they also take care of me when I get in trouble."

Matias turned his face to look up at Renaldo.

CC held her breath.

Renaldo kept his gaze in front of them. "I remember one time, after my mom found a snake in my room. I told her I found him and made him my pet. She was very unhappy with me. Grounded for two weeks. My sisters would sneak into my room and bring me dessert. I wasn't supposed to have dessert. That was part of my grounding."

Matias leaned back. "Sylvia's always yelling at me to wash my face and stay close to home."

"Sisters," Renaldo allowed a little laugh to spill out. "Such a pain, aren't they?"

Matias grew quiet, and then, almost as quiet as the wind blowing over them, a sob eked out of his tiny mouth. Renaldo waited, keeping his head forward, not seeing the tears spilling down Matias's cheeks.

"I told her I was going to Charly's, but I didn't. I lied, and that's why she's gone. It's all my fault." Matias' sorrow spilled out.

Renaldo put his hand on Matias's shoulders. CC watched Matias' tiny body shake as more sobs spilled.

"Me and Charly went to the store to get candy. We're not allowed to go to the store by ourselves. So, I told Sylvia I was going to Charlie's house and Charlie told his mom he was coming here. If Sylvia doesn't come back, momma and papa will hate me. I know they will. They won't want to be with a liar." Matias leaned into Renaldo.

"They will not send you away, Matias. They love you too much. It's not your fault Sylvia is missing."

"She wouldn't have gone through the park if she had known we went to the store."

CC's head jerked up. Someone got out of the back of the SUV, but it didn't drive away. Renaldo turned his head just enough to catch CC's eyes. Renaldo took in a long breath. "How do you know Sylvia went through the park?"

Matias pushed himself away from Renaldo. His head hung low as his back continued to shake. "Me and Charlie were on our way back when I heard Sylvia calling me. We went to our fort in the trees to hide the candy. It was almost dark, and I knew I was in trouble, so I didn't answer. But then she stopped calling. We heard someone running near us, so we ran down the street. That's when I fell and scraped my knee. I fell right in front of a car. The woman was crying and screaming when she got out of the car. I think she was mad that I fell in front of her, so me and Charly each ran home."

"Do you know who the woman was?"

"No, but I think she's the lady from that big new house on the other side of the park."

Renaldo watched and waited until Matias's tears slowed and his breath steadied.

CC pulled her phone out and opened the map. She controlled the excitement in her voice as she listed to Renaldo, who lowered the volume of his voice.

He kneeled in front of Matias and put a hand on the boy's shoulder.. "Matias, thank you for telling me your story. It's very important we're honest with each other. Now, we need to be honest with everyone else. You're not in trouble, but we need to let your parents and Detective Jarvis know what happened. The woman, or maybe even Charly, might have seen something that will help us find Sylvia."

Matias dropped from the swing, his head still hanging. Fresh tears formed, but his body no longer shook. "Okay," he said.

"Good man," Reynaldo said and led Matias inside the house.

CC sent a text to Max to meet her at the park as soon as it was dark. And then she sent a text to Eugene to stop following her and go to class.

*****

Max leaned against a tree inside the small grove in the park. He didn't wait until dark but kept to the deep shadows of the trees. He remained silent as Eugene walked in concentric circles around the spot Eugene where said the monster grabbed the girl, one hundred yards from the yellow tape the police placed where they thought Sylvia had been taken. Despite focusing on the scents of Sylvia, Matias, and his friend, and the monster, Eugene couldn't help but look up to study CC's face.

"This is the spot. No doubt about it. But," Eugene straightened her back and breathed in through her nose. "I wish I could be clearer, but the scents' change. Every time I find a spot where I know the creature has been, his scent changes."

"You smell like James Earl, don't you?" CC said.

Eugene's face dropped, and she shifted her gaze to Max. His face didn't change. "Well," Eugene stuttered. "In a way." Then she added, "But it's not him."

CC nodded. "No, it's not him."

Eugene cringed and looked back at Max, hoping he would say something. She didn't understand why the creature smelled a little like James Earl.

Max sniffed the air. "I know what you mean," he finally said. "He doesn't smell anything like the man I ran across in Austin back in '85. But it is the same man."

"Man," spat Eugene. "No man did what I saw."

"Part man," said Max.

CC took a quick breath in. Eugene stiffened and turned to CC.

"It's like," CC said, more to herself than to the others. "As though he's taking a little from all his victims. Is that possible, Max?"

Max's lips twisted, and he put his hands in his pockets. "Perhaps," he said. "There are those who say vampires steal souls. Sometimes I think we take more than just blood."

Eugene couldn't hold back the grunt that spilled out of her. "If that were the case, I'd have the heart of a squirrel."

CC giggled. "James Earl said something like that once."

Even Max smiled. "I never believed in that theory, but," He paused, staring into the trees. "What if our creature believes it?"

"That doesn't explain why his scent changes," Eugene said.

"On the other hand," CC said, but the watch on her wrist lit up and she pulled out her phone.

In the blue light of her phone, CC's face changed. Her eyes widened, and a smile flashed before her chin dropped and her eyes widened. "They've found Sylvia and another little girl taken early this morning. They're alive."

*****

"Renaldo parked the car in front of the warehouse, surrounded by emergency vehicles and news vans. "By the way, any word from James Earl?"

CC stopped halfway out of the car. "Gone. No need to look anymore," she said, letting out a long exhale.

She stood next to the car, looking at the roof of the warehouse expecting to see someone, but the sun dazzled her eyes in late afternoon sun. No one stood up there to either comfort or support her. Not at three in the afternoon on such a fine, sunny day. She twisted her neck in one direction and then the other, gathering her strength. That's when she felt the soft prick, like a feather, falling onto her shoulder.

She looked behind her. In the crowd gathered at the fence separating the brewery from the warehouse stood Eugene. Her eyes squinted up from where CC had just looked, and then she put her finger to her lips. CC wanted to laugh. No matter how flighty Eugene seemed, she was a good friend. She should be angry at Eugene following her, but her concern was so sincere, CC felt the tension in her shoulders release and the pain growing in her head disappear. A wash of calm fell over her with the realization she wasn't alone if their prey came near.

"Sorry about James Earl," Renaldo said, leading CC under the police tape. "Never took him for a runner."

"He didn't run," said CC, clearing her throat.

Renaldo gripped her arm, slowing her. "What?"

CC patted Renaldo's hand. "He's gone," she said and continued into the warehouse.

The stink of death slapped them both. Each halted, but only long enough to register the stink, and then they moved on. The sound of a generator grumbled from outside the warehouse opposite where they entered. Light forced its way into the darkest of corners, covered with dust, dirt, and neglect. As they followed the lighted path, dark patches, blackening with age, some still smeared with globules of blood, blocked their path, and they stepped around or over them.

"Sylvia was here," said Renaldo, turning a corner around a stack of old wooden crates and pallets piled high, forming a room with only enough space to enter if they turned sideways and followed each other.

Renaldo squatted down and pointed to a circle in a corner. Inside the circle, a small, clenched fist lay alone. Dark brown fingernails blackened as the blood beneath them, once streaming red, rotted on the cold, concrete floor in the dirt. The clasp of the watchband gleamed gold, reflecting the light from the LED bulb as a man from the crime lab continued measuring and taking pictures.

The crime lab man looked up at Renaldo and then CC as though expecting them. "I'm done here," he said and walked away.

CC bent close to the fist. "Any idea who?" she asked, pointing to it.

"Not yet," said Renaldo. "Lab guys are just waiting for the all clear to take it. It's not Sylvia's."

CC closed her eyes as she stood. Her breath stuck in her throat, she felt the blood drain from her head, and she wobbled. Renaldo grabbed her arm to keep her from falling. "More tired than I thought," she said. "Can I see where Sharon was kept?"

Renaldo's eyes narrowed, but he nodded and led them out of the enclosure and through a maze of crates and boxes. Bright lights flooded other enclosures where technicians flashed cameras, vacuumed specimens, and swabbed black, dried spots.

After passing the third lighted enclosure, CC asked, "How many?"

Renaldo did not turn to look back at CC. "At least four not counting Sharon and Sylvia."

"Sylvia mentioned hearing a boy crying. You said she thinks he's dead," CC said, forcing her voice to sound neutral.

Renaldo pointed to the other side of the warehouse. "Nobody, but fresh blood over there."

They walked on the outside of the maze, near an outer wall. Renaldo pointed to a wide opening where two technicians worked. "Here," he said.

CC remained outside the enclosure, watching the technicians work. Multiple black spots littered the floor alone, with half a dozen darkening red pools circled with chalk. CC shook her head.

Renaldo put a hand on CC's shoulder. "A lot of blood for one little girl to lose." He sighed. "Thank God Sylvia kept her head. If it weren't for her-" he trailed off.

"Smart and lucky. I need to talk to her."

Renaldo nodded his head. "I was hoping you'd say that."

*****

The police officer at the door told CC which room was Sylvia's. Renaldo said little as they walked down the hall.

"You up to this?" Renaldo asked. "You look beat."

CC nodded. "I'm fine," she snapped. She stopped walking to take a breath. "Sorry," she said. "Everyone keeps asking me that."

Renaldo nodded but said nothing.

The officer at Sylvia's door opened the door for them. Renaldo pushed his head past the threshold before entering. "Are you up to visitors?"

CC held her breath. She didn't hear the answer, but Renaldo looked back at her before stepping in. CC fitted her face with her best professional, uncommitted smile; corners of her mouth up, lips closed - no teeth, eyes flat.

She followed Renaldo into the bright blue room. The rainbow painted across the back wall glared at her in juxtaposition of the pictures Renaldo showed her of Sylvia on the way to the hospital. CC lowered her eyes to the figure on the bed. One large brown eye stared at her. White bandages covered half of Sylvia's face. The pink hospital cap merged into the pale, golden brown flesh of Sylvia's swollen, bruised, but otherwise smooth face. Only the lips, cracked and too red for her face, showed the beating the girl received.

CC half listened to Renaldo's greetings. Mr. Catan stood in the far corner of the room, his ashen face dulled by deep purple circles under his eyes. If he heard Renaldo, he made no sign. Mrs. Catan sat in the chair next to Sylvia's bed. She'd put on make-up to cover dark rings, but the water-proof mascara swelled on her eyelids. Her hand shook as she lifted it to pull a strand of hair away from her eyes.

"If you think this will help find the man..." she said no more.

"I'm going to find him," CC said.

Renaldo twisted to look into her face, but CC didn't look at him. She broke the first rule - make no promises, but Sylvia needed to hear the words. Her brown eye remained fixed on CC's face. There were no tears in that eye. CC recognized a woman, very young, but a woman determined to do what was right.

"And you're going to help me, Sylvia." CC stepped closer to the bed.

Mrs. Catan pinched her lips and stood. "If you think," she began and looked at her daughter's face. "We'll wait outside." She nodded to CC and held her hand out to her husband. Mr. Catan took it, and they left the room.

"I don't know why I'm trusting you so much, CC," Renaldo muttered, and as he followed Mr. And Mrs. Catan out the room.

*****

As soon as they were alone, Sylvia said, "He killed a little boy."

CC sat in the chair vacated by Mrs. Catan. "And others," she said. "But not you. You not only got away from him, you saved a little girl."

Sylvia caught her breath. "Is Sharon all right?" Her head leaned forward as though to sit up, but her one good eye closed, and she lay her head back down. "Nobody wants to tell me what's going on."

CC, relaxing in Sylvia's courage, let her shoulders drop. "Sharon will be fine. Sustained injuries much like yours, but because of you, she'll live."

"Will she lose her eye, too?"

CC shook her head. "No. A blow to her head has affected her hearing, but with time and the right tools, she will hear again in her right ear."

Sylvia took in a long, deep breath. "Good. She sounded so little. I think it'll take time to get used to only having one eye. Maybe I'll get one of those fancy new eyes I see on the Science Channel."

CC nodded. "Perhaps."

CC waited, examining the half face in front of her. Pretty, tough, determined. Fear hid behind the brown eye as it searched the room, but Sylvia checked it, wouldn't allow it to dominate her.

CC picked up Sylvia's hand and squeezed it. Three of her nail extensions glittered red and pink. The other two fingernails were rough from too much adhesive. Sylvia didn't bite her nails. "I won't let him come back for you," CC said.

Sylvia's hand gripped CC's. "But he knows where I am," she whispered. "He knows everything. I don't know what he wants."

CC closed her eyes. Something like a tickle. It grew to a tingle traveling up her arm, down the back of her neck, and into her brain. She opened her eyes. The face looking back at her was Sylvia's, but not the frightened young woman, bandaged and worn. An older face, with an eye patch and a scar running from the right side of her mouth to her ear, stared back at her. The left side of her face smiled, the left eye gleamed dark and clear, reflecting the light over the bed, and surrounding the teenager, a mist, like rain cloud on a sunny day.

CC tilted her head to match the tilt of the ghost's face as it faded. "I know what he wants," whispered CC into Sylvia's unbandaged ear. "And I will not let him get it."

Sylvia bit her lip, staring into CC's face.

CC watched Sylvia's chest push up and fall down, up and down. Her golden cheek faded. The pink turned to red and then Sylvia let out a low, long breath from between her lips. "You know he's not human. What kind of monster is he?"

That familiar tickle on the back of CC's neck started. She closed her eyes, breathed in through her nose, focused on the feeling, and bit her lower lip.

Sylvia looked away from CC. Her face relaxed, glowed with sweat, but her natural color returned. She smiled. "You're not going to tell me."

"Not yet," said CC. "We both know he's a monster. I need you to tell me everything you're not telling the police. Tell me how the fear hit you, what you saw when the shadows moved, how his smell made you sick."

Sylvia looked back at CC. "Will you promise to tell me what he is when I'm at home and he's dead?" Sylvia tightened her grip on CC's fingers. Her eyes widened as fear flashed in front of her. "You are going to kill him."

"Yes," CC nodded. "With your help, we're going to kill him."

*****

Outside Sylvia's room, Renaldo stood talking to Mr. and Mrs. Catan. He nodded as CC approached. Stanly, the bouncer from The Phantom's Menace, stood at the other end of the hall, leaning against the wall with his cell phone to his ear.

CC positioned herself so she could see both the Catan's and Stanly. She reached out and took Mrs. Catan's hand. "Sylvia's a special girl." CC watched as Stan nodded his head to her and turned to walk into a room. "I understand she'll make a good recovery."

"Right," spat Mr. Catan. "She's lost her eye. That bastard--"

Mrs. Catan interrupted him, placing a hand on his arm. "She's alive, and she's home. We'll face what comes next together. If you've finished with her, I'd like to go back in."

Before she could walk away, CC asked, "Mrs. Catan, is there anything you can tell me about Sylvia's biological parents?"

Mrs. Catan turned, her eyes wide and her lips shaking. "Biological? How?" She shook her head. "I suppose you've seen the police details. She doesn't know, Ms. Carson. My sister was always the wild one in the family. She died in Las Vegas when Sylvia was only a baby. We didn't even know she was there, or that she had a child. But Sylvia's our daughter now. She doesn't even remember Mona."

"She won't hear it from me," said CC, resisting the urge to give Mrs. Catan a hug. "The man who took her selects fostered and adopted children. You won't find that in any of the newspapers. I'm sorry for bringing it up now."

"If he comes near my family again," Mr. Catan said, taking his wife's arm. "I'll kill him."

"We'll get him," Renaldo said.

As the door to Sylvia's room closed, Renaldo turned to CC. "You're certain about the fostered kids now?" He looked down at her. His lips twisted, but he looked away before she could answer.

CC put a hand on his arm. "I wasn't certain until this morning. If Sylvia was the Catans' biological daughter, then there would be no pattern."

Renaldo nodded. "This killer is twisting his knife in me every time I think about him. I was a foster kid myself for a while. These kids have enough to deal with someone targeting them."

CC put her hand on his arm. "I know," she said.

*****

Luna sat at Max's table with her books spread out in front of her and her laptop glowing. It was the best spot to sit and watch people without being unobserved and stared at for the two large black eyes. People came and went: no one sat at the table. Sighing, she scrolled the page on her laptop to finish reading the news about the teenage girl and young girl rescued from a warehouse of horror; she thought the title over the top, explaining how the smart thinking teen used her watch to call for help. Something about the circumstances of the teen being taken reminded her of her own fright just a few nights before.

Eugene sat in the chair next to her. "I'm beat," she said. "Why are slow days so tiring?"

Luna studied Eugene's face, smiling as usual and relaxed. Today, there was something different. A tightness circled her eyes, her fast talking went on even faster and longer. Luna looked at the face of the teen on her screen. Younger than her, but not by so much. "Will you tell me something?"

"Well," began Eugene as she took in a deep breath, "First, I overslept. Poor little Bean. He so had to pee so bad, I threw on my pants and got him outside before he made another spot on the floor. CC's pissed about that, but she pretends she's not-"

"Eugene," interrupted Luna.

"You wanted me to tell you something, so I'm telling you about my morning. It was rough." Eugene's expression didn't change.

Luna giggled. "You're as weird as Max. I need to ask you a question, but I don't know if you'll tell me the truth."

Eugene opened her mouth, only to close it again as she closed her eyes and took in a deep breath. "Serious," she said, nodding her head. "Okay. I'll be as honest as I can."

Luna flipped her screen over to show Eugene the teen's school picture and the article's headline. She bent her head to Eugene and lowered her voice. "Did the monster take her?"

Eugene blinked and looked behind her at the coffee bar. "Yes."

"Oh," said Luna. She sniffed, but this time, it wasn't mucus dripping out of her nose. Her eyes teared up. Her shoulders shook, but she cleared her throat and focused on not crying. "How many has it killed?"

Eugene bit her lip, but before she could answer, Marcus called to her from the coffee counter. "Eugene, I need you."

"Gotta go," Eugene said, standing up.

Luna sighed. "I'm not a kid. And-"

Eugene reached over and hugged Luna. Luna held her breath. She kept her hand on her keyboard until the heat of Eugene's body bore through her shell and she felt the care and protection that only a good friend can provide. Luna returned the hug.

Eugene whispered into Luna's ear, "We will not let it hurt you."

Eugene returned to work. Luna still stared at the screen. The girl looking back at her looked so sweet, unconcerned with monsters, and not afraid of the dark. Luna wished she could feel that way.

*****

Constance turned off the ignition and waited in the car. If Uncle Julio found her driving his car again, he'd have a hissy, but how else could she get across town and back? It was two hours on the bus, one way. It's not like she wanted to work nights, but when else was she supposed to work if she wanted to stay in school? "Just because Wanda dropped out of school doesn't mean I want to," she muttered to herself. "I will not live here any longer than I have to."

Checking once more that no one watched, she got out and locked Uncle Julio's car. She did one more check that she was in the same parking spot, bumper just over the cement block, and diagonally parked between the faded lines. "Why's he such an ass? He doesn't drive anymore."

Her house was only across the empty lot from the run-down apartment complex and down another street. Mama would be worried if she didn't get home soon. Mama always waited up.

As she stepped into the field, she froze at the sound of women's voices. "Something else is going on. I mean, the guys around here are tough, but even they've been staying in." The voices were behind her. She walked on.

The hair on Constance's neck stood up. She turned around again. A tall, thin woman and a short round one walked back toward the apartment complex. They were right. There was something wrong.

Constance scanned the tall grasses and brush waving beneath the night's shadows. There was no one else in the field, at least no one she could see. High brush, round, prickly bushes, and mounds of packed earth cast dark blobs in an already dark field. She reached into the pocket of her uniform, wrapping her hand around the can of mace. She quickened her pace.

Ahead of her loomed the darker shape of the tall, wooden fence of a house. Streetlights from the front of the house skidded the top of the fence, filling the bottom half of the fence with darker shadows. She looked behind her again, but still saw no one and nothing moving, but the hairs on her neck continued to prick. A chill ran across her shoulders. She wrapped her arms around her despite the heat of the night. She walked along the edge of the fence to the corner where the boards were rotten and a huge hole waited for her.

"Damn," she hissed under her breath. She smelled the fresh cut cedar before her head touched the new boards. They were firmly in place. She looked behind her again. Nothing.

Constance remained close to the fence, feeling her way. Two houses down was a chain link fence. She'd climb it and hope she could do it without tearing her uniform and before the dog barked the alarm. She couldn't afford a new one.

The rustle of cloth on grass followed by a low, almost a whisper, of a growl and her feet froze where they were. She shuddered as a breeze blew across her brow, sweating with heat and fear. She gulped a mouthful of air and twisted to look behind her. A stink rose into her nose. She gagged. That's when she saw the yellow eyes, low in the dry weeds behind her. The reek rose as the eyes seemed to float toward her. They grew as they came closer, but now, a shape in the shadows like a massive head surrounded the eyes.

Her breaths came in and out as fast as her heart beat. A dog barked from somewhere nearby, breaking the spell the eyes held on her. She turned to run. Her left foot lifted, but a grip cold and static pulled her ankle behind her. She fell, banging her chin on a rock. Flecks of light flashed between her eyes and eyelids. She gulped for air, but the stink that tugged at her nose dried her mouth. Another cold hand gripped her right shoulder and pulled her to her back.

"Where's the others?" a voice or growl--or was it in her head?--said.

She said nothing. A fist smashed into her face. The stars reappeared, and then total darkness and then silence. There was no peace. When she woke, hands and feet bound, and laying on concrete, the question returned. "Where's the others?" She heard that question again and again until she heard nothing.

7

The story changes as heroes rest.
The last move forward toward the light.
The first follow, unseen in shadows.
When eyes see, the demons halt.
I'm Mary Midnight online and in your mind.
Dance in the shadows with eyes open
Or walk in the light with eyes closed.

"It's been over two weeks," said Cesar, leaning back in his chair behind his desk. "I don't like it."

CC lay stretched on the couch with Fluffy curled at her feet and Bean curled on her belly. "Eugene found some files on James Earl's computers. He was tracking properties for a client of Jane's. She sent them to Mike to see what he could knew about them."

"Anything?" He asked, sitting up.

"Not yet," sighed CC. "Might be nothing, but she sees a connection. Don't think she's some scatterbrain. If she suspects something's there, it's there. Someone's watching Sylvia?"

"Yes," said Cesar. "For the umpteenth time, someone is always watching her. Odd he took Jenny, no signs of being one of us."

CC yawned. "I know, but then we can't put our logic into his head. Luna's been very quiet. I'm worried about her. Marcus, too. Although," CC yawned again. "He surprised me."

Cesar tapped the screen on his desk. The lights in the room dimmed.

"They're taking it all in. They grew up knowing a monster watched them. I suppose they're thinking: their world is changing."

"Uh-huh," muttered CC. With the screen covering the wall of the one-way window, the sounds in the office faded to the soft thudding of beats whispered up from the floor, reminding CC she was above a nightclub. She stared at the ceiling, covered with shadows from the floor lamps. The shadows seemed longer than they were a few minutes ago. The soft beat, the dark, the heat of Bean and Fluffy relaxed her. Sleep crept on her. She was aware of it for a moment, and it disappeared as dreams faded to restful bliss.

*****

"How's the nose?" Flo asked as she poured herself a glass of iced tea.

The large man/shadow flashed before Luna's eyes, fading when the front door opened and sunlight flashed into the cafe. She forced a smile. "Better. I can breathe through my nose easily enough. Doctor said it was such a small fracture, it would heal on its own. Just supposed to take it easy for a while. No running until the breathing is easier."

"Running," laughed Flo. "More power to you. I get enough of a work-out in the kitchen." She tilted her head and drank her glass in one long drink. When she finished, she poured another glass. "Get you anything from the kitchen?"

"No thanks. Hey," Luna lowered her voice. "What did mama want with you? You were in her office talking to her for a long time."

Flo's grin grew two-fold. "Your mom's something else. She'd heard about the trouble in the complex where we live and wanted to see how I was doing. I explained the situation with the kids - you know me and Malia aren't married, so technically there's not much I can do with the kids with their grandma around. Anyway, she said she knew some folks that might help. And she knows of a sublet close to here I could get into."

"Good," said Luna. "I don't like where you live now."

"I'll second that," said Marcus, setting a bottle of water in front of

Luna. "You're drinking a lot of coffee these days. Better keep your fluids up so you heal faster." He walked away, saying nothing else.

"I wish I knew what he was up to," muttered Luna, not intending to say it out loud.

"Must be something diabolical," laughed Flo. "Whoever heard of a brother being nice to his sister? I gotta get back to work."

Business was slow for a Thursday evening. Everybody grumbled over battling the daily afternoon storms. Luna, forced to remain seated on the bench next to the cash register until mama said she was healed, slumped on her arm. The door opened, ringing the bell, and Luna sat up. Scarlett and her friends entered, laughing.

"Luna!" shouted Scarlett. "So good to see you again. What have you been up to? Seems like forever since we've seen you."

Luna's heart lifted. She missed her friends and the gossip. "Fractured my nose running. Almost healed now. Where've you been? I didn't see you in class the last couple of weeks."

Scarlett rolled her eyes. "That class is soooo boring. I just can't take the way the professor drones on and on and on. Besides, he only counts anyone absent if an assignment isn't turned in, so I upload my essays to the portal before class." She leaned on the counter and looked into Luna's face. "Oh, you poor thing. You still have black eyes. How did you fracture your nose? Oh, hi Marcus."

Marcus walked behind the counter. a forced grin lifting the corners of his mouth but nodded. "Hello, ladies. What can I get you?"

Scarlett giggled. "There are all sorts of things you could get me, Marcus, but for now, how about three of your wonderful chocolate lattes?"

"You got it," said Marcus, pulling mugs out off the shelf. "I'll call you when they're ready."

"That will be \$14.71," said Luna.

Scarlett turned her head so fast the gold tips sent a scattering of gold flakes across her shoulders. She smiled while biting her lower lip. "Of course," she said.

After half an hour, Luna strolled to the table where Scarlett and the others sat. Once again, Scarlett asked how she hurt her nose, but this time she allowed Luna to tell them how she tripped while out jogging.

"You see what you get from being out so late at night by yourself. You're lucky someone you knew was nearby to help you home," said Scarlett. "Now, me, I go to the gym every morning. Aerobics classes start at eight, and then I find a trainer to help me with the weights. They're always so helpful. That's the safe way to work out."

The other girls agreed. Luna looked up as Tommy entered the cafe from the kitchen. He waved at her.

"I better get back to work," Luna said, pushing too hard on the table as she stood.

"Careful, Luna," scolded Scarlett. "You don't want to spill our drinks, then again..." Scarlett turned her head to look at Tommy. Lowering her voice as she turned back to her friends, she added, "It might not be such a bad thing. I see the golden barista boy is back. He could mix a latte for me anytime." The girls giggled.

Luna bent over. "Would you like me to send him over here to talk to you about coffee?"

"Oh Luna," laughed Scarlett. "You're too good. Now, don't forget about the costume party next weekend. You must tell me what your costume is. I've ordered mine already - a very sexy Marie Antoinette. You could be one of my maids."

"I'll see what I can do," Luna said, and made her way back to the coffee bar.

Tommy wiped down the machines. "Why are you still talking to them?" he asked.

"They're my friends," Luna said, sitting on the stool at the register.

Tommy scoffed. "Friends don't abandon friends on the side of the road."

Luna's hand hit the bar harder than she intended. "Eugene said she wouldn't tell."

Tommy shook his head. "Luna, Marcus carried you in here so hung-over you couldn't walk. Everyone knows."

Luna cringed. Her shoulders rolled forward. Heat burned her face, and she wanted to sink under the counter. She didn't look at Tommy. "Where is Eugene, anyway? I thought she was working tonight."

Tommy's mouth formed a little smile, but he didn't look at Luna. "Saw her walking down the street as I drove up. She'll be here soon." He picked up the tub of dirty dishes. "I'm taking these to the kitchen."

The bell over the door rang as the door opened. Luna looked up to see Thad enter with a large entourage. Her face burned so hot, she pulled a napkin out of its rack to wipe her forehead. "It's going to be a long night," she muttered, then forced a smile on her face as Thad walked up to the counter and ordered.

*****

"Tat girl," Tommy said, putting the container of dirty dishes next to the dishwasher. "Why are you walking everywhere these days? I thought you rode your bike everywhere unless you're on all fours."

Eugene snorted as she dropped her backpack on the hook in the back entryway. "Got stolen the night I went looking for James Earl and ended up at Flo's apartment building."

Tommy leaned on the doorframe as Eugene pulled her apron off its hook and wrapped it around her. "There are other bikes in the shed. CC won't mind if you use one."

Eugene crossed her hands over her chest. "Seriously?" she spat. "Like she doesn't have enough on her mind without me asking to borrow another bicycle."

Tommy grinned, and his eyes sparkled with laughter. "You didn't tell her you lost it, did you?"

"Not exactly," Eugene shrugged. "I'll get it back. It's just, with everything going on, I don't know. I haven't even taken back those clothes I stole when I found Luna passed out on the street. I mean, between watching over the house, keeping my eye on the kids, and this place. Not to mention classes." Luna sighed, tapping her code into the timekeeper app on the pad next to the door.

As Eugene's fingers tapped her code, her reflection on the screen caught her attention. She looked as tired as she felt, having spent the best part of a week getting into all of James Earl's business and personal files. The last few nights, she and CC had reviewed the information on all the clients he'd been working for and compared them to the official files for the firm, those of Mike Young, and even the few new clients from the accountants next door.

When she wasn't in class or working at the cafe, Max took her to known crime scenes, hoping to find traces of the monster who murdered children. Max and Tommy rotated nights watching the LeBrere house, while Eugene worked extra hours or studied at the cafe to watch them during the day.

Nothing. For two weeks, they hunted, searched, hacked, guarded, and their prey made no move. And now she heard Luna talking to Thad in the cafe. The one thing she had no control over, the one thing that made her angry happened in the early hours of dawn when there were no vamps in the house, when there were no humans walking or driving on the street in front of the house, when everything was quiet before the city woke, when CC curled in her bed with Fluffy, Eugene heard the sniffling and tears CC would not shed in front of anyone. She pounded the enter button, breaking her nail. "They also took my favorite leather vest!" she muttered.

"Let's get your bike back tonight," Tommy said. "We could both use a diversion."

Eugene turned, squinted her eyes. "You want to help me get my bike back?"

"Why not?" he asked, grinning that ridiculous, clichéd grin no one could not grin back from.

Eugene bit the side of her lip to not grin back, but it was no use. She sighed, shrugging her shoulders. "I would, but I hate leaving CC alone--"

"She's at the club," Tommy said. "Did I tell you I bought a pickup?"

Eugene shrugged. "Okay," and turned to walk away, but stopped. The scent of night and blood floated into her from the cafe, familiar and not. Her eyes narrowed, focusing on the door between the kitchen and the cafe. Her breathing slowed, slowing her heart, her ears focused. Thad and his friends leaving the cafe. Scarlett's silly laughter going with them. Luna grumbling as she tapped on her laptop. Marcus taking an order.

She leaped to the side, twirling to face Tommy as his hand lifted from her shoulder. "Relax," he said. "It's Clay."

Eugene shook her head and closed her eyes. The scent was familiar, though she had only met him once. "On edge, I guess. What do you think he wants?"

Tommy was already in the doorway. "Let's ask."

"Coffee, dark roast only, black, with a shot of espresso," Clay said, as he stood in front of Marcus.

Marcus nodded, but he kept his eyes on Clay as he stepped closer to Luna. Luna's mouth stared at him.

"Clay," shouted Tommy as he stepped between Marcus and the counter, grabbing a large mug. "You finally stopped by. I've got this, Marcus."

"Okay," said Marcus, without removing his eyes from Clay.

Eugene scratched her chin and studied Marcus. His face was blank, but a bead of sweat formed over his upper lip and along his hairline. She reached her hand out to touch his arm when Clay spoke.

"Thank you, Tomas."

Eugene grinned as Clay accented Tommy's name the same way Max did.

"I was hoping to speak with Eugene," Clay continued. "If she would spare me a moment."

Eugene stared at him and then at Tommy, who winked at her. "Sure," she said. "I'll bring you your coffee."

"Friend of yours?" asked Luna, watching Clay sit at the table Max usually sat at.

"Sort of," Eugene answered. She leaned over Tommy to pick up a tray, whispering, "What does he want with me?"

Tommy set the mug on a tray, as he shrugged his shoulders, "Ask him."

*****

Eugene watched Clay sip the mug. The steam drifted over his dark, almost all black, clear eyes before his lids closed as the coffee hit his tongue.

"Ah," he said, lifting the corners of his mouth and eyebrows just enough to convey satisfaction. "I miss a truly good cup of strong coffee. When I was a child, a priest at the orphanage would make me a cup whenever I got into trouble. To this day, when I smell a good cup of coffee, I expect a long lecture on morality and the cost of sin. However," he set the cup on the table between them. "The lectures did not have the desired effect. I drank many cups of coffee. When I returned to visit the priest when he was a very old man, I explained to him why I was such a bad little boy. He told me he knew that's why I was bad, but as it meant my undivided attention for an hour, he was glad to share coffee with me."

Clay's little smile grew, and his face relaxed, happy for a moment.

"I'll tell Marcus you like his coffee," Eugene said when Clay said nothing.

"Please don't," he said. "It's not that good."

Eugene released a gush of air as a laugh without meaning to. She knew little about Clay. He came to the house the night James Earl died to talk to CC. But CC didn't want to plan a memorial until the monster was dead. Clay cremated James Earl's body, standard procedure in their world. It was odd, Eugene remembered thinking, that Clay hadn't asked CC to view James Earl. She assumed it would be painful, but CC was a trained investigator. Cesar had seen the body. Eugene lifted an eyebrow, realizing just how much Cesar was hanging around the house.

Clay nodded. "You are impatient," he said.

Eugene felt her cheeks blush as she shook her head. "No, sorry. I was just thinking. Why didn't you ask CC to view James Earl before you cremated him?"

Clay's face turned away from Eugene. He grew dark, as though fading into shadow. "A very unnatural sight. Eugene," Clay paused again and put a hand over hers. "He died both human and wolf."

Eugene shook her head. "No," she said, hearing the crack in her own voice. "That's not - I mean we always return to human."

"I do not understand it," Clay said. "Max and Cesar saw. They did not think it was possible either."

A shudder ran through Eugene, and a stone fell into her gut. "I'm glad she didn't see. Does she know?"

"No," Clay said. They sat in silence until Clay shrugged his shoulders and straightened his back. "I have two purposes in speaking with you today. First, you are involved in this hunt, and you are a wolf. You need to know about the state of James Earl's demise. Unnatural. Perhaps you understand it. If not, take care. I do not wish to see you in such a state."

Eugene envisioned of her body wreathing and dying both as wolf and human. She rubbed her hands together and gulped on air. "Thanks," she said.

"Second, I am here because I am concerned about CC. She has suffered a significant loss. We all have. James Earl proved himself a good friend, although not as much as CC is, but the loss is especially troubling to her, as she loved him. My profession is to aid the living. I do not know what to do."

Eugene sniffed as her eyes watered. Clay was the only person to ask about CC. The other vamps came and went, never mentioning James Earl. Eugene took a deep breath before answering. "I didn't know him long, but I liked him. Rough around the edges, but so am I. She won't talk about him, but I hear her in the mornings when she thinks I'm asleep. She cries for him."

Clay's gaze seemed far away from the coffee shop. He nodded. "Good. I feared she held too much in. You are a good friend to her. She knows you are there. This knowledge allows me to put away my concerns - for a little while. I will return when she is ready for me."

Clay left. Eugene remained sitting. "Vamps are weird," she muttered.

"Eugene," came Marcus' voice from the coffee counter. "I'd appreciate it if you would work."

"Coming," she replied, and picked up Clay's cup. He'd drunk the whole thing. "When did he do that?"

On her way to the counter, an old man stood, bumping his chair into her hip. She stopped, waiting for him to move. The old man was huge. A cane in a huge old hand lifted the man's massive frame. His gray head turned. Eugene caught her breath as eye like black marbles hidden behind a thick gray brow glared at her.

"Excuse me," she whispered.

The man snarled beneath his thick gray beard. "None for sinners on judgement day."

His voice grated in ears Eugene's like gravel stuck in the wheel of her bicycle. It broke the odd feeling scratching on the back of her neck. "Whatever, dude," she muttered and pushed past him.

*****

The evening crowd poured in. The evening crew arrived, and Luna picked up her backpack and sat at Max's usual table, spreading out her books attempting to study. Thad and his friends filled a table on the opposite side of the cafe from Scarlett, but she and her friends moved to a table next to them. Laughter erupted from their tables, followed by long stretches of Scarlett talking.

Marcus joined her with his laptop. He sat typing and smiling. From time to time, he muttered, "Yes, excellent, this is good."

Luna first glared at him, but he ignored her. Next, she slammed a book on the table. All he did was lift the laptop and settle it back where it had been.

"Marcus," she at last demanded. "What are you doing that's got you all giddy-like?"

"Wait," he said, lifting his index finger. "Got it. You heard mama talk about Midnight Bites. Well, I just booked our first act." He grinned wider than she had seen him grin since they were just kids.

"You booked an act?" she asked.

"Max suggested it first - staying open twenty-four hours. Few coffee shops downtown do. We're setting up Midnight Bites as a special time. A separate tasting menu - we can do it super cheap so keep all our student clients, but they'll be specialty desserts to bring in the higher end clientele. We already have the stage, so local, acoustic musicians. You know, one-, two-, or three-person acts."

Luna stared at Marcus. This brother was the happy big brother she remembered from childhood, always thinking, planning, looking forward to something. "What kind of act did you book?"

"Flamenco," he said.

"Did I hear you right?" Tommy asked. Luna curled her head, wondering how he got from the coffee bar to their table so quickly. "You've booked a Flamenco act?" His eyes were bright and round.

"Yes," said Marcus. His smile disappeared. Worry lines shot out from his mouth as his brows furrowed. "You don't think it's right for Midnight Bites?"

"It's perfect!" Exclaimed Tommy, smiling so wide his teeth gleamed in the light. "This is the perfect stage for Flamenco. We'll move the plants. Better get the carpenter out here to check a couple of those boards. It's been a while, and the dancers will pound them."

Marcus' smile returned as his smile widened as much as Tommy's. He pointed to the stage. "I was thinking of shifting the tables - make them more a semi-circle around the stage."

"Excellent," continued Tommy.

Luna closed her books and packed her bag, escaping the cascading workload for one silly dancer. She made her way to the office when a hand brushed against her shoulder. She turned to find Thad standing next to her.

"Hi," he said. His eyes darted to the side where his friends and Scarlett sat and back to her. "I heard you got hurt running."

Luna looked up at his beautiful brown eyes set on his beautiful, soft face. "Stupid. I tripped, banged into the back of a pick-up. It's nothing."

"Ow." he shook his head. Laughter emerged from the table where his friends sat. "It had to have hurt. You sure you should be working? Looks like you still have some darkness under your eyes."

Luna heard the laughter of his friends and the voices in the cafe, but they were far away. Thad's eyes darted back and forth until he shifted so his back was to his friends and she stood squarely in front of him. Her heart pounded in her chest, and a warmth grew inside her core and radiated out to her skin. "I'm good," she said. "Won't be running for another couple of weeks, but," she shrugged. "Not so bad."

"Good," Thad nodded his head. "Glad you're doing okay."

Her cheeks flushed, and she looked down, hoping the blush didn't show.

"Hey, Thad," one of his friends shouted. "We're heading out. Coming?"

Thad twisted to look behind him, and Luna glimpsed his friends standing, putting phones in their pockets, and pushing chairs in.

"Yeah," he shouted back. Looking back at Luna, he asked, "You going to the Halloween party next weekend?"

Scarlett's voice rose over the crowds. "Of course, we'll come. How nice of you to ask."

"I don't know," answered Luna.

"Maybe you'd like to go with me," Thad said.

"Oh," was all Luna could think of saying. She looked around him at Scarlett.

"Look," Thad said, pulling her attention back to his face, his lovely, brown, soft, caressable face. "I'd like to take you. Not just to make up for being an ass at the river party. I like you, Luna. I'd like to get to know you."

Luna cleared her throat. Scarlett and the girls walked to the door with Thad's friends. "Sure," she said. "You can take me to the party, but - um - I'm not going to drink anything. I think I've had enough of that."

"Come on, Thad," shouted Scarlett from the door.

Thad's smile fell over Luna like a warm blanket. "Works for me," he said. "Catch you later."

He left with the others and Luna walked into the office. Her nose didn't hurt at all. In fact, she couldn't ever remember feeling so well. She didn't even mind the weird old man standing near the front door glaring at her.

*****

"Why do you have a pickup truck?" Eugene asked.

Tommy grinned as he pulled between two buildings into the empty lot behind the apartment building where Flo lived. "Don't you love that new car smell?" he said.

"No," said Eugene, cringing her nose. "It's noxious."

Tommy rolled his eyes. "Wers! I'm living in Austin, Texas. What else does a young man on the move drive? Besides, it's all electric. Very chic these days."

Eugene tilted her head, listening. "Oh, yeah. I didn't realize. So, you're serious about getting back the bike." She didn't intend to sound so surprised, but she was.

"If I say I'm going to do a thing," he said. "I do it." He opened the door and stepped out. "Coming?" he asked, before closing the door.

They walked through tall weeds, hiding mounds of trash and muddy earth, until they reached the back of the building. Tommy stood still and stared at it. "I see what you mean about the fear," he said. "I thought you were exaggerating."

"If I tell you a thing," she mocked. "It's a thing."

"Finesse, Eugene. You lack finesse." Tommy smiled, and she followed him through the breezeway leading to the front of the building. A man pushing a bicycle walked across the lot toward them.

"That's it," Eugene whispered. "He took it and he still has it."

Two men came out of an apartment near them. They did not exchange greetings with the man pushing the bicycle.

"Our lucky day," Tommy said. "He hasn't sold it yet."

Eugene stepped forward, but Tommy grabbed her arm and stopped her.

"If I may," said Tommy. "We don't want a scene."

"Vamps," Eugene said, shaking her head, but stepped behind him.

"Trust me," he said, lifting his arm. "Stay here and watch the master work."

Eugene leaned against a cool, wet wall. While temperatures were falling as steadily as rain over the past week, the muggy air pressed against her skin, making her not only sticky but uncomfortable. As soon as she entered any building, cold, air-conditioned air beat into her, making her shiver. She missed the cool, dry nights of Vegas.

Tommy stepped away from her. Before he was out of reach, she whispered to him. "And he's wearing my favorite vest."

Tommy leaned against a car at the end of the lot. The man with her bicycle saw Tommy but continued walking past him, despite Tommy's greeting. Eugene shook her head, but the man stopped and turned around, walking back to Tommy. They laughed, not the laugh of strangers sharing a common joke, but the laugh of friends sharing a long-running jab at the other. Tommy stood straight and led the man to the side of the building. Eugene neither saw nor heard anything else from them.

She turned to walk back into the lot behind the complex when she saw Tommy riding her bicycle and wearing her vest. "Done," he said, jumping off the bicycle.

"That was fast," Eugene said, turning the light on her phone to look at it.

"Turn that off," snapped Tommy. "You want to be seen?"

"Oh, yeah," said Eugene.

Tommy handed her the vest. It reeked of cigarette smoke, car exhaust, sweat, weed, hate, and fear. "I should have let him keep it." She held the vest with her fingertips at the end of her arm.

Tommy grabbed it from her. "It's not that bad," he said, but held it away from him. "I'll get it cleaned for you. It'll be okay. Let's get out of here."

Eugene lifted her bicycle into the cab of the car where Tommy took it and laid it down, fastening it with straps stored in a side box. "Don't want it scratching," he said.

Eugene noticed the wide grin on Tommy's face and the rose in his cheeks. "Tommy," she said, unsure how to ask a delicate question. "You didn't kill that guy, did you?"

Tommy's cherub laughter floated over her. "No, he's very much alive. He might be a little giddy when he wakes up, but he'll have a hell of a good memory."

Eugene asked no more questions. The moratorium on killing to feed remained in effect in the city, no matter who was in charge, but Eugene knew vamps to lose their tempers or wait too long to feed and get away with killing. Despite knowing several vamps in Vegas, she was friends with none, and her curiosity piqued.

As they drove out of the empty lot, Eugene saw the man who's stolen her bicycle laying naked on the ground next to the curb. "You took all his clothes," she said.

Tommy grinned. "He enjoyed himself."

*****

Tommy parked his new truck at the back door of CC's house. Eugene turned the flashlight on her phone and fought with the lock on the bike barn until it unlocked and she pulled open the doors. Despite her best efforts, she growled as the hairs on her neck rose. Her legs widened and knees loosened as she lowered to a fighting stance.

"Wait," Tommy said. "Is he here?"

Eugene tilted her head in one direction and then another. Cars were traveling along the interstate less than a mile away. The accountants next door snored and mumbled in their sleep. Someone nearby hit snooze on an alarm clock. Similar noises came from houses down the street. A morning lark called. Dogs didn't bark. Cats didn't screech. There was no silence, no growling, no shuffling on paws or feet. The one thing that didn't belong was the odor.

"Death," Eugene said.

Tommy's eyes glared, reflecting off her flashlight. "Human, and dead a while."

"This is so bad," said Eugene.

"Put the light out. Let's see what's here," said Tommy.

Eugene turned out the light and stepped forward. Where two

motorcycles, one with a sidecar, should have been, pale pink scrubs torn and splattered with blood and gore, lay crumbled in a mound in the center of the floor. Eugene wanted to turn away, but she forced her eyes to search for a face. She gagged. A neck twisted too far. A dark, tangled mass of hair revealed where a face should be, but there was little left to call a face. The constant clicks of maggots rummaging in a dark cavity confirmed it was once flesh and a heart once beat inside it.

Under the domineering odor of decay, a trace of the monster.

"Come on," Tommy said. His voice was tight. Eugene looked into his eyes. They gleamed with the blue light of the streetlamps. "I'll call Clay. CC and Cesar need to know."

*****

Eugene jumped out of the pickup before the engine was off and ran to the front door amidst cat-calls and moans from the long line waiting to get into the club. Stanly stood at the door with the human bouncers and nodded her in. She strode through the throng of people to the steps leading to the office when Tommy stopped her.

"Cesar's over there," he said, nodding to the bar where Cesar leaned against the counter talking to a tall, pretty girl with short, black hair.

"Cesar," Eugene said, knowing he'd hear her over the throng. "We need to talk."

Cesar straightened and moved to her faster than a human should, but not so fast as to be noticed. His expression changed from smiling sex to concern. "What's wrong?"

"Another body," Tommy said.

"It's our guy," added Eugene. "Has to be."

"At CC's house." Tommy looked over the dance floor. "Is she still here? Clay's on his way to move it."

"No," Cesar was staring up at the wall of one-way mirrors. "Call Clay back. Tell him to leave it. Eugene, use one of the burner phones under the bar to call it in to the police." He motioned to Stanly, who'd followed Eugene inside the bar. "Call Max," Cesar said.

Tommy folded his arms across this chest. "CC will want to know."

"She's upstairs," Cesar said. "Sleeping."

Eugene looked up from behind the bar. "Good. She hasn't been sleeping well. I think-"

"Police, Eugene," Cesar said. "Call from down the block."

Eugene nodded as she headed to the entrance.

"Go with her," Cesar said to Tommy.

Tommy's eyes narrowed. "Look, kid," he stared, but Cesar raised his palm.

"He's calling us out. Do you know for certain he didn't follow you here? If you haven't noticed," Cesar paused and nodded to Eugene. "She's a little flighty."

Tommy burst into laughter, flooding those in earshot with smiles at mirth unlocked for. "You got balls, kid. That's why I like you. But you're right. I'll keep an eye on the wolf. You wake our charmer."

Eugene grumbled as she waited inside the door for Tommy. "I do not need a babysitter," she told him.

Tommy put his arm in hers and led her out. "It just means he likes you," he said. "And you should learn not to eavesdrop."

Eugene fanned her face with her hand as heat rose to her cheeks, hearing her mother's words from Tommy's mouth.

*****

"He's made a move," Cesar said, pouring orange juice into a tall, chilled glass.

CC stretched, yawned, and stood. "Sorry for falling asleep on your couch. Another body?"

She took the offered glass, but as it approached her lips, she stopped and asked. "What are you afraid to tell me?"

Cesar scratched his head and leaned over the bar. "He left it in your garage."

CC plopped onto the bar stool, her juice still in her hand. Neither spoke.

Cesar's eye remained fixed on CC's face. "I told Eugene to call the police and Clay to leave the body where it was. I thought you wanted the police involved."

CC realized she was thirsty and drank the glass of juice as quick as she could. Sliding off the barstool, she said, "I do. Good call. The garage belongs to Jane and Tom. That will keep the busy-bodies off my back. He left the body for me to find. Ready to go?"

Cesar stared at CC. "Go where?"

"The house," she said. "By the time we give the fur-babies a minute or two near a bush and drive to the house, the police will be there. Run interference until I'm sure Mike is there and awake enough to keep them out of the house."

Cesar tugged the knot of his tie. "You sound like you expected this."

CC smiled. "He's desperate for my company. If he's desperate, he'll make mistakes. Once Frank or Renaldo gets to the house, we can make plans. Speaking of, I better call them."

Her phone was at her ear when Eugene and Tommy entered the office. Renaldo didn't answer, but Frank did.

"Frank," she said.

Frank's voice grumbled. She could hear his siren over the phone. "CC, why the hell am I getting a call about a body at your address?"

"I just heard about it myself," she said. "It's got to be one of your missing kids."

"Damn," mumbled Frank. "I was afraid of that."

"Look," she said before he spoke again. "Keep your eyes open. This is very public for him. He wants something."

Tommy's voice interrupted her. "You're awake, good."

CC raised her hand and shushed him.

"I think I know what he wants." Eugene's voice interrupted her this time.

Eugene picked up Bean. "I'll take them out," she said.

Cesar nodded to Tommy, but Tommy rolled his eyes. "I am not a dog sitter."

"I do not need vamp junior walking around with me," Eugene said, pulling open the door.

CC put the phone to her chest. "Tommy, Eugene, outside. Cesar, get the car. Has anyone called Max?"

Putting the phone to her ear, she said, "Be careful, Frank."

"Does the whole city know already?" Cesar muttered.

"Only those who need to know," she said, and closed the call.

Cesar set his phone on his desk and looked at her. She stood still, counting her breaths.

Cesar waited, standing, watching, and saying nothing.

CC lifted her face to look at Cesar. "Let's go." She grabbed her backpack and walked out the door without waiting for a response.

*****

Luna opened the door and slipped as Marcus told her to stay in the car.

"Luna," snapped Marcus.

"CC could be hurt," Luna said as she slipped between the gathering crowd to the edge of CC's fence.

"There's no ambulance," said Marcus, taking her arm and wrapping it around hers. "That's good."

"Then why so many police?" Luna asked. She bit her lower lip and looked across the street at the empty dog park. A light breeze blew across her face. She rubbed her eyes. For a moment, she thought she saw something move inside the park. A shudder ran through her.

"I'm sure she's fine," Marcus said, tightening his grip as she shuddered.

"She is," came Max's voice from behind them.

Luna and Marcus both jerked their heads to look behind them. Max stood no more than a foot from them, arms folded in front of his chest, gazing over the heads of the crowd and the police.

"Someone found a body in the garage between her house and their neighbor's," Max added.

Luna noticed his face was paler in the streetlights than it was in the dim lights of the cafe. Only his eyes looked bright, as though reflecting the streetlights. But humans didn't do that.

"I told you," said Marcus to Luna. "She's fine. We should go home. We're just in the way here."

"How did you hear about it?" Luna asked Max.

Max didn't look at her to answer. "She called me."

From the corner of her eye, Luna caught a shape in the dog park, large, moving slower than the breeze, but steadily toward the nearest gate. Her heart sped up. Its pounding drummed in her ears. She held her breath, waiting.

An old man, a very large old man, stepped through the gate and into the circle of a streetlight. A massive beard hung long and gray, disappearing onto a face with a mustache equally gray and bushy, hiding a mouth. Gray eyebrows, more like one thick mass of gray brush, hid his eyes except for dark, almost glass-like black balls gleamed from within the thick, gray mass, revealing his eyes. For a moment, as the old man's head turned to gaze over the crown, they looked like sick-yellow eyes glowing into her.

"Luna." Marcus's voice felt like an anchor in her mind. "Luna," it came again.

She turned to face her brother. He shook her shoulders. She gasped in a mouthful of air. Her body shook, but not from her brother.

"Luna, are you okay?" Marcus' voice filled her ears and then her mind, and she stared into clear tan-brown eyes.

"I need to see CC," she said.

Marcus hugged her. Rubbing her back, he said, "I got you. You're safe." Pulling away from her, he pulled out his phone. "Let me message her. If she's not talking to the police, I'm sure she'll come see you."

"No need," Max said, placing and hand on each of their backs and pushing them to the front door. "She's at the front door. Let's go inside."

"But the police," started Luna, until Marcus squeezed her arm and he pulled her to the house. Luna looked behind once as they stepped toward CC's house. She didn't see the man, but the chill she'd felt when he arrived remained.

*****

The body still lay crumbled in the center of the garage. Men and women continued to walk around the house, in and out of the garage, up and down the street, knocking on doors. Lights flashed and the tension in Eugene's shoulders rose to the back of her neck and into her head. As much as she enjoyed city life, she did not like her territory being abused. Tonight, not only did the monster she was hunting invade her space, but police criss-crossed it, tearing into every corner and under every stone. She'd already had to replace the saucer of milk on the back stoop twice.

She sat on the stairs, watching the front door. CC closed the curtains and leaned against the old receptionist's desk while Frank Jarvis sat in the chair. Frank and Renaldo were the only police officers to enter the house, and Eugene hoped no others came in. She doubted whether she could allow anyone inside the house. Even more frightening was the thought of a stranger in her room.

"Constance Bridges, fifteen, went missing a few weeks ago," said Frank, looking up from his phone. "Worked nights as a cleaner at a hospital. Lied about her age, of course, but kept her grades up. Good kid."

"Adopted?" Asked CC.

"There's the rub," said Frank.

Eugene glimpsed Cesar sitting behind CC's desk in her office. The door was open to her office, and Frank pretended he wasn't there.

"Her grandmother reported her missing. Lived with her, but she said her daughter showed up at her house one day with little Constance in diapers. She hadn't seen her daughter in a year and took her for her word Constance was her daughter."

CC nodded. "No records of her anywhere."

"Daughter married a Marine stationed in Germany. Grandmother never met him, but it got her into the country on a special visa. When it ran out, she stayed. We're tracking down the Marine now."

"No surprise there," muttered Tommy, sitting behind Eugene.

"I know Eugene lives here, but who are you again?" Frank asked, looking at Tommy.

"Her date," Tommy answered with a straight face.

Eugene sat up and put her arm around Tommy, who did the same. "We both work at Coffee Philosophy," Eugene said.

CC raised an eyebrow, and Eugene looked away.

"What?" Eugene asked.

Renaldo walked in from the back and looked up at her. He shook his head before turning his attention to CC and Frank. "They're taking the body now. We won't be much longer."

Eugene watched CC's face pale as she stared at the heavy drapes over the window. Cesar stood and disappeared from view. He moved too fast, but Eugene thought she heard him open the drapes in CC's office. That's when she heard the neighborhood dogs. They all barked once, and then stopped.

CC opened the front door.

"What's up?" asked Renaldo. Frank said nothing but watched CC with narrowed eyes.

CC opened the door, and that's when Eugene smelled him. The hairs on her neck went up, and she choked, holding back a growl in the back of her throat.

"Eugene?" Asked Frank, and Eugene realized she was standing.

Tommy wrapped his arm around her. "Sweetie's a little peckish, and she gets weird when she's peckish," he said.

From the living room, Fluffy growled and Bean barked. The neighborhood dogs joined, but the barking moved away from the house, block by block, slow and steady.

"Look who's here," said CC as Luna and Marcus entered the house, followed by Max.

The tension in Eugene's shoulders loosened as Tommy massaged a knot out from between her shoulder blades. She looked at CC and all the faces in the room. They all looked at CC.

Frank, still sitting in his chair, pretending to look at something on his phone, also looked to CC. Renaldo stood next to the stairs waiting near Eugene, looking to CC. Cesar was back at CC's desk, looking at CC and waiting for something. Even Tommy, still rubbing that knot out of Eugene's shoulders, looked at CC. Max stood behind Luna and Marcus. He watched everyone but kept his eyes on CC. Luna looked to CC, her expression confused, biting her bottom lip, not sure what she was waiting for. Only Marcus didn't look at CC. He kept his eyes on Luna, helping her over the threshold.

Tommy called CC a charmer. That's what she was. Eugene saw it now. She wondered why she hadn't seen it before. Was it magic that made CC able to see them all for what they were? Was it that sight that made them all trust her?

Eugene wanted answers. She caught Max's eyes, watching her as he stepped over the threshold. He nodded, and she knew then they both realized how much of a charmer CC was.

"Come in," CC said.

The spell broke. Tommy still clung to Eugene's side. Renaldo looked down at them, shaking his head.

"Feeling better, sweetie?" asked Tommy, looking up into Eugene's face.

Eugene smirked at Renaldo and pulled Tommy closer. "Much better, pookie. Let's get something to eat," she said. Tommy enjoyed being pushed into her breasts too much, but it was worth the bewildered look on Renaldo's face.

*****

CC breathed in the tickle in her neck telling her Max drew near to the house. The hairs on her right shoulder were Cesar, and the hairs on her left shoulder were Tommy. The breath of wildness that lingered in her nose was Eugene. As Frank spoke, she reached out her senses with purpose. Someone was near and she didn't know who or what it was. The feeling was familiar but new at the same time.

Renaldo entered from the back door and walked through the kitchen to the reception room. No one else would walk through a strange house in their cowboy boots with such confidence.

Renaldo said something, but she didn't hear the words. The neighborhood dogs barked, but not Fluffy or Bean on the couch in the living room. She moved to the front door and opened it. The sounds of the night stopped. Across the street, standing in the shadows of the streetlights, it stood. CC tilted her head. Shadow on shadow wavered out of easy sight. A large, man-shaped shadow stepped toward the circle of light from the streetlamp but didn't enter.

"Together," whispered into her ear as the breeze pushed the curls on her neck.

"No," she whispered back.

"CC," Marcus' voice broke her connection with the beast. Marcus, with Luna leaning on him, walked up the path. Max walked behind them. "We were on our way home when we saw all the police. We thought you might need some help."

A feeling as snug as a warm blanket wrapped around CC's shoulders as she looked in their faces. "We're good," she said. "Come inside."

CC nodded as Max faded into the background and the door to her office closed. Eugene with Tommy held firm at her side followed to the living room where she deposited Luna and Marcus on the sofa before going to the kitchen.

"You want to make coffee?" She asked Eugene and laughed as Eugene pushed Tommy away from her.

"But sweetie," said Tommy with over-the-top eloquence.

"Scram, pookie," muttered Eugene. "Or Fluffy will have you for dinner. Speaking of, do we have anything around here to eat? I'm starving."

Tommy opened the refrigerator as someone knocked on the back door.

CC was almost out of the kitchen. "More company," she said, opening the door before a knock. "Come on in."

Tom and Jane entered, with Jane holding Myrtle.

"Oh my god! CC," began Jane. "It's terrible. Poor Myrtle's beside herself."

Eugene took the small dog, and CC hugged Jane. "It's over now, Jane. Everything's okay."

"That's what I keep telling her," said Tom, following the women into the living room. "Oh, I'm sorry. We didn't realize the police were still here."

Renaldo and Frank nodded and made polite but official gestures as they walked out the back door.

"Call you after the autopsy, CC," said Renaldo as he stepped out the door. His foot landed with a snap and crash. "What the-"

"Another dish? Sorry Renaldo. They keep showing up on the stoop," said CC, reaching out to grab Renaldo's arm before he slipped.

He laughed. "Whatever it takes to keep the hobgoblins happy." He winked and got in the car with Frank.

Shrugging, CC took a last look at the small parking area between her house and Tom and Jane's. The small garage/storage shed was locked. All that remained from hours of interruption was the yellow tape across the garage door. A familiar tug at her heart reminded her James Earl was not here to complain about police involvement or too many people in the house.

"You need to get rid of them," whispered Tommy to CC.

"No," said CC, looking into Tommy's face and seeing the experienced old man behind the youthful expression and perfect dimples. "We need to be good neighbors. Besides," she reached down and picked up Bean whining at her feet. "They stay until the sun is up."

*****

CC leaned her elbows on the table, clasping her mug with both hands. Its heat permeated her fingers as the steam floated into her nose. The tension in her shoulders eased. She was glad the heavy drapes and blinds kept the room dark. Since the first signs of dawn, the nervous chatter from Tom, Jane, Marcus, and even Luna and Eugene slowed. Everyone was tired, but the tension was slow to ebb.

The sound of Eugene's voice, sweet and singing as she ate her pancakes, allowed little joy in a room where everyone knew they had danced with death the night before. Eugene talked non-stop about the value of a hardy breakfast, the sweetness of maple syrup, and deliciousness of butter, her latest art project, and the artistry of her mother's tattoo work. CC wanted to laugh but shook her head as Luna used a second fork to offer Fluffy another bite of her pancakes. Luna lowered her head as her cheeks flushed. Fluffy returned to CC's side with her best pitiful and hungry look.

"Oh," Eugene continued, "Got a text from Phin, that's my brother, says he'll be in town later today or tomorrow. Loves to hitch. Stupid, I know, but he's made good time. CC, can Phin stay here a day or two?"

"Of course," CC said. "Looking forward to meeting him."

Max walked into the room with another plate of pancakes, setting a plate in front of CC. "Vegan," he said with a nod and walked out. Tom stared at Max over his coffee mug. Jane, sitting next to him with Myrtle on her lap, picked at the food on her plate. Her eyes drooped and she would fall asleep except for Myrtle continually reaching up to lick her chin.

Luna watched everyone. She sat up straight eating her food, responding to Eugene whenever she stopped talking long enough to put food in her mouth. CC caught Luna's eyes following Max out of the room and darting back to Cesar sitting at the other end of the table. He nodded to her and the plate in front of her.

"You should at least try them," he said.

She took a bite. A drop of syrup caught in the corner of her mouth, and she licked it up. Sweet maple, toasted almonds, and a hint of chipotle filled her mouth. Her stomach shouted for more, and she ate the rest without thinking. When she finished the plate, another appeared in front of her.

The vibration of a phone on the table rippled through a pool of syrup on her plate. She looked up. Cesar tapped his screen, and looking at her, shook his head.

Another phone beeped, and Tom pulled it out of his pocket. "It's Emily," he said to Jane. Looking up to CC, he added. "Our intern. I almost forgot. She wanted to come to do some extra work, even though it's a Saturday. A real go-getter, but I'll tell her to wait 'til Monday."

"No," said Jane, sitting up and shaking her head. "It's okay. If she's already here, we might as well take advantage of it. Besides, I'm supposed to deliver that report to Cairns today."

"We can put him off," started Tom.

Jane stood. "No. That's not 'til later. Max," she called out to the kitchen. "I don't know when I've had better pancakes. Thank you. And CC, thanks for putting up with my hysterics. It's just when the police said they found a body in our garage-"

"I'm glad you were here," CC interrupted. She walked them to the back door and waited until they entered their house before closing the door.

Marcus entered the kitchen carrying a stack of dirty plates. "I'll clean up, Max," he said. "I'm sure you're tired."

Max nodded and left the kitchen. CC recognized the too-polite smile and his sharp gaze.

"Dishes will wait," she said. "You and Luna go home and get some rest. I bet you're supposed to be at the coffee house at some point today."

"It's not a problem," he said and turned the faucet on as far as he could turn it. Lowering his voice, he asked, "Is Luna safe?"

CC reached for a plate and stood close enough to Marcus that their shoulders touched. "We're watching her," she said, not surprised by Marcus' question.

Marcus stopped pretending to rinse plates. "I know he's been around."

Bending over the dishwasher, she asked, "Have you seen him?"

"Last night," Marcus said, nodding.

"And before last night?"

"A few times," Marcus said, and picked up a towel to wipe off the countertop. "Mama can't handle losing anyone else. I don't think I can either."

CC put her hand on his shoulder. "That's not going to happen."

Marcus folded the towel into a perfect rectangle. His mouth formed a firm line across his face. "I know the police can't help us with this, but you and Uncle Frank talk. I've seen you at the cafe. He knows?" He took in a long breath and let it out slowly before looking at her. "I don't know why, but I trust *you*."

CC nodded. "I'm on your side. Frank knows enough to keep an eye on you two and your mom. He's one of the good guys."

"Luna," Marcus called to the dining table, "Let's go."

Luna pushed away from the table. "Coming."

When she stepped back into the house after seeing Marcus and Luna drive away, Cesar was sitting behind her desk. Max leaned on her desk, and Tommy and Eugene sat on the small sofa in her office.

"We have to do this now?" she asked, knowing the answer.

8

Luna adjusted the straps on her costume and put her shoes on - flats. She curled her lip, looking at the shoes. Her costume was perfect except for those black flats. The black vest with red stitching over the red silk shirt with its long puffy sleeves tied with neat, black bows, the flowing black skirt with the red chiffon petticoat and the bedazzled bat earrings made her the perfect vampire for the Halloween party. But her shoes. She'd bought new, lovely, black boots with four-inch spikes and laces to her knees. They would make the costume perfect. But when she slid the right boot on, her toes squealed in protest, and when she stood, she wobbled.

"Flats it is," she said. "No way I'm falling over and breaking my nose tonight." She looked at her reflection in the mirror over her dresser, applied deep purple lipstick, and twirled. The skirt shot out into an enormous circle. She giggled and pulled her vest down and her collar up, revealing a thick line of cleavage. "Get a load of this, Scarlett," she muttered.

"Luna," shouted Marcus from downstairs. "Aunt Jasmine's here."

Luna pulled the small black bag holding her phone and credit card over her head as she leaped down the stairs.

"Hi there, Luna," Aunt Jasmine's voice rang through the house as she charged in. Jasmine stopped and looked at Luna. "And what are you supposed to be? Jackie, are you ready?"

Marcus took Aunt Jasmine's overnight bag. "I'll put this in the car for you. Mama's already put her bag in."

Luna looked up, watching Aunt Jasmine's eyes appraise her costume. She stood and twirled. "Isn't it fun?" she said.

Marcus shrugged. "You look nice."

Luna put her hands on her hips as Aunt Jasmine shrugged her shoulders. "I'm a vampire, duh!"

"I think it's perfect," said Jackie, coming out of the kitchen. She kissed Luna's cheek. "Now you be careful tonight. College parties are notorious for the amount of alcohol that flows. Drink nothing you didn't see poured into your cup."

Luna gulped. "Yes, Ma'am. I'll be careful." She looked at Marcus, but he had already stepped through the door. "And you be good, Mama. Girls' weekends are notorious."

"I'll keep her in line, don't you worry about that," laughed Aunt Jasmine. "Are you ready Jackie? Frank won't leave until he sees us getting in the car."

"He should come in," Jackie said and walked to the door. She didn't call Frank but closed the door. "I think we have time for a cup of tea. Don't you?" Jackie pulled Jasmine to the kitchen.

Luna squinted, watching her mother and aunt walk away. She knew the look on her mother's face. She was up to something. Aunt Jasmine had it too once she realized her sister would not let her just leave. They were twins in everything.

Luna sat on the stairwell and caught sight of Marcus standing in front of the house with Uncle Frank. She searched for an excuse to step outside to hear what they were talking about. She and Marcus didn't talk to Uncle Frank unless they had to. He only married Aunt Jasmine last year, but Luna remembered the first time she saw him, standing with other cops outside her house, when Tony disappeared.

She stood and ran into the kitchen when she saw Marcus and Frank shaking hands and Thad's car pulled up behind Uncle Frank's.

"Mama, Thad's here. I'm going," she yelled from the entrance way.

"No, you're not," replied her mother, returning to the entranceway. "He can come to the door like a civilized man."

"Mama," whined Luna, but she had to stop as Marcus and Uncle Frank walked in.

"You ladies heading out soon?" asked Uncle Frank. "I gotta get to work."

Aunt Jasmine's head popped in the doorframe to the kitchen. "Chill, Frank," she said. She nodded her head to Jackie. "Come back here and help me for a sec. You've got plenty of time."

"But Renaldo said-"

Aunt Jasmine interrupted him. "Never mind about Renaldo. Come here." She stepped into the entranceway and took him by the arm to the kitchen. "Now," she added when the doorbell rang.

Luna felt her face burn and heart sink as Marcus grinned at her before opening the door.

"Hi, Luna," Thad said, standing in the doorway. He wore an old-time black suit and a white wig. Luna admired his shining brown eyes and easy grin, despite the silly costume. "Love your costume. Vampire, right?"

"Yes," Luna said, trying not to giggle out loud.

"You must be Dr. LeBrere-Smythe. I'm Thad Miller. Pleased to meet you." Thad shook Jackie's hand.

She nodded her approval to Luna as she left them at the doorstep. "You two have fun tonight. Marcus. You sure about holding down the fort tonight?"

Marcus grinned. "Tommy and I have everything covered," he said. "Midnight Bites will run smooth as silk."

"I should be there," Jackie sighed. "But when Jasmine said she had reservations for a spa weekend, it sounded too good to pass up."

"It is, Mama." Marcus said. "You deserve a little time on your own. You have fun. Luna, you and Thad get out of here and have fun, too. I'll work like a dog all night long."

Luna laughed. Mama going away for the weekend, Marcus having fun with his cafe, and she was going to a party with Thad. The night couldn't get any better.

Thad let her out the door and to the car. He opened the door for her and closed it as she got comfortable and pulled her seatbelt on. Mama and Aunt Jackie pretended to not watch her getting into the car. Uncle Frank and Marcus openly watched. Luna waved, and Marcus held his phone up to her.

"So," Thad said. "Sounds like you've got a whole night on your own." He started the engine and waved as Jackie waved them off. His smile slipped into a frown as Uncle Frank looked at them and crossed his arms over his chest. "Who's the big guy?" he asked.

"That's just Uncle Frank. Never mind him," Luna said. "I can't wait to see Scarlet. She wanted me to dress like one of her maids."

*****

It was a sweet ride. Eugene wanted to feel awkward riding James Earl's motorcycle, but she didn't. It was made for her. Despite their differences in height, it took only a quick shift to set the footrest back and make a perfect fit. She leaned into a right turn, and the bike followed with the grace she expected from a custom cycle. A slight press of her foot, and the engine kicked in, reaching highway speed faster than the surrounding cars. She turned her head to check behind her and sped past the cars in front of her.

Ahead of her, Austin glittered as it grew larger with each second. One property left, not too far from the house, but surrounded by warehouses converted into modern distilleries, shops, and bars. Eugene agreed with the others that it was an unlikely location for their monster to hide.

And yet, Eugene sniffed out traces of their prey at each property. They knew his hiding spots. They would find him. She would kill him.

Instead of bad roads and trucks, the long road of warehouses flowed straight between two rows of new metal buildings. Cars parked bumper to bumper on both sides of the road. The lots around three of the warehouses were full of more cars puttering back and forth until a car pulled out of a spot, and then they converged as one. The music from live bands in the warehouses across the street merged into a single, chronic heartbeat. Eugene drove past a replica of an old-time still at the end of the road. The place was full of music spilling out of the tasting room onto open air seating and a food truck with a line of people wrapped around it.

The warehouse she wanted sat behind this one. Turning off the main road, the first of multiple potholes slowed her. She parked the cycle next to a row of cycles parked along the side wall of the distillery. Two men in leather vests and long chains dropping out of their jeans pockets leaned against the wall watching her park. One man nodded to her as she removed her helmet and walked toward the open-air seating area. She nodded back, no longer worried about James Earl's bike being stolen.

The smell of tamales grabbed her attention as she passed the food truck. Whiskey and gin flowed in abundance inside the distillery, but outside people laughed, sipped, talked, and ate in subdued tones. Her phone vibrated in her pocket.

Location? said CC.

Eugene grinned. *Distillery, want me to pick up?*

Getting dark, come home, said CC.

Eugene's grin widened. *Checking first. Phin arrived?*

Not yet, replied CC.

She put her phone in her back pocket when it vibrated again. *Where?*

This time, it was Phineas. She couldn't help the smile spreading across her face. He'd left two years ago for the Wilderness, but he'd always stayed in touch. She skipped before she stopped to text her location.

Putting the phone back in her pocket, she meandered, occasionally skipping in excitement, down a narrow alley between the back of the distillery and the fence separating it from the old, falling warehouse behind it. A quick look at the crowd to ensure no one noticed her, and she stepped into the alley and darkness. She listened. No one said anything about seeing her. She reached up with her right arm. Her fingers could just touch the top of the fence. One more look around her, and she leaped over the fence, landing on both feet.

The noise from the distillery shifted to a muffled murmur. There were no lights, but her eyes adjusted. The moon, just full, tugged at her chest.

"No," Eugene whispered, even as the scent of mice and bats tickled her nose. No hunting on paws tonight.

Eugene straightened and walked toward the warehouse, which as she moved closer, she saw showed signs of repair: a new metal plate screwed in here, fresh paint over rust there. She walked to the front of the warehouse, where a new door and very shiny lock stood ajar. On either side, new plywood with new screws covered the windows to an office. And somewhere, faint and clear in her ears, a whimper. A small heart beat faster than it should.

Her own hair tickled Eugene's neck as it rose. She breathed in a long, deep breath into her nose, and flowing from the crack in the doorway, the scent of death, her prey, and someone very young. Eugene rubbed her fingers together. The wolf's hackles rose. She looked up, hoping to see the moon, but it hid behind a cloud. She reached for her phone, but the whimper turned to cry, "I don't know."

Eugene stepped into the warehouse office. She crept low to the ground searching for footprints, something to follow, but the floor was clean in the office. Another door on the opposite side of the empty office stood closed between a wall of windows. The warehouse was dark.

Skin hit skin, and bone cracked. "Where's the others?" a voice roared, a familiar voice, a voice as human as it was not human. Eugene turned to the knob of the door. It clicked, echoing in through the warehouse.

An angry roar filled her ears as it bounced off the empty walls. The wolf charged.

In the center of the warehouse lay a child, huddled, bound, and shaking with fear. Above the shadow of a man who was not a man turned to face the wolf. The shadow roared again and charged Eugene.

Eugene leaped, landing on the creature's front. Her teeth missed its neck but caught its ear. Blood spilled into her mouth, but massive hands pushed her off. She landed on all fours between the shadow and the child. She spun as a wooden board slammed into her. Nails bit into her side as she flew across the dirty concrete. She yelped but turned to stand, ready to leap. The creature moved to her again. She was ready for an assault, but not for the flash and bang of a gun. A bullet ripped into her side, stinging as it passed through flesh and muscle and tore into her lung. She howled, as long and as loud as she could, before rising to charge the creature again, but it vanished into the night.

The child sniffled. Eugene limped her way to the child, falling flat on her stomach as she reached him. Brilliant blue eyes filled with tears stared at her. She forced her face to his and licked his tears and blood pouring from his nose.

He tried to move his arms, but his bonds prevented him. He slid his body close to the wolf. "I think you scared him away," the boy said and lay his head on her side.

His heartbeat was strong and fast. From the row of new warehouses came people howling and laughing. Beyond the warehouses from the homes across the freeway, dogs howled. One howl caught her attention. Five, maybe six miles away. A familiar long howl answered hers. Phineas knew where she was.

Eugene sighed as the boy continued to whisper to her. "It'll be all right. You scared the monster away." He didn't stop talking, finding courage in his own tiny voice.

Eugene closed her eyes as blood flowed out of her body, and she wondered if she would see her brother before she died.

*****

CC sat her phone back on the coffee table and picked up her keyboard. "To many places." She changed a dot from blue to orange. "Eugene's at the warehouse on distillery row now."

Cesar leaned forward on the couch. "We can't monitor all these places, and that's assuming he doesn't know we know his hiding places. We're going to need help."

"Agreed," said CC. "I know Max doesn't want to bring anyone else in, but," she stopped, sitting up straight and listening.

The howl, long and searching, reached CC's ears only a moment after Cesar's.

He stood, turning to face the front door. "That's Eugene."

Fluffy ran in from the kitchen, barking, with Bean close behind.

"Go," CC said to Cesar. "I'll follow."

Cesar tossed his car keys to her. "My car's faster." Cesar vanished before Fluffy barked again.

CC shook her head. "No, Fluffy. Watch the house. He knows where we live."

Bean, running as fast as he could in his cast, ran to CC's side. "No, Bean. You stay."

CC grabbed her backpack, leaning next to the coffee table. Reaching in, she pulled out her handgun in its holster, took a deep breath in, and attached it to her belt. "Hope I won't need this."

*****

Everybody was howling. First, the dogs in the neighborhood howled, then everyone in the backyard howled, and then everyone inside the house howled. No one sounded like a howling dog. The noise reminded Luna of her kindergarten graduation when she and her classmates all stood up and sang the national anthem, but she and her kindergarten classmates were more on key than the howlers at the party. The full moon lifted above the apartment building behind the house, providing her with just enough of a peek at it to tell her it was full. Partygoers in werewolf costumes continued to howl, but she stopped laughing when she heard the single howl of a dog so lonely, it broke her heart.

She leaned against the doorjamb leading to the backdoor. The night cooled her forehead and dried the sweat on her back. It was after ten and she'd yet to see Scarlett. Thad spent his time dancing with one girl after another. Every time he stopped, he brought her another burnt-orange cup. She smiled and thanked him, and as soon as he turned around, she dumped the sticky sweet drink and refilled it with water.

Thad pulled her into the darkened room and wrapped his body close to hers. He was firm and hot. His aftershave woody, sweet, and nice, but with her face pressed against his chest, it was hard to smell it over his sweat. They swayed back and forth. His hands rubbing her back and buttocks. She sighed and melted closer to him.

A shadow fluttered across her peripheral vision in the far corner of the room. She started but saw no one. Thad's right hand reached down her thigh and inched her skirt up.

"Thad," she said, pulling her head away from him. "People will see."

"Come on, baby," he said, and placed his mouth over hers.

Luna's heart skipped a beat with the sudden passion, but the taste of beer and someone else in Thad's mouth made her gag.

"What's wrong, baby?" Thad asked.

"Sorry," she said, pulling further away to escape the smell of his breath. "I need to find the restroom."

Thad pulled her close to him again, kissed her, and said, "Don't be long." As she pulled herself away, he grabbed her right hand and pushed it down the front of his costume, stopping as her fingers tightened on his erection. "I need you, baby. Hurry back."

Luna turned, walking as fast as she could through the crowd to the back of the house. The house was suddenly boiling hot. She made her way to the bar and filled a cup with ice and water. Again, a flutter in her periphery caught her attention. This time, it came from outside the back door, behind the bar. She took a step closer to the door. A pair of eyes looked at her, gray, clear, and familiar eyes reflecting the patio lights. They blinked once and disappeared. She shook her head, as a feeling like a warm, soft blanket fell over her. The hairs on her neck tickled once and disappeared. She fingered her phone in its little black bag now laced on her belt after someone had fallen onto her on entering the party and ripped the strap. "No," she muttered. "Not calling Marcus."

Someone yelled, "Whoop!" The lights in the living room brightened as the music sped up. Everyone danced in the living room and everywhere else. She weaved in and out of clusters of people toward the living room. As she entered, the front door opened, and Scarlett and her friends, stunning in their Marie Antoinette wigs, embroidered bustiers, and short, short skirts, entered. They laughed and danced their way through the crowd.

Luna smiled. They were beautiful. She pulled and tugged at her costume as she made her way through the crowd to Scarlett.

Scarlett turned as Luna approached. "Luna," shouted Scarlett, "You look so cute. I thought you were going to be one of my maids. But a gypsy! So cute, isn't she Thad?"

"Vampire," shouted Luna, putting her false fangs in her mouth and grinning.

"Oh, take them out," Scarlett groaned. "Vampires are so high school. Tell everyone you're a gypsy. Thad, get me a beer, would you?"

Luna hadn't noticed Thad, but he stood behind Scarlett and smiled down at Luna. He bent over and kissed Scarlett's neck before walking away to the bar. Scarlett turned to talk to someone else. Luna backed away. Her head swam as weight pushed down on her shoulders and into her chest. She used her fingers to put a piece of ice on her neck and made her to the back of the house.

"More like Scarlet Bitch," a voice said as she walked past a group. Her companions laughed.

"If they're here," said a masculine voice. "It's time for me to go. The Scarlet Bitch is bad enough, but that group of jocs always makes trouble."

"I thought you were a joc?" asked a woman's voice.

"I'm a real joc. They're the wanna-be's." said the first voice.

Luna bumped into Thad carrying two burnt-range cups. "Here you go. Relax. I thought of you, too," he said, shoving one cup into her hand. "You're a lot more fun after a couple of drinks."

Luna nodded but didn't drink from them. "Thanks," she shouted, and watched as he moved through the crowd back to Scarlett.

She walked past the bar, out the back door. Her fingers tapped her phone as she walked around to the front. She knew Marcus would drop what he was doing to come get her. He had said he would if she called. She hoped he didn't say, "Told you so."

*****

Cesar's car drove so smooth and went so fast, CC lost count of the stop signs, red lights, and speed limits she passed. In under ten minutes, the brakes squealed in front of the abandoned warehouse, and CC ran out of the car as fast as she could through the front door. She froze. A giant wolf in flowing shades of tans and browns stood in front of Cesar guarding Eugene, still a wolf, and a child curled up with her. The wolf growled, hackles raised, teeth gleaming from saliva, and eyes shining from the headlights of the car through the front door.

"Stay back, CC," Cesar growled.

CC recognized the growl in Cesar's voice too well. She never forgot how dangerous he could be, but it was different this time. It gave her courage. The danger in his voice, directed to the strange wolf, boosted her confidence. She removed her hand from her handgun and took in a long breath and opened her mind, compiling what she felt, heard, and saw: The familiar prickle on her neck of Cesar, the soft touch, like the hair on her arm of Eugene, the similar but different feel of the wolf out front, but no other unhumans.

Eugene moaned. CC shifted her weight from foot to foot as the unknown wolf backed up and licked Eugene's face. This new wolf was huge, much larger than Eugene's, but otherwise it could have been Eugene. CC relaxed her jaw with a long breath out and forced a smile on her lips.

"You've got to be Phineas," she said, walking toward the wolf.

The wolf stared at her and lifted its head and then sat. He twisted his head to one side and then the other. He looked behind him and then back at CC.

CC took a step forward, but the wolf stood and growled.

CC put her hands on her hips. "We do not have time for attitude. You either get behind me or bite me. Either way, I'm taking care of Eugene." CC plowed forward, pushing the wolf out of her way.

Cesar straightened his tie, keeping his hand eyes on the new wolf. "Yes, she can be bossy, but she knows what she's doing."

Cesar kneeled next to Eugene and the boy before CC arrived. He spoke in a calm, low, slow voice. "Everything's going to be okay now. This is my friend, CC. You're going to like her. Eugene, stay still." He reached to touch her, and she growled.

"Eugene," said CC. "Let Cesar help. Phineas is here, in case you hadn't noticed. You three need to get out of here. I called Frank on my way here."

"Don't go," shouted the shaking voice of the little boy. "The monster will come back."

"He's not coming back," CC said, reaching over to stroke the boy's head. She pulled her phone out and turned on its flashlight. "Do you have a pocketknife?" she asked Cesar.

"Never needed one," Cesar said.

CC kept her voice soft and her gaze on the boy. "See if you can cut his bonds. Will you tell me your name?"

"Luke," the boy answered. "You have a big dog."

Phin moved behind Luke. He lay on his stomach and licked the boy's hands before biting on the plastic ties binding them together.

"Yes, he's a big dog but he won't bite you." CC said. "Now, we need to get you home."

"But what if the monster comes back to the house?" Luke asked as CC bent over and picked him up.

"I can walk! I'm not a baby. The dog is hurt. I think he was shot," Luke complained.

CC nodded and helped Luke to his feet as Cesar lifted Eugene.

Eugene bared her fangs as Cesar reached to lift her.

"Like you're walking out yourself," Cesar muttered. He cleared his throat. "I'll take her to the doctor right now," Cesar said to Luke.

"Are you sure the monster's gone?" asked Luke, taking CC's offered hand.

Eugene dropped her head, allowing Cesar to pick her up. As he did, she licked his nose.

Cesar's face pinched and sniffed. "There's such a thing as carrying a role too far."

Phineas ran to the front door and barked once.

"Yes," said CC, leading them out of the warehouse.

CC opened the back of Cesar's car, and Cesar lay Eugene on the back seat. Phineas jumped into the back as Cesar removed a blanket and gym bag from the back. "Sweats in the bag," he said to Phineas.

Cesar closed the door. "I'll take her to the safe room at the club. We can protect her there."

"Good. Frank will be here any minute. Better you were gone," CC said, pulling Luke away from the car.

Cesar narrowed his eyes and looked around. "I don't like leaving you alone." He lowered his head to her ear, adding in a whisper. "He could be anywhere."

CC shook her head. "No. He's gone. I don't think he expected to be found. If he had, he'd still be here. Take care of Eugene. Phineas is a nurse."

"CC," Cesar said, eyes scanning the area.

CC put her hand on his shoulder. "We're good. I noticed the bikers over there." She pointed to the distillery behind them.

"You're going to trust bikers to keep you safe?" Cesar spat his words.

"Please. They're all cops," CC said, rolling her eyes. "Recognized two of them. As soon as you pull out, We start screaming. That reminds me." CC opened the passenger door and pulled out her backpack. She removed her gun from her waistband and handed it to Cesar. "You better take this."

Cesar said nothing else as he got in the car and raced away as fast as the car would go.

CC kneeled down in front of Luke. "First rule to survive is learning to yell for help. You up for that?"

Luke nodded. "Will the dog that saved me be okay?"

"I hope so," CC said. She stood feeling a tug at her heart, realized she liked Eugene and didn't know if she would survive. Lifting her face, she watched the moon over the trees and houses across the freeway. "I think she will. Now, as loud as you can."

They both yelled "Help!" until two men in jeans and leather vest jumped over the tall fence and came running toward them.

*****

"I love Flamenco," Tommy said, leaning against the coffee bar and watching a dancer in her red satin gown argue with one of the guitar players.

Marcus handed a drink to a customer and smirked, "A bit out of your league."

Tommy turned to Marcus with raised eyebrows. "I'm talking about art," he said. "The dance and music fit together like," Tommy paused as a customer asked Marcus for a chocolate latte. "Like chocolate and coffee. Each is excellent on its own. Each is bitter by nature, but combined, flavored, sweetened, it weaves tales of love and loss." He sighed and returned to watching the dancer argue with the other guitarist.

"I know what Flamenco is," snapped Marcus. "I hired them. How I got them I don't know."

Luna, sitting on her usual stool, but tonight shifted to the side of the coffee bar butted in. "What's to know? They're for hire and you were hiring."

Tommy smiled at Luna and said nothing. Marcus took a deep breath before answering her. "This troupe's from Spain touring the U.S. We shouldn't have been able to afford them."

"Oh," Tommy said, standing up straight. "One of the guitarists just left. I'll lay you odds there's been a lover's spat."

Marcus dropped the cup he was filling. "No," he muttered. "They can't. Look at the crowd. They're all here to see her dance."

"So," Luna began, with her face scrunched together. "Why did they agree to perform here?"

"I got this," said Tommy, and he rounded the bar to head off the dancer stomping her way to the restroom.

"Great," muttered Marcus. "What are we going to do?"

Luna sighed and stood. "I can call mama."

"No, you won't," Marcus said. "I'll take care of this. Besides, she's at the spa with her phone off. She needs a weekend on her own."

Before either could step away from the coffee bar, Tommy and the dancer were laughing their way to the stage. Luna strained her ears over the noise of the crowd to catch what Tommy was saying to the guitarist, but only snatches came to her, and they were all in Spanish.

"I didn't know Tommy spoke Spanish," she said to Marcus.

"Just goes to show," started Marcus, but Flo entered with a young woman at her side.

Flo's grin was so wide it almost broke her face. Two boys, in clean jeans and new tee shirts, walked in behind them. The youngest one yawned, but his eyes were wide. "Hey, guys. This is Marla," Flo said.

"The Marla?" asked Luna, grinning and winking at Flo.

Flo's cheeks burned bright red. "Yeah," she said.

Luna let the happiness spill from Flo's face as she introduced Marla and the kids engulfed her. "Hey," Flo said as Marla took the boys to a table. "Is your mom around? I really want to thank her for helping me find a new place for us. It's close enough I can walk here, and for Marla to get to her new job downtown."

"She'll be back Tuesday," said Marcus. "You can talk to her then. Take a seat and relax. Show's about to start, I hope."

Tommy returned to the bar. "Luna, you'll have to take over for me. I'll be on stage." He winked at Luna, his face glowing as he walked up to her.

"Seriously?" Marcus spoke before she had a chance.

"You don't mind, do you?" Tommy's face continued to smile. "Been a while since I've played much Flamenco, but Daniel listed their repertoire, and I know it all. This is going to be fun." He turned and walked back to the stage, where he picked up a guitar left by the other musician and strummed to tune it.

"Just goes to show," Luna said, laughing as Marcus' dropped jaw.

The other musician signaled Marcus as he and Tommy sat on stools. Marcus lowered the lights in the cafe and turned on the spotlights. First, one guitar strummed a melody and then the other answered. The dancer stood between them, posed, long and lovely. Her castanets clicked a slow, long rhythm, and the guitars exchanged barbs. The dancer and Tommy were beautiful.

Luna watched Tommy's eyes close and his mouth grew sad. His fingers danced up and down the strings, and still his eyes remained closed. And then he and the other guitarist joined in a new melody combining to form yet another one with the beat of the castanets and the clicking of the dancers' heels following and leading the story.

Luna felt the song grow inside her. She reached over and took Marcus' hand. "They're great," she said, squeezing.

Marcus smiled at her. "Can you believe Tommy?" he asked.

"House is full," she said as she looked around her. Standing room only remained, and no line formed for drinks. All attention was on the dancer.

"I'm glad you called me tonight," he said without looking at her.

Luna squeezed his hand again. "Sorry I had to, but I needed to get away from that party."

Marcus nodded as the front door opened. He moved to stand behind the counter as the new arrivals placed their orders before turning their attention to the dancer.

Luna watched as he made their drinks, enjoying his expression of contentment. Marla said something to Flo and picked up one of the little boys and placed him on her lap. Flo put the other boy in her lap and offered the chairs to the latecomers. Between sets, they were busy.

She helped serve. Flo went into the kitchen to pull out pastries meant for tomorrow's crowd and prepared more snacks as they sold out. As the final set began, Luna returned to her stool, drinking iced tea and fanning herself. She appreciated how Tommy managed the extra crew during his break. The cafe was still full. And then she realized Marcus wasn't there.

* * * * *

By the time Frank arrived, paramedics had Luke in the back of the ambulance, cleaning his cuts and bruises while a sergeant from the party talked to him. CC sat on a stool at the bar enjoying the bourbon the owner insisted on her having as more police arrived and stories circulated among the guests. Frank sat next to her, his arms folded over his chest and his fingers scratching the hair on his chin.

"Another?" asked the owner from behind the bar.

"No," CC answered, holding her hand over her glass. "Didn't know I liked bourbon until tonight, but more than this, and I'll be on the floor. Thanks."

The man laughed and moved to pour drinks for other guests.

"Gotta know your limits," Frank said, eyeing CC with his face toward the crowded tasting room.

"Yup," CC muttered. "How's Luke?"

"He'll be fine. Taking him to get checked out." Frank raised his mouth into a disgusting smirk. "His dad didn't even know he was missing. CPS will keep him for a few days."

"Good," CC nodded. "Want me in tomorrow for a statement?"

Frank turned to face her. "Luke keeps going on about a big dog that scared away the *monster*. There's blood splatter and gun residue in there."

CC didn't look at Frank. "Makes sense if you think about it."

Frank raised an eyebrow.

"You saw all the rodent and bat droppings. Stray dog wanders in looking for a meal. It's big and frightens the kidnapper. He shoots, wounding the dog, which gets pissed and attacks. Kidnapper runs away. Dog limps off to lick its wounds."

"Hmmm," muttered Frank. "Couple of the guys mentioned a tall, skinny girl with *killer sleeves* walking toward the back earlier in the evening. Where's your house guest, Eugene?"

CC looked at Frank this time. "In bed asleep." She added, *I hope* under her breath.

Frank's face turned red, and then he bit his bottom lip before asking in a whisper, "Was this the same guy we've been looking for?"

CC nodded and took another sip of her drink. "I do like this," she said. "Too bad I have so much to do."

The hair on CC's neck pricked at her and she sat up. "Frank,"

Frank stood and lifted his hand. "No, CC. Just get the SOB before another kid dies. Luke got lucky tonight."

She nodded as he walked away. As she took the last sip of her drink, she turned to see her reflection in the mirrored wall opposite the bar. Max and Clay stood on either side of her, towering over her.

They were so much alike, yet so different. Each tall and almost wraith-thin. One with such pale, white skin he could be ill. The other, with his dark brown skin but so pale of face, could also be ill. Yet, each carried himself wired, loose, ready to pounce. Each wore their hair long. One's dark hair hung loose and shaggy. The other wore long dreadlocks neat, pulled together with a black velvet ribbon.

Their eyes. Their eyes were the same. Dark, forbidding eyes that stormed one moment and tore into you the next. Eyes that disappeared if she looked straight into them, looked at her now. Small, ordinary. She was so ordinary, standing there in her jeans and tee shirt, long red curls splaying on her shoulders, and a face full of freckles, but these two nightmares befriended her, followed her. Realizing how much she had changed over the past year, she wanted to laugh.

She shook her head to break her sudden melancholia as Clay spoke. "I didn't think he'd ever leave. I like Frank, but sometimes he is too thorough."

"He's a good guy," CC answered. "Why are you two here?" Turning to look up into Max's face, she added, "I thought you were keeping an eye on Luna."

"She called Marcus to pick her up," Max said, motioning for a glass of bourbon. "I left her ensconced at the I with Tomas. And I'm here because I heard Eugene call."

"As am I," added Clay.

"Oh." CC couldn't help the surprise in her voice. "I wasn't into the party scene in college either. Clay," CC looked Clay up and down. While dressed all in black, he was not wearing his usual gloves, jacket, and top hat. "You are very un-undertaker. I like it."

"I hurried to get here," he said as the bartender set a flight of glasses in front of him. "It's been a long time since I hurried anywhere. Almost as long since I've tasted this." He closed his eyes and sipped from one glass. A smile perked up his lips. When he opened his eyes, he set the glass down, in the same spot it had been. "I still don't like the stuff. If my services are not required, I shall return home."

"This monster is getting bold, Clay," Max said.

CC shook her head. "No tonight. He didn't expect Eugene to find him."

Max shrugged his shoulders and said nothing, but Clay put a hand on CC's arm. "Do nothing rash, CC. I cannot afford to lose you."

CC smiled and looked up into Clay's pale but dark brown face. His dark, clear eyes with their crow's feet and silver tipped eyebrows were as honest as it ever was. His concern flowed so openly from him she hugged him. "I'll be careful, Clay. But you, too. This monster knows too much about us to not know about you."

"Perhaps," Max started, but stopped when CC shook her head.

"You will not suggest I hide."

"No," Max said, holding his glass under his nose and smelling. "I am going to suggest something unpleasant, though. Our prey wants Luna. We can use her."

"I don't like using children," Clay said, pulling a credit card out and handing it to the barman.

"Why did he grab Luke?" CC asked aloud although she directed the question to herself. "He's as human as human can be."

"He's been mistaken before," said Max. He paused and tilted his head before looking down at CC.

CC stood. "He thinks leaving me the body will make me talk to him."

Max nodded. "You've made it clear you won't."

"He watched the night we called the police about the body in my garage." CC crossed her arms. "He didn't expect that, and then Eugene finding him tonight."

"Is he running out of places to torture?" asked Clay lifting another glass to his nose.

"He can't cope," Max said and looked at Clay "We've been around long enough to see the signs."

"Agreed," said Clay.

Can't cope?" asked CC.

"Those who do not change with the times," said Max.

"Crumble under their weight," finished Clay.

CC stood. "Cesar told me why so few of you live long. It's the same thing, he's very old."

Max nodded. "And time is catching up with him. You're a woman and should submit to male authority."

CC snickered, but Clay replied. "That's so not going to happen."

"He's pissed he was almost caught tonight," CC said, grabbing her backpack. "We need to get to Luna and Marcus."

Clay pulled a set of keys out of his pocket. "Would you like my car?"

"No, thanks," CC said. "Eugene rode here on James Earl's bike. I've got the keys."

"I'll drive," Max said as he pulled the keys from CC's hand. "Why Marcus?" He shook his head to CC. "We'll get there much faster if I drive."

"Marcus is Luna's brother, he's adopted, and if either of them is going to change, it will be him." CC headed to the door and stopped releasing neither man followed her. "Come on. You don't see it?" She shrugged her shoulders. "Guess there is something to this charmer or touched thing. Clay, will you check on Eugene? I can't think straight not knowing how she is."

"Delighted to," answered Clay. "I hope her brother doesn't attack me."

*****

Eugene lay on the bed on her side. The ride in the car was almost as painful as being carried. The pain rushed through her shoulder and lungs and down her back. Her entire side pounded with each breath. She knew she needed to change, but the pain demanded she not.

"Sorry, kid," said Cesar, standing next to the bed. "It's got to hurt. But you know you need to change. There's nothing we can do until you do."

Eugene growled.

"Fine," Cesar said, lifting his arms in surrender. "I'll call a vet."

Eugene barked. She wanted to shout, but the bark had taken her breath.

The bed bounced. A fresh wave of pain flooded her synapsis, sending sparks through her snout. Fluffy licked her face. Eugene tried to push her away, but her paws wouldn't move.

Fluffy stopped licking and barked a warning as a much louder bark answered her. The bed shook again, and the brown wolf lay next to Eugene, whining.

"Phineas," said Cesar. "Can you get her to change?"

Fluffy in front of her and Phineas behind her flooded her with warmth. A paw wrapped around her from behind, but as she breathed in, the scent changed. An arm, long and strong, wrapped around her. "Lil' sis," came the voice, so much like hers but deep and resonate. "Come on. I know it hurts, but you've got to do it."

Eugene growled, but only a whimper came out. She hated it when Phineas called her Lil' sis, but as his warm body surrounded hers, and Fluffy continued to lick her face, she changed.

She howled as the pain of the bones bent, reformed, and muscles and tendons twisted around them. The howl turned to a scream, and she felt other hands grabbing her shoulders and holding her down.

"Breathe, Eugene," came Cesar's voice. "We've got you." Eugene couldn't see through the darkness that was her vision.

"One little prick," came Phineas' voice. A needle went into her arm.

"Ow," Eugene muttered even as a wave of disconnection washed over her.

"That's my lil'sis," said Phineas.

"Prick," muttered Eugene. "Only three minutes," was all she could say as sleep and a warm blanked wrapped around her.

*****

Luna eased off her stool and walked into the kitchen. Flo and Marla sat at the tiny chef's table near the pass-through window. Flo leaned back in her chair, sipping her iced tea as the younger boy curled up asleep against her breasts. Marla smiled up at Luna.

"Is Marcus back here?" Luna asked.

Flo shook her head.

"He said he was going outside to cool off a little while ago. I haven't seen him since," Marla said.

Luna nodded and wove through the crowd to the front door. People stood outside listening to the music, chatting, smoking, and drinking coffee. Marcus was not there. She walked down to the sidewalk. Parked cars filled the curb of the street and more eased their way up and down Twenty-First Street. She sent him a text and went back inside.

He didn't reply. A lump formed in the bottom of her stomach. She went into the office. The lights were off, and he wasn't there. Still no reply, so she sent him a message and sat on the couch, trying to slow her heartbeat.

The music filled the small office, but she didn't hear it. Her breath quickened as a familiar fear, a fear that settled into her bones so long ago, resurfaced. "No!" she said to the fear. "You will not take Marcus, too."

Luna walked to the window. Her hand shook as she grabbed the pull cord to the blinds. Another deep breath. She closed her eyes. "I will not be afraid." She opened her eyes and pulled the cord. The parking lot was full of cars. The co-op on the other side stood lit with life. No yellow eyes looked at her.

"Think, Luna. Think."

"CC said welcome to the family." Eugene and CC found her and cleaned her up the night of the party on the river. CC rescued her when the monster chased her. "CC knows what to do."

Luna checked her phone once more for any communication from Marcus, and then she pressed CC's speed dial button.

*****

Eugene stretched her body and winced. "Ow," she muttered.

"You're going to hurt for a while," Phineas said.

She opened her eyes. "You're here." Eugene smiled. "I thought maybe I dreamed you were here."

Phineas sat next to her on a bed in a dark room with black walls and no windows. His tanned skin glowed against the black headboard. Small table lamps on either side of the bed provided the only light. Eugene sniffed, smelling blood and night. She tried to sit up, but her head spun, and she fell back onto soft pillows wrapped in black.

"Where are we?" she asked.

Phineas lifted her head and gave her water. "A safe room. We got you here in the nick of time," he said. "Had I been any later, you would have made the news again."

"It wasn't my fault!" she said and reached to smack his side with her left arm. She missed and her arm went in a different direction.

Phineas pulled her to him and hugged her. "I'm so sorry," he said. "I should have come sooner. You almost left me. Please don't do that again."

Eugene strained to hear her brother's voice, but sleep called to her even as she felt something warm and wet dripping onto her face.

Phineas sniffed. "It's the drugs. Just go to sleep. You'll feel better in the morning."

"Was it silver?" Cesar's voice asked. Eugene didn't know where it was. She couldn't open her eyes.

"No," answered Phineas. "But the bullet pierced her lung. It almost got her heart. She'll sleep 'til tomorrow, but she'll be okay, sore, but okay."

"Good. I was just starting to like her," Cesar said. He chuckled. "Love the picture of her running down The Strip."

"It wasnnn faul," Eugene tried to say, but her mouth wouldn't work.

"Thought so," Cesar said.

Someone else entered the room, vamp by the smell. "I'll report her condition and return to my home." It was Clay's voice.

"Better stay here," Clay said. "He's taken Marcus, Luna's brother."

Eugene gasped. One eye opened. Phineas still sat next to her on the bed. Her head against his chest.

He stroked her head. "We got this one, Eep. Go to sleep," he said.

"Stop callllinn me tha," she mumbled. Her eye closed.

"What are you calling her?" asked Cesar.

"Eep - Eugene Elizabeth Plumb," said Phineas. "Our folks had to be stoned when they named us both Eugene. I call her Eep. She calls me Epp - Eugene Phineas Plumb."

Clay's voice was the last Eugene heard until she woke the next day. "Even I agree. You two are weird."

* * * * *

Luna curled her arms around her legs. The blanket wrapped over her shoulders warmed her, but she still shook. CC sat on the couch next to her, eyes closed, feet on the floor, breathing in and out with slow, deliberate breaths. Max paced back and forth in front of them.

Max stopped pacing and looked at CC. "I don't like it. Too risky."

CC's shoulders slackened, and she looked at Max. "This is our best shot of finding Marcus. Now please, sit down."

Max sat in the overstuffed chair next to the couch. "CC, If you can see through his eyes, he can see through yours."

CC breathed in deep, closing her eyes. "I know."

Max looked at Luna, then back to CC. "Let me at least send Luna to safety."

"No!" Luna said, louder than she intended. She sat up, putting her feet on the floor, and sitting close enough to CC to feel the warmth of her body next to hers.

"She stays with me," CC said, not opening her eyes.

Luna reached over and took CC's hand.

"Trust me, Max," said CC, her voice took on a dreamy quality, as though she were in another room, not seeing them. "Both of you, please be quiet. I'm new to this."

Luna squeezed CC's hand and let the blanket fall off her shoulders, no longer cold. Fear continued to prick her insides, but for the first time since realizing Marcus was missing, hope trickled into her mind.

"Ew," CC whispered. She reached out her free arm. Her thumb and fingers pinched her nose. "Cigarette smoke," she said, and turned her head away from her hand in disgust. "It's too dark to see."

"What else do you smell?" asked Max.

CC forced her fingers away from her mouth and took in a long, slow breath through her nose. Her chest filled so much, Luna felt her heartbeat through her arm. It was steady, confident. It assured her everything around her was real.

"Cold," CC said. "Beer."

Max slide close to the edge of his chair. "Do you hear music?"

"Yes," said CC. "Too much. Near. Laughter. Voices. Cars, but over there." CC opened her eyes and faced Luna. "Sixth Street. Somewhere close enough to hear and see it, but someplace cold and dark.

Max stood. He looked at the door and then at CC and Luna.

"It's not enough for me, but you know something," CC said.

"If he's on Sixth Street, I can find him."

CC stood. "Go. We're going to Cesar's safe room. Killing him is your job."

Max nodded and was gone.

Luna jumped to her feet and spun around. "Where?" she started. "But he was…"

CC's shoulders shrugged. The worry around her lines disappeared as she smiled. "Don't think I'll ever get used to that. Let's go."

"I have to find Marcus," Luna said. "I can't go to some safe place while that monster-"

CC put her hands on Luna's shoulders. "Breathe. Marcus is only bait. He wants us looking for him. He wants us to lose our way."

The fear in Luna's guts twisted again. The hope disappeared. She tried to slow her mind from racing toward the worse, but there were too many questions. The only question that she could ask was, "Why is he doing this?"

"You're special, Luna. You and Marcus are. You see things others don't. You smell, hear, even taste things differently than others, and you know it. I'll explain later. For now, please trust me. I want both of you alive and well."

Luna gazed into CC's eyes. That trickle of hope returned. Her heartbeat returned to normal, and her chest breathed in and out as it should. "Promise you'll explain it all," she said. She turned away from CC and picked up the blanket, folding it. "When I'm ready, explain it. Not until then."

"You got it," said CC.

CC picked up her phone. "Just in case, I'm getting us a little backup." She tapped on her phone and held it up to her ear. "Renaldo, I need some help."

*****

"Stop the car!" shouted CC.

Renaldo skidded to a halt. "Jesus, CC. What the-"

CC opened the door and ran for a tall man standing outside the parking lot entrance next to the Phantom's Menace. Approaching him, she reached for her gun, but remembered she gave it to Cesar. Renaldo pulled his own gun and followed.

"What's wrong?" asked Renaldo, eyeing the tall man in front of CC.

CC turned. "This is Phineas, Eugene's brother. It's a trap." She turned back to Phineas. "What floor?"

"Fourth," he said. "Saw him on the monitor. He's staying away from the guests. Cesar sent me out with them to warn you."

"Alive?" CC asked.

Luna stepped forward, grabbing Phineas' arm. "Is Marcus alive?"

"Yes," Phineas said, tapping Luna's hand. "Pretty sure he's unconscious, but he was breathing."

"Eugene?" CC asked.

"Asleep," said Phineas. "I gave her a strong sedative once I got her to change. Her body will heal itself."

"Something happened to Eugene? Is she all right?" began Luna.

"What a minute," Renaldo interrupted. "What's going on, CC?"

CC didn't look at Renaldo but stared across the street. "The monster we've been looking for kidnapped her brother, Marcus, earlier this evening. I was sure he was somewhere on Sixth Street. I didn't think he'd be here."

CC pushed her senses to seek what was around her. "I can't feel him anywhere close. Maybe." She stopped and shook her head. "Doesn't make sense."

"We have to get to Marcus," Luna insisted, and tugged on Renaldo's arm.

"Yes," said CC. "But we move slow. Renaldo, you know the drill. Phineas, could you-" She paused before adding, "do your thing?"

Phineas' eyes darted from Renaldo to CC. "Thought you'd never ask." He grinned and pulled his shirt off as he turned to walk into the garage, but stopped and turned back to CC. "Cesar said you'd want this." He gave her her gun in its holster, turned around kicking off his shoes as he walked into the darkness of the parking garage.

"Thanks," CC said, as she placed the holster on her belt and turned the safety off the gun.

"What-" Renaldo said pointing to Phineas, but CC raised her hand.

"You'll find out soon enough," she said. Before Phineas disappeared, she shouted, "Do not engage it."

She looked up and down the street. Bars were closing and restaurant employees streamed out of back doors, chatting and laughing. A van carrying a group of cleaners pulled to a stop on the street next to the club. The driver got out and opened the back of the van. Five men and a woman got out and distributed supplies to each other. Another car arrived and parked behind the van. That driver got out. She distributed hot drinks, and they all stood drinking and chatting. "We can't leave Marcus unprotected until sunrise.

"What happens at sunrise?" asked Renaldo.

"I don't get it either," Luna answered. "But she knows what she's doing."

Before crossing the threshold into the garage, CC sent a text to Max and Cesar, letting them know what was happening. "Max can't be too far away," she said, and gripped her gun with both hands. "Luna, do not leave my side. Renaldo, you know how you always fuss at Frank for not wanting to talk about certain things? This is one of them."

Renaldo followed CC's example, clicking off his gun's safety and gripping it, ready to shoot. "What kind of thing are we talking about?"

"You won't believe me 'til you shoot it." CC led them into the garage.

They followed the one-way arrows up. At each point where the drive curved up and in the opposite direction, they slowed. Phineas took the lead, remaining ten feet ahead of them. Renaldo remained behind them. CC kept Luna at her side.

As they approached the curve leading them to the fourth level, CC signaled a halt. She focused on the gun in her hands and leaned against the wall separating the twist from third to fourth level. Cold slipped through the concrete, chilling the sweat on her back into little fingers of ice. The fourth floor of the garage. There were no cars on the fourth level. Phineas crouched low, his lips snarled up, ready to growl or bite. CC eased her head around the turn. Marcus laying huddled on the floor, his back to her. She couldn't see if he breathed.

Luna's fast breaths whispered in CC's ears. The girl's eyes, so beautiful, narrowed into slips. Her shoulders, hunched with worry only an hour ago, pulled back. With a deep breath, Luna pushed herself away from the wall. Her right foot inched forward.

CC pushed her back to the wall, shaking her head. "Trap," she breathed.

Luna's eyes widened, and she gulped in a full breath. "He's right there."

CC squeezed Luna's shoulder, nodding. "Stay here." She pushed herself from the wall but looked back to see Renaldo stepping forward. "Let me," she mouthed to him. "Keep her safe."

Renaldo and then Luna nodded.

CC sighed. Weeks of hunting for this killer, yet it only took a moment for someone else to die. She stepped next to Phineas. "Keep watch," she whispered.

Deep shadows scattered across the concrete floor. The monster could wait for them in the depths of them. The sounds of Sixth Street faded to nothing in her ears, as she strained to listen for the fall of feet or paw, a growl. She breathed in through her nose, searching for the stink of the creature over the smell of life flowing up the road next to them.

A final shake of her shoulders and she ran to Marcus, crouching beside him. Without looking at him, she lay her hand on his shoulder. Warmth. A steady rising and falling, and with a jerk, he sat up.

"Get away!" he shouted, then slumped when CC looked him in the face, putting a finger to her lips.

"Can you move?" she mouthed hoping he could see her lips moving.

He nodded, twisting to use his hands to push up from the floor. CC reached to help, but Luna ran to him, wrapping her arms around him. He gripped her back.

CC hissed in a breath, motioning Renaldo and Phineas to her. With Luna's help, Marcus stood, and arm in arm, they followed CC. She led them toward the staircase on the far wall. If they could get to the third floor, she could get them into the safe room. Max would arrive, find the monster, and kill it.

Marcus favored his right leg, but with Luna's help, kept the fast pace CC set. CC stopped at the entrance to the stairwell, holding her hand up to stop everyone. CC leaned forward to look up. There were no windows in the stairwell above them. Red safety lights turned the dark opening into a bloody fog, but she saw neither movement nor heard any sound above the gentle hum of the lights. She took two steps at a time until she could twist her head to see above and below the next flight of stairs.

She turned to motion for the others to follow and froze as Marcus pushed Luna toward CC.

"Stay away from my sister!" he shouted.

A gunshot echoed through the garage. Someone screamed. She didn't know if it was Marcus or Renaldo.

Luna fell onto the stairs. CC jumped over her, landing in front of Marcus in a crouch. She pointed her gun, ready for an attack. Instead, an old man stood where Marcus had been laying. He leaned on his walking stick, staring at her through matted, gray eyebrows and bushy beard.

"You brought the other," he said.

"No," CC said. "You won't kill anyone else."

"God commands us to smite all demons!" shouted the old man.

CC first felt and then heard Luna gasp as she reached and pulled Marcus to her.

"I'm okay," CC heard Marcus say.

"No," CC said again. "You are a murderer of children. God does not want that."

"Children of Satan! I deliver them to God before he can put his claws into them." The old man took a step forward.

"I will shoot you," CC said. Only then did she realize she'd lowered her gun. She lifted it again, aiming for the old man's chest.

He stopped. "No," he said, shaking his head. "We both serve God's will in this. You are only a woman, easily confused. I will guide you on our journey."

"That's the old, grouchy man from the cafe," Luna whispered.

CC wasn't sure if Luna meant to tell the information to her or Marcus. Behind the old man, CC watched as Phineas stalked up the ramp, skipping his front left paw, which even from a distance CC could see hung limply from its arm. Renaldo lay on his side next to her. Blood trickled off his forehead. "And now you kill lawmen, those sworn to protect the righteous," she said. She blinked, and Phineas leaped, sinking his teeth into the back of the old man's neck.

The old man roared. It echoed through the parking lot. His body twisted and grew. Massive hands twisted Phineas and threw him across the parking lot and over the barrier to the street below. He turned, facing CC and Renaldo again. His voice grew with his body. It resonated deep and lonely. He pointed to Renaldo. "Not dead. I defend myself, but I know who he is. I will not kill him unless he pursues the wrong path."

The hairs on CC's neck lifted and waved. A prick on her neck told her Max was near. She forced breath through her throat. "Who are you?"

The creature or old man lifted his head. "I'm the Reverend Doctor Cairns, slayer of the wicked, defender of children's souls. You and I are chosen by God to rid the world of Satan's spawns. Though you're only a woman, you will be my right hand."

CC shook her head. "I'm only a woman, but I'm a woman with friends. And you will no longer kill children who may or may not become unhuman anymore."

A growl rolled out of Cairn's mouth. "Stupid woman! I am commanded by God. You will not presume to tell me His will. He gave us the gift to see into souls, to see those who are damned. He even gives us their hearts so that we may continue to do His will."

Cairns lifted his cane above his head and charged CC.

A gunshot echoed through the parking garage. The bullet his Cairns in the forehead. He fell with a great howl.

"Got the son of a bitch," said Renaldo, pushing himself up.

"Stay down, Renaldo," shouted CC as Cairns roared again and sprung to his feet.

"What the-"

CC shot, hitting Cairns in the chest before Renaldo could say more.

Once again, Cairns screamed, but this time blood sputtered from his mouth even as it continued to run down his forehead and into his eyes. His face contorted between a wolf, a man, and a demon. White fangs gleamed from his mouth under a shaggy gray beard.

Cairns continued to charge, but Max dove at him from behind, grabbing his neck and pulling him back. CC squatted next to Renaldo, putting a hand on his arm to prevent him from shooting Max. She risked a look behind her and found Marcus leading Luna down. They both looked up at her. When she turned back to face the battle. Cesar stood in front of her, his eyes reflecting the red safety lights in the stairwell giving him a demon look. An animal snarl lifted the edges of his lips, revealing his long, white teeth, ready to bite. He held a long blade in his right hand.

"Get them to the safe room," Cesar growled more than said.

She helped Renaldo to his feet as Cesar disappeared before she could answer him.

"Leg," muttered Renaldo, bending over to grip his knee. "Broken."

"Lean on me," she said. "Marcus, Luna, third floor."

Marcus turned Luna around and together they hobbled to the third floor. The steel door to the club was open. Clay waited for them. He pulled Luna and Marcus in. As he reached to help CC with Renaldo, he shut the door. CC heard the click of the lock behind it.

"What?" muttered Renaldo, even as CC turned him to face behind them.

Cairns stood on three stairs over them. The gray hair or fur covering his face matted as blood continued to flow. A long knife stuck out of his shoulder. "Demon!" he shouted to CC. "You've joined the league of Satan!" He wobbled forward and reached behind him, pulling the long knife out of his shoulder. He raised it over his head. "Suffer not a witch to live!"

CC shot. A shadow fluttered past her ear. Max swung his arm and a long silver blade sliced through Cairns' neck. His head fell off. It bounced down the stairs to CC and Renaldo's feet. The face distorted, its lips twisted as though to speak, and its dark eyes glared then faded to nothing.

"Holy shit," muttered Renaldo. "Frank and I are going to have to have a long talk." He might have said more, but his leg gave way and he fell. Max caught him.

CC stared at the face until Cesar stood beside her. Blood splattered his face and clothes. It ran down his chin, but his eyes glowed and his lips smiled. "Not such a wicked bastard after all." He bent down and picked up the head, sitting next to the body that in death, shrunk down to human size.

"Phineas," CC said, looking around her.

"He limped inside," said Clay, opening the door. "None the worse for the beating. I'm sorry I had to close the door, CC."

CC nodded as Cesar offered him his hand and he led her inside. "You did the right thing. The kids are safe."

Luna ran to CC. "You're all right!" she shouted and hugged CC. "Clay wouldn't let us open the door. I was so worried."

Marcus walked outside the door and stared at Cairns' remains. "He looked bigger."

"He grew as a beast, but he was always a small man," said Clay, and led Marcus inside.

*****

"So, I should convey these words to the Señora?"

CC didn't recognize the voice. The Long Island accent was the thickest she'd ever heard. With her hand resting on the door handle, she listened.

"Yes, along with my compliments," said Cesar. "I send a case of our finest from the vineyard."

CC's eyebrows raised.

"A most excellent offering. Then I shall repeat your words exactly as you have stated them. You may be well assured of my exactness," the Long Island man said. "The Señora will be most pleased, understanding, of course, that how she thinks is her own business, not mine, but I believe, and I speak from my long acquaintance with her in these matters, she will be pleased."

"Thank you, Teaser,"

"And I believe the lovely Catherine Carson you so fondly speak of is at the door," said Teaser.

CC felt her face flush, but whether from the compliment or from being caught listening at the door, she wasn't sure. She opened the door and walked into Cesar's office. Cesar stood shaking hands with a short, broad man wearing a fedora and an ugly, moss-green suit with matching shirt and blood red tie. The man's nose stuck out from beneath tiny, dark eyes hidden under the brim of his hat. His smile, for all the mystery of the rest of his face, revealed large, not vampire, white teeth and bright red lips.

"It is most sincerely my pleasure to make your acquaintance, Ms. Carson," said Teaser. He took her offered hand and raised it to his lips. "I shall look forward to the time when we might," and he turned his gaze to Cesar, "with all due respect and permissions, meet and converse on the ways of the worlds." He touched the rim of his hat with his hand, nodded to both Cesar and CC, and left.

"Who?" began CC, but Cesar shook his head.

"Another story," Cesar said.

CC squinted her eyes as Teaser closed the door. "I've never seen anyone like him," she said. "Not human."

"Not human," replied Cesar.

He pulled a bottle of sparkling wine from the ice bucket and opened it.

"I hate it when you say things like that," she said, crossing her arms. "And when you get all godfather-like."

Cesar smiled. "I know." He poured the wine and offered her the glass. "It's New Year's Eve. Let's not worry about what we have no control over."

CC smiled and turned her attention to the dancefloor below them. Lights flashed to the steady beat of the music. The crowd on the floor danced and laughed. Their anticipation for midnight filled the air with electric anticipation. CC reached her hand to her neck and brushed her curls away. Fluffy reached his front paws to the window and barked. CC followed Fluffy's gaze to the second-floor bar, where Luna stood with Marcus. They laughed together, pointing to people on the dance floor.

CC smiled. "They're happy again. And Max tells me the cafe is doing well."

"Let's hope it lasts," Cesar said. "That family deserves a break. Renaldo's back from leave? Everything okay on that end?"

CC narrowed her eyes but smiled. "What you really want to know is what he's telling people. We're good, and because Frank Jarvis is his partner, the entire LeBrere family has closure." She shook her head to stop CC from asking more questions. "No, I don't know what he told them. Whatever it was, well. When I went into the cafe this afternoon, I saw the mom. She was laughing and talking to her sister."

"Hmm," said Cesar.

"Irritating, isn't it?" CC said with as much snark as she could muster.

Overhead, lights flashed. Bartenders filled plastic flutes with sparkling wine. Waitstaff carried the trays of the wine through the crowd. Voices rose as midnight closed in. The largest of the video screens flashed the time: Eleven fifty-five.

CC pet Fluffy. "Five more minutes, Fluffy."

Fluffy looked up at CC, then turned to take her usual place on a cushion near Cesar's private bar. Bean, already curled up on his own cushion, lifted his nose to Fluffy before re-curling to return to sleep.

Cesar pulled out his phone. "Sorry," he said. "Business."

CC pushed her nose to one side with a finger. "It's just business."

Cesar grinned and bit his lip, trying not to laugh. CC didn't recognize the dialect he spoke. An offshoot of Mandarin, one language she knew but not enough to comprehend what he said. She turned her gaze back to the crowd. It was the most anticipated New Year's party in the city of Austin. She'd never seen the bar packed over capacity and was glad she was in Cesar's office and not downstairs.

The tone of Cesar's voice changed from casual to formal. She watched his reflection in the window as he stood and hung up the phone. "Sorry about that," he said.

"I'm used to that with you," she said, feeling neither neglected nor offended at being left alone to watch the crowd. "Are you really going to close the bar?"

"Venturing into other fields," he said, standing next to CC. "That was my friend in Hunan. This new SARS bug is bad. It shut most of his businesses down. At least I have a little warning."

"He thinks it will reach here?" CC asked.

"It's already here, and too many people are depending on me." Cesar lifted his glass and pointed to the dance floor. "Not just vamps. Most of the people who work here are human."

Below her, Luna and Marcus chatted now with Eugene and Phineas. Smiles and laughs abounded. She caught her breath as the image of James Earl appeared in a memory smiling like when they met Eugene. She moved her hand to wipe away a tear forming in her eyes.

Cesar tapped a button on the control panel in front of him. The roar of the crowd filled his office as they began the countdown to the New Year. "Five, four," filled her ears.

"We'll get through this, CC. None of us are alone," whispered Cesar in her ear.

"One! Happy New Year!" roared through the speaker before Cesar tapped the button to close the speaker.

Below her, Marcus lifted his glass to his sister and new friends. Eugene raised her glass first to Cesar and CC, and then to her new friends.

"To new beginnings," said Cesar.

"Yes," CC said, tapping her glass to his. "Old friends and new friends."

Sirens roared through the bar as red, blue, and white lights flashed. Laser lights cut swaths through the fog spilling from the rafters to bathe the dancers in the cool, wet air. Cheers erupted as foam flew from hidden nozzles. It was the best place to welcome the New Year, and CC felt at home.

L.K. Latham writes Urban Fantasy and poetry that's about as dark as the chocolate she loves. She spends her days weaving tales of vampires, werewolves, and other creatures known to Dance in the Shadows of the Moon. When not writing, you'll find L.K. baking with chocolate and wine. In the evenings, she rests with a class of bourbon - made in Texas, of course, and waiting for last year's grapes to become this year's wine.

A recovering educator, this native Texas settled in the Austin area with her husband. She enjoys living in Texas as much as she enjoys the wines of Texas, perhaps a bit more than some of its inhabitants, but that doesn't stop her from admiring their spunk and veracity in the face of overwhelming facts.

Join L.K. Latham to receive updates and free short stories in the world of *Midnight Whispers* and beyond at https://lklatham.com